Praise for Denzil Meyrick and the D

'Denzil Meyrick's DCI Daley has won a loyal army of fans
since he first appeared in *Whisky from Small Glasses*'
Sunday Times Crime Club

'Universal truths . . . an unbuttoned sense of humour . . .
engaging and eventful'
Wall Street Journal

'In high demand across the globe . . . Readers instantly
warm to Daley'
Daily Mail

'Good atmospheric writing . . . moments of chilling horror
. . . a fine example of tartan noir'
Allan Massie, *The Scotsman*

'You'll have a blast with these'
Ian Rankin

'A top talent, and one to be cherished'
Quintin Jardine

'Spellbinding . . . one of the UK's most loved crime writers'
Sunday Post

'A compelling lead . . . satisfyingly twisted plot'
Publishers Weekly

A note on the author

Denzil Meyrick was born in Glasgow and brought up in Campbeltown. After studying politics, he pursued a varied career including time spent as a police officer, freelance journalist and director of several companies in the leisure, engineering and marketing sectors. Denzil lives on Loch Lomond side with his wife Fiona.

Also by Denzil Meyrick

Terms of Restitution

DCI Daley thriller series
Whisky from Small Glasses
The Last Witness
Dark Suits and Sad Songs
The Rat Stone Serenade
Well of the Winds
The Relentless Tide
A Breath on Dying Embers
Jeremiah's Bell
For Any Other Truth
The Death of Remembrance

Tales from Kinloch
A Large Measure of Snow
A Toast to the Old Stones
Ghosts in the Gloaming

Short stories
One Last Dram Before Midnight

For more information
www.denzilmeyrick.com
and www.birlinn.co.uk

NO SWEET SORROW

A DCI DALEY THRILLER

Denzil Meyrick

Polygon

First published in Great Britain in 2023 by Polygon, an imprint of Birlinn Ltd.

Birlinn Ltd
West Newington House
10 Newington Road
Edinburgh
EH9 1QS

www.polygonbooks.co.uk

1

ISBN 978 1 84697 637 7
eBook ISBN 978 1 78885 583 9

British Library Cataloguing-in-Publication Data
A catalogue record for this book is available on request from the British Library.

Typeset by 3btype.com, Edinburgh

For my wife Fiona

'The woods are lovely, dark and deep,
But I have promises to keep,
And miles to go before I sleep,
And miles to go before I sleep.'

—'Stopping by Woods on a Snowy Evening',
Robert Frost

PROLOGUE

Eleven years earlier

The children stood in the long caravan, their father's blood splattered up the sides of the boy's white trainers. He was tall for his fifteen years, face pockmarked by acne. His sister, three years his junior, used her elder sibling like a shield against the three police officers who stood before them in the cramped space. A bloodied carving knife lay on the vinyl floor of the cooking area like a punctuation mark between the youngsters and the officers of the law.

The uniformed men offered only platitudes, anxious to assess the situation rather than lay hands on the children. They were painfully aware that, as first responders under these circumstances, their job was to contain the situation until somebody with the right qualifications appeared to deal with the horror before them.

That someone was Emily Kilvington, a detective sergeant in Lincolnshire Police's Child Protection Unit. Having had to force her way through the crowds on Skegness's seafront, then navigate a difficult path in between caravans and holidaymakers in the labyrinthine holiday park, she was late. Late was her middle name. Harassed, and finding it hard to focus, she stepped into the caravan, nodded to one of her colleagues, and took in the scene.

The day was sticky and hot, even for July. Kilvington wiped a film of sweat from her forehead, pushed back her blonde hair, and knelt in front of the siblings.

'Hi, my name's Emily,' she said softly.

The boy stared past her to the uniformed officers. Both children remained silent.

'Lads, wait outside, would you?'

'You sure, boss?' He was the oldest of the three, with a gnarled face.

'If I wasn't sure, I wouldn't have asked you, Dalton.'

Constable Dalton leaned in to her. 'We haven't searched them. Waited until you arrived, like they told us. Pretty obvious where the murder weapon is, mind you.' He nodded to the bloody knife on the floor.

'I hadn't noticed that – or the body lying behind them. Top marks for observation, Terry!' said Kilvington without whispering, making the boy snigger at the obvious sarcasm.

'You're in charge, sergeant.' Dalton sounded less than pleased. He jerked his head to his colleagues, and they left the caravan.

'What're your names?' she asked, having to crane her head up to meet the eyes of the boy.

'I'm Sam. She's Charlie – Charlotte. Broughton, that's our second name.'

'Hi, Charlie,' Kilvington tried, hoping to entice the girl out from behind her brother's tall frame.

'Hi,' the girl replied, without showing herself.

Kilvington nodded and smiled. Her priority was to keep the children calm, while making sure they left the murder scene and were properly checked over, medically, forensically and mentally.

'Okay. Is this man your dad?' Kilvington took in the body. The face was mottled grey, the distinct colour of death. His lifeless eyes stared up at the ceiling, as his blood congealed around him like a frozen pond. It had emanated from a dark wound in his now still chest.

'Yeah,' said Sam. 'He's our dad.'

'*Was* our dad.' The voice came from the girl. She peeked around her brother's shoulder.

'Yes, I'm sorry,' said Kilvington.

Sam shrugged. 'Everybody dies sometime, don't they?'

'That's true,' said Kilvington. 'Is your mum around?'

'She's dead.' Sam's reply was without emotion.

The caravan was stiflingly hot now, almost unbearable. Kilvington was aware of a bead of sweat trailing down her nose. She banished it with a flick of her hand. This wasn't the time to unpick the whole story. That would come later. 'Listen, we need to get this sorted, okay?'

Sam inclined his head a fraction.

'My priority is your wellbeing. Do you understand that?'

Sam shrugged.

'I want you to come outside with me. Don't worry, nobody will see you. We've shut off this part of the site. We'll get you checked over in the hospital, then we can chat properly. Is that fine with both of you?'

'We can't stay here for ever, can we? said Sam in a matter-of-fact way. 'What do you want us to do?'

Kilvington got to her feet. 'I'll take you and your sister outside. There's an ambulance waiting to drive you to the hospital. I'll come too.'

3

'Whose side are you on?' Charlie asked.

'You might not believe this, but I'm on your side.'

'But you're a police, right?' said Sam.

'Yes. Though, remember, we don't all do the same job. I'm here to look after you. But I can't do that here.'

'Our dad *was* a police.' The past tense was emphasised. Charlie stepped out from behind her brother. She was thin, dressed in a pair of shorts and a faded T-shirt.

This information took Kilvington aback, but she tried not to let it show. 'I see. Where did he work?'

'Manchester. That's where we're from.'

'Okay, we can talk about this once we get you sorted. Are you ready to go?' She smiled at them both.

Sam nodded to his sister. 'Come on, let's do this.'

They walked towards Kilvington.

Just as they were at the detective's side, Charlie looked up into her face. 'My dad used to say that kids get a beating from police. Said he'd beat us himself if we got caught doing stuff. He used to do it anyway.'

Kilvington was about to reply when she felt a sharp pain in her side. She grabbed at it, her mouth gaping open. When she felt her own warm blood flow over her hand, she screamed.

1

'You gonna believe this?' DS Brian Scott was sitting opposite Daley in the glass box. He was leaning back on a chair, feet up on the big desk, reading the local newspaper.

Daley was standing, examining a huge map of the peninsula on the wall. 'I'll believe anything now. After what we've seen in our careers, who knows what's going to happen, eh?'

'True, big man, very true. It's like Miranda's box every day in here, so it is.'

Daley raised his brows and carried on running one finger down the main road into Kinloch. Carefully, he studied every turn-off, side road and farm track as he went. 'What's the latest in the *Kinloch Herald*?'

'It says here that a group o' climbers fae Oxford University are coming here to walk the Peninsula Way next week. They're acclimatising themselves for Everest.'

'What's so amazing about that?'

'They're camping, Jimmy. It's December – bloody freezing.'

'Colder on Everest.'

'You think? I near froze off my haw-maws last week when you had me on that obs job doon at the bus terminus. I'd bet you it was warmer at base camp that night.'

'You know the score, Bri. We have that intelligence from up the road that drugs are being smuggled into the area on public transport. That means the bus or the plane.'

'Or the ferry.'

'Hard to keep tabs on the ferry when it only operates between May and September. As you've pointed out, this is December.'

'But when did we get that intel again, big man?'

'The middle of October. Do you listen to any of the briefings?'

Scott thought for a moment. 'If I remember right, it was me who did that one.'

'It was! Even less excuse.'

'You know me, Jimmy. When I'm up there it's all aboot presentation and that. I was having problems wae my iPad, if you remember.'

'I remember the Rangers' team photo appearing at one point. Oh, and a picture of you on holiday in Spain.'

'Ach, I throw these in to lighten the load. You know that.'

'You don't know how to work it, you mean.'

'It's something different every couple o' days. You switch the bloody thing on, and it looks totally different to what it did the day before. It's like jumping into the motor no' knowing where the steering wheel is. How can they no' just leave stuff alone?'

'Updates, Brian – progress. Mind you, it's not that long ago you were drawing cartoons on that old whiteboard we had at Stewart Street. I suppose I should be grateful.'

'Tommy Rogan! Dae you remember that prick? He used to go mental.' Scott laughed heartily.

'He's dead,' said Daley absently.

'Eh? Tommy's deid? Man, he was a decent bugger, mind.'

Daley sighed at his colleague's ability to shift his assessment of a person depending on whether they were dead or alive. For Scott, death clearly involved elevation to sainthood. There were a few notable exceptions, but in the main this was his default position as far as the deceased were concerned.

'He was younger than me. The big C, I bet. He smoked like a lum.'

'No, he jumped in front of a train after years of being mocked by his colleagues because of his buck teeth.'

'Right.' Scott looked suddenly guilty, remembering the cartoons he'd drawn on the whiteboard so long ago.

'Nah, only kidding. It was a heart attack.' Daley rubbed his own chest at the very thought.

Scott dunked a chocolate Hobnob into his tea. 'Aye, he'd a hell o' a diet, mind you. His idea o' healthy eating was having one pie instead o' two for his lunch.'

'I just can't work it out. They must be offloading the drugs somewhere between here and Glasgow. But we've had observations all the way up and down. Nothing.'

'Could just be a false lead – a red herring.'

'It could, I suppose. But you know the source was sound.'

Scott shrugged. 'Aye, the best.' He looked down at his shirt, where a lump of chocolate had been dislocated by the hot tea and landed there. 'Oh, ya bastard!'

Desk Sergeant Shaw appeared through the open door just as Scott was in mid-expletive. 'Another operation gone wrong, Brian?'

'No. Look at the state o' this.' He pointed to his stained shirt. 'Ella hates me eating chocolate. Says it clogs up the arteries. I'll need to try and get this off. It's evidence!'

'Sir, new intel from Glasgow in your inbox,' said Shaw.

'Och, just tell the man. All this inbox-outbox stuff is driving me up the wall.'

'A party of fifteen backpackers just boarded the bus in Glasgow heading here to Kinloch. They want us to check them when they arrive.'

Daley sat heavily in his big chair. 'What's the betting it's the Oxford University Mountaineering Club?'

'Sorry?' said Shaw.

'Next week they're coming, Jimmy. It said so in the paper.'

'Which is dated . . . ?'

Scott turned to the front page of the *Kinloch Herald*. 'Friday – aye, you're right enough.'

'Okay. Brian, a nice piece of overtime for you. When does the bus get in, Al?'

'Six sharp, sir.'

'Why me again? It's bloody awkward having to search poor folk coming off a bus. Probably never done anything wrong in their lives. That bus is like the slow horse to China as it is, without getting someone poking up your arse wae a torch when you get off.'

'Who else is going to supervise it?' said Daley.

'You've no' done one yet!'

'Right. Let's work this out.' Daley pointed to his chest. 'Me, chief inspector.' He pointed to Scott. 'You, sergeant. Simples!' He smiled broadly. 'Why don't you take a couple of hours off? You can have that shirt sorted before Ella gets back from work.'

'Aye, true,' said Scott, stroking his chin.

'How's she getting on, Brian?' Shaw asked.

'Just fine. She needed something to keep her mind occupied. Working behind the bar in the County's just the thing.

She did bar work when we first got married. You know my Ella, she can bring a tear to a glass eye wae those jokes.'

'Learned all she knows from you, eh?' Shaw turned on his heel and left.

'What's up wae him, Jimmy? He's had a face like a squelched plook for weeks.'

'His wife's left him. Don't tell anyone. He told me in confidence.'

'Don't tell anyone? This is Kinloch. They likely know why she left, who she went wae and where they're shacked up!'

'She's at her mother's in Livingston. It's just some time apart.'

'Huh! I've heard that before. Sure, my Ella was heading for New York no' that long ago.'

'Only because you were permanently pished, Brian.'

'That's over now.'

'I hope so.'

'Trust me. And wae Ella behind the bar at the County, where would I go?'

Daley smiled. 'Brian, I've known you all these years. You're like a bloodhound when it comes to whisky.'

'Don't you mean a St Bernard?'

'We've been through this dog thing.'

'I suppose.'

Daley swung his chair back to face the map. 'We've got to get to grips with this new drug supply. Four overdoses in the last fortnight alone – one fatality. They're cutting it with fentanyl. It's a bloody epidemic up the road.'

'It'll be cut wae other shit, too.'

'Yeah, that's what they're saying at the lab.' Daley swung back round. 'I'm worried about Alasdair.'

9

'Who?'

'Alasdair Shaw – the man who was standing there a couple of minutes ago.'

'Right, I see. Because of his wife, you mean?'

'Yes. Remember, I know what it's like, Brian.'

'The only difference is that he's got a broken heart, and you were delighted.'

'Not true!'

'And the band played on.' Scott levered his feet off the table and stood. 'Right, I'm off.'

As Daley watched his old friend go, he marvelled at his skill in distilling everything down to the lowest common denominator. For Brian Scott, the world was black and white. Sadly, when it came to marriage, and just about everything else, Daley's world was distinctly grey.

2

The winter sun sparkled on a calm sea in shades of gold and red, as though trying to make itself too striking, too spectacular – too handsome to die behind the sea heralding the darkness of night. The woman stood on the rocky shore, admiring nature's own light display. Of badly preserved middle age, her grey hair straggled in the breeze, eyes unblinking. When she could watch a sunset, she would. And by the look of things, this one was going to be spectacular. She fancied that the aurora borealis might even appear – there was something in the air.

Behind her, just through the pine trees on a short rise, stood a crumbling house. It was of the Georgian period and seemed incongruous by a beach here on Scotland's west coast. Buildings like this were much more likely to be found in the leafy suburbs of Glasgow, or any other city in the country. But here it was, four big windows looking out over the bay, a vision in slate and granite.

She mumbled to herself as she gazed at the setting sun, which was beginning to flame and rage. Night was the enemy, day her only desire.

She reached into the pocket of her faded rain jacket and removed a brown leather bag. Worn smooth by age and use, it was tautened to a pucker by a lace drawstring. The woman loosened the knot and opened the bag. With thin, bony fingers, she delved inside and removed two objects from within, then pulled the drawstring tight and placed the bag back in her pocket.

Just before the sun nodded below the horizon in a cacophony of colour and splendour, she raised her right arm and propelled one of the objects through the air into the sea, then repeated the process with the other. Her eyes now closed against the blazing reds and golds from the protesting sun, she mumbled an incantation, her lips moving silently, her voice little more than a whisper.

As though perfectly choreographed, just as the sun disappeared the woman spread her arms wide, raised her face to the heavens and shouted, 'Let him live!'

This outpouring over, she lowered her head, muttered something else, then turned on her heel and progressed back up the beach towards the small path and home.

Caught in faint flickers of the fading day, two severed fingers – deathly grey, almost black – bobbed gently, before being caught in the first shaft of light from the moon.

'Gosh, isn't that glorious!' The young student tugged at the jacket of the man beside her.

They stared out of the windows of the 929 coach from Glasgow to Kinloch. There was only an echo of the day left in the far west, as the dark curtain of night spread across the sky. But it afforded a fleeting, almost incandescent scene, picking out rocks, trees and lapping waves on the shore in a stark, almost unnatural way.

'No sign of the Northern Lights, I see.'

'Nate, that's so typical of you. Fabulous is never enough.' She punched him playfully on the arm.

'I have high standards, Tracy.'

She laughed. 'Why do you keep calling me that? It's not my name.'

'But Delphine makes you sound like pottery.'

'So you say! It's the outcome of having a French mother. I didn't have too much influence on it, to be honest. Well, maybe more than you think.' She winked.

'You'll always be Tracy to me.' He enjoyed the way her eyes focused on his lips, on him. As he spoke, she beamed. 'You can call me Gary. There's a guy who rooms just down from me – Gary Brown. Isn't that a quintessentially brilliant name?'

'No!' she said through her giggles.

'But it's so inane, so – perfect.'

'Aw, Nathan Farringdon doesn't like his name – diddums.' Delph mocked him further by petting her lip.

'Come on. I'll be Gary and you're Tracy. We could buy a semi-detached in Reading or Staines. I'll get a job in a factory; you can smoke and push out a couple of sprogs with ADHD or something like that.'

'You're such a snob. Has anyone ever told you that?'

He laughed. 'Yes, as a matter of fact.'

'When everyone else is tearing through Lee Child or James Patterson, there you are with your well-thumbed copy of Marcus Aurelius.'

'We're Oxford undergraduates, Tracy. Who reads James Patterson?'

'Ha! Just a billion or so. My friend Emma reads Danielle Steel.'

'Fuck, that's bad.'

'We should pick up some Scotch books while we're here, Nate. Go with the flow.'

'No, thanks. Weary old detectives with stressful marriages and drink problems? It's a stereotype, Tracy. Quite frankly, I find it offensive. And by the way, don't call Scottish people *Scotch*. That's a drink. They'll hate it.'

'So, not afraid to make a fool of poor Gary Brown or people from Staines, but call a man Scotch and you're all Jeremy Corbyn.'

'Who?'

'Says the PPE undergraduate.' She ran her long fingers through his curly brown hair thoughtfully. 'Your problem is that you've never had problems. Not really.'

He gazed into space, expression suddenly blank, as the bus jolted along. 'You think?'

'You're tall, dark and handsome. You make Harry Styles look like Prince Harry.'

'But he managed to snag Meghan. And you ain't no Meghan, babe.' Nate's good humour had returned.

She punched him on the arm again. They kissed, embraced and whispered sweet nothings to each other, much to the disgust of Effie Morrison from Machrie, sitting two rows behind. She'd attended a Glasgow hospital to have an ingrown toenail removed. That alone was enough to leave her in thoroughly bad trim; the last thing she needed was a courting couple.

So, as life aboard the coach went on, as they wound up and down the winding road by the sea, the nearer to Kinloch they came.

3

Hamish had taken to walking in the evening. He was aware that time was hot on his heels. His GP had told him that the route to longevity was less whisky and more exercise. While he'd taken note of the latter, the former had proven to be – as yet – unattainable.

'Och, I should have been dead long ago. What's the odds?' he muttered to himself as he ambled along the esplanade, the loch to his left. He paused and looked across at the harbour. There sat his little lobster boat, bobbing on the dark waves under the harsh glow of the pier's acetylene lights. He'd decided that the time had come to sell her. And while he wasn't sure how much she'd make, the thought of being without a vessel to sail was a much greater concern.

Names, faces and the old days flashed before his mind's eye. There was his father, Andy, Duncan, Peeny – so many, and all of them gone. He could picture his mentor Sandy Hoynes holding court at the head of the quay. But the man he'd so admired had been dead for almost half a century. It was the trouble with getting old: everyone you knew and loved steadily disappeared. Ultimately, he supposed, his eventual demise would be like parting from strangers – meaningless. Who was left to grieve?

A large gull eyed him from its perch on top of a tall lamp-post on the quay. No doubt there was some warmth to be found there on this cold December night. As he stared into the water, thinking of nothing in particular, a cold hand gripped his heart. At first, so strong was the sensation, Hamish feared he was in the throes of a coronary. But as he endured it, the old man realised that this was that old, familiar feeling of dread and premonition. He'd felt it first on the day his father had died. It was as though the death of the man who'd given him life had opened up a portal to something other – the pull of the *thin places*.

This time, though, it was bad – very bad. Even the jumbled dreams and notions in the aftermath of Annie's death hadn't hit him as hard. Hamish leaned against the seawall to steady himself.

'Oh, Hamish!'

The voice came from behind. Hamish screwed up his eyes. It was rare that he experienced anything quite as visceral. Footsteps, coming nearer – the fear and sense of anticipation was almost palpable. The fisherman wanted to scream at this wraith to leave him alone.

'You've had a few tonight, auld fella, eh?'

Hamish snapped his head round. Standing before him wasn't some unimaginable ghoul, but his friend Detective Sergeant Brian Scott.

'I'm perfectly in possession of my senses, I'll have you know, Brian,' he said breathlessly.

'That won't last long, then. It's nearly quarter to seven.' Scott had consulted his faithful Casio G-Shock. And, true to form, hadn't noticed that the old fisherman was in any distress.

'Do you ever think about the day you're going to die, Brian?'

'Nah. I've near died enough to no' worry aboot it. See, when you get shot a few times, you tend no' to think about such things. Mind you, you're fair getting on, Hamish. It's no wonder you've half an eye on the cemetery.'

'A master of tact and diplomacy, right enough. That's what Mr Daley always tells me aboot you.'

'Auld misery guts. Likely still up in the office fretting on something rather than going home, I suppose.'

'Are things no' so good between him and Liz again?'

'Are things ever good between him and Liz, Hamish?'

'Och, good people, both o' them. I just wish they could find each other once mair.'

'And I wish I could find a bottle to sink into. But we all know where that would end. They've been at this for thirty-odd years, Hamish. They'll be at it for a good few more, trust me.'

Hamish glanced at the still water. 'I'm no' so sure aboot the future, Brian. The whole thing's bloody impenetrable.'

'Right, time you snapped oot o' this. We'll take a wee trip to see my wife, eh?'

'Aye, that would be most welcome. Though I'm no' sneaking you a dram, mind.' Hamish wagged his finger at the policeman.

'You can't sneak anything past my Ella. Trust me, I've tried. I'm no' stupid enough to want to drink again. Not now. Some folk can enjoy it. I cannae, and that's just a fact. It's either sober or heid in the toilet, that's me.'

They made their way along the esplanade, crossed the road and on to Main Street. Hamish pulled the collar of his pea jacket up over his cheeks. 'Man, what took you out on a night like this, Brian?'

'A fool's errand. Aye, and some unhappy students.'

'In the course of your duty, I shouldna wonder.'

'In the course o' a wild goose chase. Still, we can get a heat at the fire in the County.'

In no time they were walking through the doors of the hotel, past the staircase and into the bar. Being a Monday, the place was quiet, with only a handful of drinkers dotted here and there. Ella stood behind the bar, polishing a pint tumbler.

'My goodness, I thought Fran and Anna were deid,' she said.

'Fine legs they had in those kilts,' said Hamish. 'I fair admired them.' He adopted a distant look.

'You see, that's what sobriety does for you, Hamish,' said Brian. 'You get all kinds of mad notions.' Then to his wife, 'A large dram, my dear. And some watery pish for myself. You choose.'

'Lighter fluid is looking good this month,' said Ella waspishly.

'You see, that's no way to talk to your customers. The community buy-out folk won't be happy wae you at all.'

'We're just lucky that the place is still open,' said Hamish. 'Man, there's some terrible pubs in Kinloch now. If it's no' weans running aboot, it's TVs blaring, music, games machines. Nobody seems willing just to sit doon and have a dram and a good yarn any more.'

'I know somebody that would sit and have a dram wae you any day o' the week.' Ella presented Hamish with his whisky.

'You're undermining my self-esteem, Ella,' said Brian.

'Now we've got the five-step programme. Heaven help us!' Ella handed her husband a ginger beer and lime.

'If it's helping Brian, it must be a great thing, as far as I'm concerned,' said Hamish.

'See, that's how it's done, Ella.' Scott folded his arms triumphantly.

'I'm no' saying there's anything wrong wae the whole idea. But wae him to deal wae, they're needing more steps – it should be the thirty-five-step programme.'

'Ella, you're a tonic,' said Hamish. 'I never thought I'd ever be back in the County again, never mind laugh in it.' Suddenly his expression was sad.

'You still miss her, Hamish, I know. But I'll do my best to keep you cheery.' Ella bustled off to serve another customer.

'She seems happy enough, Brian. She's been here a few months now, eh?'

'Different person. I don't know why we didn't think of it a long time ago. I felt the place was empty when the weans left. Goodness knows how Ella felt.'

Hamish swirled his dram, considering this. 'Maybe Liz could come and help her. I'm thinking that might help the lassie find herself again.'

It was Brian Scott's turn to think. For a long time, he'd willed his friend's marriage to endure. But as the years marched on, it became ever clearer that staying together for their son's sake only served to make Jim and Liz more and more unhappy. That said, Jim Daley would do anything rather than speak about his domestic situation. And on the rare occasion Scott visited the house on the hill these days, the atmosphere felt dense enough to push through. 'I'm no' sure Ella and Lizzie would dae so well working together,' he said, aware that this was an understatement.

'Shame.'

No sooner had the old fisherman spoken than the big front door of the hotel swung open and noise of a commotion in the lobby drifted through the hatch to the drinkers at the bar.

'Help! Please, anyone!' The voice was disembodied.

Scott rushed out of the bar. Before him he saw a man trying to sit a youth in a chair. The man was of late middle age, and clearly struggling with the task in hand. The youth's head lolled as though he was unconscious, a stream of dark saliva slipping down his chin.

'What's this?' said Scott, helping seat the younger man.

'Sergeant Scott, it's yourself. I'm Darren Barr. We played golf together once.'

'Aye, I remember that charity day. I can hardly swing a club. What's up wae this lad? Drugs?'

'I think so. Can't get any sense out of him at all.'

Scott lifted the lad's head and pulled open one eyelid to examine the eye. There was nothing there, his pupils just tiny pinpricks barely moving in the light. 'He's in a bad way. Where did you find him, Mr Barr?'

'Just in Kintyre Road. Where the workshop used to be. He was just lying there – I thought he was dead.'

Scott checked the unconscious man's pulse. It was weak but steady.

'I've told that lot to stay in the bar. Can I help?' Ella arrived at her husband's side.

'Aye, do me a favour and phone an ambulance.' Then, in a quieter voice, 'And gie oor Jimmy a bell. Tell him I could dae wae a word.' Ella rushed off. 'What's his name, do you know?'

Barr nodded. 'He's Alex Watson's boy, David. I hardly recognised him, he's that thin. He was at school with my own son. Though they weren't friends.'

'What age?'

'He'll be seventeen now. Went to college in Glasgow. Hasn't done much for him, by the look of things.'

Scott tilted David Watson's head back. 'Can you hear me?' He slapped the young man's face gently. 'Wake up, son. Come on!' Watson's eyelids flickered but didn't open.

'Thank goodness, he's still with us,' said Barr.

'He is at the moment. The sooner we can get him to the hospital, the better it'll be.'

Ella appeared back at Scott's side. 'The ambulance is on its way, Brian. Can I do anything else?'

'Did you get Jimmy?'

'There's no reply.'

'On his mobile?'

'No. It just went to answerphone.'

'Bugger! Listen, Ella, keep speaking to the boy. Give his face a gentle slap fae time to time.'

'Is he going to die?' The colour drained from her face.

'I hope not.' Scott got to his feet and walked to the County's main entrance. He dialled a number on his mobile then held the phone to his ear. It went straight to the answering service. 'Jimmy, it's me. I need you down at the County. Another drug overdose, by the looks o' things. Just a lad. But he's one o' the worst I've seen.'

Scott ended the call and thrust the phone into his pocket. He wondered where his boss could be.

4

Daley was in the garage of his home, lying face down on the floor.

'Lever yourself up on your hands and arch your back. Trust me, it'll ease the pain,' said Liz.

'It won't make it worse – you promise?'

'It won't. It's just a basic yoga move. You've seen me do it a hundred times.'

'I have?'

'Yes. You just weren't paying attention.'

Daley propped himself up on both hands, and without moving his legs pushed his torso up off the floor.

'How does that feel?'

'Sore!'

'Okay. Now, gently ease your head back as though you're trying to look at the ceiling.'

Daley obeyed, as gently as he could, but the pain became so great he eased himself back on to the floor with a groan.

Just as Liz was about to speak, James junior poked his head round the garage door. He took one look at his father lying stock-still and looked up at his mother.

'Is Daddy dead?' The question was matter-of-fact.

'No, he isn't dead. He's got a sore back, so he's trying to make it better,' Liz replied.

The boy took in the scene sceptically before saying, 'His phone's been ringing.' With some difficulty, young James fished a mobile out of his pocket and handed it to his mother.

'See who it is, Liz,' said Daley in a voice that was a mix of a moan and a whimper.

Liz pressed the screen a couple of times. 'It's Brian – of course it is.' She listened to the message.

'What's he saying?' Again, the pained whisper.

'Something about a drug overdose. He's at the County, wants you to go to the hospital.'

'Help me up, will you?'

'I'll help too, Daddy,' said James junior.

'You're in no fit state to go anywhere. Not until you've seen a doctor,' said Liz.

Daley forced himself on to one knee with a grimace.

'See? This is madness, Jim.'

'Dial Brian's number and give me the phone, will you?'

Reluctantly, Liz followed her husband's wishes, handing over the mobile with a right-lipped expression.

Daley held the mobile to his ear, his voice strained. 'Brian, what's up?'

'You okay, big man? You sound a bit off.'

'I've hurt my back. I can hardly move.'

Scott lowered his voice. 'This boy isnae good, big man. I don't know if he'll make it, to be honest.'

'Shit. This has to stop. It's the stuff cut with the fentanyl, you reckon?'

'Got it in one.'

'So?'

'The paramedics are here in the hotel lobby working on him. As soon as he's fit enough, they'll get him up to the hospital. I'll get a hauld o' his parents, Jimmy. It's a bad one.'

Daley lay with his back on the floor, phone still at his ear. 'Shit!'

'Shit!' shouted James Junior.

Liz glared at her husband.

It took DCI Jim Daley longer to get out of his SUV than it had to get in. His back was agony now, making him feel almost faint. All told, the time it had taken him to get ready and out of the door was a new record in tardiness.

He limped into Kinloch hospital and made for the emergency ward. Sure enough, Scott was seated in the corridor, idly thumbing through a magazine. 'What's up wae you?' he said.

'Like I said on the phone, a sore back.'

'Sore? It looks as though you've got a great rock on your back, big man. Sit doon; it'll make you feel better.'

'That's not going to be possible, Brian. I'll stand, thank you.' Daley grimaced again as yet another spasm sent pain shooting down his spine.

'Happened to me once.'

'What did?'

'The kind o' problem you're having right now, Jimmy.'

'What did you do?'

'I went to that chiropodist bloke, dae you no' remember?'

'Chiropractor.'

'I cannae remember his name. But anyway, he put me right in a couple o' minutes. I walked in there like Quasimodo and came oot like Nureyev.'

24

'There's an image, eh? What did this bloke do?'

'He worked part-time at Asda – in the butchery department. But the rest o' the time he fixed backs. Man was a genius.' Scott looked puzzled by his friend's expression.

'What did he do to you?' Daley asked after a stunned moment.

'Just grabbed me and pulled me aboot a bit.'

'Was it painful?'

'Nah. Just a few clicks and pops and I was brand new.'

Daley clenched his teeth again as another spasm caught him. 'They'll be a while with that poor lad, eh?'

'Definitely. He's in some mess. If we don't get a handle on this shit, some poor bastard's going to die. Hope it's no' this fella.'

'Shit, I hope not. I can't understand why they do it. It's not as though the whole drug-using community don't realise how dangerous this stuff is.' Daley thought for a moment. 'Do you think you could pull me back into shape, Brian? I mean, if it's as easy as that, eh?'

Brian Scott, never a man to shirk a challenge, nodded enthusiastically. 'It cannae be that hard, Jimmy. If the butcher can get the job done, why no' me, eh?' He looked Daley up and down with a critical eye. 'See, you're standing at a funny angle there. I'll just get behind you and tug you back in the right direction. Hey presto!'

'You could choose your words more carefully. But, okay, I'm willing to try anything to get rid of this pain.'

'Just the job.' Scott took up a position behind his friend. He assessed the situation in what he considered a professional manner, even taking time to stroke his chin, apparently deep in thought. There was no doubt that Daley's right shoulder was considerably lower than his left, his back at an unnatural angle. 'Okay, Jimmy. I've isolated the problem. Just you stand still, I'll have you sorted in a jiffy.'

Before Daley could reply, he felt strong hands grab his neck and shoulders. Scott was trying to force his right shoulder up, the other down. The pain was so bad that it sent flashes of light through his vision. 'No, stop!' Daley bent forward in an attempt to rid himself of Scott's attentions.

'Just one mair tug, big man. Come on, don't be a baby.'

Scott pulled at Daley's right shoulder again. The big man screamed, collapsing against a wall bent over in agony, his hands propping him and his erstwhile chiropractor up. Meanwhile, Scott had been pulled forward, and because of Daley's great height looked as though he was trying to grab a piggyback.

'What on earth is going on here?' Staff Nurse Murphy took in the scene. DCI Daley was doubled in two, his arms outstretched against the wall, while Scott held on to his shoulders, his face red with effort.

'It's my back, nurse. Brian was just trying to straighten me out.' Daley spoke through gritted teeth.

'What the pair of you get up to in your free time is entirely a matter for yourselves. But let me tell you both, it won't be happening in this hospital. Do you understand?' She folded her arms to emphasise her point.

'Hang on, doll,' said Scott, as he stood up and brushed himself down.

'*Doll*? To whom do you think you're speaking?' Staff Nurse Murphy eyed him less than amicably.

'This man's in pain. You should be helping him, no' trying to cast disruptions.'

'Aspersions, Brian,' said Daley, his face still contorted.

'It would seem you police officers have little in the way of tolerance to pain. Who can forget your peanut episode, Sergeant Scott?'

'Here we go. Yous never miss a chance.'

'That poor lad next door fighting for his life, while you pair are up to – well, goodness knows what out here. Please remember where you are. The doctor will be with you directly.'

'Great. Thank you,' said Daley, his jaws still clenched, as she marched off.

'I don't think he's coming to see you, Jimmy. It'll be to tell us aboot the lad, how he is, you know.'

'Shut up, Brian. As soon as I'm better I'm going to break your neck.'

'Aye, it's true what they say – no good deed goes unpunished, that's the truth.' Scott straightened his tie.

5

The man stared from the window of his caravan out across the dark sea. He was sipping at a can of beer, the lights in the room switched off. The moon was casting a ribbon of light which appeared to end at his window. It was as though it was trying to tell him the time was right; the time was now.

He placed his right hand against the cold window. He had two missing fingers. He passed his hand across the deep scar on his face, and then against the glass, throwing his head back at the tiny hint of sensation left in the remaining digits. In moments, his mutilated hand was balled into a fist. His expression changed from blank to something more redolent of simmering hatred.

He would only ever blame one person for his plight.

But revenge would be sweet, and it would come soon. He sensed it; he knew it. This was something he'd always been able to do: sense when something big was going to happen in his life. And he'd had an eventful one. Sadly, few if any of the experiences stored in his memory were enjoyable. In fact, most were indescribably terrible, at the hands of people he should have been able to trust, people who should have cared for him. But they were all life lessons. Life had taught him to hate – hate with a passion.

Moving away from the window, he lowered himself back into his chair, picked a joint from the small table beside him and fired it into life. The cannabis cracked as he drew deeply on the reefer, its sweet, earthy taste tickling his throat as it travelled down to his burning lungs. This was pleasure rather than pain. This was his only relief from the self-hatred that followed him around like a ghoul: always there, sometimes out of sight, at others dominating his every sense, every emotion.

Some of his friends liked heavier drugs, others found oblivion in alcohol. He preferred the gentle balm of weed. For him, it was like sinking into a feather bed, a mother's embrace. Not that he could remember such a thing. Drink and coke drove you wild. He liked to think of cannabis as protection against the elements, a personal roof against the raining problems of his world. After all, everyone needed something, some kind of crutch to see them through the battering that life pitched at everyone.

His gaze shifted around the room. A photograph of his parents took pride of place on a battered shelf. A ramshackle coffee table with one bent leg sat before him. There was a motheaten rug in front of an electric fire that buzzed constantly. He had no choice but to use it, though, as the weather had turned seasonally cold and he had no other form of heating. A stolen television was wedged into a corner. On it played a Netflix documentary, the sound muted. It wasn't a service he paid for. Like almost everything in his life it was done on the fly, a hack here, a dodge there.

Next to the television were two shotguns. One was sawn off, the other complete with its long barrel. He smiled at the sight of them; they were his instruments of revenge. And after such a long time, at last he would have that revenge. That, alongside a buzz from his smoke, afforded him comfort. But then he stared at the remains of his fingers once more, and the comfort was gone.

She'd taken everything away from him. It was all her fault. But although life had taken away most of his chances, he'd finally been given the opportunity to get even, to get straight.

He remembered them asking him questions in the plain white room.

'*Whose idea was it? Why did you do it? Was it planned?*'

'*No!*' he'd yelled. '*It was her!*'

Nobody believed him. Not until the kind man in the smart suit had appeared. He listened to everything; he understood.

Getting to the right moment had taken time. But now that time was near.

'Bastard!' The oath echoed around the caravan.

In Kinloch hospital, Dr Frisland was showing Daley and Scott an X-ray plate against an illuminated viewer.

'Now, if you look carefully, you'll see what I mean.' He pointed at the skeletal image of a skull.

'There, a hairline crack?' said Daley.

'Yes, right first time. This young man not only nearly killed himself with these horrible drugs, but he's also been hit over the head into the bargain. Hit hard, too.'

Scott squinted at the X-ray, his reading glasses perched on his nose. 'Nasty. Good on you for spotting that, doc.'

'It's not the fact that we know that it's happened, it's the way it's been done, sergeant.'

'Wae a big hammer, I'd say,' said Scott.

'Not so, I don't think.'

'What, then?' Daley asked.

Dr Frisland shook his head. 'I'd say a clenched fist. Like so.' He bunched his fist and hammered it down, side-on. 'A person of immense personal strength. None of the soft tissue around the skull has been damaged – save for bruising, that is.'

'What are you driving at, doc?' said Scott.

'Well, it's a very clean, accurate strike. From my limited knowledge of brutality, I'd have to say I'd have been rather proud of myself if I'd executed that particular piece of work. Hit this man just in the right place to cause maximum damage.'

Scott made a face. 'You sound like an undercover psychopath, if you don't mind me saying.'

'Would you have to be trained to be able to do this, I wonder?' Daley asked absently.

'I'd say so, Jim. Ex-army, some profession that values people who are able to damage another without a weapon.'

'Bet any gent of your profession could do it, eh?' said Scott.

'No, not a chance. I could break a finger, maybe an arm. But this is artistry. You've no idea how difficult it is to do – such force.'

'You're a real admirer, then?' said Daley sarcastically.

'No, inspector. I'm interested by the physical – how things happen to the body. But you'll be pleased to know that young Mr Watson will survive, for now at least.'

'For now? What do you mean?'

'I mean that we have his liver, heart and kidney functions restored to something approaching normality. But there's no knowing what damage those organs have sustained. That will manifest itself later on in life. Toxicity of this kind almost always leaves some mark on all but the most robust individuals. That's why I can't get my head round why they want to do this to themselves. What's to be gained by spending one's time in a permanent fug?'

'That's puzzled me for years, doctor,' said Daley.

Scott looked on without comment.

Daley moved to stand up straight but yelled out in pain.

'Bit of trouble with your back?' said Frisland.

'You could say that. I must have jarred it earlier. It's been agony for hours.' Daley grimaced again.

'I'll give you some pain relief. Co-codamol, I think. But you'd better get to your GP as soon as you can.'

'That's the stuff, Jimmy. Once you get a few pills doon your throat, you'll be brand new. They co-codamol are top notch. Make you feel like a million dollars, so they do.'

'Are you in the habit of taking them, sergeant?'

Scott smiled. 'Only when I get shot.'

'Is that a frequent experience?'

'Mair frequent than I'd like, doc.'

'They tell me you have a peanut allergy.' Frisland's face was a mask of insincerity.

'Aye, very good.'

The detectives looked on as Frisland went in search of painkillers for Daley.

'At least the lad's going to survive. I hate this. There doesn't seem to be anything we can do. Everything we try, we hit up against a dead end.'

'We can look forward to more of it, too, Jimmy. The junkies can't get enough of the new fentanyl shit.'

'This isn't just dealing for money. I'm convinced there's a sadist at work here.'

Scott furrowed his brow. 'Whatever religion he is, it'll mean a bundle mair work for us, and that's for certain, Jimmy.'

Daley looked at Scott and sighed. He knew he wouldn't be able to apply his mind to enlightening his sergeant until the tablets arrived and the pain went away.

6

Nate was slouched at a table in the hotel bar, while Delphine pretended to be interested in what fellow student Salazar Brandt was saying. He'd climbed Everest as an Eton schoolboy. This gave him the opportunity to set himself up as the unofficial mentor of their expedition group, and he was showing Delph endless images of his ascent on his phone, a tortuous story behind each picture.

'Hey, Salz, mate. Do you think you could give us a little space?' Nate yawned and leaned back in his chair, effortlessly louche.

Delph glared at him, but Salazar excused himself at once.

'Fuck, I'm sorry, guys. You'll understand once you've experienced it yourself. It gets to you, man. The big rock is something you'll never forget.'

'Yeah, you said.' Nate yawned again.

Salazar made his way back to the bar, where two of the less popular undergraduates were boring a young waitress.

'That was really rude, Nate.' Delph slapped his hand.

'Were you going to sit here all night listening to that? Fuck, I was bored titless. You attract that type of person, you know. Remember that folk singer in the Dordogne?'

'He was lovely!'

'He wanted to shag you. Had no qualms about making his intentions clear, right there and then in front of me. I wanted to cut his bloody hand off so he couldn't play that awful thing any more.'

'It was a bouzouki.' She stared at him. 'Why do you say such terrible things?'

'Like what?'

'Cutting people's hands off, stuff like that. You do it all the time. I find it really distasteful.'

'Less of the petted lip, Delph. You know I can't stand all that right-on PC stuff. I keep it real!'

'Some of my friends think you're boorish.' She took a gulp of her pint.

'I'm from Kensington. You can't be *boorish* there.'

'More likely to be Russian.'

Nate made a face. 'Not so sure about that these days.'

'Whatever. You should try and be more tolerant. You'll gain friends.'

'I don't need *friends*, Tracy. I've got you.'

'Well, I have friends, and I intend to keep them.'

'Like Emerald Tweedie, you mean?'

'Em is lovely!'

'She's like a twenty-one-year-old grandmother. All that baking and knitting. I can't stand her.'

Delphine folded her arms defensively across her chest.

'Time for the cold shoulder.' Nate snorted his derision. 'I'm going to bed. We've got a twenty-mile hike tomorrow, remember. It's going to be cold, too. Might be some snow up on the path, they say.'

'Goodnight. I'm staying for another drink.' She averted

her eyes.

'Why not? You can maybe toss Salz off under the table when he gets to his summiting story. That should be fun.'

'Yes, I think it might. Better fun than sitting here watching you look bored and uninterested.'

Nate gestured expansively round the room. 'I'm sorry. I mean, this is all so entertaining. Some shitty little hotel on the end of a peninsula that looks like a knob.'

'You're the knob, Nate.'

He ran his hand through his hair. 'Right, that's enough for me.'

'You're the one who was so keen to come here, remember?'

'I beg your pardon? You were desperate to come on this little trip. *Christmasy,* you said. All whisky and snow is what you promised. A chance to get away together before we get eaten up by our families over the festive season.'

'When it comes to families, it's before yours eat you up, you mean.'

'Bollocks! You were invited to Buckinghamshire for Boxing Day. What's your problem?'

'Lucky me! Boxing Day, but not Christmas Day. I'm not good enough for that.'

Nate massaged his forehead with one hand. 'Here we go. You know what Teddy is like. He isn't keen on having anyone but his family round the table on the big day. My sister's husband is only there on sufferance, for fuck's sake.'

Delph sighed. 'Why don't you call him *dad* or *father*? Why *Teddy*?'

Nate shrugged. 'He likes to be called Teddy. You can't hang a man for that, surely?'

'I suppose not. Bit odd, though.'

'You'll be quite happy in your little cottage with Mummy and Daddy. Where is it again?'

'Daddy's taken a place in Cornwall – by the sea, as a matter of fact. I'm looking forward to it.'

'What are you worried about, then?'

In the corner, three of their more inebriated companions struck up a raucous rugby song.

'Everywhere we go they murder that shit.' Nate shook his head.

'I'll come with you. I can't stand all this male bravado.'

'I knew you would. Come on, Tracy. Salz's loss is my gain.'

'You think?'

Nate put his arm over her shoulder, and the pair made their way back to their room.

7

It was just after three in the morning, and Kinloch's streets were deserted, save for one figure staggering down Main Street. The young man was tall, but hunched over, dragging his feet along the pavement, occasionally stumbling into doorways or bouncing off cars and the plate glass windows of the emporia along the way.

Under the glow of acetylene, everything looked stark – clinical, almost – and sounds carried clearly: the dead-eyed windows of flats, the fleeting black shadow of a prowling cat, the rattle of a drinks can being propelled along the road by the fresh breeze, the distant wash of waves breaking on the sea wall, and the flashes from primed alarm units above shop doorways, like tiny beacons in the night beckoning the day.

The young man lurched on, his moan of pain echoing up a close before he carried on his zig-zagging path and crashed into a large refuse bin, over which he slumped for a few moments.

He was trying to focus to get his bearings. But some instinct told him that his destination was just down the road, and if he could keep going, he'd find help.

He forced himself off the bin with a yell of pain. The sheer shock of it all made him feel like passing out, though he was barely in possession of his senses at all.

What was left of his journey encompassed little more than a hundred metres. Yet he managed to collide with another car and a wall before tripping over the kerb and flying headlong on to the road, where he lay silent and still.

This shift was normally a long one for the two police constables in Lima Mike Three, a marked police car used to patrol the streets of the sleeping town. Little happened during the week – not on the night shift. There was the odd domestic dispute, arrests for drunkenness, and if you were lucky, a break-in. But all in all, it was quiet until the weekends. Unless the drugs war flared up again, as it had the previous evening.

Constable Ellie Ferris yawned as they took the long arc of the esplanade at the head of the loch connecting the two parts of Kinloch that had once been separate towns. The lights at the quay were bright, though nothing moved under them, and there were only fleeting glimpses of the moon between the low clouds. The few boats left in the Kinloch fleet bobbed at anchor, outnumbered – even at this time of year – by pleasure craft of all shapes and sizes hugging the pontoons.

'I could just go for a sleep, Davie,' said Ferris. The trouble with the night shift was that, as soon as you were acclimatised to staying up all night then sleeping during the day, it was time for a couple of rest days then on to something else. This being the first night of their shift, the pair were still slightly disoriented.

'I'll never get used to nights,' said Constable Davie Lee. 'The wife hates them even more. She can't stand sleeping alone.'

'Huh. We'd a special back in Govan like that. She just made sure there was always somebody with her every night, if you get my drift.'

'Aye, you get all sorts in this job, Ellie.'

They turned left off the roundabout along a stretch of road between the town's twin piers. Lee slowed his speed as they stared out across the loch, making sure all was in order in the harbour. It was automatic – mechanical, almost – but had to be done, and it was bred into the bones of police officers everywhere: check, check, check.

Instead of coming off this tiny stretch of road the locals called the 'dual carriageway', he turned the vehicle back the way he'd come. Two lanes separated by a narrow median strip had earned this section of road its name. It was a legacy of an old narrow-gauge railway that used to ply its trade between the coal pit at Machrie and the harbour: long gone, but never forgotten.

Back on the roundabout, they took the turn on to Main Street.

'Wait a minute, Ellie. What's that?' A man was lying in the middle of the road, only metres away from the King's Hotel.

'I hope he hasn't shat himself,' said Ferris, a look of distaste on her face.

'It's the spew I can't stand. Really gets me right in the gut.'

They pulled up alongside the stricken figure and emerged from the car. Lee bent over the man and held two fingers to the artery in his throat. 'He lives!' he said as his colleague made her way round, ready to grab an arm to haul him into the vehicle if they couldn't rouse him back to consciousness. A man lying drunk in the road was no strange sight anywhere in the country these days.

'Now, think on what you were taught, Davie. This person could be ill. Don't *assume*: it makes an *ass* of *you* and *me* – remember?'

Lee smiled at the old phonetic trope they'd picked up during training. The police service was full of little nuggets like this, all designed to teach the mind never to take anything at face value.

'You'd need to have no sense of smell at all not to assume here, Ellie. Guy smells like a brewery.'

Instead of a witty riposte, his colleague stood, her hand over her mouth. She reached for the Airwave radio clipped to her stab-vest. 'Two-seven-two, over.'

'Go ahead, two-seven-two, over.' The reply was instant.

'Requesting an ambulance on Main Street at the King's Hotel. Make it quick, Bobby, over.'

Constable Davie Lee looked surprised. 'What's up?'

The man lying on the road stirred. He tried to speak, then let out a howl of pain.

A look of concern spread across Ferris's face. 'Check this out, Davie.'

Lee hurried to her side, where the man's left arm was stretched along the tarmac. Two fingers had been removed from his left hand, the stumps that remained cauterised black.

8

Despite the early hour – it was just after five in the morning – the bar at the King's Hotel was busy. The entire Everest Expedition party sat wearily at the tables spread round the room. There was a low murmur of gratitude when a night porter arrived with a tray of coffee and toast from the kitchens.

Brian Scott took in the scene, his face grim.

'What's up with you?' said Daley.

'This is the cream o' our youth, eh? Can't say I'm impressed, Jimmy.'

'To be fair, they were travelling all day yesterday. Have you seen the time?'

'No' unusual for us to be up and aboot at this time, is it?'

'We're police officers, Brian. We can't do a nine to five.'

'Unless you're a lazy bastard in the Courts branch.'

'Some good cops in the Courts branch.'

'You're just saying that because you were nearly in it after you leathered that dentist.'

'Thank you for your kind words, my old friend.' Daley took a deep breath, marvelling at the efficacy of the painkillers he'd been given by the doctor at Kinloch hospital. Despite leaving him feeling a bit sleepy, the pain was greatly diminished; his state of mind had improved too. Normally, when called out in the middle of the night, Daley was like a bear with a sore head. Now, however, he felt a certain joie de vivre. Most unusual, but he rode his luck, hoping his mood would remain buoyant. Now they had coffee and toast, Daley reckoned the university party would be ready to divulge any information they could supply regarding one of their own now languishing in Kinloch hospital.

Daley stood and banged a teaspoon on his own mug of coffee. It sounded shrill in a room where tired undergraduates were more intent on a caffeine hit than conversation.

'I'm DCI Daley, and this is DS Brian Scott. I apologise for getting you out of your beds at this hour. However, I have some bad news.'

'Has my tutor died?' shouted one lad who was failing in his attempts to grow a beard. 'I owe him an essay.' This to thin laughter.

'What makes you think that?' said Scott, narrowing his eyes into a gimlet glare.

'Can't stand the bloke, that's all. Just a joke, officer.' The young man now looked rather sheepish.

'Let me give you a lesson in life, son. See, when you're dragged out your bed at five in the morning to speak to the police, it's best no' to bother wae the jokes. Got it?'

Daley cleared his throat and continued, marvelling yet again at how his colleague rarely if ever practised what he preached. 'One of your friends was found in the street a couple of hours ago. He was under the influence of strong narcotics, and I'm sad to say he'd been the victim of a serious assault.'

'Who is it?' shouted two of the group at once. Still half asleep, they hadn't bothered to work out who from their party was missing. Now there were anxious glances around the room.

'The injured party is one Salazar Brandt. I'm sure you all know him.'

Delph had been leaning her head on Nate's shoulder. On hearing their fellow student's name, she sat up and looked at Nate, her eyes scrutinising his face.

Daley continued. 'I know some of you will be firmer friends with Mr Brandt than others here. But I have to speak to you all as a matter of procedure. Remember, no matter how small you may think the detail, the information contained within could help us find out who did this. So, try to remember everything you can about last night.'

'It's no' as though it's that long ago. And yous are supposed to be right brainboxes, no?' said Scott rather unhelpfully.

Daley resisted the temptation to raise a disapproving eyebrow and carried on. 'Professor Tang and her colleagues will bring you up one by one to either myself or DS Scott. The sooner we get this over with, the better. And, please, try to recall the events of last evening as accurately as you can. I'm sure you all want to help Mr Brandt.'

'Fuck, I hope we don't get that sergeant. Looks like a real bastard,' Nate whispered to Delph.

She stared back at him blankly.

'What?'

'You weren't very nice about him last night, Nate. I hope you haven't done anything stupid.' Her lips were pursed, expression formidable.

'Oh, come on, Delph. We've been in bed since midnight – together! Don't you think you'd have noticed if I'd slipped out to do Salz a mischief?'

'You know how I sleep after . . . well, after we've made love.'

Nate shook his head angrily, and whispered to his girlfriend through gritted teeth, 'Be very careful what you say to these detectives, Delph. They don't mess about up here. They arrested Teddy once in Glasgow when he was younger. Gave him a good kicking, apparently. All he'd done was have a piss in the street.'

'I'm sure his attitude had nothing to do with that. I mean, he's such a pleasant person.'

'He is if he's in the right mood.'

'And that happens when?' Delph folded her arms as Professor Tang appeared at their side.

'Okay. Miss Harker, please step forward and speak to DCI Daley. Mr Farringdon, you'll be interviewed by the sergeant.' She moved on to the next table.

'Shit, I knew I'd get him.' Nate sighed then yawned. 'I hope we'll get the chance to catch another few hours' kip.'

'So typical of you, Nate. No thought whatsoever for poor Salazar. We don't even know what they did to him.'

'A good going over was just what that boring bastard needed, if you ask me.'

'Go tell that to the detective. See how you get on.'

Nate slouched across to where DS Brian Scott was sitting behind a table.

'What's your name, son?'

'Nathan Farringdon.'

'How do you spell all that?' said Scott with more than a hint of irritation.

'Is it so hard?'

Scott bent his head and stared over his half-moon reading glasses. 'Lose the attitude and spell your name, son.

Mistakes lead to injustices. We wouldn't want you caught up in something you didn't do just because we didnae catch your name properly, would we now?'

Nate looked at the police officer wearily and spelled out his name.

'Good. Now we can get on wae the details.'

'Sorry?'

'We can proceed wae the interview. Have you got cloth ears?'

'I just find your accent a bit hard to follow. Is that a crime up here?'

Scott cleared his throat. 'Did you speak to Salazar Brandt yesterday evening?' The words were individually formed, delivered in a slow, halting yet intimidating fashion.

'Not really.'

'Dae you mind me asking what you're studying?'

'Politics, philosophy and economics. Why?'

'Makes sense. Well, you're no' in the House o' Commons now. Answer the fucking question!'

Nate shook his head in frustration. 'Okay, he was at our table. But he wasn't speaking to me.'

'Who then?'

'My girlfriend, Delphine Harker. She's with your colleague now.'

Scott looked across to where Daley was deep in conversation with a young woman. 'You got lucky, eh?'

'She's very beautiful, I know.' Nate sat up in his chair. 'Listen, can we please get on with this? I'm knackered, and we've got a twenty-mile hike later today.'

'Lucky all they wars were last century. We'd never have won wae kids like you having such a fondness for their beds.'

'Take your tropes somewhere else.'

Scott realised that he'd somehow been insulted, but being rather hazy as to the meaning of the word *tropes* he decided that discretion was the better part of valour in this instance and carried on regardless.

'One more time, Mr Farringdon.' He smiled. 'What was discussed between you and Salazar last night?'

'Nothing really. He was showing my girlfriend pictures on his phone. I was bored. I told him so. He went. End of story.'

Scott leaned back in his chair. 'Fair to say that you and he aren't the best o' pals, then?'

'I barely know him. Just spoken to him a few times in the club. I have no opinion of the guy either way. I just object to having someone force his way into my company, that's all.'

'You're the jealous type, then?'

'What? No, not at all. Listen, not long after he left our table, Delph and I went upstairs to bed, where we stayed until you woke us and brought us back down here. I was with her the whole time. So, whatever happened to Salz – and I do feel sorry for him – it wasn't me, okay?'

'If you say so. Mind, I'll be checking your partner corroborates what you've said.' Scott scribbled some notes.

'Can I go now?'

'Hang on.'

'What for?'

'I'm no' a quick writer, that's what for.' Scott glared at him for a moment, then continued with his pen.

Nate leaned back in his chair and angled his head towards the ceiling, letting out a long sigh.

'Right. One last thing. How did your girlfriend react when she heard the way you spoke to Mr Brandt? I mean, it sounds rather rude. Not many lassies would enjoy that.'

'She gave me grief about it for a couple of minutes.'

'Maybe learn some manners, son. In our short acquaintance, I can tell you right now that you'll just piss folk off with the way you behave.'

Nate flung himself forward in his chair, his hands suddenly balled into fists.

'Some temper, too, eh?'

Nate was aware of footsteps behind him. Daley pulled out a chair and sat beside Scott, all the time not taking his eyes off the undergraduate.

'What now?' Nate shook his head in irritation.

'Did you tell DS Scott what you threatened to do to Mr Brandt?'

'I'm sorry?'

Daley consulted his notes. 'Is it true you threatened to cut his hand off, sir?'

'Not his, no, and anyway it was a joke – nothing more. Fuck, this is bizarre.' Nate turned in his chair to look for Delph, but she was nowhere to be seen.

'Do you know what happened to Mr Brandt?' said Daley.

'Just what you've told us.' Nate shrugged.

'Someone cut off his fingers,' said Daley dispassionately.

Scott grimaced. 'You and that temper, son, eh?'

'Will you both listen to me!' Nate thudded a fist into the table. 'I had absolutely nothing to do with what happened to Salazar Brandt. I know what I said to Delph, but it was said in jest. I don't even know why she bothered to tell you. I've been with her all night.'

'Methinks he dost protest mair than he needs to,' said Scott, secretly proud of his mangling of the Bard.

'I'd like to speak to you at greater length, Mr Farringdon.

Brian, please inform Professor Tang that we intend to take this young man to the office for further questioning.'

Nate shot to his feet. 'No way! I've heard stories about the police in Scotland. If you think you'll amuse yourselves by using me as a punch bag, think again. I want to call my father.'

'You'll be able to call him once we get there. And for your information, I don't *amuse myself* by using anyone as a punch bag. Just tell us the truth and you'll be fine.'

Nate slumped back in his chair. 'I don't believe this, I really don't.'

'I find it hard to believe you don't have any other forms of amusement, Jimmy.' Brian Scott left in search of Professor Tang.

9

She looked out as dawn broke through the trees and across the restless ocean. Despite the cold, the sky was clear, and birdsong filled the air. She pushed open the stiff sash window and breathed in the chill morning.

'Good morning to me,' she said in a bright voice.

Having taken her fill of the dawn, she wandered back to the low coffee table where she had left the French press and her mug and checked her watch, making sure five minutes had elapsed. Depressing the plunger then lifting the pot, she poured the hot coffee into her mug, put it to her nose and enjoyed the brew's aroma.

She thought back on her early experiences with coffee. Her father had been addicted to the stuff, so he saw nothing wrong in cooling some down and letting his four-year-old daughter experience it for the first time.

'You can't beat the Java of a morning, lass,' he would say as he smacked his lips at the first sip of the day. She smiled at the memory.

She had no idea how many days had passed between that day and this, but realised that it must be a very long time. She recalled holding a mug of coffee under his nose as he lay motionless in the hospital, little more than skin and bone. She'd told herself that it would reinvigorate the man to whom she owed her existence. But every vestige of his former self was gone.

The room was large, with a high ceiling, ornate plaster cornices and a parquet floor. Only an old leather armchair and the coffee table occupied this space, and they were situated in the very centre of the floor. She took another drink, then scratched at a stain on the floral dress she was wearing. The swirling pattern had faded; she realised how much when a shaft of sunlight caught it. She couldn't remember the last time she'd looked in a mirror. Come to think of it, she struggled to remember if she possessed such a thing at all.

It was funny, she thought. She could remember the days when she looked in mirrors all the time. Her teenage years hadn't been the happiest time of her life; she was never sure if the reflection she perceived was a true representation of how she actually looked. Though she thought it conceited, she felt that she was as pretty as any girl in her class – certainly more so than Tamara Stevens. But it was Tamara who turned heads, Tamara who was invited out to pubs by older boys, even though she was far too young to visit such places.

Come to think of it, it was Tamara who told the girls all they needed to know about men and making love. She remembered hanging on her every word.

'But where are you now, Tamara? I know, you're dead. I saw your dead eyes and your grey face. I watched them take you away in a black bag. No boys, no pubs, no fancy necklaces that day, *Tamara*.' Her tone was mocking, words echoing round the empty room. 'And you looked like shit, too.'

First, she smiled, then the smile turned into a giggle, then a manic laugh.

'Fuck you, Tamara!' She sang the words over and over again, until a wave of melancholy swept over her.

'*Why can't you just get back to normal? You were clever; you had a good job. What's wrong with you?*'

It was her mother's voice. Not in the cold empty room but in her head.

'*Answer me!*'

'No, I won't answer you. You ask me that question all the time but I'm never going to answer you. Not ever!'

'*You're an embarrassment. Letty next door is an accountant now. What are you? Tell me, what are you?*'

'At least I can go out the house. You're the odd one, not me, Mother!' She bunched her dress between two clenched fists, thudding her feet into the wooden floor in her rage. 'You haven't been out of this house for fifteen years. Not since Dad died. You're not right!' She screamed the last few words.

Exhausted, she slouched in the chair and reached for the mug. It was almost empty and what remained of the coffee was cold.

'*Cold as a witch's tit!*'

She turned round, trying to place this new voice.

She remembered she had wanted someone to put her right for so long. Now, here they were.

'*It's in your head, you know that. They're all in your head.*'

'*Cold as a witch's tit!*'

'Leave me alone, Mother! I want to hear the other voice!'

She sat stock-still for a few moments, her eyes so tightly closed it hurt. She willed the new voice to speak to her again, but the words were gone.

She held out her fist and propelled it against her own face. Again and again, she felt the pain; heard flesh on bone; felt the first seep of blood as it found its way between her fingers.

That was the time to stop. That was the time to stop.

She cowered from the imaginary blows, trying to get away as far as she could from the pain. She screamed. 'Please just leave me alone. You must! I will be better. You can't keep doing this!'

She fell to her knees, curled into a ball and placed her fingers in her ears.

'La-la-la-la-la.' It began as a whisper and ended as a *cri de coeur*.

As quickly as the fit had begun, her body relaxed and she rolled over on to her back, the expression on her bloodied face blank once more.

10

Kinloch police office was a busy place. Still following the intelligence tip on drugs being brought to the area on public transport, and now with two mutilated young people to deal with, resources were stretched.

Daley studied the images of each victim: one with missing digits and the other a broken skull. Yet again, he tried to think who could do such a thing. But having seen his fair share of ghastly inhumanity, he wasn't surprised. There seemed to be no depths to which people couldn't sink in terms of wickedness and cruelty. He thought of his own son. What horrors would he face in his life? It was a notion he had to banish quickly before he became melancholy.

Shaw appeared at the door of his glass box with some papers to be signed. His face was pale and drawn, and his uniform hung off him in folds.

'How are you faring, Alasdair?' said Daley.

The sergeant shrugged. 'I'm just trying to get on with it, sir. What is there to do?'

'Any word from your wife?' Daley held up his hand. 'If I'm overstepping, please say.'

'No, not at all. It's good to have someone to talk to, as a

matter of fact.' He took a seat opposite the DCI. 'It's just like talking to a stranger. I asked her if I should apply for a posting, if Kinloch was the problem.'

'We'd be sad to lose you. You're the glue that keeps this place together.'

'I don't think there's any danger of that. She made it plain the problem wasn't where we live, it was me.'

'Oh, I see. If it's the job – well, it's not everything, you know. So many marriages are under strain because of the way we're forced to live our lives. It's hard for the one left to bring up the kids, balance the books, keep the house going, juggle another job while we obsess about our work.'

Shaw nodded balefully. 'I rather think I could be working in any job, and nothing would be any different, Jim. When it's gone, it's gone. I just have to get used to that.'

'Not so good. You'll be missing the children.'

'I'm missing everything. I never thought this would happen. We were a wee family – a unit, you know. I thought we were solid as a rock. I never thought for one minute she was so unhappy.' He looked close to tears.

'If it's any consolation, I know how you feel. Remember, my door is always open, okay?'

'Thanks, sir.'

Daley signed the papers and Shaw made his way back to his desk. You either sank or swam in this job as far as marriage was concerned. There seemed to be very little in the way of a halfway house. Some couples struggled on for the sake of their children, or merely because neither party could think of anything else to do. But some partnerships were like rocks. Daley watched Brian Scott hard at work behind a desk in the CID suite. Though his old friend and his wife could fight like demons, he knew there was an almost unbreakable bond there. True love that could never be breached by the demands of the job, by money – by any exigency.

Again, Daley remembered how much he envied the man.

As he stared, he saw Scott take a call, write some hurried notes, then get up and make his way towards him.

'Some severed fingers have been found on a beach, Jimmy.'

'Where? Who?'

'Up on the Largie. A dog-walker. I just spoke to her there. She's standing beside them, doesn't know what to do.'

Daley blew out his cheeks. 'I sometimes wonder what we'd do without dog-walkers, eh?'

'It's a dangerous occupation as far as I can tell, big man. Fancy a run up the coast? I can take Potts with me, if you want.'

'No, I'll come with you, Brian. Hopefully the fresh air will clear my head.'

'That'll be they painkillers you keep flinging doon your throat. Better watch wae those things. I've a cousin in Cambuslang. He hurt his back at work, and they put him on those pills. Three months later he was snorting coke.'

'Your cousin, you say?'

'Aye. Big Donnie. Good joiner, by the way.'

Daley nodded. 'If you see me rolling up a tenner, just take it off me.'

'That's you mocking me again. I'm serious! One minute you're getting relief for your pain, the next it's doon to the local dealer for a bag or two.'

'Here's hoping you don't hurt your back. I've seen you drink plenty. I don't fancy enduring you on drugs.'

'Nah, no' me, Jimmy. I've got a will of iron when it comes to that type of thing.'

Idly, Daley pondered on Scott's iron will as they headed for the car park.

The university party disembarked from two minibuses at the bottom of a rough path that meandered up a steep hillside. Professor Tang looked harassed as she paid the drivers in cash for their services then made her way back to the group of weary undergraduates.

The party could have begun their walk at Machrie, but their time was limited, and Tang wanted to make sure they all had what it took to camp out in cold conditions, and all that brought with it.

'Okay. Let's get last night out of our minds and concentrate on what's ahead. Both here and in the future, right? We focus, and we move on. When we get to the top of this hill, we'll get our bearings. Then we split up into the pairs we talked about last week. This is an exercise in map-reading and basic survival.'

'How is Salz?' asked a bearded student.

'He's as well as he can be. His father is on the way, and he's out of danger.'

'But he's still missing fingers. They won't grow back. He was going to be an architect,' said a blonde girl who looked near to tears.

'It's a tragedy, of course. Let it be a lesson to us all. We can never let down our guard to the possibility of violence. Even in beautiful places like this, awful things can happen. I'm sure the police will catch whoever did this terrible thing. But it should also act as a warning not to become involved with drugs. Here are the consequences writ large. Now, let's go.' Tang checked the straps on her bulky rucksack and was first to step out on the path, followed by a ragged column of her charges.

Nate pulled Delph back. They were the very last in the group.

'Leave me alone! I still can't believe that you ended up in a police station because of your attitude. You're a total arsehole, Nate.'

'*I* still can't believe you grassed me up! Why did you mention what I'd said about cutting that guy's hand off? You know it was just a throwaway remark.' Delph searched his face, but it registered only anger and resentment. 'Come on, say something! Four hours I was up there. Then they ask me a few stupid questions and let me go. It was an exercise in humiliation, nothing more.'

'You humiliated yourself, Nate. I've told you so many times that the way you treat people will get you into trouble.'

'*You* got me into trouble.' He poked his finger into her face. 'All you had to do was confirm we'd been together in bed. Not only could you not manage that, you felt it necessary to tell stupid tales into the bargain. Fuck's sake!' He glared at her.

'I was always brought up to respect the police and tell the truth. That's all I did. I was sound asleep until we were asked to go back down into the bar. You could have gone anywhere, and I wouldn't have known. That's the truth.'

'You really amaze me, do you know that?'

'Why? Is it maybe because honesty is a concept lost on you and the rest of your family?'

'Okay, so this is the real reason you were such a twat last night. Jealousy is a terrible thing, Delph.'

'Jealous of what? Your slippery banker father who helped preside over a global financial meltdown and walked away with even fuller pockets? No, that's nothing to aspire to.'

'Aw, poor little Delph on her high horse. What is it your

father does again? Oh yes, I know. He owns a couple of shops. You know, Teddy warned me about you. About getting involved with a *scholarship girl*.'

'Fuck you!' Delph strode forward, shouting to the three girls in front of them to hang on.

Nate clenched his teeth as he watched her go. If there was one thing his father had taught him, it was to despise betrayal.

He turned and looked out across the mirror-calm sea. An island lay off the coast, three windmills clearly visible, barely moving in the still, cold air. They'd only been seeing each other for a few months, but even in that short time Nate had known he was falling in love. Yes, he was angry that she'd told the police about his empty threat, but deep down it was no reason for ending their relationship.

He would have to do what he hated most: eat humble pie. However bitter it tasted, he would eat what he had to.

He trudged up the hill after the rest of the party.

11

Truth be told, Andrew Mitchell hated being told what do by a woman. But he'd done it without question. The money was good, and he loved money. It outweighed anything else in his life – just about.

He heard the car pull up in the drive, and quickly switched off the porn movie he'd been watching on the TV. Luckily, their cottage was a remote one, not in the town but on its edge. It could only be accessed by the long gravel driveway, which suited him for two reasons. He'd grown up in a grim block of flats in one of Glasgow's schemes. Both his mother and he had been miserable, constantly short of money and subsequently food. He'd still been in primary school when he started doing favours for local dealers. They gave him a few quid in return. Nothing to them, but a godsend for him and his mother.

As he grew older, Mitchell's criminal career blossomed. He was big and strong – very strong – and by the time he was nineteen, in between working on the door as security for nightclubs owned by his gangster pals, he was sent to hand out beatings to those who had defaulted on financial arrangements with the mob, or simply irritated them.

He smiled as he watched his wife get out of the car with his son and twin daughters. It was half-day at school, and the sight of them skipping into the house made him happy. No stinking lift for his kids to negotiate, no bullies ready to extort money from a five-year-old boy who had to find his own way home from school as his mother was spark-out drunk on the sofa after a lunchtime vodka session with her pals.

His children grew up in splendid isolation, surrounded by fields of cows and sheep, breathing fresh country air, not the grime and pollution of the city. They wouldn't have his life, they'd have a start that he couldn't have imagined.

The fact they were isolated with only one lane to access the house suited his profession. If you dealt drugs, you were vulnerable. Simple as that. But he could keep an eye out for the police, rivals and even nosy neighbours. The bungalow boasted powerful security lights to the front and rear. He was ready to face all comers.

He smiled at his wife as she came into the room, but she didn't respond, instead calling back to the kids, 'Go and get changed, and you'll get some pizza. Yous are getting nothing until you do, got it?'

'I'll have pizza, Nadine.' He smiled again as she turned to face him.

'You'll have fuck all. Don't think I didnae hear you on that phone when I left. I forgot my purse. I'd to come back for it. Who's the lassie?'

'Eh?'

'The one you were talking to all fucking quiet an' that. You know fine who I mean.'

'It was business, that's all. You said you don't want to know anything aboot that. How come it's all changed?'

'Nah, dae you think I'm stupid? The only business you have with her is getting intae her knickers.'

'I never thought you were so jealous, Nadine. It's doing my heid in! I swear, I've nothing to dae wae her like that. It's money. Aye, and we all know how much you like that, wae the expensive shoes and the handbags.'

'Well, who's up at the main road in the big black motor wae the windows blacked oot, eh? Did you no' expect me hame so soon?'

Mitchell darted to the window. It was over three hundred metres to the house from the main road. He squinted in the grey afternoon light but couldn't make out any vehicle. 'Fuck all there, Nadine. You're at it, so you are.'

'I'm telling you, if they're no' there now, they were when I turned in. Believe me if you like. I don't care!' She flung her handbag on to the sofa and stormed off.

Mitchell stood at the window and gazed out. Paranoia was part of what he did for a living. He refused to give in to it.

He sat back on his recliner, wondering whether the money from the voice on the phone was worth the hassle.

12

Like most dog-walkers in Daley's experience, Mrs Irene Wilkes was diligent when it came to guarding what she'd found on the beach. A small car park overlooked the short stretch of sand and rock where she'd been walking Reg, her spaniel. Told not to move the pair of severed fingers she'd come across, Wilkes had kept a leery eye on the spot from her car, just in case anyone should happen upon the beach and make a similar discovery.

'I'm not quite sure what I'd have said, Mr Daley. Probably that I was on police business.' Mrs Wilkes reached into the footwell of her little car and produced a large thermos flask. The snow was heavy now, obscuring any views of Islay, Jura or Gairsay. The wind had dropped to a whisper.

'Good idea bringing some tea wae you in this weather,' said Scott. Daley examined the fingers, both in separate evidence bags, as they stood beside Mrs Wilkes's car.

'Aye, I always take a wee flask with me in the winter. At my age, a summer's day can feel chilly.' She unscrewed the lid of the flask. 'It's coffee, by the way. Would you like a drop?'

'Why not?' said Scott with a smile. He took the plastic mug and sipped at the contents, then winced and handed it back to Mrs Wilkes. 'You like your coffee strong, eh?' he said, a doubtful look on his face.

She winked. 'It's the only way, son.'

'Okay,' said Daley. 'We'd better get these to the lab. I'm sorry you made such a gruesome discovery, Mrs Wilkes.'

'Och, I used to work in the old Co-op fleshings. Back in those days, health and safety just wisna in it.'

'I bet.'

'The boys would be cutting the tips o' their fingers off left, right and centre. It wisna a pretty sight, mind you. But you get used to anything.'

Daley raised his brows. 'I daresay.'

'I'm thinking folk sometimes got a wee bit mair than they bargained for wae their Sunday joint, if you know what I mean. These boys were rough, some o' them.'

'Fuck me,' said Scott under his breath.

'If you wouldn't mind coming into the office and making a statement, I'd be obliged to you,' said Daley. 'DS Scott and I have photos of exactly where you found the fingers. Your statement will complete what we need.'

'One o' them was only a couple o' feet away on the shingle. Reg found the other one, didn't you, boy?'

At the mention of his name, Reg stuck his head between the two front seats and barked twice, as though answering her question.

She looked out across the beach, where heavy snow was now falling. 'We used to bring the weans here – me and my late husband.' She inclined her head, the sense of nostalgia palpable. 'But they fled the coop years ago, and my husband died in January.'

'No' easy, right enough,' said Scott.

'Enjoy your youth while yous have it, boys.' She looked them both up and down. 'Mind you, you pair are past the first flush, if you don't mind me saying,' she added, laughing.

'Thanks again. If you can take a run up to the office tomorrow morning, I'll be obliged to you,' said Daley. 'The desk sergeant will know why you've come.' He smiled. 'Good-bye. And thanks again.' He trudged off, pulling his collar up against the weather.

Scott lingered by the old woman's car.

'Dae you want another slug o' coffee, son?'

'No, thanks. And neither should you. You cannae be driving about drinking coffee laced wae whisky, Mrs Wilkes. Near blew my heid off.'

'It's just a drop. Wouldna get a fly drunk.'

'Still, promise me the next time you fill the flask it'll be coffee only, eh?'

'If you say so.'

'That I do. Get yourself down the road before this snow gets any worse. Good day to you, Mrs Wilkes.' Scott smiled as he followed Daley to the unmarked police car.

The university party had split up into different groups. Each had been handed a map with a slightly different route to the village of Tarbert, at the end of the Peninsula Way. With the snow lying at this height, it would be a better replication of the foothills of Everest than anyone had expected.

Nate and Delph were navigating their way through a dense forest of pines in silence. Delph was the first to speak. 'We've only got two and half days to get through this.' She gestured to the map.

'It's hardly a challenge.' Nate was still sullen. 'We'll walk for another four hours or so then find a pitch. Easy.'

'If you say so, boss.'

'Listen, I'm sorry. But I still can't work out why you did it.'

'He asked me what you said. I told them you were a bit sarcastic about Salz. Then he asked again. I'm not good at lying, that's all.'

'Clearly.'

'Oh, come on!'

Nate leaned down and kissed her on the cheek. 'You look quite cute with all that snow on your beanie.'

'It's a "toorie" up here, remember.'

'Okay, a toorie,' said Nate in a mock Scots accent. 'We'd better get on or we'll never make it to this Tarbert.'

'Thank goodness! I thought we were splitting up over this.'

'Never, Tracy. Unless you grass me up to the cops again.' Suddenly, Nate put his finger to his mouth, hushing her.

'What's up?'

'Listen. I thought I heard something . . . footsteps . . . I don't know.'

'Are you frightened?'

'I'm being serious, Delph. It's not as though we don't already know there're some odd people around here. Just ask Salz.'

'Look, the rest can't be that far away. I feel sorry for Salz, but I knew he was doing drugs. So who on earth's going to stalk us up here?'

'Doing drugs? You kept that quiet. How did you know he was on drugs?'

'In the summer. He was in the Grafton, absolutely out of his head.'

'You didn't take anything, did you?'

'Yeah. Just some crack but it did nothing for me. What do you think, Nate.'

'Where was I when all this was going on?'

'Capri, remember? You invited me then told me that there was no room in the villa your father had rented.'

'Oh, yeah. Bloody Aunt Camilla said she wanted to go. I remember now. I did apologise.'

'Not your fault, Nate. But can we please remember that when we annoy each other, it's not always anyone's fault? Let's get going. It's freezing when we stop.'

'Okay, truce. This way, I think, Tracy.'

Delph laughed, and the pair followed the path, oblivious of the puff of freezing breath drifting through the trees behind them.

13

Daley despatched the two reporters waiting outside Kinloch police office with a curt *No comment*. Yet again, he'd have to run the full gamut of the press, anxious for every detail of the local lad and the Oxford student who'd been so viciously attacked in the last few hours.

That this place – like so many others – had a drug problem was one thing. It was a tide that was almost impossible to resist. Where once the town's young people were initiated into the drinking culture in local hostelries, now they sought the chemical delights of illegal substances. The detective often thought it was time to legalise these controlled drugs. He realised that this view was still a minority one within police circles, but something had to be done: that was a simple fact.

The day was cold, a sharp wind howling up Main Street from the grey loch. The sky was a matching steel, flakes of snow dancing through the air. Not heavy, as it had been up on the Atlantic coast of the peninsula, but promising to be. Most of the shops were sporting their Christmas finery: leaping reindeer, elves, tinsel, and of course Father Christmas. This normally made him feel festive, but for some reason it all felt hollow, tainted by the assaults and the flow of drugs into the area. Now there was the extreme violence that accompanied the trade. With still a couple of weeks to go before the big day itself he was already exhausted. He couldn't help think that the whole festive season now lasted far too long. Certainly, much longer than it had when he was a boy.

Daley turned into the County Hotel. Being just after lunch, the bar was quiet, but he could hear voices from behind a large Christmas tree. One that looked to be in the process of decoration.

'You have to put that fairy atop the thing – it's tradition. Aye, and I daresay calamity is guaranteed if you don't.' Hamish's voice was as indignant as it was instantly recognisable.

Daley made his way through the bar.

'It's yourself,' said Hamish with a smile. 'Can you please talk sense into this woman? She has to understand that certain observances must be maintained, whether she likes it or no'!'

'I thought Brian was difficult,' said Ella, halfway up a stepladder.

'He is,' said Daley.

'Well, he spends more time with you than he does with me, Jimmy.' Ella made her way down the steps gingerly, Hamish holding out his hand by way of steadying her. 'You're a gentleman, Hamish,' she said.

'It's a matter o' practicality, to be honest, Ella. I'm working on the basis that if you come a cropper on they steps, there will be nobody aboot to pour a drink.' Hamish sucked at his unlit pipe by way of emphasis.

'Charming.' Ella made her way out of the room, reappearing behind the bar. 'Now, Jimmy, what can I get you?'

'Can I trouble you for a coffee, please, Ella? I'm finding it hard to keep my eyes open, to be honest.'

'It's the drugs. Brian told me all aboot it.'

Hamish took a seat at his usual table. 'Man, that's bad news, right enough. Even the polis are contaminated by this menace. I must say I'm shocked, Mr Daley.'

'They're for his back, dolt. But I know fine how potent the damn things are. I had to take them when I broke my ankle thon time. I was that oot o' it Brian's antics didnae even bother me.'

'They're good for the pain. But I just can't stay awake.'

'A good strong coffee it is, Jimmy.' Ella trooped off to fetch it.

'Did you manage that wee favour for me, Hamish?' Daley sat down stiffly at the table.

'I did that, Mr Daley.' The old fisherman reached below the table for a faded canvas bag which he plonked down between them. 'I had a word wae the boys doon the quay this morning for weather details and the like. You reckoned these digits hadn't been in the water for long, eh?'

'That's what they said up at the hospital. No more than forty-eight hours.'

Hamish shook his head wearily. 'I canna understand what's happening to this place. It used to be a quiet wee toon. Now we've a' this cruelty.'

'These are warnings, Hamish. Some drug gang's signature warning. It could mean a lot of things, but we reckon it means a change-up. I don't need to tell you how much worse the abuse of drugs is becoming.'

'Barely a soul under forty in the pubs these days. They're all away getting fixed up, or whatever they call what these poor buggers are doing.'

'I know.' Daley rubbed one eye wearily.

'Before you fall asleep, I'll show you on my wee chart. They tell me that there are contraptions for everything these days, but I've always preferred good old-fashioned paper.' Hamish pulled out a scroll from his canvas bag. He removed the rubber band that was holding it together and spread the miniature chart across the table. 'No' the full size, you'll understand. But when you're oot on a wee lobster boat, you don't have the luxury o' a chart table or the like. This will gie you an idea, if nothing else.'

'Good.' Daley leaned over the table, grabbing at his back as a twinge shot up his spine.

'A sore back is a cruel master, Mr Daley. You should go and see auld Duncan.'

'Who?'

'He worked wae the Chinese for years up in Glasgow – one of their medicine shops. Now he treats half the toon. I had problems wae arthritis in my fingers. Ten years ago or more, it must have been.' Hamish stretched out the fingers of one gnarled hand by way of demonstration. 'Man, they were turning into claws. At one point I couldna hold a glass in this hand, it was that useless. A terrible thing, as you can imagine.'

'That must have been awful for you.'

'There's nae need for sarcasm. I'm trying to help you.'

'Sorry.'

'Anyhow, I gave up on the doctors. All they wanted to dae was fill me up wae pills – you know the way. A blue tablet here, a capsule there. The worst o' it all was I couldna take a dram wae the bloody things. I don't think I've ever been mair miserable in my life.'

'Sounds horrible. How did you manage to go about the fishing?'

71

'They gave me a young lad fae one o' these government schemes. He was useless. In any case, after I threatened to throw him overboard when he dropped a cracking big lobster back over the side, he demanded to be taken back to port. I never saw him again.'

'Well, I can see his point, to be fair.'

'I wisna really going to fling him overboard, you understand.'

'No, I didn't think so, Hamish.'

'For a start, I'd never have been able to get a grip o' him wae this hand in such a state.'

Daley nodded, saying nothing.

'But that's where auld Duncan comes in. I went to see him and told him what the matter was. He went pottering into his kitchen and came back wae a brew. Man, it was foul. But I was desperate, so I drank it. He gave me a wee hessian bag to take home wae me. Och, looked like a bunch o' twigs an' that. But he telt me how to make the tea he'd given me.'

'And it worked?'

'Aye, it worked. Look at my hand.' Hamish stretched out his fingers once more.

'Chinese medicine. Liz is always on about stuff like that.'

'And she's right. Think aboot it, Mr Daley. The Chinese knew all these things when we were still living in huts. They invented gunpowder, you know.'

'Yes. We could have done without that.'

'Ach, you're missing the point. If they hadn't done it, we'd have likely caught up. Some clever Scot, I daresay. Man, we've invented just aboot everything else. But their medicine is nothing short o' a miracle.'

Daley thought for a moment. 'This auld Duncan. Is he still

72

plying his trade?'

'Aye. He's a good age, mark you. But he's still going aboot his business. He lives up a close in Long Road.'

'How did he end up working as a Chinese doctor?'

'He wasn't a doctor, Mr Daley. No, not at all. He was the handyman – janitor, if you like. But he kept an eye on what they were aboot. Man, I'm just glad he did.'

Daley looked at Hamish doubtfully. 'You say he treats half the town?'

'I know what you're worried aboot. But there's no illegal drugs involved. Just bits o' bark, and herbs, and the like. I would gie him a go, if I were you.'

'I'll keep it in mind.'

Ella arrived with Daley's coffee; a strong brew that was pitch-black in the small cup. She also brought Hamish a dram. 'Are you planning a trip?' she said, looking over Daley's shoulder at the chart.

'You never mind, Ella Scott. This is polis business. Isn't that right, Mr Daley?'

'I see.' Ella chuckled and returned to decorating the tree.

'So, what can you tell me, Hamish?'

The old man pointed to the west coast of the Kintyre peninsula. 'A strange set o' circumstances have combined over the last few days.'

'Yes?'

'Out at sea there's been an offshore wind. A bugger o' a thing, by all accounts. But the nearer the coast you get, it becomes onshore.'

'I see.' Daley rubbed his chin, looking confused.

'You're no' getting it, are you?'

'No, not really. Sorry for sounding so obtuse, Hamish.'

'Your fingers float, right?'

'Yes, they do. We checked.'

'But because of the coastal onshore wind, they canna float out to sea. Well, no' in the last three days or so.'

'So that means they were disposed of locally?'

'It does. And given the winds and tides – well, they may have travelled south by a couple or three miles. But nae mair than that.' Hamish squinted at the chart. 'If I'd to guess, I'd say they likely entered the water somewhere around here.' He stabbed his finger at a small bay. 'It's just a guess, mind you. But I've learned a few things over my years at sea.'

'I know you have.'

'You look disappointed, Mr Daley.'

'I suppose part of me wished that they'd been washed ashore from far away.'

'Och, it would be a bit o' a coincidence – given what's going on here – for fingers from somewhere else being washed ashore. Do you no' think?'

Daley took a gulp of his coffee. 'Thanks, Hamish. You've answered that question, at least.' He paused for a moment. 'Wait. How did you know I was talking about severed fingers? I never mentioned that.'

Hamish shrugged. 'Ten years here and you still don't get it.'

'It's Kinloch. That's what you're going to say.'

'I am.' Hamish leaned across the table. 'How's the boy – the one fae Oxford?' He winked at the detective.

'You'll have to set your townsfolk on that one, Hamish. My lips are sealed.'

'Och, you canna blame a man for trying, right enough.' He sat back and took a long swig of his dram, while Daley pondered on a growing list of problems.

14

Though the young man in the bed had sallow skin and dark hair, his face still looked pale. He was wearing a hospital gown that was loose over his left shoulder, and his left arm was contained within a wire frame, keeping it suspended in mid-air, off the bed and protected from the shift of sheets and blankets. On his hand was a ball of dressings, covered with what could easily have been a shower cap for a very small head.

Scott felt sorry for the lad as he lay there asleep. To be disfigured at any age was bad enough. But to suffer such an act of cruelty when you had the rest of your life in front of you – well, that was worse.

As though sensing someone beside his hospital bed, the patient's eyes flickered open.

'Hello, son – Mr Brandt. How are you feeling?' said Scott.

Brandt regarded the policeman with big dark eyes. 'How do you think? Who are you, anyway?'

'I'm Detective Sergeant Scott. I know it's a pain in the arse, but you'll appreciate that we've got to ask you a few questions if we're to catch who did this to you.'

Brandt nodded his head wearily. 'If you must. But I tell you now, I don't remember a thing.'

'Aye, but we can start from when you do remember something, eh?'

'I was with my friend up in the hotel room.' Brandt sighed.

'That would be Mr Sherrington, yes?' Scott read the name from his notebook.

'Tim, you're right.'

'What were you doing?'

'Just chatting, you know, about the trip. It's exciting being part of this Everest gig. I can't wait to see the place again.' He stopped and looked down at his arm, encased in the wire frame. 'Though that's not going to happen now, is it?'

'Don't say that, son. The human body is an amazing piece o' kit. I've been shot twice, you know.'

'You look okay on it.'

Scott tapped his forehead with his right index finger. 'It's all up here. You have to get your heid roon what's happened. Get your shit together, if you don't mind my language.'

Brandt smiled. 'I've heard worse. I know I'm at Oxford, but life doesn't begin there, you know.'

'No, I'm sure. But heed what I have to say. If you start feeling sorry for yourself, well, it'll stay wae you.' The detective did feel slightly guilty as he imparted these words of wisdom. After all, after each occasion he'd been shot, his descent into the bottle had been spectacular. Only Ella had managed to drag him back to sobriety. Still, he remembered one of Jim Daley's favourite sayings: don't do as I do.

'Who shot you?'

'Bad people. A bad person, to be exact.'

'So, he shot you twice. What year was that?'

Scott screwed up his face. 'The first time was years ago.

The second much mair recent. Och, I'm bad wae dates. You'd have to ask my wife.'

'So, the same guy shot you twice, years apart?'

'Aye, that's right.'

'You must have pissed him off!'

'I wisnae exactly patting him on the back, neither,' said Scott with a touch of indignance.

'No, of course. Sorry.'

'Okay, let's get back to you and Tim in the hotel. What were you talking aboot?'

'I don't know. This and that, nothing important.'

'I've spoken to Tim, son.'

'Yeah?' Brandt looked bewildered.

'He was telling me that you boys had run out of cannabis.'

'Fuck, he's so stupid!' Brandt raised his eyes to the ceiling.

'He's worried. It's natural. He was telling the truth to try and help us to help you. You should be doing the same.'

'Yes, right, fine.' Brandt sighed. 'You know as well as I do that you won't catch the person who cut off my fingers. These people never get caught. They're sociopaths.'

'I've managed to catch a few in my time. Gie me the chance.'

'Yes, we wanted a smoke, and, no, we didn't have any shit. So what?'

'And you volunteered to go and try to find a dealer?'

'I did. You're not investigating me, are you? Don't you think I've been through enough?'

'No, I'm no' investigating you. But I want to know what your plan was.'

'Plan?'

'A smart boy like you doesnae just walk out o' his hotel in

77

a strange place in the hope he's going to find a dealer. Who did you speak to?'

'I don't know what you mean.'

Scott stared into Brandt's face. He wasn't much younger than his own son Will. He recalled just how close *he'd* come to a nasty end by getting involved with the wrong people. 'Was it someone in the hotel or just a random stranger that told you where to go to find drugs?'

Brandt turned his pale face away from the policeman.

Scott was about to ask a third time when the door to the private room burst open. Nurse Gavney excused herself then took Scott's place at Brandt's bedside.

'Good news, Salz. Your dad is just off the phone. He's in Glasgow right now. He'll be down this afternoon. That'll cheer you up.'

The patient looked at her for a moment. 'You think?'

'Ah, come on. He tells me he's come all the way from Dubai. I hardly see my dad and we live in the same town.' She laughed to try to lighten the mood.

'He has his own jet, nurse. He can fly wherever he wants.'

'How lovely! That must be so great. His own jet, imagine.'

Brandt fixed her with a stern gaze. 'I don't want to see him. I can do that, right?'

Nurse Gavney looked confused. 'You're just saying that. It's the shock of what you've been through.'

Brandt was wired to a drip and a heart monitor. The latter's bleeping became insistent.

'I don't want to see him. How hard is that to understand?'

She cleared her throat. 'I'll leave you to speak with Sergeant Scott. Mr Patterson will likely come in to see you. He's a lovely man. You can have a word with him about your dad.'

'I don't want to talk to anyone about my dad, and I don't want to talk to him. I'm an adult. I should have been consulted before he was informed.' Brandt lay motionless, but his eyes had a staring, wild look.

'Okay, okay.' Nurse Gavney backed off. 'Please try not to get upset. You've been through so much. I'll come back and see you in a while, all right?'

Brandt nodded.

Gavney raised her eyes to Scott as she left the room.

'I take it you and your auld fella don't get on?' said the detective.

'You could say that.'

'How so?'

'Could we not talk about this, please? I'm fed up with people treating me like a child. I'm twenty years old.'

'Fair enough. None o' my business, son.' Scott studied the young man with the missing fingers. Age was an odd concept, he decided. When he'd been twenty, he'd felt sure that he knew all he needed to know. But as the time between then and now stretched inexorably, he'd realised that he'd really known nothing at that tender age.

'What are you thinking about?' said Brandt.

'I'm wondering why you're trying to protect the person who told you where to find what you were looking for.'

'Fuck, Tim again.' Brandt shook his head.

'Yup. Sensible lad, worried about his mate, that Tim.'

'Idiot, if you ask me.'

'So, tell me who told you where to go.'

'If Tim told you, why do you need me to confirm it?'

'Because he doesn't know where you were told to go, just that you were going. I know it was Malcolm Baird that you spoke to. He works the bar at the hotel, right?'

'No comment.'

'I'll have to speak to your father when he arrives. He's bound to have questions, son.'

Brandt's face changed. 'Please don't tell him about the drugs. Honestly, I'll be really unhappy if you tell him things that are between me and the police.'

'I'm really unhappy right now, Salz. That's what folk call you, isn't it?'

'Yes.'

'I'll be speaking to Mr Baird, so all this nonsense is point-less. Where did he tell you to go to get the drugs, Mr Brandt?'

Brandt sighed, his eyes filling with tears. 'Sixty-eight Long Road. He said that I was to stand in the close and wait. Somebody would come with what I wanted.'

'And what happened when you got there?'

'That's just it. I don't remember. I can barely remember leaving the hotel. The next thing I know, I'm in here, minus my fingers!'

Scott had been round the block often enough to know the desperate truth when he saw it. Lies were sometimes hard to define. But the truth was always much more apparent.

'I'm not shitting you, I promise.'

'I believe you.'

'What's going to happen to the barman? He was just helping us out.'

'If that's what he thinks counts as help, then he's much mistaken. Don't you worry about anyone else. Just concentrate on getting better.' Scott smiled. 'I know you think this is the end o' the world. It's no'. But you have to remember, somebody else might no' be so lucky.'

Brandt nodded. 'And what about my father?'

'We'll cross that bridge when we come to it, Salz.'

'He's not my real father, you know. I was adopted.'

Scott shrugged. 'You seem to have fallen on your feet, mind you.'

'I may have fallen on my feet. But the landing was scary.'

Scott searched his face. Here was a young man who was no stranger to pain and upheaval. The detective hadn't thought of that. He'd considered the party from Oxford University to be a collection of spoiled, over-privileged brats, seeking the thrill of danger that was all too familiar to their peers who didn't enjoy such advantages. He'd been wrong, and silently cursed himself for it. Nobody should be judged by their perceived place in society or apparent wealth. The mind of the richest on the planet could be as troubled as the man begging in the gutter; only their preoccupations differed.

Scott bade the patient farewell and left the hospital feeling nothing but sympathy for Brandt. But something troubled him, and despite mulling it over, he didn't know why. He decided to pay a visit to Malcolm Baird.

15

The forest was grey in the dying light of the winter evening. Nate and Delph had, at the second attempt, managed to set up their Hilleberg Staika tent. It was one of the best money could buy: solid, roomy enough, and more than up to the demands of anything a cold winter's night in Kintyre was likely to demand of it.

Nate checked that the guy lines were pegged out securely enough, while Delph worked inside making sure their sleeping system was ready. They'd opted for two sturdy Rab sleeping bags, Trekology inflatable camping mattresses, and closed-cell foam mats to provide protection from the rough, stony ground, as well as the encroaching, leaching cold.

They were both hungry. Delph decided she'd have the dehydrated reindeer stew, while Nate picked the pasta bolognese. Though dehydrated meals didn't sound appealing, years of making rations to military specification had seen manufacturers hone the process down to a fine art, ensuring their meals were as tasty and satisfying as anything you could find in the average restaurant. In any event, this is what they'd be eating on Everest, so they had better get accustomed to it.

Nate boiled water on a spirit stove; Delph scribbled in her leather-bound diary under the light of two LED lanterns. They could hear the distant wash of the sea. And as darkness encroached all round their little haven, the noise of the forest became apparent. There was the urgent rustle as a creature dashed through ferns, the mournful wail of deer, the flutter of birds seeking the best roosting spot high in the fir trees that towered all around.

Between their branches, the stars twinkled. The weather had cleared, and a cold night was in prospect – down to as low as minus four Celsius, the forecast said. But with the best of kit, huddled together in the tent, they knew they'd be plenty warm enough.

'This is delicious,' said Delph as she tucked into her reindeer stew.

'Lucky you. Mine is bolognese.'

'Aw. Why didn't you take the meals you like?'

'Because, Tracy, by the time we got there, the best stuff was gone. We had to go and see Tabby, remember?'

'Poor Tabby. She has no luck with men. Her last boyfriend was a bastard.'

'Freddie? I liked him. Bloody good scrum half.'

'Yeah, loves a bit of a scrum, does Freddie. But usually with anyone else but Tabby.'

'What do you mean?'

'Isn't it obvious?'

'Delph, if it was obvious, I wouldn't be asking.'

'Well, he's obviously gay.'

'Freddie?'

'Yes, Freddie.'

Nate shrugged. 'Well, that's his business, isn't it? I know

that where you live in Wiltshire they still like to persecute homosexuals. But I must inform you that in the rest of the world it's normal.'

'Not when you're going out with my best friend, it isn't.'

'Okay, he's bisexual then. So what?'

Delph glared at her boyfriend. 'He told her he just wanted to make sure. She was nothing more than a guinea pig.'

'I can see the resemblance. It's her cheeks.'

'It's shit, that's what it is. He was invited to her parents' for Christmas and everything.' A confused look spread across her face. 'But you should know all this.'

'Why?'

'Because you were there when she was telling me.'

'Oh yeah, all that crying and drama. I was playing Genshin Impact. Sorry, it's immersive.'

'You really are a twat, Nathan.'

'I hate being called Nathan.'

She cuddled into him. 'But I know what you do like.'

'Be serious, Trace. For a start, we'd burst our inflatable mats. And secondly, you clearly have no knowledge of the male condition in extremely cold weather.'

'What?'

'I had to go for a pee a while ago. It took me ten minutes to find it.'

'Honestly!' She laughed.

'Didn't you bring some wine?'

'It's in that plastic water bottle.'

Nate reached across to Delph's rucksack and searched about until he found the wine.

'What have you got in there? It weighs a ton.'

'Women's things, that's all.'

84

'Women's things?' Nate reached behind her again and hauled the rucksack on to his lap.

'Leave it!' Delph made to grab it.

'Now, now. Play nice, Tracy.'

'Give it to me, Nathan.' Delph's face was expressionless.

'We just spoke about this. I don't like being called that.' He opened his mouth to say something else, but before the words could come she caught him on the cheek with a clenched fist. Instinctively, he recoiled, letting go of the rucksack. She grabbed it and pulled it over to her side.

'Why did you do that?' Nate was rubbing his cheek, where a red weal was already appearing.

'How many times? You never learn to leave my stuff alone. Fuck, you're such a spoiled brat!' Delph levered herself up, scrambled back into the tent and hauled her sleeping bag over her head.

'You're crazy, do you know that?' Nathan grabbed the head torch at his side. 'Fuck this, I'm going for a walk.'

The caravan was cold, condensation dripping down the walls because the gas fire was burning at its highest setting in order to fend off the cold.

He was drowsy, slumped in front of a cartoon. A half-eaten plate of microwave food sat before him on the table, beside a can of obscure IPA that was supposed to taste like melon.

His doze was disturbed when an urgent knock sounded at the door.

'Okay, give me a fucking second!' he shouted, knocking over the beer and cursing once more. Blearily, he made his way along the threadbare carpet, reached for the door handle and pulled. First, the cold darkness caught his breath. But there was nobody standing outside.

He padded down the metal steps in his stocking soles. 'Who is it?' There was no reply.

He swore again, sick of the kids who shared this little estate of unfortunates; people society deemed unworthy even of bricks and mortar, discarded in tin boxes to eke out miserable days packed together like sardines, barely a few feet between each rusting caravan. He'd been lucky; his van was at the end of a row, so at least he had room to breathe.

'You little bastards knock on my door again and I'll fucking cut you, got it!' he roared. It was likely to be one of the growing band of feral kids who were the offspring of his venal neighbours. He spat on the frozen ground and turned back to the metal steps leading up into the warmth.

However, for some reason, the hairs on the back of his neck stood to attention. The caravan was in darkness. And though he didn't remember turning off the lights before stepping outside, it was something that wouldn't have been unusual. It was one of the things he did automatically, not triggering a memory – even in the short term. Everyone did it, didn't they?

But when he flicked the switch back on, in his chair before the TV sat someone else.

16

The following morning in Kinloch dawned free of snow, but still icy cold. Daley had decided to walk in to work in an attempt to rid himself of the malaise induced by his painkillers. As he crossed the esplanade, the loch was calm under a flawless blue sky. Fishing boats bobbed, their reflections perfectly rendered in the still water of the harbour. There were a few fishermen on the pier, their collective breath rising in clouds.

But as he strode on, Daley felt sluggish. As he breathed in the cool air and quickened his stride, he couldn't dislodge the vague notion that he might catch a nap when he arrived at the office. The impact the medication had on him was odd in other ways. Yes, the agonising pain in his back – apart from a stabbing reminder now and again – had been almost completely eradicated. But it had been replaced by this soporific calm, so at odds with his restless personality. But he had to say it was good to feel relaxed, not poised for anything and everything to go wrong in seconds.

As he stared up at the hills that cosseted the town, he was sure the shades of the various fir trees packed so tightly together were not only more varied; their colours seemed deeper, vivid in a way he hadn't noted before. He was drawn to the scene like a painter or a poet, appreciating something that he'd have normally been too preoccupied to register.

As little in his domestic or work life had changed, Daley could only ascribe this new heightened perception of his surroundings to the tablets. He'd spent a lifetime wondering why individuals chose to blight their lives with drugs. Maybe he was now gaining insight as to why they did. The very thought scared him.

He resolved to make an appointment to see his GP as soon as he could.

His long stride took him quickly up Main Street, which was, as he had become accustomed to in his time in Kinloch, a flurry of activity at this time in the morning. The enticing aroma of fresh bread rolls drifted across the road as Michael Kerr's bakery was replenished.

As he walked on, a butcher hefted a tray of freshly cut steaks on the palm of one hand, his blue and white apron dotted with spots of blood. He wore a white trilby-style hat, headgear favoured by those of his profession in years gone by. The man smiled at the police officer and bade him good morning.

Just along a side road, a large wagon was discharging kegs of beer on to a bumper mat, supplying the huddle of pubs that bordered the square. Daley remembered he'd spoken to a publican only a few days ago. The careworn man had lamented the drop-off in trade, doubting that his bar would be open in a year or so if things didn't change.

'The average age of my clientele is going up. The young folk aren't interested in beer. They'd rather kill themselves wae the drugs.'

Daley needed no reminder of this. He felt he was fighting a losing battle against narcotics. But despite the many slivers of intelligence that appeared from HQ, he knew he'd singularly failed to bring any dealers to justice. In this regard, he acknowledged he was no different from his colleagues anywhere in the country. But Jim Daley prided himself on being a cut above, a police officer capable of achieving results where others floundered.

'Good morning, chief inspector.' An old lady in a thick anorak slowed down as he approached.

'Good morning, Mrs MacCulloch.' Daley smiled.

'I hope you're going to catch the wicked people that are attacking these young lads. I'm frightened to put the light out these nights.'

'I know, it's a terrible thing. But try not to worry, I'm sure you're absolutely safe. They fight amongst themselves.'

Mrs MacCulloch thought for a moment. 'Aye, I know what you mean. But surely wae the drugs comes theft and other crimes. I'm studying criminology with the Open University, you know. It's all doon to deprivation and bad parenting, if you ask me.'

'I'm sure you're right. But I better get on and try to catch them.' He hesitated. 'And if you need any help with your criminology, just ask. I'm more than happy to have a chat.' It was a bland and disingenuous attempt at a little positive PR. But every little helped.

She nodded. 'To be honest, I thought you might be more inclined to come and seek my advice. You don't seem to be making much progress, if you don't mind me saying, Mr Daley.'

Daley recognised that he was in line for a lecture on the cause and remedy for drug abuse. Quickly, he made his excuses and carried on up the hill towards the office. 'Bloody criminology,' he muttered under his breath. In Daley's opinion, those responsible for the nation's tertiary education were wasting their time on many subjects, criminology and media studies being two of them.

Thoughts of the latter were prompted by the sight of two reporters standing at the gates leading into the car park. What was the point of inculcating legions of would-be journalists into the ways of a newspaper industry that was already struggling against the tide of social media and fake news? The big detective had endured a long and frequently strained relationship with the ladies and gentlemen of the press, but in these days of trending this, influencing that, and downright lies he had begun to mourn their passing. Still, he resented being harangued first thing in the morning.

'Any further forward with the mutilator, DCI Daley?' said an impossibly young man, holding a smartphone out towards the detective's face.

Shit, they were working up a name for the idiot who was doing this. It was the last thing he needed. 'No comment, son,' Daley replied.

The other reporter was older. Daley knew him from way back in his days as an ADC at Stewart Street. Michael Ross was of the old school, as cunning as a fox, but fair and even-handed. He was a crime reporter for one of the broadsheets.

'Any chance of a word, Jim? For our mutual benefit, promise.'

Daley's first inclination was to politely turn down this offer of mutual assistance. However, as he was getting nowhere with his inquiries, it was time to look at other options. *If you're lost in the desert, accept any help that's forthcoming*, as Brian Scott would have inevitably counselled in such circumstances.

When Daley nodded Ross through, the younger man tried to follow.

'Hey, three's a crowd, son,' said Ross as he and Daley disappeared up the steps to reception.

Automatically, Daley expected to see Shaw at his post. But in his place sat a probationary constable, looking nervous at the arrival of his boss.

'Where's Sergeant Shaw?' said Daley.

'Phoned in sick, sir. Sergeant Thomson said I should fill in – sir.'

'Okay. Just make sure you note everything, log all calls et cetera. And if you don't know something, ask. Sign this gentleman in as a visitor then show him through to my office, okay?'

'Nae bother,' said the constable, completely forgetting protocol now he had something to do.

By the time Daley had stopped at the coffee machine and settled himself in his glass box, Ross was knocking on the door.

'Take a seat, Mike. What do you have for me?'

'No coffee for me?'

Daley laughed. 'What do you think this is, charity week?'

'Okay, I do have something, but I'll need you to give me something back, big man.'

'I'll see what I can offer you once you tell me what you have. Come on, Mike, we're both old hands at this caper. You need stories, and I've got them.'

'You show me yours first. Is that it?'

'Got it in one.'

The reporter leaned forward in his seat. 'The Oxford boy – the one who lost his fingers.'

'What about him?'

91

'His father's heavy. I mean *big-time* heavy.'

'In what way?'

'On the surface he looks like a respectable businessman. He's rich – I mean *mega rich*.' Mike Ross reached into his thick jacket and pushed a photograph of a middle-aged man in an expensive suit across the desk. Iron-grey hair, thinning but stylishly cut, framed a tanned face and a pair of designer spectacles. 'This is him. Werner Brandt.'

'And heavy how?' Daley asked.

'He's an industrialist. Petrochemicals, that type of thing. Mostly out of Germany.'

'Is he German?'

'Austrian. He has joint Austrian and British nationality. Spends most of his time in Buckinghamshire, from what I can tell.'

Daley shrugged. 'Don't see anything dodgy so far.'

'He's a fixer for various Eastern European states, Jim. And that normally means gangs, as you know. Alleged links to the Kremlin, too. As the story goes, he supplies Russia with chemicals that are "hard to source", if you get my drift.'

'This is the reason you're down here covering a rural turf war, then. I wondered why.'

'Listen, we've been working on a story for two years now. He's part of it. It's focusing on UK business and its connections to organised crime across the globe. You'd be surprised, honestly.'

'Actually, I don't think I would. But fortunately, cleverer men than me will be heading up the fight against that kind of thing.'

'Aye, and the band played believe it if you like. There aren't many detectives in Police Scotland as smart as you, DCI Daley.

You can't pull the wool over my eyes. Too long in the tooth.'

'I wish. But I don't get it, really. What happened to his son was – well, it was unfortunate. But I can't see it being related in any way to the Russian mob. The lad was just in the wrong place at the wrong time.'

It was Ross's turn to shrug. 'I believe he's coming here this afternoon – the father, I mean. He was booked onto the service plane yesterday, but that's just a ruse. He's flying down in his own private jet.'

'Impressive. And it's all good to know, Mike. But I don't see any potential for an international incident down here, do you?' Daley yawned.

'Fuck me, Jim. It's not eight o'clock and you're ready for your bed.'

'Bad back. I'm not sleeping well.'

'Is this a *bad* back or one of the *retirement* variety?'

'The former. Bloody agony.'

'Take my advice. Don't let them give you those horse pills to take away the pain. My brother did in his shoulder playing golf last year. They gave him these opioids to get him through until he could have an operation.'

'And?'

'Poor bastard got operated on three months ago. But he can't get off those pills. Needs them just to stay normal. He's had to tell the doc all kinds of shit to keep getting the prescription.'

'I'll bear it in mind.' Daley felt his heart sink, but changed the subject. 'So, what can I do for you?'

'Just let me know if Brandt takes your fancy, that's all. Remember, he's involved in all kinds of shit. Illegal arms to the former Soviet states, the Palestinians, blah blah. There have been various attempts to investigate him, but to no avail. He's too well connected not to be dangerous, if you see what I mean. He may be untouchable.'

'Meaning?'

'UK security services. It's hard to tell, but go carefully with him. Playing both ends against the middle.'

'And you're the people to snag him?'

'Might sound unlikely, Jim. But we're left-field, under the radar. He's probably never heard of the paper.'

'I'll keep a watching brief, Mike.' Daley leaned forward and offered the reporter his hand, wincing as he did so.

'Sore, eh?'

'Very. But I'm sure my meds'll sort me out.'

'Meds? Remember what I said about those pills.' Ross placed his card on Daley's desk. 'I'm staying at the County. Bloody awful hotel, but the barmaid's good crack.'

'Until you find out who she's married to.'

'Who? Some local bigwig, no doubt?'

'No, Brian Scott.'

'You mean *your* Brian Scott?'

'I do.'

'He hates me. It's after that carry-on with the corruption allegations, remember?'

'Not your finest hour, Mike.'

'No, we got it wrong. But you're not seriously going to try and tell me that Police Scotland is squeaky clean?'

'It's clean round the bend in this office.'

'Ha, I'm sure. Thanks for the heads-up on Brian. I'll stay out of his way.'

'Good idea.'

Michael Ross departed, leaving Daley alone with his

thoughts. Up until now, he'd had no doubt that the young Oxford student was the victim of a random attack in the turf war that was building in Kinloch. But still, his father brought another set of problems to Daley's patch. People like that brought the potential for trouble of all kinds. It wasn't unusual for some of that to rub off on their families.

Daley's attention was drawn to the tiny calendar on his wall. Somebody had put it there – certainly not him. Above the dates was the print of a painting by Matisse. For a few moments he stared at it, admiring the vivid blue colours and the skill of the artist.

'Shit! What's wrong with me?' he mumbled under his breath.

17

The bright morning shining red through the walls of the tent had roused her from sleep. Blearily, she checked her watch; it was almost six thirty. Delph Harker turned to where Nate should have been lying in his sleeping bag. Instead of his bulky shape, there was nothing. Nate wasn't in the tent.

She thought about this for a moment, remembering the argument they'd had just before she had turned in the night before. He'd gone for a walk, and she must have drifted off before he came back. If he came back at all.

Quickly, she unzipped her sleeping bag and pushed herself out of it. The moment she left the cocoon, Delph felt the temperature drop. She grabbed her down jacket and trousers, pulling them on against the cold. She'd slept in her thermals; it didn't do to be too well wrapped up in a sleeping bag unless the temperature was outrageously low. If you were too warm, you began to sweat, and moisture of any kind was the enemy of the wild camper. It was better to be cold and dry than wet and lukewarm; Nate had drummed that into her.

She fished in the bottom of the sleeping bag to retrieve her boots. There was nothing worse than putting on frozen boots on a frosty morning. So, the rule was to stuff them into your bag if there was room. As she slipped them on, she was pleased to note that her body heat had been enough to keep them from freezing solid.

Delph tied perfunctory knots in the laces. She'd do it properly later. She was surprised to find her heart thudding in her chest at the thought of her missing partner.

She leaned across and unzipped the tent: inner first then the fly. Bright sunshine flooded the little space, and she had to shade her eyes. The cold air hit her like a punch to the stomach. Though only protected by thin walls of fabric, it was amazing how much warmer it was inside the tent than outside.

Delph shuffled out of her temporary home on her backside and forced herself up off the cold hard ground. The sun flashing through the trees was at just the right angle to blind her, but as her eyes became accustomed to the glare she searched through the firs. No sign of Nate.

'Where the fuck are you, Nathan,' she muttered. Then, louder this time, 'Nate, where are you!'

She stood in the frost-sparkling morning, awaiting a reply, but none came, and she swore loudly, sending something rustling through the undergrowth. She ducked back inside the tent and pulled her gloves and woollen beanie from a dry bag, trying to rationalise the situation. Surely, he hadn't been stupid enough not to return to the tent just because they'd fallen out? Yes, it was only the west coast of Scotland, but in freezing temperatures your life was at risk wherever you found yourself.

But, she told herself, he had a really good sense of direction, and she was sure he'd taken a head torch when he'd stormed off the previous evening. This, combined with the fact that he was never more than a few inches from his phone – well, surely, he'd be able to find his way back, or at least be safe somewhere. After all, she needed him.

'Nathan!' she called, stepping away from the tent, her boots breaking through the frosted grass and pine needles.

Her own phone was in a small pocket in her thermals, where it had been all night, safe from the cold. She pulled off one glove, fished the phone out from under her down jacket and speed-dialled his number. The mobile bleeped loudly in her ear. When she looked at the screen, she saw she had no signal.

She put the phone in the inside pocket of her jacket and walked on a few steps. This was serious. She decided to have a poke about their campsite. If there was no sign of him, she would need to find a phone signal and inform the team leaders. They'd been through rigorous safety protocols before they left Oxford. After all, this was a rehearsal for the real thing, the trip to Everest.

'Nathan!' she called again, sending a small flock of protesting birds into the air.

Behind her, there was the sound of a cracking twig. Delph spun round to face the noise. But there was nothing to see, certainly not her missing partner.

'Shit, it's like a crappy horror movie,' she muttered to herself, turning back to carry on her impromptu search. But just as she squinted once more through the bright morning sun, it was suddenly blocked from her view. A tall figure rose in front of her, and clamped a gloved hand roughly over her mouth.

Daley pulled up outside Alasdair Shaw's home, a neat little house on the outskirts of the town. He'd been worried about his sergeant since he and his wife had parted ways. And since the usually dependable officer had failed to turn up for work that morning, he reckoned his concerns weren't misplaced.

Daley parked in front of the house, noting that all the curtains were closed. He hadn't intended to knock with such official gusto, but it came so naturally as to be automatic. He remembered Liz complaining that he knocked his mother-in-law's door in much the same way, sending the occupant jolting out of her chair with alarm.

He waited for a few moments, but there was no sign of movement or sound from behind the front door. The big detective was just about to bend down and shout through the letterbox when a car pulled up on the road beside his. Brian Scott jumped out of a blue saloon, then took the garden path to where his friend was standing.

'Is he no' answering?'

'Aye, he's standing in the doorway. Can't you see him?' Daley shook his head.

'Nae need for sarcasm, Jimmy. I've been worried aboot the boy. Nobody knows better than me what it's like to encounter a bump or two in the road.'

'A bump or two? Your life's been like crossing the Alps in your bare feet. But not everyone's as resilient as you are, Brian.'

'Needed to be, too. If there's anyone who's suffered they slings and barrows, it's me.'

'Arrows, Bri. Slings and arrows.'

Scott nodded sagely. 'Now that makes sense, Jimmy. I could never understand why folk were flinging barrows at some poor bastard. Mind you, they'd have flung anything at you where I came fae. Dae you mind that ned, Peter Miller? He flung his wean oot the landing window at a couple o' cops trying to serve him wae a warrant.'

'A baby? That's disgusting. He was a real lowlife.'

'Nah, the boy was in his teens. I'm no' sure if big Pete flung him or the boy jumped. But you never know wae these kind o' folk. I mind watching wae my mother fae the front garden.'

'*Watch with Mother* where you grew up was very different to the one most of us enjoyed as kids, eh?'

Scott shrugged. 'It made a change. We usually watched my faither come home pished and fall over.'

'Happy days.'

'Och, it wisnae the worst. When you see what happens with kids these days. Even the posh ones are fat bastards that don't go oot. Staring at screens a' day – it cannae be good for you.' Scott rubbed his chin. 'Have you knocked the door, Jimmy?'

'No, I've just been standing here hoping my very presence would be enough to alert him to the fact I was here.'

'That won't work.' Scott leaned across and hammered the door knocker repeatedly.

'I'm so glad you're here, Brian.'

'Don't think twice aboot it.'

Despite their efforts, however, there was still no movement from within Shaw's home. This time, Daley did call through the letterbox, but to no avail. He tried to kneel down far enough to take a look through the small opening but grabbed his back and shot back to his feet in pain.

'Thought your breeks were for the off there, Jimmy.'

'It's my back. You give him a shout, will you?' Daley grimaced as he searched his pockets for a pack of pills.

Scott squatted in front of the front door and levered the letterbox open. 'Oi, Al! The boss is here. He wants to talk to you. Hurry the fuck up!'

'If only I had your way with words, Brian. It's poetic, in many ways.'

'Haud your wheesht, big man. I cannae get a handle on what's going on.' Scott was still on his hunkers, one ear pressed to the letterbox.

'Very sorry.'

Scott frowned. 'I think I hear something. It's like groaning, or something. Have a listen yourself.' Scott got back to his feet and ushered Daley towards the door.

'What kind of groaning?'

'How many kinds are there?' Scott looked nonplussed.

'Okay, I'll take your word for it.' Daley nodded to the door. 'Do your worst, Brian.'

'Kick it in, you mean?'

'What do you think?'

'Modern doors are nae use for that caper. You need a mair subtle approach.' Scott thrust his hand into his trouser pocket and produced a small bunch of keys.

'Please tell me they're not what I think they are, Bri.'

'Okay, they're no' what you think they are.' He selected a key and inserted it into the barrel lock on the door. He twisted it a few times, his tongue between his teeth, but to no avail. He removed that key and tried another. It took four different keys before he managed to open the door.

Daley was first through it into the hall. 'Alasdair, are you there?' He walked down the hall, Scott behind him.

'What's that smell, Jimmy?'

Daley shrugged and walked on. He pushed on the door to his left. It opened to reveal a chaotic lounge. There were discarded takeaway cartons on the coffee table, and a few empty beer cans scattered on the carpet. A portion of a meal had landed on the carpet and was growing mould. 'Shit, this doesn't look good.'

Scott looked surprised. 'How? He's just no' had time to put the shit in the bin. His wife's away, remember. Gie the poor guy a break, Jimmy. You want to see oor place when Ella takes off on one o' her trips up the road.'

'You're a model of domestic emancipation, Brian. Does it ever cross your mind it's not her job to clean up after you?'

'I catch the crooks, she does the dishes. What's wrong wae that?'

'So much, I don't know where to start. Anyway, she's got a job now. You'd better pull your weight, because I tell you, if she leaves you, it's goodnight, Vienna.'

'Never mind Vienna, goodnight Brian, too.'

Daley held up his hand. 'Wait, I hear something.'

The detectives stood motionless in the untidy lounge until Scott raised his eyes. 'Coming fae upstairs, Jimmy. Come on!'

They hurried out of the living room and took the stairs at the end of the hall. Photographs of Shaw's children hung in the stairwell, close-ups of them at various ages.

'There it is again, Jimmy. That groaning.'

There were four doors on the landing, each one tight shut. Daley pushed at the one he came to first. It was a child's bedroom. The wallpaper was bright and colourful, featuring a cartoon character Daley didn't recognise. But the place was tidy, bed made, and some clothes were laid out across the duvet, as though its occupant was still in residence.

Scott pushed opened another door. It was the master bedroom. The large bed was stripped down to the mattress, covered only by a dirty-looking quilt. On the wall was a large photograph of a couple on their wedding day. The man was dressed in a kilt and smiling broadly, his new wife gazing lovingly into his eyes. Daley recognised Alasdair and Jill Shaw, much younger and happier back then, by the look of things.

'Here, Jimmy!' Scott's call was urgent.

Daley stepped back on to the landing. Scott had opened the door opposite the master bedroom, into what turned out to be the bathroom. Lying naked save for a pair of boxer shorts, propped up against the bath, head lolling, was Alasdair Shaw. His own vomit was slathered down his chest on to a fluffy bathroom mat, and a syringe, empty of its contents, stuck out of his arm, held there by a hypodermic needle. Shaw was mumbling incoherently. He tried to open his eyes a fraction, but failed.

Daley pulled his mobile from his pocket. 'This is DCI Daley in Kinloch. An ambulance for Mill Lane. Make it quick!'

Scott leaned over his colleague. Gently, he removed the needle from Shaw's arm. Reaching for a towel that was hanging over the side of the bath, he pulled Shaw's mouth open to check that nothing was obstructing his airway. Carefully, with Daley's help, he laid Shaw on his side in the recovery position. 'What the fuck, Jimmy?'

'I don't know, Brian. I honestly don't know.'

Shaw muttered something which neither of them understood.

'Poor bastard,' said Scott, and he meant it.

18

Werner Brandt looked out of the small window of his private jet. They were due to land at Machrie airport in ten minutes.

Idly, he gazed at a grey sea, white sandy bays, wooded hills and snaking little roads hugging the coast. Travel no longer held the fascination for him it once had. He was usually too preoccupied or merely uninterested to take in the scenery of whichever landscape he happened to occupy at any one time. Private air travel had that effect. The world shrank to a fleeting blur of images. The great globe and all its problems and wonders swished by beneath him, as though existing in another dimension.

He glanced at his half-million-dollar Patek, a gift from a grateful Arab potentate. It wasn't even three in the afternoon, and already he could see lights in the windows of small dwellings dotted here and there as they flew down the length of the peninsula.

Though he was on his way to recover his adopted son, Brandt's thoughts were elsewhere. This was an inconvenience, an embarrassment. He despised instances of both. He'd only arrived back from Moscow a couple of days before Salazar managed to get himself into trouble. For Brandt, it was a hard thing to accept. Though he knew his son was – apart from his missing fingers – quite well, he cared little for his welfare. He, adoptive parent or not, had been disrespected by default, and there was only one way to right that particular wrong.

Brandt felt the phone vibrate in the inside pocket of his Huntsman suit. He checked the name before taking the call.

'Mr Brandt, where are you?' The voice was accented, English.

'The more pertinent question is where are you, Stanton?'

'We'll be with you this evening. Just getting organised. Had a little scoot round yesterday. Found out what we needed to know.'

'Good. I want this quick, clean and likely to impart the right message, do you understand?'

'You know you can rely on us.'

'I know you are in charge of my son's wellbeing. In that, you have failed, singularly.'

There was silence on the other end of the phone for a few seconds. Then: 'But we agreed. What could happen to him in that backwater? Remember we had that conversation, Mr Brandt?'

'Oh yes, I remember the conversation well. But you are paid to assess risk, and you got it terribly wrong, didn't you? After all, he could have been killed.'

'A chance in a million.'

'And yet, that chance came to pass.' Brandt looked out of the window at a small boat struggling through the grey sea far below. 'You failed to tell me that my son has a drug problem. Why?'

Again, a pause. 'He just dabbles – I'm sure of it. A little grass, nothing else. Tell me what kid his age doesn't?'

'Yet here we are. Me flying to this bloody awful place to extricate Salazar and get him proper care. You and I will have words, do you understand?' Though Brandt's English was fluent, a trace of his Austrian accent was evident in the menace of his statement. He ended the call without ceremony and placed the phone back in his pocket.

'Landing in five minutes, sir.' The voice over the aircraft's speaker system was confident. Brandt only hired the best of pilots, most of them ex-military. Though they came from a number of countries, they were ready to fly their boss anywhere at a moment's notice. And though their boss was strict – and often rude and gruff –the financial rewards were such that they could never hope to match them elsewhere, in the public or private sector. Hence, Werner Brandt's pilots – all his staff – were loyal to a man and woman. Their relationships were cast in symbiotic respect.

The aircraft began to lose height, ready for landing.

Brandt saw them arc out over the sea before a smooth descent to a long runway, somehow disproportionate to the little town it served. He pressed a button on the console at his side. 'Thank you, gentlemen, a pleasant flight. Be ready to leave at any time. Make the necessary arrangements with the authorities.' He picked up a sleek leather briefcase from the floor of the aircraft, unbuckled himself from his seat and took to the aisle.

'Good afternoon, sir. Transport has been arranged. A car is waiting.' The flight attendant was a tall Asian man, dressed in a grey suit.

'Thank you. I may need you to accompany me later if my son is too fragile to be moved. Be ready, please.'

'I can arrange a medevac facility, if you'd like, Mr Brandt?'

'No, that won't be necessary. But I might stay, and I'll need your administrative support, if that is the case.'

'Very good, sir.' The attendant inclined his head and smiled.

The plane's door swung open, and the flight crew greeted him as he took the stairs to the runway. The airfield's fire truck was in attendance. Faces stared from the vehicle, but then, deciding nothing was amiss, they turned away and the truck rolled back down the tarmac.

Brandt stood before his private jet and breathed deeply. The air held notes of the salty sea and damp earth.

'Shithole,' he declared, before striding off towards his transport.

19

'You absolute bastard, Nate!' Delphine was hunched up in their tent. 'Look, I'm still shaking.' She held out a hand to better demonstrate this fact.

'It was a joke.' He sighed. 'We didn't exactly part on very good terms last night, did we?'

'Trust me, we're on even worse terms now, you ignorant prick!'

'You know, Tracy? Sometimes when you're angry I can hear an entirely different you.'

'What? And don't call me Tracy. The novelty has worn off, okay!'

'Woo.' He fluttered his hands under his chin sarcastically. 'You do sound different sometimes, though, that's all I'm saying.'

Ignoring this, Delph continued. 'What were you doing all night, tell me that?'

'You don't think I was out alone in the woods with no shelter, do you?'

'Where else were you? With Stephanie Culshaw?'

'I worry about you sometimes. We share the same tutor, that's all.'

'Huh! You'd like to share the same bed with her. I see how you drink her in.'

'I was sleeping beside you in the tent. You were sound when I arrived back, and you were the same when I woke up this morning. I went to find some firewood. Thought we could warm up. I have a secret, you know.'

'Oh, I know you have secrets. Everyone knows that. With a father like yours, it would be impossible not to.'

'Give Teddy a break, will you?'

'*Teddy*. It even sounds sleazy.'

Nate pulled his rucksack from the hard ground. 'I'll just fling this away. I don't have an appetite now anyway.' He produced a small plastic box from the rucksack. 'It's a shame, though. Eggs and bacon on a cold day. There's nothing like it.'

'Where did you get them?'

'Little farm shop, just the other side of the trees. I got some cream, too. Thought it might make our instant coffee taste a bit better.' He grinned.

Delph shook her head. 'You see, this is what always happens. I get *so* angry at you, then you just do things like this.'

'I'm just lovable, admit it.'

'What worries me is you're too much like Teddy.'

'Fuck, don't say that.' Nate laughed.

'Okay, let's make a bloody fire then! I'm starving.'

Yet again, Daley and Scott found themselves heading to Kinloch hospital, this time worried for the welfare of their colleague, Sergeant Alasdair Shaw. Daley pondered on whether or not it would be appropriate to contact Shaw's estranged wife, tell her how close her husband had come to death. But, he reasoned, once a marriage was over, it was over. Apart from his, of course. With the Shaws, the Gordian knot had been cut. He'd never managed to do that with Liz – he doubted he would ever have the strength.

Daley's mobile rang. Quickly, he parked the car and answered on the car's Bluetooth system.

'Yes, sir. How can I help you?' *ACC Cunningham* was emblazoned across the screen on the dashboard.

'I don't know what it is about you, Daley. But trouble seems make its way to Kinloch to find you and your DS.'

'What now, sir?'

'More intel.'

'On the drug supply?'

'No, on a potential visitor who's making his way towards the town as we speak. May be there already, for all we know.'

'Who?' Daley looked puzzled. Beside him in the passenger seat, Scott was all ears.

'Amil Rashton. It's not his real name, but it's what he's gone by for so many years we must assume it's his chosen moniker and he's sticking to it. Came from Jamaica when he was a kid. Learned all he needed to know in south London. He's dangerous, Daley. Make no mistake.'

'Never heard the name, sir.' At his side, Scott shook his head in agreement.

'Gangland fixer, reputed hitman et cetera et cetera. This information comes from MI5. He's been under surveillance for years. Could be a number of reasons. Might be something to do with the lad who had his fingers cut off.'

'But Brandt is just a student, sir.' Though Daley knew all about Brandt senior, he was interested to hear what the ACC would have to say about this enigma of a man.

'All I'll say is, watch out. I want you to be extra careful in your dealings with Brandt senior and this Rashton.'

'Of course. Do we have anything on Rashton?'

'Fellow traveller with Winston Blears. His muscleman that does, if you prefer.'

'And anything I should know about the lad's father?' There was the bait.

Cunningham cleared his throat. 'Nothing you need to know, Jim. Your job is to keep your eye on Rashton and Blears. I hope your sidekick is in appropriate shape. We don't want him stumbling all over this in his cups. Last bloody thing we need.'

Scott, who'd been listening intently, raised two fingers towards the screen across which Cunningham's name was displayed.

'He's in fine fettle, sir,' said Daley with a smile.

'Well, make bloody sure he stays that way.'

When the call ended, Daley blew out his cheeks.

'What's up, Jimmy?'

'He's not telling us the truth. That's what's up, Bri.'

Scott looked confused. 'Eh?'

'I need to get you up to speed with a few things surrounding Mr Brandt senior. He's also on his way to Kinloch. But our Assistant Chief Constable didn't see fit to tell us that.'

'Who's this Brandt guy? I tell you something, his son doesn't like him.'

'I'm not surprised.' Daley switched the engine on. 'I'll fill you in on our way to the hospital, Brian.'

'Fine wae me.' Scott sniffed. 'And if any proof was needed, it's easy to see what the bosses think o' me up the road.'

'I'd say they think just about the same as they've always thought, Brian.'

'Aye, that's the problem.'

'Think of poor Alasdair. Even you've not managed to get that far down.'

'You think? There've been times I just wanted to end it, Jimmy. But I can't understand what's happened to Al. Straight as a die, so he is. Who'd have thought he'd get into the drugs? I mean, we've all had marital problems, but I didnae see you shooting up when your Liz was running aboot wae half o' Stewart Street. You're a better man – that's a fact.'

'Gee, thanks, old pal. You really know how to make a man feel good about himself.'

'Don't mention it, bud.'

Now in silence, they made their way to the hospital.

20

Hamish walked up from the quay a richer man. He'd just sold his lobster boat to Jock Meenan, a fisherman from Tarbert. As Hamish had done before him, this new owner had decided that his days of chasing proud shoals of fish were over. But rather than cut all ties with the sea, he would keep his hand in with some creels.

Hamish remembered the day he'd let the *Girl Maggie II* go. She was a small vessel, needing only two or three crew members. But for him, she represented his life and all the people he'd known and loved. Every time he set sail from Kinloch harbour, he remembered his father, his mother, Sandy Hoynes and a whole host of others who'd shaped him as a fisherman, who'd made him a man.

Though he missed the pelagic trade, lobster fishing took him out on to the sea. Most fishermen, though they revelled in their time onshore, were maritime in attitude: more fish than men, as Sandy Hoynes often said. It was their natural element, and Hamish was no different.

He stopped and gazed back down the quay at the diminished fishing fleet that lay at anchor in the harbour. He wondered how long the industry could sustain itself in

Kinloch. On the pontoons next to the old quay were a handful of sleek hulls and proud masts, the manifestations of the hobbyist. When he'd been a lad, only the wealthiest could afford a sailing vessel for pleasure. Now working men and women were taking to the waves, feeling the wind in their faces, smelling the salt in the air. The sheer joy of being set free on a different plain was intoxicating. But were working boats soon to be a thing of the past?

These were very different days. Hamish could never have conceived of this time of computers and the internet. The whole idea baffled him. It was odd how something you couldn't hold, and couldn't see, could be all around, could create such wealth for those involved. There was no honesty in it at all, as far as he was concerned. It was the emperor's new clothes, a will-o'-the-wisp, a sea haar: nothing of substance.

But then, what substance did he have now? No direction in life, no plashing waves, turning tides, shifting wind. No life apart from hanging about waiting for it all to end. Finally – and he'd felt it for a while – all that remained was sitting in death's waiting room, trying to find anything to distract himself from encroaching oblivion. The whole concept wasn't just troubling – it was terrifying.

Hamish looked at the cheque he'd been given in exchange for his boat. It was a tidy enough sum – more than he'd been expecting, if he was honest. Maybe more than she was worth. It was strange to think that the numbers on this small piece of paper represented the final payment he'd ever receive from a career that had sustained him for a lifetime.

His first inclination was to get the cheque paid into the bank then go for a dram. But, he reasoned, throwing alcohol on top of his current mood would only make him melancholy.

Hamish stared at the loch. It was slate-grey, the surface rippled by the wind, the tide on the ebb. *On the ebb*. That neatly described his new circumstances. Hamish wasn't sure if the sale of his boat was responsible for the unfamiliar empty feeling in his gut. Maybe it was one of his more undefinable notions. Whatever it was, he could feel a harsh chill marching up the street, howling through shop doorways, lifting tiles, hammering at windows, harrying his very bones.

There was no particular reason for this feeling. Annie was gone, as were most of those he'd ever loved. However, the sensation was real. It was visceral, a real wind of change – change for ill, he reckoned – tugging at his bunnet.

He heard a voice behind him. 'Hamish, are you lost?' Mrs McLean was younger than him, but nonetheless no longer in the first flush of youth. He'd known her as a child.

'I'm fine, lassie,' he said. 'I'm just contemplating the world and all the changes I've seen in my life.'

'Aye, we all do that from time to time.' She gestured expansively round Main Street. 'Look at this, for instance. Hardly a soul about, and Christmas just roon the corner. I wisna born yesterday, as you know. But this is the least festive I've felt in my life. It's as though there's a pall over the place.'

'Funny, I was just thinking that myself.' Hamish gazed up at the dull sky.

'You should take a turn to the County and get some cheer about yourself. My Ian swore by the restorative powers o' whisky, and no mistake.'

'There's no doubt that a dram can lift a mood. Mind you, it's not always the case. At least, that's the way I'm feeling today, Jenny.'

'And you're no' alone. I was speaking to my sister on the phone this morning. Fair scunnered, she is. And canna explain it, either. Anyway, I'd better be on my way before we both burst into tears.'

'Take care, Jenny.' Hamish watched her go, feeling no better for their conversation. But she was right: there was hardly anyone about. The place was eerily quiet. There was something malign in the air, he could sense it.

Hamish turned on his heel, deciding to clear his head with the long walk home. It's what kept him fit. And given most of his route was beside the sea, it meant that his connection to that element was maintained in some form, at least.

He thought about what Jenny had said. If he felt glum, so did the sisters. He'd known for a long time that he could touch his feelings and see or feel events yet to come. He played on it, as most people realised. But he was aware of something else. Everyone had the ability to sense the onrush of the future; you just had to know what you were experiencing. There was a stark feeling about Kinloch today; an empty, sick-of-life blanket of sadness, with no apparent cause.

As Hamish stepped out on to the road, a loud car horn sounded. He scurried back on to the pavement just as an oversized SUV flashed past. It was black, black like his mood. Though Hamish wasn't cold under his sea jumper and pea jacket, he shivered.

Daley and Scott were beside Shaw's bed. The sergeant's face was almost as pale as the sheets upon which he lay. He looked hollowed out, broken, as though all the life and joy had been sucked from him. In all honesty, he'd aged ten years in the weeks since his wife had departed Kinloch.

'I'm not lying to you, sir.' Shaw's voice was weak, almost a whisper. 'The last thing I remember was standing on the doorstep looking for my keys. After that, everything is just confused – a jumble – until you both arrived. It was like being outside my own body.'

'So, you've no' been injecting the drugs, Alasdair?' Scott looked unconvinced. 'They'd fair make you feel as though you were having an out-of-body experience, right enough.'

'I swear to you both, I've never so much as smoked a joint in all my life.' His eyes widened in a silent plea that the detectives should believe him.

'I want you to get some rest, Alasdair.' Daley leaned over the forlorn man. 'They've given you meds to make you feel better. You'll be back to your old self in a couple of days, I promise.'

'Please, I'm not lying, Jim. You have to believe me.' Shaw grabbed Daley's arm weakly.

'Of course I do. We need to get to the bottom of this. But that can't happen until you're well. I'll come back and see you tomorrow. Do you want anything, Alasdair?'

Shaw turned his head away. 'I want to see my wife and kids. Can you do that for me?' His words had a hopeless, throwaway feel.

'Just try to keep calm. There's nothing that can't be fixed, you know that.'

'He's right, Al. And even if that's her on her toes for good, there's plenty mair fish in the sea,' said Scott.

Shaw whimpered and turned away.

The pair took their leave, Daley taking long strides down the hospital corridor.

'Hold the bus, big man. It's no' a race.'

'Do you have to be so insensitive, Brian?'

'It's just a fact, Jimmy. There's no point getting yourself into the state he's in o'er a deid relationship. Imagine going to the lengths o' sticking yourself wae that shit. How's that going to help anything?'

'You don't believe him?' Daley pushed through the exit doors and out into the car park.

'No, dae you? The only truth I can see is, if we spend any mair time in this hospital, we might as well move the office up here.'

'You've got to admit, it's not like the man.'

'He's embarrassed! Who wouldnae be, eh? If you found me wae half o' Colombia up my arm, I'd say the same things. He's likely been at it for a while to block oot the pain.'

Daley stopped in his tracks. 'You haven't thought of the consequences, Brian.'

'Which are?'

'If – and I mean *if* – Shaw's been taking drugs, then he's vulnerable. We all know how little luck we've had following up tip-offs.'

'You don't think he's been warning the dealers? Man, first you're all sympathetic, the next thing you're condemning the man to a fate worse than death.'

'He's the heartbeat of the office, you know that. He has access to virtually everything.'

'Aye, but this is Alasdair Shaw we're talking aboot.'

'I know. But look at the state he's in.'

'But he says he was jumped, Jimmy.'

'You believe that now. You shift with the wind, Bri. Your loyalty is admirable. But it's misplaced. And in any case, we should respect what he says by investigating it. That's my point.

If he's lying . . .' Daley didn't finish the sentence.

'I suppose it's better than your usual, thinking it's always me in league wae the crooks.'

'It's a regular consideration, Brian.' Daley smiled. 'And that was a joke, before you go off the rails.'

'You're a funny guy.'

'We owe it to Alasdair to listen. To investigate on that basis. Do you agree?'

'Aye, sure, Jimmy.'

'Good. Because if there is someone attacking police officers, you know what happens. The big guns come out.'

'And I get shot.'

'Optimist to the last. Listen, I want you to post someone at Alasdair's door. Just in case.'

'You're the boss.'

The pair made their way across the car park and climbed into Dalcy's car just as a black SUV pulled into a parking space. A well-dressed man in his fifties, followed by a striking younger woman, got out. Both were dressed sombrely in dark suits. The man's hair was either grey or ash blond; it was hard to tell as it was gelled back and short. But despite his middle years, he looked fit, his height exaggerating this impression.

'Nearly as big as you, Jimmy.'

'I know who he is, too.'

'I can take a wild guess. It's the Brandt boy's father.'

'Got it in one, Brian.'

The man passed in front of Daley's car. He nodded at the policemen and carried on, the young woman walking slightly behind.

'I smell money,' said Scott.

'Yes, and none of it very clean,' Daley replied.

21

Despite the cold, she was sitting on the beach wrapped up in a thick overcoat. She'd had the garment for a long time. A relic from another life, or so it seemed.

The winter sun was disappearing in the west, but not in the spectacular way it often did. Tonight, it was cloudy and cold. A chill easterly was gaining ground: in this place, a harbinger of snow. It was as though someone was slowly leaching the light from the scene, like draining a body of blood. The gunmetal sea darkened to inky black, the rocks becoming jagged teeth on a dead, jawbone shore. The cry of seabirds no longer echoed up the beach, through the trees and to the hills beyond. Apart from the wash of the tide, all was silence. It was the way she liked it.

She pulled the coat more tightly round her bulky frame. She knew she was gaining weight. It was the inevitable outcome of a diet that came pre-prepared in boxes and bags, ready to be placed in a microwave. Then there were the sweets, crisps and large glasses of wine she consumed just to retain any sense of sanity.

The more she thought about it, though, the more madness appealed. Surely it was respite from her memories, the ghosts that scarred and battered her with a wicked persistence, its intensity swollen with every passing day. Once she'd been too busy to think, her life an onrushing tableau of things to do and places to be. Now that there was nowhere to go, nothing to do, entropy had engulfed her. It was like tonight's sunset. She was slowly disappearing over her own horizon in darkening shades of grey: unlamented, unseen by a world which – while mindful of the end – only had time for fading beauty and the death of brilliance. The demise of the average, the humdrum, the mundane, merited not even the twitch of a curtain or the glisten of a single tear.

She buried her face in the ample collar. She couldn't remember the last time she'd had it cleaned. The sheer banality of this thought surprised her. Perhaps she wasn't being engulfed by solipsism after all. Maybe the existential pull of normality, of things that had to be done without praise or comment, still had a place in her life. How large a portion of every existence is devoted to the drudgery of endless chores: cleaning, washing, tidying? The endless *to-do*.

You washed your knickers well today. This was a sentence that was never spoken. Yet, she reasoned, if this simple act remained undone, what would be the outcome? A question of hygiene – surely that would be most pertinent. But that was never the case. Filthy clothes were a symptom of a sliding awareness. She knew this from experience. The question was always the same: a loss of interest, of self-respect, or the onset of madness. Soiled knickers were the ultimate arbiter: the grimier the skin, the greater the insanity.

These jumbled thoughts weren't mere flights of fancy. Such questions had been asked of her on the slow path to becoming nothing – well, nothing of any substance, at least.

Filthy underwear had nearly brought about incarceration. Her freedom was preserved by a doctor who took pity on a woman with whom he'd once worked.

Go, get away from here! Go somewhere they can't find you.

She pushed herself off the sand, feeling the clicks from protesting knees and the ache in her back. It often crossed her mind to find the resolve to sit out all night in cold weather like this. It would be the closest she'd ever come to suicide. Thoughts of swallowing pills or cutting into her own flesh were out of the question. The passive act of just sitting there appealed. The only physical actions required were stepping out of the door and finding a suitable place – a suitable place to die.

Not tonight, though. The pull of wine was too much. She wanted to bathe in the oblivion of alcohol. It was all that soothed her now. There were no kind words left; the reassuringly welcome press of flesh on flesh was a distant memory. Solace could only be found in things, not people. The knowledge that nobody knew or cared was at first depressing. But now, the acceptance of the fact that she too cared nothing for herself or her fate was in itself a comfort. Things were just the way they were. Only the means to the end were of any consequence.

Despite the darkness, she made her way sure-footedly through the spaces between rocks and boulders. It was a short journey she could have executed with her eyes shut; it was the retentive study of where things were. After all, she'd little else to commit to memory. Remembering the path along the beach to her front door had become her life's work. Well, that and managing to obtain the stuff of life – ready meals, sweet-meats and wine – without human contact. But a friendly voice on the phone and the anonymous use of a credit card had helped her cross that little hurdle. Her groceries were delivered every Thursday, by means of a cardboard box at her door.

The cardboard box crossed her mind because, through the trees, under the vestibule light, she could see an object matching that description on the front doorstep. She stopped for a minute, desperately trying to remember what day it was, but couldn't get a handle on it. But if the box was there, it must be Thursday. She supposed that with Christmas on the way, the man whose voice on the phone represented her only human contact must be busy.

She lengthened her stride. The grocery delivery was her one distraction. Though she purchased the same items every week, sometimes there were surprises. Occasionally, certain items weren't available, so substitutes took their place. It was the random hand of fate that thrilled. She'd learned to appreciate this like a wrapped birthday present. An alternative curry, the substitution of one custard for another, filled her with joy.

Of course, she could have changed her order. After all, she phoned it in every Monday at nine-thirty. The same items, week after week. What she enjoyed was the mystery of it all. Wondering if something would be different, a departure from the norm.

She stopped in her tracks, a short distance from her own front door.

What if these were the new things, unwanted deliveries?

She studied the box under the light of the single bulb. It looked like her grocery order. And though the day of the week remained a mystery, she was reasonably confident that this was the work of the kind shopkeeper.

Her confidence was tinged with disappointment, though. She always stood behind the net curtains that covered a bedroom window when she heard his van roll on to the gravel drive. She caught a fleeting view of the top of his head as he left the driver's seat and made his way to the back of the van. His hair was dark, with wisps of grey.

Only once had he stepped back, looking up in her direction rather than going about his business. It was as though he sensed her presence, her searching gaze. She'd retreated into the dark of the room, absolutely sure he couldn't see her. But she could still see him.

The little episode reminded her of an Edward Hopper painting in motion. She remembered falling back on the bed and bringing herself to a climax, this fleeting glimpse enough to engender desire. A signal event in itself.

No, this was her grocery delivery. In any case, the other things – the things she banished from her mind – arrived in little padded envelopes.

To the sound of her quick footsteps crunching on the gravel, she hurried over to the box. As always, the flaps weren't taped or stapled shut; rather they were folded neatly to form a closure.

She tore at the cardboard. And stopped, the very breath caught in her throat. She had to force herself to breathe as the ghastly sight made her stomach churn and tiny prickles shot down her arms and legs. Sheer terror banished her fight-or-flight response; it was as though she was rooted to the spot, unable to shout or scream, paralysed by revulsion and fear.

The disembodied head stared back at her with glassy, blank eyes.

22

Daley and Scott decided to end their day at the bar of the County Hotel. Brian, in a touching and rather old-fashioned way, liked to pick his wife up from work, just in case any ill-doers lurked with intent. After all, alcohol did funny things to people, and he knew it.

They sat at their usual table at the back of the bar. At first, when they'd first arrived in Kinloch, the hotel's clientele were reluctant to share their watering hole with gentlemen of the constabulary. But in the years that had elapsed they had become most welcome. Scott's antics had become the stuff of legend in Kinloch, and rather than lose respect for the detective who struggled with the bottle, the townsfolk recognised a flawed but honest man and a good police officer. Scott was brave – he'd been shot twice and attacked with intent by a dry-roasted peanut. Here was a man of action who could be called upon at any time to save the day.

Daley had a slightly different reputation. He was more cerebral, buttoned-up. Despite his large frame, everybody knew him to be the brains behind the outfit, but nobody wanted to get too close. Stories of a volcanic temper and the meting out of summary justice were well known. If Scott was the brave soldier, Daley was the general who would happily take up the cudgels and do what had to be done himself, if required.

Now Scott shook his head. 'You'll have heard Hamish sold his boat, Jimmy?'

Daley looked up from his whisky. 'No, I hadn't heard. I knew he was thinking about it, mind you.'

'I heard he's stoating aboot like a wet Tuesday. I suppose it's understandable after all these years. It's like one o' us trying to think what to dae when we retire, eh?'

'I don't think so, Bri. Our job only takes up eighty per cent of our available headspace.'

'Speak for yourself. I'm lucky if it gets forty per cent o' mine.'

'That explains a great deal. But with Hamish it was his love, what he lived to do. I think he'll take it really hard.'

Scott looked at his watch then called to Ella, who was busy clearing a table of empty glasses. 'Has the auld fella been in today, honey?'

'Aye, you're sitting there,' she replied. 'If you mean Hamish, no he hasn't. Do you think he's okay?'

'He's just sold his boat, Ella,' said Daley. 'Bound to be a bit of a wrench.'

'Aye, like when Brian walks past a distillery, I daresay.'

'I'll dae the jokes, darling,' said Scott

'Oh, great! That'll be fun for us all. I mean, me and Jimmy have only heard them a thousand times before.' She bustled off with a tray of empty glasses.

'Come on, let's take a run down. Liz is at her friend's tonight with James. Some perfume night or something. And Ella won't be done here for a good while.'

'Aye, that's a good idea, Jimmy.'

The detectives drank up. Hamish had been a good friend to them both. It was time to pay some of that back. And, as Daley mentioned when they stepped into his SUV, if there was any gossip to be had about recent events in the town, Hamish was the man to impart it.

They'd had a hard day trekking through thick pines, then heading up a steep rise on to a ridge that overlooked the sea far below.

While Nate was busy with the spirit stove, Delph was lying in the tent, wrapped up in a sleeping bag, cold and miserable.

'Why are we doing this?' she said with a sigh.

'Because we want to experience all that life can offer while we're young enough to enjoy it,' Nate replied.

'I suppose.'

He looked at his watch. 'These meals will be ready soon. I'm just making some tea.'

'What is it tonight?'

'You have the choice of chilli or bolognese. And we have boil-in-the-bag dessert, too.' He waved his hands in mock celebration.

'Wow, that's just fabulous.' Delph struggled out of the tent, yawned and stretched. She looked out across the sea. There was no twinkling moonlit ribbon tonight. Instead, the water looked flat and sullen, lit only by a fleeting shift of stars through the clouds. Her eyes were drawn to the foreshore, just below where they'd pitched up. The dark shadow of pines was unmistakable, but in their midst, not far from a tiny bay, she could see dots of light. 'Do you think that's some of the other guys?'

Nate joined her, following the line of her finger. 'Nah, that's a house, not a tent. Big one too, by the look of it.'

'Who'd want to live there? It's in the middle of nowhere.'

'Somebody, clearly. Anyway, think of the views. We're going to spend our lives crammed into some boxy pad we'll pay a fortune for in Islington. Imagine waking up to this every day. I know which I'd prefer.'

'Yeah, but think of your social life. The occasional dinner at Angus and Morag's talking about fence posts and broth.' The sarcasm was palpable.

'Who on earth are Angus and Morag?'

'They're a generic construct. But you can see them if you try.' Delph put a finger to her lips. 'He's big but overweight. Unruly hair and a bushy red beard.'

'And she's dumpy with one of those bubble perms my grandma used to have.'

'Woo, *grandma*. How posh.'

'Why? What did you call your grandmother?'

Her face became blank. 'Nothing. She's dead. I never met her.'

'That's sad. What about the other one?'

'What other one?'

'What do you mean?'

'Most people have a brace of grandmothers, you know. One for each parent, normally.'

Delph shrugged. 'Nobody ever mentioned her.'

'Which one, your mother's mother or your father's mother.'

'My goodness, wouldn't you think maternal and paternal sound better for people with our education?'

'Ha! You know what I mean. Don't go all sociologist

128

on me, Tracy. You're just avoiding the question. What about this mystery granny?'

Delph looked down at the lights in the trees again. 'My father never talked about her. I mean – *never*. I remember asking about her when I was a child. I knew everyone else had two nanas, and I'd been told the other one was dead. But nothing about my paternal grandmother.'

'Talked? Your father hasn't kicked the bucket, has he?'

'Talked, talks – a slip of the tongue. Do you have to be so pedantic?' She folded her arms defensively.

Nate studied her in the shadows. He'd hung a USB lantern outside the tent to see what he was cooking. In that diffused light she could have been a film star. Flaxen hair, high cheekbones and a button nose. Her eyes were big too, almost unnaturally so. They gave her a wickedly coquettish look sometimes. But Delph excelled at hiding her feelings. He knew that her family had problems: financial difficulties, he remembered her saying. He felt as though he was catching another glimpse of her background now.

'What are you staring at?' she said.

'Just reminding myself how beautiful you are, Delphine.'

She smiled. 'I'll need something to eat first.'

'First?'

Her laugh tinkled on the cold air. 'And if you're worried about bursting your mat, why don't you do me up against a tree?'

'In this cold? You're keen.'

'I want to road-test your stamina in all conditions before I buy.'

'You make me sound like a Land Rover.'

'A girl's got to know how sustainable her partner is.'

'Come on, let's eat!'

Delph chose the chilli, tucking into it as Nate made the tea. 'I don't think we'll bother with dessert. What do you reckon?'

'It depends what you mean by dessert, Tracy.'

They chatted away, eating their meal from two foil pouches. They were blissfully unaware of the light footsteps on the frozen grass only metres away from their tent.

23

Hamish looked surprised when he opened the door to Daley and Scott.

'Man, it's yourselves. Don't tell me the bomb's dropped and you're here to see me through the end?'

'All the fun o' the fair in this hoose, Hamish. Can we no' come in?' said Scott.

'Aye, aye, of course. You'll forgive the upheaval.'

They made their way past clothes, boots and some ancient-looking kitchen appliances that would have looked more at home in a museum. A food mixer that must have been made in the fifties sat next to a rusty pressure cooker, an old tin tray was piled high with old biscuit boxes, mainly of the shortbread variety, while a wooden crate of empty whisky bottles was placed outside the bathroom door.

'Are you having a clear-out, or planning a yard sale, Hamish?' said Daley.

'Ach, most of this stuff belonged to my mother. I should have carted it out long ago. I just didna have the heart, somehow.'

'Hey, does this suit me?' Brian Scott was wearing a faded corduroy Breton cap. 'Bit on the large side. It would fit you, Jimmy.'

'That cap belonged to Sandy Hoynes, my old skipper. A finer man never drew breath, and that's a fact. If it weren't for him, I wouldna be the man you see before you today.'

'He liked a dram then, eh?' said Scott.

'He did. But what are you implying, Brian?' Hamish looked rather indignant.

'Just joking, auld fella. Keep your bunnet on.'

'I remember you talking about him. I stood at his grave with you. When – well, you know,' said Daley sadly.

'When we buried Annie. A day I'll never forget.'

Scott picked up a rusty carving knife with a bone handle. 'Is this sharp enough to cut my ain throat? The Chuckle Brothers o'er here.'

'Come on through,' said Hamish.

The old fisherman's lounge was every bit as chaotic as the hall. Cardboard boxes, wooden crates and other items were dotted about the room.

'Just move stuff to get a seat, boys,' said Hamish, as he sat down and began tamping some tobacco into his pipe. 'I'll get the kettle on in a moment, Brian. You help yourself to a dram, Mr Daley.'

Daley moved a box from a chair and sat down. 'I'll have a cup of tea when you're ready, Hamish. I've got the car.' He looked round the room he'd become so used to over the last few years. 'If I didn't know any better, I'd say you were flitting.'

'A moonlight job, at that,' said Scott.

Hamish sucked his pipe into life, sending clouds of blue tobacco smoke into the small room. 'And you'd be right, Mr Daley. For that's just what's happening.'

Brian Scott looked shocked. 'You're no' heading for one o' they retirement homes, are you? You'd hate that, Hamish.'

'No, no retirement home. Just call them what they are, Brian: knackers' yards wae bibs and entertainment on a Wednesday. Not for me. I have somewhere very different in mind.'

'Where?' asked Daley, looking puzzled.

'I have a cousin in Perthshire. A nice wee village, it is. Beautiful up there. I've always liked it. His wife died a wee while back and he's fair lonely. He and I always rubbed along uncommon well. We're o' an age and enjoy similar things. And I daresay the same sentiment as far as annoyances go, too. It'll help him wae household costs and the like. Me too. Man, the price o' the electric alone is enough to frighten auld black waistcoats himsel'.'

'Aye, right,' said Scott. 'You're having us on, Hamish.'

'No, I am not. I'm deadly serious. The time comes when you have to accept what's happening in your own life. I sold my boat the other day. I have a wee bit money put away. High time I broadened my horizons before there are nae horizons to broaden. Kinloch's been my home all my life. It would be a shame if it was the only place where I ever took off my bunnet ready for bed.'

'But all your friends are here, Hamish. The people who love you,' said Daley.

'Aye, it's true to say there are folk – like your good selves – who hold me in great regard. Rightly or wrongly, mark you. I'm glad o' it, all the same. But as for friends and family, well, they're all gone. I live in a place full o' ghosts, and that's a fact. You wait till you both get older. You feel as though you're just hanging aboot, wae everyone dropping deid all around.'

Hamish took another puff as the detectives looked on, not knowing what to say. 'The wee lassie was the last. My Annie.

When she went, well, that was it. I promised I'd look after her. She lost her parents too young – her mother, at any rate.' He hesitated, looking as though he was about to say something. In the end, he remained silent, though there were tears in his eyes.

'You never let anyone down with that promise, Hamish,' said Daley.

The old man's eyes flashed. 'No, I did not keep my promise. For where is she now? A rickle o' bones up in the cemetery, gone long before her time.'

'That wasn't your fault,' said Scott. 'You cannae blame yourself, neither.'

'I should have seen what that bastard Macmillan was at. I knew he wasn't to be trusted. But there I was, happy soaking up whisky instead o' taking note o' things that mattered. That wee lassie was the last thing I cared aboot. Och, yous will never understand.'

'Try me,' said Daley, just as his phone burst into life in his pocket. 'Hold that thought, Hamish.' He answered the call, looking detached at first, but soon his face broke into an expression of incredulity. 'Where was this? Do we know the victim?' He listened intently.

'You stay put until we get a chance to have a good natter wae you, Hamish,' said Scott in a low voice. 'You promise?'

'Aye, that much I promise. But, Brian, I'll never be on a proud wave again. And living so close to the sea – well, if you don't mind me saying, it's like you having a bottle o' whisky tied roon your neck you know you'll never be able to touch.'

Scott nodded thoughtfully. Though he'd never understood the devotion many people in Kinloch had for the sea, Hamish's words made sense, he supposed.

Daley ended the call. 'Sorry, it's back on duty for us. But we'll see you again soon, Hamish. Do you hear?'

'And it'll be good to see you both, as always.'

The police officers hurried out of the little fisherman's cottage by the loch, the island looming in the darkness, perhaps a harbinger of things to come.

Hamish watched their headlights disappear through his old brown net curtains. He ambled back to his chair, and was soon joined by his namesake, Hamish the cat.

'Well, son. A change o' scene will do you good too. We're just getting old, you and I.' The animal lay with its head on his lap, purring contentedly, as the old clock on the mantelpiece ticked steadily on, as it had done for seventy years and more.

They drove down a long gravel drive, the distinctive flash of blue lights pinpointing their destination. Daley parked beside two police cars. He and Scott made for the house.

DC Potts had been in charge of the crime scene until their arrival. It was to him that Daley turned before entering the dilapidated Georgian mansion that looked so out of place here, beside woods and the small bay.

'What do we have, Potts?' said Daley.

'A severed head, and that's about it, sir.'

'What about the woman who reported it?'

'She found it, sir, but she didn't report it.'

'Sorry?' Daley looked confused and irritated at the same time. He placed one hand on the small of his back and leaned into it, trying to banish the pain that had been increasing in intensity for the last couple of hours.

Potts consulted his notebook. 'A Mr Wanley was the reporter, sir. He owns the shop in Taindale.'

'What's that all aboot? Was he here when she found it?'

'No, sergeant. It sounds as though he's the only person she has any contact with. She phones in her grocery order every week, and he delivers it.' Potts gestured with his hands in a bewildered fashion.

'Where is he?' said Daley.

'At home, I assume, sir.'

DCI Daley closed his eyes, his nostrils flaring. 'How long have you been in this job, son?'

'Twelve years, sir.'

'Then for fuck's sake try and use some common sense. I want to speak to the man who reported this. Now! And smarten yourself up while you're at it. Take us to the occupant first.'

'Yes, sir.' Potts automatically stood to attention before showing Daley and Scott into the house. He led them into a high-ceilinged room with ornate cornices. For all its grandeur, it was sparsely furnished, with only a table and one easy chair sitting on a worn red carpet.

Potts looked about quizzically.

'What's up?' said Daley.

'She was here a minute ago, sir.'

Scott grimaced. He knew his old friend wasn't in a good humour and sensed what was to come. 'Jimmy, take it easy, man,' he said from the corner of his mouth.

Daley ignored him. 'You've lost the man who reported this, as well as the woman who found a severed head in a cardboard box sitting at her front door. Isn't that great Potts?'

'Not really, sir.' The detective was moving nervously from foot to foot.

'Bloody well go and find her!' Daley's voice echoed round the cavernous room. His fists were bunched at his sides.

As Potts ran off to find the lady of the house, Scott looked his boss up and down, without comment.

'What's wrong with your face?' said Daley.

'I think you know what's wrong with me. You shouldnae have bawled the lad oot like that. There's no point.'

'I tell you what there's no point in, DS Scott. There's no point in having you train younger officers. Because they all develop the slapdash habits you've been allowed to indulge in for so long. Don't think I don't blame myself for the way you behave. I've been your gaffer for long and weary – too long, maybe.' Daley stormed across the room and stared out of a window.

'No' like you to be like this, Jimmy,' said Scott flatly.

'Oh, no? Maybe it's time for a change. Things aren't running right. I'm fed up with it.' He spun round, ready to berate Scott some more, but yelled out in pain instead, holding his back with both hands.

'Can I ask you a question?'

'It better be a sensible one,' said Daley through gritted teeth.

'When's the last time you took one o' they painkillers?'

'I had one this morning before I came to work.'

'Well, if you don't mind me saying, the effects have well and truly worn off. To be honest, you need to get your back fixed pronto. Because this is the first sign o' dependency, old buddy.'

Daley frowned then hung his head. 'Sorry, Brian. I feel like shit – irritable, you know. But I can't be addicted to them already.'

'Aye, you can, like I told you. Those bloody things are a nightmare.'

Daley made his way back across the room just as the door creaked open.

In the doorway stood a woman whose hair straggled over a dishevelled police sergeant's tunic of a style popular a decade before. It looked as though it had been stuffed in a box and left there for years, gaining a multitude of creases and holes, probably courtesy of moths.

'PC E2192 reporting for duty, sir.' The woman drew herself to attention before formally saluting Daley and Scott.

'That's what you want fae all your witnesses,' said Scott.

Daley looked on, his eyes wide with disbelief.

24

Delph was finding sleep hard to find. When she looked at her watch, it was just after five in the morning. Nate was snoring softly by her side, his head almost entirely enveloped by his mummy bag.

Delph realised that her claustrophobia was at least partially responsible for the cold she now felt. She found it almost impossible to bury her head in a sleeping bag the way her boyfriend did. The end result was a chill that spread up her nose, on to her face, and seemed to thread its way through her body like a malevolent snake, intent on chilling her to the bone.

She turned on to her back, staring into the gloom. Another thing she couldn't bear was darkness. To that end, Nate made sure that one of the little LED lanterns they used to light the tent was left on at its dimmest setting to get her through the night.

Delph regularly found the wee small hours a challenge. Being a light sleeper, the least thing woke her up, a state from which a return to the arms of Morpheus was almost impossible. She berated herself for thinking of not being able to sleep as a banishment from Morpheus's arms. Oxford had affected her that way. At first, she'd found spending time with so many brilliant students unnerving. In the main, her upbringing hadn't prepared her for rubbing shoulders with the public school elite, some of whom freely conversed in Latin as though they were sharing a joke down the pub. Her first roommate, a quiet, bird-like girl from Ipswich, had been identified by NASA as a potential employee. Soon she was whisked off to Harvard. It was a rarefied atmosphere for which her secondary modern education had ill prepared her. However, her thoughts on Morpheus were proof that maybe she was thinking on a different plane these days.

Delph thought about Salz. What an awful thing to happen. But the world was cruel. She knew that for a fact. Everyone was here to perform a function. It was simple.

Nate mumbled something in his sleep. She listened carefully, holding her own breath in case he was whispering the name of another woman. But his utterances made no sense, and she soon tired of the whole thing. She nudged him in the back, and he mumbled something else she couldn't understand before returning to a more peaceful sleep.

Random thoughts filled her head as the cold night chilled her further to the bone. After a few more freezing minutes, she remembered that Nate had given her a hand warmer, which she had placed in one of the pockets of her down jacket. She rummaged about, found it and activated it. Soon, she felt its warmth, and sighed with the simple pleasure of holding the little pad between both hands. It wasn't much, but it was better than nothing.

Another check of her watch revealed that it was just before five thirty. Delph closed her eyes, her heart suddenly thumping in her chest.

There was something moving outside. A slow thudding noise was increasing in intensity with each second. Delph held her breath again. After a few seconds of silence, she thought that whatever it was had thought better of getting nearer to the tent. But just as she sighed with relief, there it was again. This time the sound appeared to be coming from only a few feet away.

'Nate, wake up!' She thumped him in the back to rouse him from his slumber. 'Nate!'

'What is it?' His words were slurred, eyes still half shut.

'There's something outside the tent. Please wake up.'

'I can't hear anything. Just let me go back to sleep.'

Just as the words left his mouth there was a snap, metal on metal.

Nate shot up in his sleeping bag, arms still pinned to his side by its intentionally snug fit. 'You're right!' He tried to wriggle free of the bag, but just as he did so something hit the tent, knocking the little lantern from the loop on the roof to which it was hooked.

For Delph, the next few seconds seemed to drag on for hours. The tent was in semi-darkness, with only the lantern lying on the groundsheet a source of illumination. She heard a shearing sound, like a zip being pulled but much higher pitched, felt a chill wind against her face, and screamed.

'Fuck off!' This came from Nate as he struggled with two pairs of strong arms. The tent had been cut open and two figures cast in shadow were tugging at him, trying to drag him through the slash they had made.

Delph reached for her rucksack as the struggle continued. She was acting on sheer impulse now. She found the walking pole that was attached to the side of the bag, pulled it clear with one sharp tug, and swung it – still folded in two – at one of the shadows, feeling as though she was helping Nate when she heard a muffled oath.

But it wasn't enough. Between Nate's frantic cries of panic, she could hear grunts of exertion from whoever was attacking him. Blindly, she swung the folded walking pole again. This time, though, all she succeeded in doing was catching Nate a glancing blow on the temple, enough to send his head flying back and induce a cry of pain.

Out of nowhere, Delph received a blow to the chest, knocking the wind out of her lungs. She fell back, with the familiar feeling of gasping for breath that wouldn't come. By the time she had recovered a deathly silence reigned. The scarred tent was flapping in the breeze, stars visible through a great hole through which Nathan had been wrenched from her side.

Delph's first instinct was to run. She forced herself up out of her sleeping bag and through the slash in the tent. She knew the pine trees became denser just behind their campsite. Running blind, her hands held out in front of her to prevent a collision with an unseen object, she tripped, hitting the ground hard. She pushed herself back to her feet, but a few staggering steps later her right shoulder collided with the trunk of a tree. This time, she managed to stop herself from falling by crashing into another pine.

Feeling she'd made sufficient progress into the safety of the thicker part of the forest, she stopped, her back against a trunk, and tried to calm her thudding heart. The last thing she needed was desperate gasping of air to give her away.

She stood, propped up by the tree, for almost half an hour, able to see nothing in the darkness of early morning. She was shivering now, her teeth chattering, and just when she knew she'd have to seek temporary shelter back in the tent, she heard a distant rumble. It was the unmistakable thump of a diesel engine, far away, at the edge of her hearing.

25

Werner Brandt knew how to manoeuvre people round to his way of thinking. After all, he'd been doing it most of his life, from the backstreets of Vienna to palaces and corridors of power across the world. It usually made little difference where one was or to whom one spoke, human nature being much the same in Austria as it was in Azerbaijan. There were exceptions to prove this rule: some megalomaniacs who ran countries like their own fiefdoms, which, in fact, they were. These man –they were always men – could be tricky. But pretty much, people were the same across the globe, driven by greed and ego, and the need to be recognised as outstanding in some way. In real megalomaniacs, these traits were merely amplified – sometimes deafeningly.

He found the staff at Kinloch hospital no different. He noticed that they had a poster appealing for money for scanning equipment pinned to the wall of the waiting room. He had his assistant produce a cheque book, and on the spot donated five thousand pounds. The money meant nothing to him, but it bought him leverage. Now, he walked along the hospital's corridors as though he owned the place. He was even given permission to take a short cut through the nurses' station in order to avoid the long trek to where his son languished in one of the side rooms.

'So grateful, staff nurse. Thank you,' he gushed to a bespectacled woman before entering his son's room. She fawned in reponse. He'd heard her being extremely rude to another visitor just as he'd arrived, and the man was clearly upset by her attitude. Secretly, he hoped that she'd try it with him, just to have the pleasure of quickly wearing her down. But she was instantly, if rather unfortunately, obsequious.

He opened the door to the private room without knocking. His son was dozing, a pair of oversized headphones over his ears.

'He seems to be doing well in himself,' said the staff nurse. 'He was a bit reserved. But I suppose that's understandable. Such a pleasant young man.'

'I'm sure you're right. He's quite sensitive, you know. He'd been very badly treated before we adopted him as a child. He needed to be handled with the utmost care. But we got there in the end. We love him very much, my wife and I.' Brandt smiled beatifically.

'I'll leave you to have a chat. Just ring the bell if you need anything.' The staff nurse bustled off, no doubt ready to berate a less impressive visitor.

Brandt studied his son for a moment. His face was pallid, arm held in a scaffold to keep the injured hand safe from knocks. Brandt senior had harboured high hopes for the boy he'd only adopted to appease his childless wife. He had considered that Salazar might join his organisation when he left university, but deep down he had known that was unlikely. Salazar Brandt was heading for a middling degree and seemed to lack any ambition other than to make endless mistakes, scrape mediocre grades and conduct a very active social life.

In any case, he lacked any ruthlessness or cunning, and could never survive the jolts his father's line of work served up on an almost daily basis.

Without ceremony, Werner Brandt tugged the headphones from his son's head. The young man was violently thrust into wakefulness, instinctively tugging at his disfigured hand, which made him cry out in pain.

'Why are you lying asleep at this time of day?' Werner Brandt's question was as lacking in care as it was in thought.

'Father. Have you found me a new hospital yet?'

'I've reconsidered.'

'Why?' Salazar looked wary.

'Because if you're admitted to a hospital back in civilisation, you'll become an even bigger embarrassment than you already are. I've made other arrangements.'

'I see.'

'No, you don't *see*. You never do. That's the fucking problem.' Werner leaned into his son's face, sending flecks of spittle into his eyes. 'My entire business is about reputation, and you're destroying it with your reckless behaviour and your pathetic addictions. Don't you see that your weaknesses make me look weak too?'

'I'm not an addict. I use drugs recreationally.'

Werner grabbed his son by the throat, slowly tightening his grip as he spoke. 'If you spent more time studying and less on your *recreation*, perhaps your grades might improve. Maybe you wouldn't be a source of shame.' He let go of Salazar's throat, leaving his son gasping for air.

'You're a monster,' the young man spluttered.

As though nothing had happened, Werner Brandt was transformed. He walked to the end of the bed and began rearranging a vase of flowers sent to Salz by his fellow students. 'These are nice, but some are dying. You must always weed out the weak, Salazar. They pollute everything else.' Though his words were sinister, his tone was now bright, breezy – conversational, even.

'I'm not exactly in any shape to attend to the flowers myself.' Salazar nodded to the bulbous dressing.

'I'll get you a hook.' Werner smiled.

'Thanks.'

As the older man returned to his side, the close proximity of father to son made the younger man shrink away in the bed.

'You know I'm only angry because I love you, yes?'

'Yeah, I know.' Salazar sounded less than convinced.

'You know, sometimes, there is only one way to right a wrong.'

'Which is?'

'*Do unto others . . .*' Werner didn't finish the biblical quotation. But the inference was plain. 'We will find those who did this to you, and we will do the same to them.'

'I don't know who did it.'

'Listen, Salazar. This is a small town, with very few people. An idiot could find out who did this to you.'

'The police don't know. Sergeant Scott told me.'

'Scott?'

'He was the policeman who interviewed me when – when it happened.' Salazar's eyes began to fill with tears.

Werner sat on the bed. 'You don't cry in my presence. You know this.' His voice was almost a whisper, but the accent had shifted. Now there was a distinctly Teutonic edge to his words.

'I can't help it. Look at me, Father. I'm fucked up! I want

to kill myself, never mind just cry.' Salazar turned his head away.

'Well, I've heard worse ideas. But unfortunately, such an act would upset your mother very much. As you know, I love your mother. So this act of contemptible self-pity cannot happen. Tell me you understand.'

Salazar didn't reply.

'Tell me! You have three seconds.'

Salazar could remember this threat from his childhood. At least his father had stopped counting down.

'I'm not going to do anything stupid.'

'Good.' Werner patted his son's cheek. 'Progress, at last. Now, all I want you to do is tell me what happened. I need to know exactly.'

'I don't remember.'

'Try.'

'I'm telling you, I don't remember anything! How many times?'

Werner rubbed his chin thoughtfully. 'I must ask myself a question. It's a question for which there is only one answer.'

'Which is?'

'Why would you try to save the person who did this to you? If I were you, I'd be thirsting for revenge. Revenge of the most satisfying kind. But you don't seem to care. I wonder why that is?'

'Maybe I think it's better to forgive, Father. Have you ever thought about the concept of forgiveness?'

'No, I haven't. You see, people only forgive for a reason. Perhaps it's to conform with their religion. But I know you are an atheist. You're too clever to believe in God. That again shows misjudgement. You're not clever. Nobody is clever enough to know the immensity of the universe.'

'Please don't lecture me on religion, Father.'

'I know you think yourself to be moral and me wicked. Despite this, you take drugs produced by ruthless gangs all over the world, but it's okay because you have the morals of an unbeliever. You think that makes you superior. It doesn't. I don't think I know better than the Almighty. In fact, I'm in awe of him. I am frail, and that frailty makes me vulnerable. But because I believe in more than just myself, frailty dissolves away. You have no such luxury.'

'Okay.'

'I have known you since you arrived at our home as a child. A miserable Arab boy from a hell-hole country. Your mother was a prostitute, your father a petty thief. A little kid with snot dripping down his nose who couldn't stop crying even though he'd won the lottery of life by being adopted by me.'

'You're so full of shit.' Salazar had recovered from being suddenly ripped from sleep. He was determined not to submit to his father. The line had to be drawn here. After all, he had nothing to lose. He lay in a hospital bed, disfigured and miserable. His father was powerless to make him feel any more depressed.

'Back to why you won't give up those who did this wicked thing to you. I have an idea.'

Salazar felt a sudden shiver up his spine.

'You have something to lose by telling me. Now, of course, I wonder, why would my son give a damn about some petty drug dealer in a place he'd only been for a matter of hours? Can you tell me?'

'No. I don't know what you're talking about.' That answer came too quickly. His father's raised brow was enough to indicate that he'd noted this.

'Let's hypothesise further. Let's say that you weren't on the search for drugs in this awful place just for yourself. Let's say that you were acting for someone else – a girl, maybe. I know you have a weakness for pretty girls, even though all they do is use you for their own ends in the hope of money. It's happened many times.' Werner smiled wickedly, his artificially whitened teeth reminiscent of fangs.

'I don't know where you get this stuff, Father.' The retort was bold, but there was nothing behind Salazar's brown eyes to back it up.

'Like a book.'

'Sorry?'

'I can read you like a book – a very bad book, at that. I picked one up in the waiting room here. The hero kicks in the door, and off we go. Pathetic.'

'This is shit.'

His father stood, buttoning his jacket, clearly preparing to leave. 'I'm meeting your tutor later today. I'll be sure to ask her who you're close to at Oxford.'

'Leave Professor Tang out of this! Anyway, she won't tell you anything. All she thinks about is chemistry and Everest.'

Werner pulled on a pair of black leather gloves. 'Oh yes, she will tell me.' He buttoned up his jacket, a garment that cost more than most family saloons. 'You see, Salazar, I can't hurt you. I would hurt my wife at the same time, as I've said. For some odd reason, she loves you.' He made a face. 'But I can hurt just about anyone else. Do you understand? Anyone who hates you, anyone who loves you. Anybody at all, in fact.'

Salazar shook his head, his face flushed with panic.

'Whoever your little friend is in all this, I'll identify them. If you care for them at all, you'll tell me what happened.'

He looked at his platinum Patek. 'I'll let you think about this for a few hours. But one way or another, I'll find out who did this and why. Then I will bring them to justice – my justice, not this plod *Scott*'s.'

26

Daley, Scott and a younger man were staring through one-way glass into the police office's largest interview room. A social worker with bobbed fair hair was speaking to the woman who'd found the severed head in the box. Emily Kilvington had refused the advice of a solicitor, but procedure dictated that she have someone with her.

Though the local doctor who'd examined her was no expert in the field, he reckoned that she was suffering from a form of schizophrenia, though he was unable to rule out post-traumatic stress disorder. While she appeared at times to be utterly without reason, there were moments of absolute lucidity.

'She'll need to see someone better qualified than me in this discipline, Jim,' said the doctor, a young man with a shock of carrot-red hair. 'But given the gravity of it all, and the fact that she's not under investigation, I can sign it off.' He hesitated. 'You're not investigating her, are you?'

'How many times has someone sent you a heid in a box, doc? There has to be a reason for it, and we'll have to keep an open mind,' said Scott.

'I think it more likely she is a victim, Dr Healy. Either way, we have to find out what's happening. I'm sure you understand,' Daley added, in a more reassuring tone.

'I'll have to be in here. If she becomes too distressed, the interview will have to be halted.'

'You fill your boots, doc. I'll get someone to bring you a coffee,' said Scott. 'It's like the pictures, only real life, eh?'

'That's okay. I try not to consume caffeine. I advise you both to do the same.'

'Steady on, big man. I've just managed to cut oot whisky. Gie a man a break.'

'It'll be hard at first. But eventually you'll feel the benefit of it. Better sleep, less stress. It's amazing how we abuse ourselves without knowing.'

Scott grimaced. 'Funny, you look like a man who's nae stranger to self-abuse, right enough.'

'I beg your pardon?' Healy looked put out.

Scott winked at him. 'Just a wee joke, nothing mair.'

'If you don't mind waiting here, doctor, we'll get ready for the interview.' Daley gestured to the door, and he and Brian Scott left the room.

'What's wrong with you? Can you even tell me?'

'What dae you mean, Jimmy?'

They were in the corridor, Daley towering over his detective sergeant.

'This woman is a former colleague. We owe her some respect. She resigned after being stabbed. She nearly died. No wonder it all got too much.'

'I've been shot – twice. You don't see me prancing aboot mad as fuck.'

'That's a matter of opinion.'

DC Potts appeared round the corner.

'Sir, can I have a quick word?'

'Yes, Potts. But ASAP, please. We've an interview to conduct.'

'You'll want to hear this, sir. SOCO have been going through Ms Kilvington's house, as you know. They found four severed fingers in a kitchen cupboard.' Potts produced his phone. He showed Daley and Scott an image of the four blackened digits placed against a yellow ruler for perspective.

Daley shook his head. 'I just can't understand this.'

'I'm telling you, big man. Mad as a box o' frogs. She's lopped off some poor bastard's napper and his fingers too. Hey, we have to make the connection between her and these attacks on drug users.'

'So, she's running a drug-smuggling empire in her state of mind? Come on, Brian.'

'She could be putting it on. Has that crossed your mind?'

'Don't be ridiculous. Look at the state of the house. If she's trying to pull a fast one, she's very thorough.'

'What aboot they actors?'

'What actors?'

'Them that dae the method acting. They cloak aboot for months pretending to be the character they're going to play. I saw a documentary on it wae Ella. Imagine that.' He thought for a moment. 'For me, that woman could be up to all sorts, and we wouldnae have a clue.'

'Right, let's get in there. Potts, thank you. Good work.' Daley was painfully aware he'd treated Potts more harshly than he'd intended in Kilvington's house. He'd taken some painkillers in the last hour, which meant that not only was the agony of his back reduced to a dull ache, but he also felt content, relaxed, even.

Potts returned to his duties, while Scott and Daley entered the interview room and sat down opposite Emily Kilvington and Catriona MacPhail, the social worker. Daley attended to the introductory formalities, and the interview proper began.

'Miss Kilvington, I hope you're recovering from the shock of last night?'

Emily Kilvington nodded. 'Yes, sir. In our line of work, you get used to anything, don't you?'

Scott looked puzzled. 'Oor line o' work, you say?'

'Yes – being police officers. Catch up.' She rolled her eyes at Daley.

'That's something I'd like to cover with you if that's okay,' said Daley.

'What do you mean okay?'

'Your time in the police?'

She smiled. 'Oh, I know that things are different up here in Scotland. But we're all colleagues under the skin, are we not?'

Daley shuffled through some papers. 'I have a document here from Lincolnshire Constabulary, Miss Kilvington. According to this, you left their employ almost eight years ago. You'd been off sick for quite a long time after the incident in which you were injured.'

Kilvington's eyes flicked between Daley, Scott and the social worker. She leaned forward in her chair. 'Would it be okay to have a word in private with you, DCI Daley?'

'You can say anything in here, in front of my colleagues.'

Her eyes darted to MacPhail and she held her hand up to the side of her face, hiding her mouth from the social worker. 'What about her?' she whispered.

'It's absolutely fine, Emily. Mrs MacPhail is just here to

make sure you're okay. You can speak freely in front of her and DS Scott.'

Kilvington's gaze shifted to Scott. 'He's a sour bastard, isn't he? Don't worry, sir. You get bastards like that in every station in the country.'

'I'm sure you do,' said Scott. 'Listen, lassie. You left the police a good while ago. I know we all never *leave* the job. But you're a civilian now.' He said these words as though he was trying to make himself understood to someone who didn't speak English, his delivery slow and deliberate.

'Why's he talking like that?' Kilvington looked bewildered. Daley sent Scott a warning glance from the corner of his eye. 'I'm not in Lincolnshire Police. I know that.' She sat back in her chair looking most indignant. 'Do you think I'm mad or something?'

Daley saw Scott's mouth open and kicked him under the table, making Catriona MacPhail look questioningly at them both.

'If you're no' in Lincolnshire Police, where are you now?' said Scott, trying to be at his most diplomatic.

Kilvington appeared to be taken aback. 'Special Branch, where else?'

'Aye, right,' said Scott under his breath.

'I see,' said Daley quickly. 'Who do you report to?'

'That's a confidential matter, sir. I'm willing to inform you in private, but not here.'

'Okay.' Daley smiled. 'We'll do that later. But can I ask you, why do you think you were sent a severed head?'

Emily Kilvington leaned back in her chair and sighed. It was as though the question itself was beneath contempt. 'That's what they do to unsettle you.'

'Who dae?' said Scott.

'Any number of people: OCGs, Russia, Mossad – the bloody French. You name it, they'll do anything to try and break an officer. Especially when they know I'm getting close. The French are the worst.'

'Close to what?' said Daley.

'I can't tell you, sir. Not without clearance. I'm sure you know that.'

'Can we get to the heid – the head,' said Scott, moderating his accent for the English woman.

'It's a head. You must have seen it yourselves.'

'We did, Emily – you don't mind me calling you Emily, do you?' said Daley.

'No, not at all.'

'Do you know who it belonged to? Can you identify the victim?' Scott asked.

Kilvington put a dirty finger to her lips. 'You know, that's the strange thing. I thought I did recognise it. But – well, you know how these things are. It's like having a word on the tip of your tongue that just won't come.'

'DCI Daley doesn't have that kind o' problem,' said Scott. 'He's like a walking dictionary, aren't you, big man?'

Ignoring the remark, Daley carried on. 'Nobody knows better than you what I'm trying to achieve here, Emily. We share the same job.'

'I know, sir. You're trying to identify this person. I understand.'

'If I were to show you some images – you know, the face – do you think it might jog your memory a bit?'

'I suppose it's possible, sir. I'll have a go, if you want.' Beside Kilvington, Catriona MacPhail looked uneasy.

'Please feel free to turn your head away, Mrs MacPhail. I'm going to show Emily an image you may find upsetting.'

'I'm fine, DCI Daley. Honestly,' said MacPhail. 'I *am* a professional, after all.'

Daley shuffled through his papers again and produced an A4 image of the head that had been sent to Emily Kilvington in a cardboard box. The face, grey, mottled and lifeless, eyes closed, was pictured in full colour. Daley slid it across to Kilvington, who leaned forward and studied it carefully.

'You know, it's so annoying. There is something familiar about that face, but I just can't get my head round it.'

Beside her, Catriona MacPhail pushed back her chair, hand over her mouth. She mumbled something indistinct before turning her head and vomiting copiously on the interview room floor.

'That's no' very professional,' said Scott.

27

Liz had dressed down for her visit. She was wearing a blue Italian leather jacket, designer jeans and a pair of outrageously expensive white Crown Northampton leather trainers. At the last minute, she decided to leave her matching Radley bag in the car, carrying only a specially gift-wrapped basket of fruit into Kinloch hospital.

She breezed through the main doors, heading for where she knew she'd find the unfortunate Alasdair Shaw. Liz – now well known in Kinloch – was well used to the attention she received in the town. As expected, she attracted more than a few looks from patients and staff alike as she strode on. But when she noticed a cleaner talking to an auxiliary nurse and smirking behind his hand, she sighed. 'What's so funny?'

The man looked in the opposite direction, while the nurse bustled into a side room.

Though she knew the circumstances behind Shaw's hospitalisation, Liz was still shocked to see a police officer seated outside his room.

'Good afternoon, Mrs Daley,' said the constable dutifully.

She smiled at him and knocked.

'Come in.' The voice behind the door was weak.

'Alasdair, how are you?' Liz placed the fruit on the table at the end of the bed.

'Mrs Daley – Liz – thank you. I didn't expect many visitors. Apart from my colleagues, obviously.'

'I thought you needed cheering up.'

Shaw blew out his cheeks. 'I do. But I'm not sure if anyone will manage that right now.' He stared at the bedsheets balefully.

'Oh, come on. I don't know exactly what happened to you, but I do have some idea of what you've been going through outside that.'

'Jill leaving, you mean?'

'Yes, exactly that.' Liz pulled up a chair and seated herself by the bed. 'Can I get you anything else? I didn't know what to bring, hence the fruit. I'm not sure men appreciate flowers the way they should.'

'I like fruit. You're very kind.'

'When I say I know what you've been going through, I don't just mean I know what's happened to you.'

'Oh?'

'I mean I know what it's like when you think you're going to lose someone you love.'

Shaw swallowed hard. 'Yes, of course.'

'Don't be embarrassed, Alasdair. I know every one of you knew about Ms Dunn. You'd have to be blind not to have noticed. I've been around police officers for too many years not to become acquainted with the gossip in a workplace.'

'It was a difficult time.'

'It was, Alasdair. But I never would have wanted it to turn out the way it did.' It was Liz's turn to lower her head.

'A tragedy, by any measure. Out of the blue. Really sad.' Shaw coughed feebly.

'That's just it. You never know how things will turn out. I thought I'd lost Jim for good. Goodness knows, I deserved to.'

Shaw shook his head. 'I don't think she's coming back, Liz. In fact, though I miss her and the kids more than anything in my life, I know she *can't* come back.'

'What do you mean?' Liz was confused. She was used to her husband talking but not saying anything. It appeared that this was a trait he shared with his colleague.

Shaw closed his eyes, as though in prayer. 'I need to tell somebody, but I have nobody to talk to.'

'Tell what? I mean, you can try me. Apart from my husband, most people find me easy enough to talk to.'

Shaw reached out, touching her arm. 'I don't want to make things awkward for you, Liz.'

'Things are rarely anything but awkward for me, Alasdair. And if you think I'm going to go running with anything you tell me to Jim, well, think again. He gets paid to do what he does. I don't.'

Shaw cleared his throat. 'I don't know where to start.'

'Anywhere that suits. Just take your time.'

'Jill and I were young when we first met – still in school, would you believe.'

'Gosh, I didn't know. A school romance that lasted. None of mine did. And there were a few,' she added rather ruefully.

'We went our separate ways for a while. I didn't see her again until I was on the beat in Glasgow. Jill was a student. I was walking down Sauchiehall Street on the night shift. She was coming out of a club a bit worse for wear – and we bumped into each other.'

'So you took it from there?'

'Sort of. She had another boyfriend. But that was complicated.'

'Life's complicated, Alasdair.'

'We started seeing each other again – on and off, you know. She was studying chemistry, got involved with some post-grad research. But, eventually, we got it together. It took long enough, mind you.' Shaw smiled at the memory.

'Okay, so you get married and find yourselves in Kinloch.'

'Yes. A bit down the line, but that's basically it.'

'Do you mind me asking why it took you both so long to get together? Properly, I mean?'

'Jill came with an expensive friend. What's that saying: *there were three of us in the marriage*?'

'Another man. Shit, Alasdair, you should have walked away.' Liz placed a hand on her chest. 'Sorry. It's easy to judge. And I don't know anything about the circumstances.'

'If it had been another man, it would have been easier.'

'A woman? Wow!'

'No. Though I suppose you could call it a heroine.'

Liz Daley's mouth gaped open. 'I'm so sorry. That's just awful. I mean, she always seems so normal. Not – well, you know.'

'We've worked hard to keep it under the radar. Being a chemist, Jill knows what to do – what to take and how much, how to source high-quality stuff. Just enough to keep withdrawal at bay. It's been really hard. I nearly walked away – more times than I can count. Should maybe have had the courage of my convictions and gone through with it. But I love her. And I adore our children. I just couldn't. It's been so tough at times that sometimes I think I'd be better off dead.'

'Don't say that. You have a lovely family now. There's nothing that can't be fixed.'

'I thought that, too. Until recently.'

'Please, tell me about it.'

'I was slow on the uptake at first. You know, late up with the kids for school. Not looking after herself properly, barely eating. I thought she was depressed. I tried all I could to help her out of it.'

'She couldn't cope with it – as she had been, I mean?'

Shaw eyed Liz warily, trying to gauge her likely response. 'This is the part you'll find difficult.'

'Try me, Alasdair. I'm not going to run to Jim with this.'

He looked to the ceiling, plainly trying to gather his courage, deciding whether to go on or not. 'It was a phone call – to my mobile. Random guy on the other end of the line, so it was odd. I wasn't sure how he got my number.'

'Okay, and . . . ?'

'He tells me he's sending me a picture.' Shaw closed his eyes tight shut, as though desperately trying to banish the memory. 'It was disgusting. Him and her – you know.'

'Shit.'

'But that wasn't the worst of it. Turned out that he was her dealer. Jill owed him money.'

Liz was almost too scared to ask the question. 'A lot?'

'Thousands. More than we could afford to pay, that's for sure. She'd told me she was only spending a few hundred on the stuff. That she was able to cut corners – you know, because of her knowledge of chemistry.'

'Okay, Alasdair, I know I said you could tell me anything, but this is where it gets difficult.'

'Trust me, I know.' His eyes wouldn't meet hers.

'This dealer – was he the one who assaulted you? Left you for dead, as Jim said.'

'He's going to kill my children, Liz. I don't know what to do.' Shaw broke down, his body convulsing again and again in heart-wrenching sobs. 'What happened to me was just a warning. I don't know his name. He wanted information from the office. I refused at first. But he just kept coming . . . threatening . . .'

Liz sat on the bed and held him. 'We'll work something out, I promise.' But as she tried to calm the man who'd almost been killed trying to protect his wife and children, the only solution she could see was telling her husband. The very thing she'd promised she wouldn't do.

28

Semple's Hotel overlooked the sandy white shore. Even though it was early afternoon, the leaden sky already held the promise of the night to come. And in winter, that came early.

In this gloom, colours popped. The orange buoys lying beside some tattered nets were picked out like bright sweets in a jar. The hotel owners had just bought a new red van. It stood out against the gloomy sea and sky like a bright, shining prize, bringing at least the notion that the dark days of winter would soon slip away, and the light of the summer sun would bring colour, hope and visitors back to this beautiful part of the world.

Ludmilla and Jakub Mazur had first visited Scotland soon after they were married. They'd travelled across the country and learned to love the place, and they'd felt instantly at home in this little hotel the moment they'd walked through the door. There was no particular reason for the sense of wellbeing it engendered within them. After all, it was like nowhere they'd ever lived as children or adults. Yet there was such beauty in the rocky coast that faced the Atlantic with jagged determination, it stole their hearts. In ten years, they'd saved up enough to sell the family business – a shop in Gdansk – and make their dream move.

In the summer, tourists appeared regularly. Ludmilla was a fine cook, and her Polish twists on Scottish dishes brought people from far and wide, anxious to try this fusion cooking. In the winter, however, money wasn't as easy to come by. Their local clientele was scattered in farms, cottages and little steadings up and down the coast. And though the community tried their best to support the business, the long nights and short days could be as cold financially as the weather.

The festive season provided some relief. Customers arrived for meals, drinks and even nights in one of the hotel's five rooms, anxious to capture the spirit of Christmas in a place that wasn't spoiled by the greed of commercialism.

The old man sat at a table next to the bar, his unlit pipe clenched between his teeth. 'Ach, I've never had the time to travel the highways and byways on land, Ludmilla. I've spent my whole life on a wave, chasing shoals o' one fish or another.' Hamish smiled as he nursed the small glass in one calloused hand. 'And man, that was a fine piece and bacon you made me. It's like nae bacon sandwich I've ever had, and that's a fact. What is it you dae to it?'

'My mother was Hungarian. She swore by paprika. I add a tiny drop of fresh cream and paprika to the bacon before it is served. People like it.' Ludmilla wiped her hands on the white apron that encompassed her ample waist.

'I tell you something. I'll be doing the same thing wae my mince an' tatties – aye, and maybe the haggis too.'

'I'm not so sure that it would work with haggis, Mr Hamish. Though I've only once eaten it, the taste would be wrong, I think.'

'Not at all.' Hamish waved a hand dismissively. 'I'm sure no bugger knows what's in a haggis anyway. They put all sorts in there to flesh the puddings oot. My mother telt me that MacAndrew the butcher used to grind doon his ain nail clippings and cook them in his haggis.'

'No!' Ludmilla put her hand to her mouth in horror.

'Mind you, my mother wisna that fond o' auld MacAndrew on account o' the fact she was sure he was fiddling the ration during the war. Never forgave him, neither. So, whether he did or didna dae it is open to question.' Hamish looked round; the bar was still empty. With a sigh, he searched in his pocket, retrieving a handful of coins. 'Another dram, if you don't mind, dear.'

'What brought you here? You're not driving, I hope?' Ludmilla placed the glass under an optic, laughing nervously.

'No, no' driving. Though I mind the days when the farmers would jump into their cars wae a good cargo on board and drive doon some right perilous roads. There was nae traffic in they days, mark you. No' like today. You take your life in your hands turning right oot o' Long Road into Main Street, let me tell you. I took the bus here. I'll get another back just after four.' Hamish consulted his battered pocket watch.

'It's good of you to come. You're more than welcome, Mr Hamish.'

'Hey, less o' the *Mr*. It's just plain Hamish, a good Scots name, and no mistake.'

'What is your surname?'

Hamish hesitated. 'I just go by Hamish. You canna spoil perfection wae another name. And in any case, it just gets confusing for folk wae all they names.'

'Here you are.' Ludmilla placed the glass in front of Hamish on his table.

'I'm going off to Blaan tomorrow. Man, you've got to keep your hand on your ha'penny doon there, an' no mistake.'

'Your what?'

'It's an expression. You have to have your wits aboot you, for they're a parcel o' rogues in that village. Descended fae smugglers, near every one o' them.'

'Goodness! I remember smugglers in Poland when I was a girl. They used to come with all sorts of things we couldn't buy. Levi's, Sony Walkman . . .' She bit her lip in thought. 'Betamax video player! Sadly, we couldn't afford such things and had to buy the Polish versions, usually made in the Soviet Union.'

'Could they no' make video players and jeans, then?'

'They made them. But the jeans were big and baggy.' She smiled. 'I was young and slim in those days. We wanted American jeans. We saw them in magazines smuggled from the West. The shoes, dresses, the haircuts. It was a different world back then.'

'Much mair with it now, I daresay.' Hamish took the first sip of his new dram.

Ludmilla shrugged. 'We can buy these things now, this is true. But in Poland, the prices are so high that nobody can afford them. And with young people now, the old Soviet fashions have returned. They wear the jeans and the shoes that I hated and love them.'

'Would you believe I used to have a quiff?' Hamish executed a complex manoeuvre with one hand above his head. 'You know, like Elvis.'

'Oh, my.' Ludmilla laughed heartily, finding the notion of this bald old man sporting such a haircut highly amusing.

'It's no' that hard to imagine, is it?' said Hamish, a little put out when she was unable to stop laughing, tears running down her face.

'No, not that funny.' She wiped her tears of mirth away with a hankie. 'Since the winter has arrived, it's been very quiet. It's nice to have a customer who is so entertaining. It makes me happy.'

'That's a good thing, lassie,' said Hamish. 'Life is here to be enjoyed.' A dark shadow passed across his face. 'Though sometimes there's precious little to enjoy.'

Sensing his change of mood, Ludmilla offered him a slice of one of her Drozdzowka cakes. 'I don't know if you have a sweet tooth, Hamish. But the people here tell me it's a bit like cakes you have here in Scotland.'

Never one to look a gift horse in the mouth, Hamish tucked into a large slice of the yeast and plum cake and declared it delicious. 'Man, yous know a' aboot cakes in Poland, I can tell you that. There's a wee café on Blaan I like to visit. The lassie there is a fabulous baker. You should swap ideas – recipes and the like. It's a' aboot cross cultures these days.' Hamish took another bite of cake and thought for a moment. 'I like to think that we did oor bit for a' that multicultural thing back in the sixties. When I was at the fishing, you understand.'

'Did you go to some exotic places?'

'Islay, for one. And damn me, if there were ever bodies in need o' proper civilisation, it's them. Passingly good at whisky, mark you. If you like that sort o' peaty, medicinal stuff.'

'My husband and I should go for a few days, I think,' said Ludmilla.

'I widna go as far as that.' Hamish washed a large bite of cake down with more whisky. 'Yous'll no' understand a word they're saying. For a start, they've a hoor o' an accent. You'll be right scunnered trying to understand a word o' their havers.' He bit into his cake again, happy that a valid point had been made.

'I see,' said Ludmilla, unsure that she'd understood much of what he'd said. She was just about to ask more about Islay, the island she could see from her kitchen window, when the door swung open and a figure staggered into the bar.

'*Do diaska!* What is this?' The Polish landlady rushed to assist the new arrival.

Hamish got to his feet, alarmed by the sight of the young woman. Her face was streaming with little rivulets of blood, her coat – a thick down jacket, torn here and there – had feathers bursting through the holes. Her dark trousers were filthy, her hands were bleeding, and she had a nasty bruise over one eye.

'Help me, please,' she croaked as she sat down heavily on a chair.

'Lassie, what's happened to you? What's your name?' said Hamish. 'Get her a dram, Ludmilla – on me, you understand.'

'I don't like whisky. And my name is Delphine – Delph.' Tears began to flow down her cheeks, mixing with the blood coming from the pinprick wounds on her face.

'Nonsense. There's nothing better than whisky to ease your pain and anguish. I've been drinking it all my life, and it's never done me anything but good – mainly.'

'They took him!' she wailed.

'Took who?' Ludmilla had arrived with a bowl of warm water, into which she'd poured a little disinfectant. 'This will sting, I think. But it's best to be done.' The Polish landlady sat opposite Delph and began dabbing her face with the water using a little cotton wool.

'Who did they take, and when?' Hamish asked.

'My boyfriend, Nathan. We were camped up on the hill. We're going to Everest.' The words tumbled out of Delph's mouth.

'Well, you're away the wrong way,' said Hamish under his breath, earning a silent rebuke from Ludmilla by way of a frown.

'Why would anyone be taken from a hillside here in Kintyre?' Ludmilla looked confused.

Delph wailed again. 'His father is rich. I don't know. I think he's been kidnapped.' Despite the warmth coming from the crackling fire, she was shivering from head to toe. 'I had to hide in case they came back for me. It was so cold. When I couldn't take it any more, I came down the hill to try and find help. There was no path, and I got lost.' She fell into Ludmilla's arms, sobbing miserably.

'My husband is in Kinloch getting provisions. Could you call the police, Hamish? The telephone is behind the bar.'

'Aye, I'll get them, don't worry.' The old fisherman hurried off to call Kinloch police office.

Dalcy was in his glass box, studying the vexing images of the severed head.

'If you ask me, it's no' the only severed head around here,' said Scott.

'Meaning?'

'*Meaning*, that lassie Kilvington lost her heid years ago by the look o' it.'

Before he could admonish his colleague, Daley's laptop pinged with an email notification. He opened it and read the contents.

171

'Have they identified heid the ba'?' said Scott.

'No, but they've confirmed part of Ms Kilvington's story. She did work as a detective sergeant with Lincolnshire Police – the Child Protection Unit.'

'Bugger me, there must be loads o' frightened weans aboot in Lincolnshire if the likes o' her are protecting them, Jimmy. What aboot the Special Branch carry-on?'

'No mention. But we can't be sure until we dig a bit deeper. I've alerted our lot. They'll be able to find out if there's any truth in it.' Daley read more of the email. 'It says Kilvington inherited a property in Scotland from a great-aunt. Also, that she'd been traumatised and on sick leave when she took off – vanished. She was consulting a psychiatrist after being attacked on duty. It was a long-term thing.'

'She should have kept going.' Scott coughed, noting Daley's expression. 'So, she wasn't lying aboot that either?'

'See, not everybody matches up to your jaundiced view of life, Brian.'

'Okay, she's a cop who had a hard time. That happens to all of us. You don't see me bounding aboot like a mad thing. And I've had plenty to jump aboot for.' Another glare from his boss was enough to shut him up.

The phone on Daley's desk rang.

'Daley,' he answered. He nodded his head as he listened. 'Yes, I know the place. Liz and I had a meal there last summer.' His tone was conversational until: 'What?' The expression on the detective's face became almost incredulous.

'What noo?' said Scott in a whisper.

Daley ended the call. 'One of the Oxford students has been kidnapped from their tent. Happened this morning. Our friend Nate. His girlfriend is at Semple's Hotel.' Daley frowned.

'What else?'

'Hamish is there. He phoned it in.'

'The way things are going, as long as the lad has all his limbs and his heid's no' in a box, he should be grateful, Jimmy.'

'Come on, we'll attend. Tell Potts to inform Division.'

Scott dashed out of the glass box, found Potts and set him to work. 'We'll need to organise a search party, into the bargain, son. Get to work on that when we're away.'

'What about Mr Brandt?'

'Eh?'

'He's coming to see you at four.' Potts grimaced.

'He'll just have to wait. Better still, tell him to come back tomorrow. We've got a situation here.'

Scott grabbed his warm jacket, then with Daley in tow headed for the car park.

29

Werner Brandt had chosen to take rooms in a hotel a few miles away from Kinloch in Machrie. The establishment was good enough but fell below the standards to which he'd become accustomed. However, he reasoned, his stay would be short.

He stood at the large window, looking across a golf course. It was getting dark now, and a few hardy golfers were wending their way off the eighteenth tee, no doubt ready to warm themselves up and quench their thirst at the nineteenth, back in the modern clubhouse with its panoramic views of Islay, Jura and the Atlantic beyond.

He sipped at his wine, well below the quality he usually enjoyed. Still, it helped lift the burden of gloom that had fallen on his shoulders since he arrived in this godforsaken place.

To the left of the course he could see the cold, grey Atlantic. The horizon was almost out of sight in the darkness. But Werner Brandt felt as though he could almost touch the eastern seaboard of the United States of America. One of the few places he truly felt at home now. His great mansion in New England, where he resided in splendid isolation looking at this same ocean, was his solace and joy. America was his real home, his estates in England and Austria almost only for show now, and the use of his extended family. In his business, it paid to misdirect. Few people – not even his son – knew about the New England property. He spent a lot of time *away*.

That was the way it would stay. For while Brandt appeared to eschew the western democracies, being a vociferous advocate for the Russians, the Chinese and many rogue states, his paymasters sat happily in Washington. It was a tricky tightrope to walk, but he was a master of the discipline, and that skill had made him rich – very rich.

As he took a sip of wine, screwing up his face at its lack of sophistication, the mobile in his pocket buzzed.

'Speak,' he answered without ceremony.

The response was a short one. 'We have him.'

'Where?'

'It's remote, no prying eyes.'

'So you've managed to do in a few hours what the local constabulary couldn't achieve in months.'

'We do have an unfair advantage, sir.'

'That's what life is all about.' Brandt sneered as he made the comment.

'What do you want us to do, sir?'

He thought for a moment. Usually, his business was plied in a very sharp suit, far away from the harsh, unforgiving world that was reality for so many. But it did no harm to remind oneself of the darker side of the trade he'd chosen. A good way to keep one's hand in, he reckoned.

'My son. Is he being appropriately looked after?'

'Yes. We have taken covert but highly effective measures to make sure he comes to no harm in the hospital.'

'Good. Send him word that I won't see him this evening.'

'Yes, of course.'

'Then pick me up near the hotel I told you about. Be discreet. There is a golf club next door. Be in the car park at five. On the dot, remember.'

'Of course, sir.'

Brandt clicked the phone off. He thought about telling his PA that he was going out, but she was busy in the room they'd had set up as an office. She had to focus on making sure his son spent the least possible time in hospital. Yes, Kinloch was out of the way. But in his world there was no such thing as getting lost. Anyone could be found. Anyone, anywhere. They had a window of time, while the boy recovered enough to be taken to Austria, where he'd be treated on his own properties under the supervision of the best specialists there were. His son's injuries would be marked down to some accident or other. Nobody would hear about the stupid student who was cut down on the streets of a nothing town in the middle of nowhere.

But first, he needed a base, somewhere he felt at home.

What to do with Salazar after his treatment was another matter entirely. He would have set him adrift, had it not been for the protective hand of his mother. Time was running out, though. Not for the first time, Werner Brandt pictured the car crash that would take his son's life. He, of course, would be devastated. His wife would be inconsolable. But time healed all wounds, if not completely, certainly adequately. He must decide soon, before the young man who bore his name caused him any further humiliation.

Brandt flung back the rest of the wine. It was swill anyway. He opened the wardrobe and selected clothes most suited to the next task in hand.

To be prepared was everything.

When Daley and Scott arrived at Semple's Hotel, two paramedics were already attending to the young woman's wounds. Though they recognised Delphine Harker she was no longer the pretty, confident young woman they'd met only two days before. Her eyes were sunken, her face swollen and bloody, the blonde hair matted and dull.

'How is she, George?' Daley asked a paramedic he knew.

'Touch of hypothermia, but not as bad as it could have been in this weather.'

'Why not as bad?'

'She knows her stuff. The best of gear, and she kept moving. Helps you stay alive when you're exposed to the elements for any length of time in weather like this.'

As he listened, Daley could see flakes of snow brushing against the un-curtained hotel windows. There was nothing to be seen beyond but darkness.

'She's suffering from shock more than anything, Jim. I've given her something to help.'

'Have I time to speak to her?'

'Yes, but go easy. I want her in hospital within the hour. Just to be on the safe side.'

'It's getting to be a busy place – the hospital, I mean.'

'The less time I spend there, the happier I am.' George patted Daley on the shoulder and left him to speak to Delph.

With Scott busy interviewing Hamish and the hotel's landlady, Daley made for the young woman by the fire, who was wrapped in blankets and cradling a mug of tea.

'So, we meet again, Delphine. It's DCI Daley, remember?'

She looked at him, a plaster here, the smear of ointment there. 'Of course I remember you. You put my boyfriend in

177

a cell. I hope you're pleased with yourself.' She sniffed away a tear.

'It was you who couldn't vouch for his whereabouts.'

'I was just telling you the truth. I was asleep! You know, I was brought up to respect the police. But you're all as bad as each other.' She looked away.

'As bad as each other? What does that mean?'

'Nothing. The police in Oxford are just as bad – oh, I don't know.'

'Let's not think about that at the moment. Tell me about Nathan. We really need to find him quickly.'

'What else do you want me to say? He was taken away by two men – they slashed our tent. He's been kidnapped!'

'And we've taken steps to make sure they don't get far. We've set up roadblocks.'

'That's impossible. I'm not stupid, Mr Daley. It took me three hours to get here. I was lost and I had to stay hidden as much as I could from whoever it was that took Nathan. Just in case, you know?' This time she was unable to stop a fat tear meandering down her cheek. 'They could be anywhere by now, and you know it. Your roadblocks won't work when the bird has already flown.'

'Please, you're going to have to trust me, Delphine.'

'Please call me Delph. I hate Delphine.'

'Sorry, Delph.' Daley noted that, despite her predicament, the young woman's spirit was far from broken. He had questioned young people who had endured much less yet were inconsolable when it came to a police interview. Whatever she felt about the authorities, she had no fear of them. 'I know that you just wanted to get away from where you camped as quickly as you could, but do you have any idea where that was?'

Delph shrugged. 'Nathan was doing the navigation. I didn't pay much attention, to be honest. He likes doing the *man* thing. You know, beat the path for his woman, that kind of shit. In many ways, he lives in another century, like the rest of his family.'

'Why do you say that?'

Delph tossed back her head. 'Fuck, are you going to arrest him again, if we ever find him?'

Daley sighed. 'No, it was just a question.'

'They're posh – *very* posh. His father is a big noise in international trade, whatever that really means.' Her shoulders relaxed a fraction. 'Listen, I know you deal with lying scumbags most of the time. But I'm not like that. I value honesty. It's a thing for me, yeah?'

Daley nodded, impressed by her candour. 'What about your phone?'

'I must have dropped it. When I was coming down the hill I tried to see if it had a signal. You know, to get directions from GPS. It must have fallen out of my pocket in all the panic.'

'It will be somewhere, though. We have your number, I think. I'll have someone check it.'

She nodded. 'If you think it will help.'

'We have to know where you were, as close as we can get. Nathan, does he have enemies that you know of? People who wish him ill?'

'Well, he's arrogant and full of himself, but generally people like him. He's pretty decent underneath it all. Thankfully, he doesn't see much of his father. I'm sure that helps. So, no, I can't think of anyone who would wish him harm. Not in this way. It's the money, I really think that.'

'Okay, his family are rich, I understand. Where can I find their details?'

'Just phone his college – St Dunstan's. They'll give you all you need.'

Daley was ready to go and have a trace placed on Delph's phone when she grabbed his arm. 'I do remember a couple of things that might help.'

'What?'

'For a start, they took him away in a Land Rover – an old diesel model. I recognised the sound it makes. My father has one – they all sound the same, trust me.'

'Excellent. Thank you, Delph. That helps.'

'And there's something else.'

'What?'

'I just remembered. My head's a mess with all that's happened.' She brushed her hair from her forehead. 'Wherever we were camped, below – on the beach – there was this odd big house.'

'Odd? What do you mean? In what way?'

'It looked like it was lost. Before you say it, I know there are big houses in the countryside. But this one looked out of place – like it should have been in a town.'

Daley fished his mobile from his pocket. He scrolled through some images, then showed the phone to Delph. 'Like this one, you mean?'

She squinted at the image in the flickering light of the fire. 'Yeah, that's it – I think. Remember, I was looking at it from above, but, yes, I think that's the place. How did you know?'

'Because I'm a detective.' Daley stood. 'Listen, take it easy. I know they're sending you to hospital for a check-up, but you'll be okay. Try to keep calm. I'm sure we'll find Nathan.'

'Please try. Honestly, right now, I don't care if you fling him in a cell. I just want to know he's safe.'

'She just burst through the door. Damn near collapsed,' said Hamish, as Brian Scott took notes.

'She was very distressed,' Ludmilla added. She still looked shocked by the recent events.

'How long have you been here for, Mrs Mazur?' said Scott.

'Eighteen months, no more.'

'And your husband runs the hotel wae you, aye?'

Ludmilla frowned. 'Yes, he does. He's in Kinloch getting the car serviced. He had banking and other things to do. But I can't get his mobile telephone.'

'I wouldna worry too much aboot that, lassie,' said Hamish. 'I don't carry one o' the damned things, but I hear plenty folk saying they canna get a signal when they're in the toon. Well, parts o' it, at least.'

'You should have one, Hamish,' said Scott. 'At your age, it might just save your life. If you fall, for example.'

'I know you polis are all keen on the deep state, Brian. But let me tell you, I'm no' leaving myself open to identity theft and the like. I'm taking plenty risks at my age wae health as it is, without catching a virus fae my own phone.' He nodded sagely. 'And I'm no' wanting the Russian president knowing my every move.'

'Why, have you had words wae him?'

'No, no' at the moment. But I bloody well would if I could lay hands on him.' Hamish's fists clenched and his expression changed to grim determination.

'I'm sure he'll steer clear o' you, auld fella.' Scott looked puzzled for a moment. 'How come you're up here boozing, anyway?'

'I asked him this, too,' said Ludmilla.

'Do you think my braces are tied to the toon cross, Sergeant Scott? I'll have you know I've spent a lifetime going to new places and meeting different folk. Just because I'm retired doesna mean to say I'll never leave Kinloch again. And anyway, the bus is free to folk o' my age. It's fair liberating, so it is. I'm working up to a trip much further afield, if you must know. And you know my plans for a move to the east.'

'Where? I wouldnae go to Moscow, if I were you. No' wae a mobile phone in your pocket, at any rate.'

'No, nor Moscow. I've spent enough time in Port Ellen to get an idea what Moscow's like. No, I'll be taking a trip to Oban, if the roads don't clog up wae snow. Man, I hate the time after Christmas – it's as bleak as a minister's appointments, so it is. Aye, and wae me officially retired I might as well make the best o' it. Before I leave, that is.' He looked at the anxious landlady. 'No' before I die, you understand.'

'Oh?' said Ludmilla, a hand to her mouth.

'Don't listen to him, Mrs Mazur. He'll outlast me and that's for sure,' said Scott.

'I hope you don't mind me saying, Brian, but that's no' an altogether ridiculous notion. What wae the way you've abused yourself, and all.'

Ludmilla looked between the pair of them, utterly bewildered by the exchange. She'd been warned that the Scots could be a dour lot, though in her experience that hadn't been the case – until now.

'Be sure to call us if anything else happens in the hotel,

okay?' Scott closed his notebook and put it back into the inside pocket of his jacket.

Daley beckoned from the doorway. 'You finished, Brian?'

'Aye, you could say that. According to Hamish, anyway.'

The detectives left Semple's Hotel, leaving behind the stricken student, the paramedics, Hamish and a rather confused landlady.

30

Werner Brandt had been picked up by an ageing SUV, as arranged. New cars attracted attention. But as long as they still worked well, their more venerable counterparts could move around barely noticed. Just another clapped-out car on the road.

The trip had taken them towards Kinloch, before they turned right up a rough track. The driver stopped beside a tiny white cottage, one that looked as though it hadn't been occupied for many years.

Brandt took in his surroundings. They were in the hills above Kinloch; he could see the lights of the town to his right. Under a pale, waning moon, he spotted a farm in the distance between the cottage and a lochan. In the distance, a sheep bleated plaintively. That aside, the place was as quiet as the grave. Appropriate, he thought.

The cottage was almost as dark inside as it was out. The first room they entered was empty of furniture, with only a broken-down fireplace to remind anyone that people had once lived here. Brandt could barely imagine it.

He was shown through to a smaller room – a bedroom. An old iron bedstead sat in the middle of it. Tied to this broken-down bed by hand and foot was a young man. He was large and dark-haired, his eyes wide with terror, a piece of filthy cloth tied across his mouth. He stared at Brandt desperately, taking in his dark clothes and tanned face. The place was lit only by one small gas lantern, which hissed on a shelf on the corner.

Flanking the captive stood two other men, both dressed in black, their faces masked by balaclavas. One was shorter than the other, though they were both imposing. The taller of the two whispered into Brandt's ear briefly and handed him a cloth bag before returning to the shadows.

Brandt, who was not masked, leaned over the figure tied to the bed.

'So, you are the one who likes to disfigure my family? My goodness, that was a mistake.' His Austrian accent made him sound like an upper-class Englishman, with clipped vowels and a mocking intonation. He turned to his driver. 'Take off his gag,' he commanded.

The young man struggled as the cloth was being removed.

'Remember, if you cry out, you will never leave this place alive. That, I promise you.'

'I don't know why I'm here.' The voice was desperate, pleading.

'It's quite simple. For what reason I'm not sure, but you saw fit to remove my son's fingers. Do you remember?' Brandt spoke as calmly as though he was discussing the weather.

'No, I didn't!'

Brandt put his fingers to his lips. 'What did I say? Don't cry out.'

'I'm sorry.' The young man began to sob. 'Please, you must believe me.'

'Yet my men are the best in the business. They have been trained to flush out little bastards like you, and they are very good at it. I have to say, I must take their word before yours.'

Choked pleas drowned out the sound of the hissing lantern.

'But I am a fair man. I believe in the Scriptures: *an eye for an eye, a tooth for a tooth*. You are aware of this, yes? Please just nod if you are. I'm very sensitive to sudden loud noise. It upsets me.'

The figure on the bed nodded through his tears.

Brandt hefted the cloth bag. From within he produced a hunting knife, its keen blade so well polished that it flashed even in the dim gaslight.

'No, please, please don't.' The trussed-up man spoke quietly, not wanting to incur his captor's wrath, but he worked his legs desperately, as though attempting to force his way through the hard springs of the rusting bed in order to escape his fate.

'This is fair, no?'

'No. I didn't do it. I promise you!'

Brandt stopped, one finger to his lip, apparently deep in thought. 'It would not be fair to remove your fingers if you are, as you say, innocent.'

'I am! I don't know what happened to your son. I'm sorry that it did. But I didn't do it.'

Brandt looked at his henchmen. 'Have you made a mistake?' His voice was incredulous, as though he believed what he'd been told by the captive, and was ready to admonish his men for their error. He cocked his head to one side, looking at the smaller of the two. 'You promised me this was the guilty man. You know how I hate mistakes.' Brandt's expression was one of contrition as he stared back at the bed, but suddenly it changed. His eyebrows arched, his features contorted.

'Please, no!' The young man struggled against his bonds.

Brandt thrust the knife into his chest, over and over again. Blood splattered the executioner until his victim's heart stopped and the dark blood became a trickle, the ear-splitting screams silenced.

Brandt looked up at his men. 'Clean up, and get rid of this garbage.'

He walked outside into the cool night air. He could see the lights of Kinloch shining beyond the lochan. He drew a deep breath. It was refreshing, replenishing. He felt reinvigorated, every sense fizzing, his pulse racing. Nothing made him feel younger, better, stronger. It had been too long. The only thing that made him truly alive was death.

People were gathering outside Semple's Hotel. Locals, and those from the Oxford Everest party who'd been rounded up and brought back down the hill, were anxious to help find their fellow student. Professor Tang – in charge of the training exercise that was rapidly turning into a nightmare – was speaking animatedly on her mobile, gesturing with her hands, her face a mix of expressions, none of them happy.

'If she's no' careful, she'll take off,' said Brian Scott. The detective sergeant was cold and miserable. Being in the hotel on a chill night like this, with its blazing fire and fine selection of malt whiskies, had allowed the tiny voice inside his head room to speak. That voice reminded him how much he longed for the soothing oblivion of alcohol. But he knew he had it mastered. He banished the notion.

Daley was biting his lip, watching the little crowd of people in the car park as they chatted under the security lights, their breath rising in an orange cloud, soon to be eaten up by the black sky. 'This isn't the time or the weather to have anyone searching the hill.' He looked at Scott. 'Do you agree?'

'Aye, I do. But by all accounts, this lad's family are worth a fortune. They'll want him found, Jimmy. Money talks, you know that.'

Tang had finished her call. She looked agitated as she approached the police officers.

'What are your plans, DCI Daley? I've just had a very worried parent on the phone. Let me tell you, Nathan's father is not a man I'd care to fall out with.' She rubbed her temples to relieve the stress of it all. 'I wish I'd never conceived of this little jaunt. Who would have imagined that these things could happen in such a quiet, rural place?' Tang looked between them with a helpless, bewildered expression.

'You should have read the newspapers, ma'am. Bloody nightmare, up here. I could tell you a tale or two, and that's a fact,' said Scott.

Before he could relate whatever tale of disaster was on his mind, Daley intervened. 'We're all under pressure to find Nathan. But putting a search party out on the hill in this weather, not to mention in the dark, would be highly irresponsible, Professor Tang.'

'I don't know if you will have much choice in the matter, inspector. In my experience – and it is a long one at such universities – powerful people usually get their own way. And if they don't, it turns out badly for the likes of you and me. The college wanted to cancel the trip after what happened to Salazar. I persuaded them it was just one of those terrible things that can happen anywhere. I fear I was wrong.'

Daley's mobile rang. He looked at the screen and walked away from Scott and Tang. The caller was ACC Cunningham. He had a good idea what the coming exchange would be all about. 'Daley. Hello, sir.'

'This is a real mess, Jim.' There was clearly to be no preamble, no niceties to be observed. 'I doubted the wisdom of this expedition when that lad had his fingers amputated. I was right!'

'The professor in charge has just said the same thing, sir.'

'Bloody idiot. Why can't these people sit smoking a pipe in some old pub or whatever it is they do in Oxford. Well, you'll be pleased to hear that we have no choice.'

'What do you mean, sir?'

'Get every man you can together and get them on that hill pronto!'

'But, sir – members of the public are here offering to help. It'll end up with someone else getting lost, injured or worse.'

'Obviously, don't let the public participate, Daley. I had you down as having more sense.'

'I'm on the spot, sir. And here's my sense. Nobody should be up there tonight, police officers or otherwise. It's below zero, pitch-black, and threatening to snow. There's a mountain rescue team who are taking a cursory look. They're used to these types of conditions and the terrain, and they are definitely not staying out all night.' Daley lowered his voice. 'I don't think for a minute that the young man is still up there. He's been taken. We should widen our search. Not just a few road checks around the peninsula, sir.'

'Well, obviously, Jim. And I'm putting that in place. There are members of the Support Unit on their way to you right now. But listen – and this is the crucial point – if the lad has been abducted, what chance do you think we have of finding him?'

'Sir?'

'Don't play dumb, Jim. I've read the girlfriend's statement. It's very persuasive. In the end, they'll break cover and ask for money. That's what kidnappers do. Until then, we play this down.'

Daley screwed up his face. He was aware that Tang and Scott were taking in his reaction to the call. He turned his back to them. 'What do you mean *play this down*? Are we just to pretend that this lad has vanished into thin air, shrug our shoulders and tell everybody it'll be okay?'

'Don't be such a man of the people, Jim. You know we'll struggle to find him if he has indeed been kidnapped. And we can't let those who did it think that we suspect anything. Could put the lad's life in danger. Then where would we be? We must show willing by putting some bodies up there to at least look as though we're doing something. In the meantime, we put it down to some misadventure. Getting lost, foolishness, that type of thing. For the press, you understand.'

'Are you serious?'

'Yes, have no doubt about that. Your job, DCI Daley, is to keep a lid on it all until we decide what to do. That won't be until tomorrow.'

'How?' Daley was angry now, and the tone of his voice betrayed it.

'I know you've come to think of Kinloch as your little fiefdom. But you're a client king, Jim. You'll do as you're told or someone else will reign down there. Do you understand? When the press arrive, you tell them that there's a search in progress for a missing student who got lost on the hill. You shut up anyone who tries to say otherwise. And that includes the girlfriend. Tell me this is imprinted on your mind.'

'Who got to you? The parents?'

'Just do as you're told and await my instructions. End of conversation.' The line went dead.

'Problems, Jimmy?' Scott shouted.

'Is there ever anything else, Brian?'

31

Against Tang's wishes, Delph had discharged herself from the hospital and booked into a local hotel. She wanted to be alone. Space to be able to think.

She sat in the bed in a musty room with a gurgling radiator, staring at the phone she'd been given by Tang. The message was dull and annoying. She'd known it would be before she opened it.

Delph removed her earbuds and slumped back on the bed. She could see Nate's face, the panic in those last few seconds before he was taken, as she struggled with his attackers. He looked terrified. She wondered if he'd had an inkling of what might happen. His family were so rich that the danger of his being kidnapped must have crossed their minds. Or maybe it was a thing that just happened to someone else. She'd read about notable kidnapping cases in the seventies. They had often ended in tragedy.

But her real focus was elsewhere.

Delph picked up her phone again and accessed her banking app. She smiled when she saw the figures on the screen. Money was important to her; she had always had to work for it. Her parents were – she hated the expression – comfortably off.

But that comfort was tied up in a large mortgage, two cars, good holidays, nice clothes, and the multitude of other baubles the middle classes considered essential to make life worth living. There was little left over to help her. She probably had more liquid cash than they did. All they had was debt, and a lot of it.

Delph didn't want her life to be that way.

She checked the time. Should she call the police station again? She knew it would be pointless, that they'd tell her nothing. But it was *good form*, as her father was fond of saying, so she clicked on the number for Kinloch police office. The young woman who answered sounded harassed, not properly engaged in the conversation, but when Delph asked if there was any news about her boyfriend, she could hear a change in tone.

'The search is ongoing. We'll let you know if we find him.' Hesitation. 'I mean, I'm sure we will find him. You can't get far in Kintyre.' The officer laughed nervously. 'He's probably taken shelter somewhere for the night. Nathan is experienced in the outdoors, as you know. Try not to worry too much.'

Delphine could have argued; she could have told the police officer that her boyfriend wasn't hiding out in some bolthole awaiting rescue. But the woman had obviously said what she'd been told to say, read off a pre-prepared script. The brief time they'd spent in conversation was an exercise in futility. The constable knew she wasn't telling the truth and Delph knew she knew it. How much of life was taken up by such pointless shit?

Delph considered this for a few moments before rising from the bed, slipping on her trainers, checking her hair and brushing her teeth. By the astute use of make-up, she'd managed to cover the little dots of dried blood where she'd been hit in the face by thorn bushes and branches on her way down the hill. Even so, her body bore other injuries, thankfully covered by her clothes. For a moment, she reminded herself of a woman she'd stared at long ago, but the moment was fleeting.

She left her room, walked down the faded carpet of the stairs and entered the hotel bar. There was only one customer, a man in his middle years, staring blankly at a pint glass, idly twirling it round between his thumb and forefinger. By the look of his miserable expression, the glass was half empty rather than the reverse, she thought.

'Yes, how can I help you?' A middle-aged woman appeared through a door behind the bar. She would have been pretty in her day, but the passing of time and life's exigencies had lined her face. Delph found this harrowing. How does anyone cope with getting older? She liked and hated thinking about such things in almost equal measure. The process would take her own looks, her own youth, one day. It was as well to be prepared. But the woman smiled, and seemed friendly, so she took a seat on a bar stool.

'Can I have a gin, please? Nothing fancy, just plenty of gin, tonic and ice.'

'Don't worry, I know the feeling, darling.' Ella Scott poured a double measure into a long glass. 'I can sink into a gin or three myself – more often than I should.'

The drink was set in front of her, and Delph paid with a card. One of the things she hadn't lost.

'Aye, none of my regulars in tonight. But, och, it's always the same wae Christmas coming up. Everyone saves up to spend all they have in a couple o' days, don't they?'

'Yes. Unforgivable excess, if you ask me.' Delph sipped her drink.

Ella was washing a pint tumbler. She took in the young woman with interest. She knew all about the party of students from Oxford, and Kinloch was abuzz about the young man who'd been mutilated. The story that he was so distraught he'd had to be restrained lest he take his own life was definitely a Kinloch special. But nonetheless, at least she had an interesting customer to pass the time with. 'And where are you from?' she asked.

Delph considered the question quickly. She was aware that the locals would realise that she was one of the Oxford party. And to be honest, she wasn't in the mood to describe her complex background. 'I live in Oxford. I'm one of the students you've probably heard about.' She raised her eyes. 'Infamous by now, I guess.'

'I'd be a liar if I said that you and your friends haven't attracted the local gossips. But everything does that here.'

'You not from Kinloch, then?'

'No!' Ella said this as though the very notion that she could be from this part of the world was a crime. 'I'm fae Glasgow, hen.'

Delph smiled. 'Tough, eh?'

'I can hold my own.'

'No, I mean Glasgow, not you.'

'Ach, it gets a worse reputation than it deserves. On the other hand, I am as tough as old boots.' Ella finished with the glass just as two men arrived in the bar.

'Good evening, gentlemen. How can I help you?'

'Two lagers,' said the smaller of the pair. He cast a glance at Delph. 'One for the young lady, too.' His Estuary accent was strong. 'You're a sight for sore eyes, darling. What happened to your face, then?'

Rather than engage with the new arrivals, Delph turned her attention to Ella. 'Since he's offering, I'll have a large one.' She nodded her appreciation to the man who'd bought her a drink.

'You knock yourself out, gal,' he said with a wink. 'Mind you, looks as though you've already given that a go.' He and his friend laughed at the lame joke.

Ella poured the pints, and the men carried them to a table at the back of the room. 'You watch that pair, lassie. I don't like the look o' them,' she said.

'Oh, I don't know. Quite fit, in their own way, don't you think?' Delph giggled.

'No.'

'Where I'm from, young men think floppy hair and a dance at the Young Conservatives is cool. I'm surrounded by our future political masters.'

'I can see that being a pain in the arse, right enough. But where I'm fae the young men used to think that eight pints in the local boozer and a quick fumble was the way to spend an evening.'

'Not like that now, though,' said Delph. 'Men have turned into over-groomed wimps.'

'You think?' said Ella, straightening up the drip trays so that they were symmetrical on either side of the ice bucket.

Delph glanced round. The new arrivals were huddled in deep conversation. She recalled the events of earlier that morning. 'They aren't guests, are they?'

'No, not to my knowledge, and I've been here since two this afternoon,' said Ella. 'But I'll check the register for you, just in case.' She picked up a small iPad and pressed the screen a few times. 'All we have tonight is you, a lady who's covering for someone in the Job Centre, and a travelling salesman from Elgin.'

'And neither of them look like travelling salesmen from Elgin, do they? Where is that, incidentally?'

'No, most certainly not. It's up north,' said Ella, not quite sure as to the more specific details of Elgin's location.

They sat in conversation for a few minutes. Delph didn't want to appear as though she was rushing off. And though the chat about men, shoes and music was diverting enough, she had much greater issues on her mind.

'Can I take my next drink upstairs? Would that be okay?'

'Of course. I'll miss the company, mind you.'

'Sorry, work to do. The life of a student, I'm sad to say.'

'You do what suits you, pet.' Ella poured the large gin and checked her watch. 'Another hour or so and I'll be able to close up. Sleep well.'

Delph thanked her for the drink, smiled at the men on her way out of the bar, and made her way upstairs, being careful not to spill her drink as she went. She struggled one-handed to put the key in the lock, but after a couple of goes she was back in the musty hotel room.

She sat on the bed using a straw to take a gulp of the gin, her hands shaking slightly. These men had put her off her stride, not because they were big and powerful strangers, or of what had happened to Nate. But the man who had bought her a drink had brought other things to mind.

Teddy, Nate's father, had come to mind: the same swaggering, highbrow, base charm with the hint of menace. According to Nate's stories, his father's side of the family were descended from merchant adventurers, the nouveau riche of their day. Though Nate liked to mention his illustrious ancestors, they were all on his mother's side. Delph had disliked Teddy the first time she met him, but just why was complicated.

Like many men with lots of money, Teddy tried hard to play it down – hence *Teddy* – but the fact was he was utterly full of himself because of his possessions and achievements. He was anxious to guard them from those he perceived as chancers, out to take what was his. It was clear to Delph that she was firmly in that unenviable fraternity. Teddy Farringdon had done his very best to make her feel unwelcome in his home. And though Nate tried hard to fob this off as *just his way*, she knew Teddy would much rather his heir find a young woman who suited his father's status and posed no threat to the family finances.

He'd be here soon, desperately searching for his son.

She took another slurp of gin, paying no attention to a creak of the floorboards that seemed to come from the corridor outside her door. Any lingering trepidation she felt had been banished by the soothing effects of the alcohol.

Just as Delph placed the glass on her nightstand, the floorboards creaked again, but this time the noise seemed to come from behind her.

She twisted round on the bed, ruckling up the duvet underneath her aching body.

'Hello,' the smaller man said calmly as he leaned forward and clamped a large hand over her mouth and forced her back on the bed.

32

Daley and Scott had agreed that the latter would take charge of the search for a few hours while the DCI tried to catch up on some sleep. The next day was bound to be a difficult one, filled with senior officers, the press and anxious parents. With the rank came responsibility, as his old mentor, the late Iain Burns, had often told him.

As Hamish had missed his bus because of the investigation, Daley offered to drive him back home. He was glad of the company: his back was aching, and his mind a jumble of worries. They chatted about Hamish's retirement, and his putative plans to leave Kinloch, Daley trying hard to persuade the old man that maybe now wasn't the right time to move away from everything he knew. After all, the community had been his life.

Though the fisherman had nodded sagely, he fell short of entering into any discussion on the matter. It was clearly a decision he intended to make alone, and that was that.

'They tell me you've a mad woman at the station,' he said, apropos of absolutely nothing.

'Do they now?'

'Can I sleep safe in my bed? That's all I'm asking. I'm no

coward, as you know, Mr Daley. But it has to be said that all the goings-on have put me off my stride, and I'm anxious to keep my old heid on these shoulders – for a while, at least. That's another thing to be said for Perthshire.'

'What?'

'The crime rate is a good deal lower than it is in Kinloch.'

'That's exaggerated, Hamish, and you know it.'

'You think? Look at that letter in the *Kinloch Herald* last week. It says that crime is turning Kinloch into a place nobody wants to visit. That folk would be better going to other far-flung places like Lewis or Shetland.'

'I read it. The retired headmaster, right?'

'The very man. Aye, and he isna keen on you neither, by the sound o' things. Mind you, he's as mad as a hoose on fire.'

'I'm sure.'

'Near as mad as that woman you've got in chains in the jail.'

'For a start, she's not in chains. And all I can say is that I'm sure you'll be perfectly safe. I really don't know what we're investigating at the moment, to be honest, Hamish. But whatever it is has very little to do with an old salt like yourself.'

Hamish sucked at his unlit pipe, an activity that had become as much of a habit as smoking itself, if he was honest with himself. 'But I seem to mind you've said this type o' thing to me before, Mr Daley.'

'True, but this time I'm sure you're pretty safe.'

They were nearing Kinloch now, the lights of the town glowing beyond the hills on the horizon.

'The lassie tonight,' said Hamish.

'Which lassie?'

'The one who got lost after her boyfriend was abducted.'

'What about her, Hamish?'

'She's lying.'

Daley slowed the car into a bend, glancing at his passenger as he did. 'Lying about what?' Most police officers would have taken the opinion of an old fisherman with a pinch of salt. But Daley knew from experience that this one had a sixth sense for some things.

'Of that I'm no' sure. But she's lying aboot something, I tell you.'

'But how do you know?'

'You get a feeling for it, Mr Daley. You'll remember I ignored that feeling with thon Macmillan bastard? I regret it still.'

It wasn't like Hamish to swear, but Daley knew Annie's death still weighed heavily on him. 'Yes, I remember.'

'I should have spoken up. I should have telt you or Brian. Maybe poor wee Annie would still be alive if I had.'

'You have to stop blaming yourself for that, Hamish. Nobody could have worked out what was going on there. Nobody.' But though Jim Daley uttered the words, he too doubted he'd done all he should. It bothered him, alongside every other ghost that haunted his life.

'I couldna just put my finger on it, right enough. But lying she is. I'd bet my bunnet on it.'

They drove on in silence, Daley pondering on what Hamish had said, while the old man went over and over what the Oxford student had told him. She'd seemed upset, hysterical at first. That something had happened to her boyfriend was obvious. But was she telling the truth? Or was it just the case that Hamish, following Annie's death, was going to see evil intent round every corner?

Daley navigated the narrow road along the lochside until he drew up outside Hamish's cottage. The flash from the island lighthouse illuminated the place for a split second, revealing Hamish the cat sitting on the window ledge.

'He's a loyal soul, right enough. Cats are usually quite remote, you know. He's mair like a dog, in that regard. Gie him a wave, Mr Daley.'

Though the detective felt rather foolish, he dutifully did as he was asked and waved at Hamish the cat. The next flash of the light revealed the cat's back arched, and his teeth bared.

'Right enough, he's no' that keen on you. I forgot.' Hamish removed himself stiffly from the car. He leaned back in, his face a mask of concern. 'You watch yourself, Jim Daley. Do you promise?'

'Of course, don't I always? Or have you seen something to the contrary?'

Hamish sniffed the cold night air. 'You'll believe me when I say some things make themselves too difficult to see.'

'Oh yes, I believe that.'

'And some things just don't ever want to be seen and will do anything to remain in the shadows. Do you hear what I'm saying? There is nothing worse than evil with a smile on its face.'

Daley nodded. 'You get yourself inside. It's freezing.'

Hamish thanked him for the lift. But as another flash lit up the place, DCI Jim Daley drove away with something new in the pit of his stomach. It was fear.

Worse still, he couldn't explain why.

When the DCI arrived home, the pain in his back was almost unbearable. He reached into his pocket, popped two capsules from the blister pack and washed the opiates down with water from the bottle he always kept in the car. He knew that only five hours had elapsed since his last dose, but he needed the relief, and as well as dulling the pain, the pills eased his mind.

He walked into the hall to be met by Liz. She was standing in the hall with one finger to her lips.

'He's out for the count.'

Daley tiptoed past his son's bedroom door and into the lounge.

'Homemade pizza. I hope that's okay. It's your favourite kind,' said Liz, a weary note in her voice.

Daley picked up on it. 'Yeah, fine. You make lovely pizza. Everything okay?'

'Fine, I'll go get it. I've made a side salad. Just needs to be dressed.' Liz disappeared into the kitchen.

Daley sighed and settled himself into his lounger. Already, he was sure he could feel the drugs kick in. Maybe it was his imagination, for he knew they couldn't possibly have worked so quickly. Nonetheless, he didn't feel his back as painful, and his mind had stopped racing. The placebo effect, he thought. His responses were already being conditioned to coincide with taking the pills. This was something new to worry about.

Shortly, Liz returned with a tray of food. 'I didn't think you'd be in the mood to sit at the table – with your back, I mean.'

'Well, you got that right. It's been agony the last few hours.' Daley took the tray and balanced it on his lap. It had been a long time since breakfast, and he hadn't eaten.

'What would you like to drink? I know you won't want a beer. It'll be a few hours then back out, yes?'

'I'll need to be back there by four in the morning. I'll catch some sleep in this. It's quite comfy when it's flat. I don't want to disturb you both. I'll have a Coke, if that's no bother.'

Liz returned with a bottle from the kitchen. Daley always liked his Coke from a glass bottle. She sat on the edge of the couch, wringing her hands.

'What's up, Liz? You look worse than I feel.' Daley took a bite of pizza.

'I need to tell you something, Jim.'

Daley's slice of pizza was flung back on the plate. He closed his eyes for a moment. 'Who is it?'

'Who's what?' Liz looked confused.

'Who's the lucky new guy? I can't count the times I've heard the *I've got something to tell you* routine.'

'You really are a bastard sometimes.'

'Yeah, heard that before, too. In fact, I've heard all this before. You know, just do what you want. I'll get out of your hair and go and stay at the County. I mean, it's not as though it'll be the first time, will it?'

Liz sat back on the couch and stared at the ceiling. 'It's not like that. I've been struggling to know what to say to you.'

Suddenly, Daley felt another emotion. His heart sank. 'Are you ill?'

'Would it have mattered if I was? You didn't give me a chance to say anything.'

'I'm sorry. I'm just tired. But if you're not ill, what else?' Daley thought for a moment before sitting forward in his seat, almost tipping the tray from his lap. 'It's not James, is it?'

'Shit, Jim, will you just give me a chance to say what I have to say!'

'Yes, of course.' Daley sat back on his recliner.

'I went to see Alasdair Shaw. He's in a bad way.'

The tension left Daley's face. 'I know. That was kind of you to take the time. But he's out of the woods. We've got people working on catching who did that to him. I know how terrible it is. But you also know this job, Liz. Bad things happen all the time.'

'It's not as simple as you think.'

'In what way?' Daley took a bite of pizza.

Liz drew a deep breath and – despite feeling guilty for breaching Shaw's trust – told her husband, word for word, what the unfortunate sergeant had revealed to her. 'He doesn't know where to turn. I can't say I blame him.'

Daley placed the tray on the floor beside his chair. 'Well, that's my appetite well and truly gone. Did he say anything else? We've spent ages trying to catch dealers. It's new – different drugs, more dangerous. I couldn't work out how we kept hitting brick walls. Now I know. Shaw's been tipping them off.'

'Jim, will you listen to yourself. They threatened to kill his children – his wife! Look what they did to him. Have you no sympathy?'

'He should have come to me! As soon as this happened, he should have knocked on my door. Come on, Liz, you know how things work in this job!'

'You're forgetting, I'm not in your *job*. Sometimes I feel as though I might as well be. Maybe I'd get to see more of you.'

Ignoring his wife, Daley began thinking out loud. 'You know, I should listen to Brian more often. He warned me that Shaw could be on the take.'

Liz got to her feet, face flushed with anger. 'I don't know what's happened to you over the last few years. The man I married would never have reacted this way to one of his colleagues being hurt. All you see is what's important to *you*. *Your* operation to catch drug dealers. The fact *you* should have listened to Brian. For fuck's sake, if we all listened to Brian we'd be in some state. And while we're on the subject, look at the things you let him off with over the years, eh? You seem to have a blank spot for everyone – including me, may I add – unless they're called Brian Scott. Alasdair Shaw is your colleague and your friend. You should help him. And who knows, you just might be able to catch the dealers you're so fixated on. Did you ever consider that?' Liz marched out of the room.

Daley slumped back in his chair. Of course she was right. The past couldn't be changed. Only the future could be moulded to his ends – to the ends of justice.

As he thought on what to do next, the phone in his pocket rang. 'Brian, what's up now?'

'We have a very angry father here demanding to see you, Jimmy. Aye, and expect a call fae Cunningham. You'd better get back up, pronto.'

Daley glugged half the bottle of Coke, stuck a slice of pizza between his teeth, donned his jacket, and was once more out unto the breach.

33

DS Brian Scott was smoking at the side of the hotel, listening to traffic on his Airwave radio as the search on the hillside above went on. The moon was obscured behind a cloud. Where there was light – a thin grey line from the west – it rippled across the choppy sea, leaving the other half entirely dark, almost as though it wasn't there at all.

He saw the silhouette of a huge oil tanker on the horizon, and wondered briefly where it was headed. It sailed into the ribbon of moonlight but was soon lost in the enveloping darkness of shadow and the night.

Scott wasn't a deep thinker like his old friend Jim Daley; that was the road to misery, as far as he was concerned. Yet the image of the tanker on the partially revealed ocean made him think. He couldn't fathom the reason – maybe it was his age. But he'd found himself thinking about death recently. He remembered his father and mother, their lives draining away in front of his eyes. He thought of Ella, his children, and was almost instantly transported into the nagging prison of worry. His family was one of the few things that engendered angst in Brian Scott. He'd seen real evil, up close and personal, and he was prepared to do anything to save those precious to him from similar encounters.

The oil tanker was a memory now, faded out of view and from his consciousness: out of sight, out of mind. He remembered that had been one of his father's favourite expressions. It certainly applied to the old boy's family when he was down the pub on a Friday spending much of his meagre wage. But Brian Scott had no business criticising his father or anyone else who over-indulged in alcohol. He'd done plenty of that himself.

Maybe it was something about this case – or cases. A head in a box, a mutilated student, a mad former detective, and now a missing person. They might be connected, but for the life of him he couldn't work out how.

The crack of tyres on the gravel car park brought him back to the present. He nipped out the cigarette and walked over to Daley's car.

Daley got out of the car and turned to Scott. 'Where's the father, Bri?'

'You'll no' believe this, Jimmy. He's off to his bed.'

'Bed? Where?'

'In the hotel. He just breezed in, tore a strip off me, demanded to speak to you, and when I wisnae looking went upstairs.'

'What's he like – as a person, I mean?'

'Posh, brash – a prick, basically. It's a wonder he's no' a senior polis officer.'

'I get it.'

'Teddy Farringdon, his name. Who's called Teddy these days?'

'Yeah, right enough. But it takes all sorts, Bri.'

'Something funny, though, big man.'

'Tell me.'

'He was all, *you'll do this*, and *yous better do that*, until I mentioned the boy Brandt.'

'What do you mean?'

'He just clammed up. Went white as a sheet, so he did. It's as if he hadn't heard. But surely he'd know that one of his son's mates was attacked, eh? No' as though it happens every day, is it?'

'Who knows with those kind of people? They spend so much time away from their families, making money, who knows what relationships they have with their kids.'

'Oh, another thing. They tried to get you on the phone. You must have been out of range on your way up. A posh lawyer arrived at the office. Kilvington's oot. Cannae hold her, not according to HQ, anyway.'

'Fuck.'

'She must be back in that haunted hoose, eh?'

'She's nowhere else to go. Poor woman's living off a half-pension. The house came from an aunt in a will. As far as I can tell, apart from that, she's on the bones of her arse.'

'That'll explain the sumptuous furnishings.'

'Eh? How do you know that, Brian?'

'Makes sense. Nae dosh, she cannae afford furniture.'

'No, I mean the word *sumptuous*. How do you know that?'

'You're one cheeky bastard, Jimmy Daley. Don't tell me you never read they magazines that Liz buys. I read Ella's on the lavvy. It's always *sumptuous* this or *south-facing aspect* that. You pick up the lingo.'

Daley stared at his sergeant. He never failed to surprise, even after all these years. 'How many rooms do they have in the hotel?'

'Three, I think. Why?'

'I'm not bothered if they're sumptuous or not.' He winked at Scott. 'But can't be busy at this time of year. We can hot-bed it, Bri.'

'We can what?'

'Share a bed – me and you. You know.'

The expression on Scott's face was a mix of surprise, horror and disbelief.

'What?'

'Nothing.' Scott shrugged. 'A wee bit surprised, that's all.'

'Surprised how?' It was Daley's turn to look confused. 'I go up and get some kip until it all kicks off in the morning. Then you catch some sleep after. Shift workers do it all the time to save money on accommodation.'

'Right, no bother, big man.' Scott slapped Daley on the back. He looked relieved. 'Hot-bed, eh? I see.'

Daley started to go back to get something from his car, but stopped in mid-stride. 'Did you think I wanted us in the same bed – together?'

'Hey!' Scott held up his hands in a surrender motion. 'Fuck all wrong wae it if that's what you're into, Jimmy. Look at oor Will – you know.'

Daley shook his head. 'You go in, book the room and I'll get on to HQ. Oh, and see if you can grab a whiteboard or something. We'll have to try and put this shit together somehow.'

As Scott went back to the hotel, Daley returned to the SUV to call his bosses. He was dismayed to be put through to the office of the night shift manager, in this case a chief superintendent called Alex Hunter. He knew the guy from years back, so that was something, at least.

'Jimmy! Long time no hear, eh?' Hunter greeted him enthusiastically.

'You've done well. Weren't you an inspector in Lothian and Borders the last time we spoke?'

'I was. Studied for a law degree, Jimmy. Got it, too. Before I knew it, I was in the silver braid. Never looked back. You should go for it.'

'I could be the Lord Advocate and it wouldn't do my chances of promotion any good. You should know that by now.'

'Aye, well, there's been an unfortunate turn or two along the road. Doesn't make you a bad cop.'

'Let's hope you get to be Chief Constable as quickly as possible, then.'

'What can I do for you? You're down in Kinloch, yes?'

'I am. We had a witness released earlier. She was in protective custody.'

Hunter paused a moment. Daley could hear the click of a computer keyboard. 'Okay, I have it here. Released on the orders of ACC Cunningham. Just after six this evening.'

'Just as I was busy elsewhere.'

'Big name involved into the bargain, Jim. Angus Trent, no less.'

'As in Trent, Crossley and Finnigan?'

'The very man. In person, too. I have his petition here.'

'Acting for whom?'

'Kilvington. Does that name ring a bell?'

'Our witness. But she's as poor as a church mouse, Alex.'

'Does the name Beovan mean anything to you?'

'No. Should it?'

'That's who's instructing Trent.'

'And he doesn't come cheap.'

'Most expensive there is, these days. North of the border, anyway.'

211

'Okay. Thanks, Alex. Above and beyond, buddy – sir.'

'Get yourself a law degree, Jimmy. Middle management's an endangered species in this brave new world of ours.'

Daley ended the call. He used his mobile to access Companies House. There it was: Beovan Ltd. They specialised in retirement homes and prisons. He was surprised to see the company owned two or three jails he knew in England.

There were only four directors, all of whom shared the one registered address, probably a lawyer's or accountant's office. Shima Malek, Andrew Tait, Michelle Loddings and Terrance Barrow. None of the names rang any bells. Daley decided to dig further into the company the next day.

Before he left the car, Daley called Potts's number. 'Tell me. Who do we have left at the Kilvington property?'

'Sir?' DC Potts sounded surprised.

'Ours or SOCO personnel, it doesn't matter.'

'Nobody, sir.'

'What do you mean, nobody?'

'Neither our men nor SOCO. They were ordered off the premises just after you left for Semple's Hotel this afternoon, sir. Sorry, should I have said something?'

'Well, that would have been helpful, son.'

'It was because my orders came from ACC Cunningham – I thought you'd have been informed.'

Daley stared into the blackness of sea and sky. Clouds totally obscured the moon now, and only the crash of waves on the shore attested to the Atlantic's presence.

'Not your fault, DC Potts. Let me know if SOCO turn anything up in their analysis, would you?'

Potts sounded uncertain. 'Can't help you there either, sir. Sorry.'

'What?' It was barked down the phone.

'No testing, no lab work. ACC Cunningham halted the whole operation, sir.'

Jim Daley sat back on his seat. A breeze of cold night air was coming through the driver's window, which he'd left open a crack. It made him shiver.

34

Emily Kilvington opened the door of her home with no little trepidation. Due to her medication, very few such feelings touched her now. Her demons were of her own construction, residing permanently in her head. But being back in a police station had somehow brought her back to reality, albeit in a detached way. There was something about those places that was the same the world over. The hum of radio traffic in the background, the uniforms, the smell of disinfectant, the buzz of conversation, officers coming to and fro. It all made for something familiar. It took her back in time.

The big lounge looked much the same as when she'd left when she flicked on the single lamp that sat by the door. The light it cast was by no means adequate to the task of filling the room, but Kilvington preferred it that way. Bright light unsettled her, brought back memories of the sterility of hospitals, of institutions.

As she made to settle in her favourite armchair, she noticed a discarded latex glove. It must have been left by the forensic team, she was sure. Even in her depleted mental state the thought of strangers rummaging through her personal things felt invasive, unwelcome.

Kilvington had barely slept during her time at Kinloch police station. It was impossible, even though they'd placed her in a family room that was comfortable and warm, not a bleak, hard cell.

She laid her head back and tried to relax. Soon she was in the half-world between wakefulness and sleep. The time when thoughts and dreams become confused, and it's hard to separate fantasy and reality.

The girl's face was full of hatred as she thrust the small knife into her side. The boy, tall for his age, came at her, clamping his hands round her throat.

'No, stop!' she cried out.

'Police hurt kids. Our father hurt us, and you're police. You'll hurt us too.'

The look of soulless determination on the little girl's face frightened her. The small knife was twisted agonisingly in her side again and again. She tried to scream, but with the boy's fingers biting into the flesh on her throat no sound came.

Kilvington shifted in the chair as the horror that was playing out before her mind's eye became not only her past but her present reality.

She fell, the boy on top of her forcing what was left of the breath from her lungs. His steely grip loosened for a moment – enough time for her to draw a tiny amount of air into her gaping mouth. Her throat squeaked like an old door for a moment, until once again the hands were round her throat, tightening until her vision blurred, edging into darkness.

The girl was standing over her now. The blood dripping from the little blade left spots on her face. She was dying. These children were killing her.

Emily Kilvington shot forward in her chair. The silence in

the empty room was deafening. She was breathing heavily. Somehow, the pain from all those years before had left a trace in her side and neck. She could feel it now, almost as though she was back in the dingy caravan.

To settle herself, Kilvington did what she always did. She got to her feet and started bounding round the gloomy room in a mad, unrestrained dance. One for which no steps had ever been laid down, no choreography required. She flung her head forward then back, bent her knees, and propelled herself into the air. She improvised a feverish jig, stepping from foot to foot, wailing as she went.

Eventually, almost exhausted, she flung herself against a window, her hands pressing against the cold glass, bringing her manic gyrations to a halt. She was breathing deeply now, her reflection faint in the darkness of the window, the shock of wild hair tumbling down her back, almost to her waist.

Kilvington steadied herself. She took faltering steps back to the armchair. Her knees hurt, her feet throbbed, and she had the trace of a headache. But the memories were gone: subdued, at least for a while.

She decided to try to stay awake, and held her breath, praying that the visions that haunted her with such visceral clarity wouldn't return. Her grandfather had taught her the trick to help her stay awake in school. She counted to fifteen, then began to breathe again. Somehow, the action banished her fatigue.

Kilvington was staring into space, desperately trying to marshal her thoughts. She remembered the head in the box, the detective's questions, the sterile room – the lie.

She didn't know why she'd lied. She'd just felt she had to. The face wasn't instantly recognisable, but the clouds had soon parted, and she had realised whose head she stared at. The little beard was new, as were the lines in the forehead. The features were sharper, harsher than she remembered. But she would never forget his face as he stared into hers, choking her life away.

Kilvington felt a wave of sorrow wash over her. The emotion wasn't just for herself, but for the children who'd been treated so badly that the only way out they could see was murder. She felt guilty about the lie. But she couldn't think how revealing the identity of the boy, who was now a dead man, could possibly help him or her. He was gone, and, in a way, so was she. In that way, she'd died on the caravan floor – they all had. Yet even now a little voice called for reason, shouted to her to think the process through and tell the truth.

Kilvington recalled the girl with the knife being pushed to the floor and restrained by the uniformed officers. The boy being dragged off her and handcuffed. She remembered being gently lifted from the floor and carried to an ambulance. The kind words of nurses, doctors, surgeons, psychiatrists. But deep down she knew that what had happened had been her own fault. She'd wanted to protect those children, no matter what they'd done. She'd done it before, helping to save young lives from the misery of mental illness and incarceration. She'd done it once too often.

Kilvington grimaced as she saw the face of the little girl with the knife in her mind's eye. It wasn't so much her features that sprang to mind, but rather her eyes. They seemed to pulse with anger and hatred. But the most terrifying thing was the utter absence of pity. She'd never seen it before or since.

Emily Kilvington decided that she had to go to bed. She would take pills to ease her mind away from the thoughts that constantly plagued her and she would slide, unconsciously, into the sanctuary of a narcotic sleep.

Just as she was about to force her tired body from the chair, she heard it. There were footsteps outside the lounge door. There were voices.

35

Hamish stood on the pier, admiring the lines of the big superyacht that sat at the New Quay. It was the length of three, maybe four fishing boats, but sleek, almost like a big cat ready to pounce. The superstructure was rendered in a charcoal grey, giving it the appearance of a military craft. But the chairs, tables, colourful umbrellas and smartly dressed crew told a story of luxury and excess.

'How much dae you think a vessel like that would cost, Hamish?' said Tommy Gordon, a young fisherman Hamish had taught to fish with rod and line when he was much younger.

'It's hard to say, son. What wae inflation the way it is these days, the sky's the limit. Mair money than you and me will ever see in ten lifetimes, that's for sure.'

'Dae you think she could take on the Atlantic – to America, I mean?'

'You'd be right scunnered if you spent all that money on a boat only to discover the furthest she could sail was Tarbert, eh? No, this beautiful thing could take you any-where you wanted. Aye, and in comfort into the bargain. I was reading that craft like this have cinemas onboard.

Can you imagine that? Off to the pictures once you'd been fed in the restaurant and had drinks by the pool. Aye, a fine prospect, right enough.'

'I'm no' sure my skipper would be happy wae us taking in a film when we should be catching fish, Hamish.'

'Davy Duncan? That bugger's no' been happy since he won a thousand pounds on the football pools in nineteen eighty-three. Man, he fair bragged aboot the holiday he was taking his wife on. I was sick hearing aboot it at the bar o' the County.'

'Big Davy was married? I didna know that, Hamish.'

'Ach, that's where things fair unravelled.'

'In what way?'

'Well, they both went on the big holiday, right enough. But only he came back. It was a hell o' a thing, for sure.'

'That's awful. Nae wonder he's such a miserable bastard, losing his wife in such circumstances.' Tommy shook his head at the thought. 'May she rest in peace.'

'No, no. You don't have the right o' it at all, Tommy. She didna die. In fact, I think she's still hale and hearty to this very day.' Hamish took a puff of his pipe, sending blue smoke into the sky above the harbour.

'I'm confused. If they left for the holiday together, why on earth did he come back without her, eh?'

'His wife took a fancy to a Greek waiter. Bugger me, before the fortnight was up, she'd left Davy and moved in wae him. Ach, it was all ouzo, olives and lovemaking on the veranda, I daresay. There's nothing they prefer mair in these hot countries, you know. Try that here and you'd likely choke on the olive stone, get sick wae the ouzo, while your tackle retreated for good in the heat.'

'I don't fancy any o' that. Besides, my mother doesna have

a veranda, though I daresay we could have a go at a' that on the decking.'

Hamish looked alarmed. 'Wae your mother? You don't want to be at that, Tommy. It's perversion. You'd get the jail.'

'No, wae Teenie McKinlay. She's my new lassie. We're thinking aboot getting a flat.'

'Well, all I can say is, you should think a whiles on it. And remember what happened wae your skipper's wife. Cool as a cucumber, she was. Elaine, she was called. Bold as brass – och, her mother was the same. Didna gee her ginger, neithers. Just faced him up in the hotel bar and says, "Right, Davy, I've fallen in love wae Aristotle here, and I'm making a life wae him." Poor man. Though I don't care for Davy o'er much, you couldna help but feel a wee bit sorry for a fellow soul in such a plight.'

'Aristotle. Man, that's a grand name, Hamish.'

'Only for illustrative purposes, you understand,' said Hamish with another puff. 'I've nae idea what his name really was, but it's a well-known fact that Aristotle's a Greek handle. So he could have quite easily been called that.'

Tommy made a face, just as they both turned round to face footsteps heading towards them down the quay.

'Don't you be listening to that auld gossip, Tommy. Come on, I want you to help me wae the engine. The bugger's playing up again.'

'Aye, Davy, just coming.' Tommy blushed as he cast a glance at Hamish.

'Man, we were just talking aboot you, Davy.'

Tommy's blush turned pale.

'Oh aye? Nothing good I shouldna imagine, Hamish.'

'I was just saying what a grand fisherman you were. Aye, just so.'

As Tommy followed his skipper back up the quay, Davy turned on his heel.

'His name was Nico, by the way. You've been telling that tale for near forty years, you old swine. Aye, and there were nae verandas involved!'

Hamish watched the fishermen make their way off the New Quay and took a contemplative puff of his pipe. 'Ach, nae wonder she left you. You were always too smart for your own good, Davy Duncan,' he said to himself.

As he gazed at the cruiser a man leaned over her side.

'You, what do you want?' His accent was foreign, and there was no mistaking the malign intent on his face.

'I'm admiring your fine vessel. Bonnie she is, right enough,' said Hamish.

'Go away or I will turn the hose on you, old man.' He disappeared from the rail.

'You might be on a lovely boat, but you're as classless as a Tarbert fishwife.' Hamish tapped the tobacco from his pipe against the side of his heel, and made his way back up the quay.

Alasdair Shaw was now fit enough to take a turn round the hospital gardens. He still felt unsteady on his feet. The doctor had told him that the sensation would remain until his system was purged of the drugs that had been forced into his veins.

He gazed at a wall behind which sat a primary school, and heard the shouts and screams of children playing. It brought a lump to his throat as he thought about his own kids. What was going to happen to him now, he wasn't sure. He felt as though he would be able to cope with anything if his wife and family were with him, but he was equally unsure whether that would ever be the case again.

Though he tried to banish them, images of his wife being degraded by the man who'd nearly killed him passed before his mind's eye. The very thought of it all made him feel dizzy, and he had to lay a hand on the wooden fence beside the path on which he was walking in order to steady himself. Not only was he distraught at what had happened to him; the feeling of hatred he felt was something he had never experienced before in his life.

Though he was glad that he'd unburdened himself of the truth to Liz Daley, Shaw knew what would happen. Nobody could keep such a secret. Especially not when they were married to his Chief Inspector. He supposed he'd told her not only as an act of contrition, but in the sure knowledge he'd have to pay a price. As unjust as that might seem, Shaw knew he deserved it. Whether it was pride or shame, he couldn't tell. But he'd been a police officer for long enough to know that what he'd done – regardless of his best intentions and of his plight – was wrong.

Now he was just waiting for Jim Daley to arrive, for his career to be over and his very liberty in jeopardy. Alongside everything else, the direction of his life looked likely to take only one turn – downwards.

He was distracted by the distinctive, throaty growl of a diesel engine. Alasdair Shaw looked up to see a large Range Rover with smoked-out windows park at the front entrance of the hospital. The main doors slid open, and there was a flurry of activity as a patient was pushed out on a wheelchair by an orderly. Two bulky men helped the young man from the chair – less than gently, as far as Shaw could tell, at least – and manhandled him into the back of the Range Rover.

Their eyes met for a moment, Shaw recognising the Oxford

student who'd lost his fingers to the vicious drug gang that was making his own life a misery. He could see sadness and even a hint of fear behind the lad's eyes. His blood boiled.

Speedily, the SUV turned, drove away from the hospital and was shortly out of sight.

Shaw sighed as he made his way back into the hospital. Even this little jaunt had tired him. Progress was slow. But at least he knew he'd recover. The young man he'd just seen could never grow his missing fingers back.

He pictured his own children, mutilated and disfigured. The very thought almost took his breath away.

Shaw looked at the sky, then closed his eyes, while his lips moved silently. He removed a mobile phone from his dressing gown pocket.

'Hello, it's me.' He waited for the reply. 'Did you fix things?'

36

Heads turned as the large black car crept down Main Street. In a few moments, it was followed by an identical vehicle that arrived from the Machrie road. Together, they made their way towards the harbour.

Hamish had made it as far as the town hall, where he stood with a huddle of old fishermen he'd known since they were all boys. Sorley Gillespie eyed the cars with distaste.

'They'll be heading for that great monstrosity berthed at the New Quay, I daresay.'

'Monstrosity?' said Hamish. 'Man, she's a beautiful vessel. Mind you, the crew's attitude leaves a great deal to be desired. Certainly the miserable bugger that spoke to me.'

'I hear it belongs to one o' they polygraphs,' said Alan Meenan. 'A right bunch o' bastards they are.'

Hamish puffed at his pipe. 'You'll be meaning *oligarchs*, Alan. A polygraph is something you get wired up to when some police officer or the like wants to drag the truth oot o' you.'

'They shouldna bother wasting their money on that,' said Meenan. 'My wife can get the truth fae me wae just one look.'

'That's right! I wouldna cross Jessie,' said Archie Kelly, scratching under his eyepatch. 'I mind telling her I didna like her platform shoes in nineteen seventy-two. Damn me, she near took my heid off wae her handbag. Nothing short o' assault, so it was. Aye, and she's no' forgot it, neither.'

'Here, I remember they shoes. I was just going oot wae her when she bought them. I felt like a fucking munchkin walking along the road and her wae these great clubby-doos on,' said Meenan.

'Your mother should have left you in some compost when you were young. That's what my granny always used to say,' said Arthur Shields. 'She was a daft auld bugger, right enough.'

'Yous are all daft auld buggers, if you ask me,' said Hamish.

'Mind you, you'll miss us when you're off to Dundee,' said Meenan.

'Dundee! Wild salmon wouldna drag me to Dundee. A hell o' a place. I was only there once wae Sandy Hoynes. He was looking for a part for an auld engine he was trying to keep going.'

'That sounds like him, right enough,' said Gillespie. 'He'd rather have faced the Atlantic in a tin bath than spend money on that boat.'

'That's no' true.' Hamish was indignant. 'He knew the value o' a penny, and there's nothing wrong wae that. Man, the Chancellor of the Exchequer should take a leaf or two oot o' Sandy's book.'

'Good idea, Hamish. That would mean the country wouldna have to pay for anything ever again. Sandy knew fine how to keep pennies in his pocket – especially when he was in the County. Much like yourself these days, Hamish,' said Meenan with a wink.

Hamish ignored the barb. 'I learned valuable lessons in life fae him. A better man never passed that island in a boat, and that's a fact.'

There was a general murmur of agreement at this comment. For as much as Hoynes's parsimony was a joke, these men were old enough to remember a fine seaman who had helped them all in one way or another.

'I'd like to see that vessel make way,' said Gillespie. 'I reckon she'll be oot the loch before you can say Bobby's-got-the-girl.'

Heads were nodded at this suggestion. Soon, as one, like a shoal of fish, they set off from the town hall and headed to the New Quay, collectively remembering to take a sharp right at the bottom of the street. They arrived just in time to see two large men disappearing up the gangway. Shortly afterwards the tone of the engines rose, the loch churned, and slowly the luxury cruiser eased away from the quayside.

'The captain knows what he's aboot, anyhow,' said Hamish.

'Might be *she*, no' a *he*, Hamish,' said Shields.

'It might indeed. You've always been a right pedant. Aye, and it's a habit that can be fair wearing for the listener. When I said he, it was merely for something to say. Whoever it is, they're making a grand job o' skippering, and no mistake.'

The great vessel nosed its way out of the safety of the harbour. Then, as fast as was permissible – and maybe a little faster – she ploughed through the grey waters of the loch out past the island and into the sound.

'Ten to one says she's heading for Glasgow,' said Gillespie.

'Nah, away down south, I'd say,' Meenan opined.

They hung about for a few minutes. Soon enough, the cruiser was heading north up the west side of the peninsula.

'They could be off to America,' said Kelly.

'In that case, I just hope the captain – whatever sex they happen to be – knows the way. Man, it's a fair undertaking when you hail your passengers and shout, *Next stop, New York*!'

Hamish mused for a moment or two, as though this was something he'd had to do himself.

'You never sailed to New York, Hamish,' said Gillespie.

'No, you're right there. But I made it almost halfway.'

'You're just a blether, man,' said Kelly.

'I'll tell you all aboot it up at the County. Sandy hadn't long retired from the boat. Och, he wisna a well man by that time. I was the new skipper o' the *Girl Maggie*.' He paused. 'But you'll need to buy me a dram to hear the rest.'

After a few mumbles and protestations of doubt and fiscal impoverishment, the old fishermen reformed their improvised shoal and made their way back to port: in this case the safe haven that was the County Hotel.

Brian Scott looked on as DCI Jim Daley dealt with the press. And it was an unusually large collection of the fourth estate. As police officers the pair had become accustomed to the Scottish press corps. Names and faces came and went, but over the years they had gained some knowledge of individual journalists and what they were likely to ask.

Today was different. The interest of the ladies and gentlemen of the English news media had been piqued. The mutilation of one Oxford student was bad enough. The disappearance of another was just too much to resist.

Scott was gaining the distinct impression that the parents of these unfortunate offspring were of equal, if not greater interest. As soon as Teddy Farringdon arrived, the press scrum dropped Daley in mid-sentence, immediately gravitating towards the newcomer.

'Hard going, Jimmy?' said Scott.

'Just a bit. I get the feeling this guy and Brandt are players.'

'He's a bit o' a dandy, is he no'? Must be the same age as me. If I turned up for work like that, you'd soon have me back hame to change.' Farringdon's hair was grey but subtly streaked blond, his face tanned, and despite the chill of the day a green cashmere jumper was slung over his shoulders, sleeves tied together at the neck. His trousers were lilac verging on purple. In short, he looked more prepared for a day on the French Riviera than a cold day on the west coast of Scotland. Though his expression matched the fact that his son was missing, he had an easy way with the gathered journalists that spoke of much experience in newsworthy situations.

'As expected, we've found absolutely nothing on the hill, save for tyre tracks,' said Daley. 'And they were too indistinct to be of any use.'

'Just as the lassie said, eh?'

'Yes, exactly as she said. This farce centres round the parents and whatever clout they have.'

'A great deal, I'd say, Jimmy.'

'Agreed.' Daley looked on as a straggle of media folk headed back in his direction, Farringdon having bid them a sombre farewell and retreated to the warmth of Semple's Hotel.

'I'm sorry. I've said all I'm going to say today. The search and our investigation continue.' Daley pursed his lips. 'Thank you, ladies and gentlemen.' He turned to Scott in an effort to signal the end of his engagement with the press, but one of the journalists seemed to think otherwise.

'You know that neither family has any faith in the Scotch police?' The journalist held out a mobile phone ready to record Daley's response. Scott screwed up his face in anticipation of what was to follow.

'I've given you my time already, and I must get back to

finding our missing student. As I've said, there's nothing further to add at this stage.' Daley was showing admirable restraint.

'But, still, they don't think you're up to it, mate. *Toytown cops*, I heard this one say.' The journalist raised his camera and snapped a rapid burst of shots of Daley and Scott.

'Give me the camera,' said Daley calmly.

'Fuck off, Jocko. Who do you think you are?'

Daley was on the journalist in a flash. He caught the man roughly by one arm, while with the other hand he forced the camera strap over the journalist's head, unceremoniously removing it from his grasp.

The journalist sniggered. 'Big mistake, mate. What's acceptable here isn't the same as it is back in civilisation. You'll pay for this – with your job, I shouldn't wonder.'

Daley turned to him. 'For a start, I'm not your *mate*. Secondly, in my opinion, you've used racist and defamatory language. Would you agree, DS Scott?'

'Aye, a hundred per cent, sir.'

'Would you arrest this gentleman, please.'

'With extreme pleasure.' Scott, using his experience, grabbed the journalist and handcuffed him in one fluid, almost elegant motion.

'You're mad! My editor will have your bollocks, *mate*.'

'Caution and charge this man appropriately please, DS Scott.'

At this point, Scott gazed across at his boss. Only Daley could have recognised the look of confusion on his face.

'In fact, I'll do it myself in the hotel. Please excuse me, ladies and gentlemen. I have a missing man to find.' The lingering group of reporters dispersed, all but one, who approached

Daley and whispered in his ear. Daley nodded by way of a reply. He, Scott and the handcuffed journalist walked into Semple's Hotel.

'Good man, Jimmy. Had me in a bit of a spot there,' Scott murmured.

Daley removed the journalist's handcuffs. 'You do that again to me and I will charge you, do you understand?'

'What with?'

'Your use of the words *Jocko* and *civilisation* was, as I suspect you know full well, of a racist and defamatory nature.'

'Just a little joke . . . you know?' Now he was now longer surrounded by his colleagues, the journalist was rather less bombastic.

'I don't find it funny.' Daley paused. 'You're facing an investigation into workplace bullying, am I correct?'

'Where did you get that?'

'It's true though, isn't it?'

He shrugged. 'None of your business.'

'Maybe not. But being charged up here won't do your prospects much good, I imagine.'

'Okay, okay. Let me go and I'll be a good boy, inspector.'

'It's *chief* inspector. And yes, you'd better be.'

As Daley returned the camera, Scott looked on.

'Have to say I'm surprised, Jimmy.' The pair watched the hack slope off.

'Because?'

'I thought you were going to go full-on dentist there, big man.'

'Time and place, Brian. Besides, my back's too bad for that shit.'

'There is a problem, though.'

'Which is?'

'Cunningham's on his way. He'll be here sometime after lunch. And you know what that means. They called when you were doing the presser.'

'Fabulous.' Daley was staring out of a window that faced the sea. 'Now there's a thing, Brian.'

Scott followed his line of sight. The hotel was on a rise, overlooking the beach and a small jetty. Farringdon and his retinue were making their way down to it from the hotel. A tender was on its way towards them. In the middle distance, the sleek lines of a luxury cruiser was visible, dark and impressive. 'Some boat, Jimmy. How the other half live.'

'Yes, but who's he going to see?' said Daley.

'How should I know?'

Daley cast his eye over the shoreline. Bobbing just off the beach sat an RIB. Daley walked to the bar and addressed the young man who was busy polishing glasses. 'Whose boat is that – the RIB, I mean?'

'Belongs to the hotel, sir.' The barman had a tag on his shirt announcing that his name was Angus.

Daley turned to Scott. 'I'd like to have a good look on board that boat, wouldn't you, Brian?'

'If you're asking, no, no' really.'

'Come on, where's your spirit of adventure?'

'When it comes to boats, my spirit o' adventure is just where you'd expect it to be, Jimmy.'

'And that is?'

'Nowhere.'

Daley smiled. 'Who do I need to speak to to take us out to that ship?'

'The bosses are away into Kinloch. They needed supplies.

You know, we didn't expect all these people.' He gestured round the room, where some tired police officers dozed in chairs after being up most of the night in search of the missing student, and a small huddle of journalists compared notes in the corner.

'That's a shame,' said Daley.

'No, it isn't,' said Scott.

'I'm sure they wouldn't mind if you took her out. Yous being the polis, and all, you'll know a' aboot boats if you're working here, eh?'

'Yes, absolutely,' said Daley emphatically.

'The only experience you have on boats is watching me drown and battering some bugger half to death on one.' Scott was speaking, but his lips didn't move.

'Looks calm enough, anyway.' Ignoring his sergeant, Daley watched as the Farringdon party boarded the tender.

'I do the lobsters when I'm no' at this,' Angus continued. 'Plain sailing between here and that cruiser. The water gets deep quite quickly, but there're no rocks or that to speak of.'

'*To speak of,*' said Scott quickly.

'The keys are here behind the bar.'

Daley removed the phone from his pocket, pressed the screen then put it to his ear. 'DC Potts, it's me. I want you to look for a connection between Werner Brandt and Teddy Farringdon. Speak to Gartcosh if you have to.'

'Does that mean we can stay on dry land, Jimmy?'

'No, it doesn't, Brian. I've not been able to work out what connects all this – still can't. But if these men just happen to be bosom-buddies, and their sons just happen to have encountered difficulties while here in Kintyre, well, it's worth a look, wouldn't you say?'

'No, no' really.'

Angus was still speaking. 'The boss lets some guests take her oot. As long as they know what they're doing, and they don't go too far.' He handed Daley the RIB keys. 'Just watch the trim if it gets a wee bit choppy, but I don't need to tell you that.'

'No, of course not.'

Scott looked as though he was facing execution. 'Dae you think you're doing the right thing, Jimmy? What the fuck is a trim when it's at home, eh?'

'No, I'm not sure I'm doing the right thing. But how many times have we done that in our careers? I want to see how they react when we arrive. Brandt is on that boat, I just know it.' He turned again to the barman. 'How do we get out to the RIB, Angus?'

'No problem. She's anchored to a pole on the beach. Just haul her in and off you go.'

Daley smiled. 'There you are, Brian, no problem. We get on the boat, and we'll be there in a jiffy.'

He hefted the keys and strode out of the bar, Scott at his heels.

'This is madness, big man.'

'You've been on boats loads of times since we've been here.'

'Aye, and near died every time.'

'Don't worry, Brian. I'm in charge.'

'How many boats have you skippered?'

Daley hesitated as though he was thinking deeply. 'None. But come on. How hard can it be? Straight line to that big boat, and we get a chance to shake the tree and see what falls out.'

'Was that one o' they rectangular questions you keep banging on aboot?'

'Rhetorical, Brian. Listen, I have a feeling about this. Come on.' Daley hurried down the corridor and left the hotel via the back door.

'God save us,' said Scott as, reluctantly, he followed.

37

Alex Ronald had not enjoyed a good sleep. And since he was a farmer, sleep was an important commodity. Early mornings and late nights contributed to his general exhaustion. But it was his life. The animals in the byres dotted around the farmstead had been restless from early evening onwards. Ronald had learned to trust them, knowing they possessed senses that mankind had maybe never enjoyed, or more likely had forgotten.

Following his breakfast of choice – porridge, tea and orange juice, followed by bacon and eggs – the farmer began his day. The yard needed scraping, and some fencing had to be repaired. He jumped on his quadbike and made his way up the hill towards the lochan and the more far-flung parts of his property. There were sheep on the hillside, and they had to be checked regularly.

The snow flurries the night before had lain for a while but soon melted on daybreak. The white stuff tended to lie on the south end of the peninsula only in the most severe winters. The sky was iron-grey, promising some kind of precipitation, most likely rain, and because he'd taken care to wear his long johns below two jumpers and a gilet, he was, if anything, too warm. A murder of crows was flustered by his presence, their harsh, grating calls echoing down the hill in a sound that reminded him of the many winters he'd spent at this farm, the place his parents had taken on as tenants and he now owned.

Ronald had to stand up on the stocks at the pedals as he neared the brow of the hill, leaning forward, using his weight to stop the quadbike from toppling backwards. It was an old model, and possibly dangerous. But this land was his land, and he knew every inch of it, from the wetter low fields to the hill where he kept his sheep, from the little cluster of trees beside the loch to the ruined cottages that had supported families long, long ago. There was barely a tussock of grass that he didn't recognise, and so attuned was he to the land that anything out of place drew his attention.

As he crested the hill, tyre tracks on the field between the lochan and Mains Cottage immediately caught his attention. He turned the bike to the left and was soon on the shores of his own little loch. A heron stood sentinel across the water from where he stopped the bike.

He stroked his chin, deep in thought, as he examined the deep ruts caused by the passage of SUVs. The tracks were recent, perhaps from earlier that morning or the night before; it was hard to tell. There had been two vehicles. Their tyres were distinct, making the identification easy. Their path could easily be followed from where he was to Mains Cottage, about a quarter of a mile away on a rise.

The farmer revved his quadbike and sped across the intervening field. Rural crime was the worst it had ever been in his lifetime. And though there was little of financial worth to be found up here, the presence of the SUVs could be an indication that someone was scouting out his property for potential theft. Or it was possible that some idiots were simply using his land to test out their new toys. Either way he wasn't happy.

He drew up outside Mains Cottage and stepped off the bike. People had no right to invade his property, certainly no right to steal what was his. The thought of it made him livid and, if he was honest with himself, not a little fearful. Normally, the gangs that targeted farms weren't populated by opportunists, but rather by hardened criminals, organised and determined. Some of his friends had been attacked recently at the very tip of the peninsula. But what was to be gained here, at this derelict cottage? He didn't know. But it was where the SUV tracks terminated.

With the engine of the quadbike now silenced, Ronald expected to hear the familiar sounds of the place: the craw of corvids, the bleat of a sheep, perhaps the call of a robin or blackbird, all set against the wash of the sea, only a couple of miles distant. But everywhere was silence. Even the wind appeared to have dropped. He could barely feel it on his face.

To his left, Atlantic rollers broke on the shore near Machrie. Between there and the hills that cosseted Kinloch lay a long, flat stretch of land where once an ancient ocean had held sway. He could see the island at the head of the loch, distant and immovable, like a guardian set to protect the place it had watched over since the dawn of time.

Everything looked the same, but he felt a tingle in the air: the notion that something had shifted, was out of place. Alex Ronald felt the hairs on the back of his neck prickle and rise.

When he approached the little steps of Mains Cottage, he

knew why. Dark footprints were visible on the worn stone. The traces weren't the brown earth of the land, but something altogether different, with a rusty-red tinge to them.

He was a big man, well over six feet tall, bulked out by hard work and a rich diet of red meat and dairy. Nonetheless, Ronald felt a shiver of fear as he stepped into the little lobby where occupants of this tiny dwelling had hung their coats and barred the door against weather and the world.

The patterns of well-shod feet were frozen in a choreographed dance before the crumbling fireplace. They had the same dark red hue as the ones outside. He remembered finding a pair of venerable wire-rimmed spectacles here when he was a boy and wanting to take them home as a keepsake, but his father had counselled to the contrary.

'Best to leave what's left of those who lived their lives here be, son. It'll no' dae any good to disturb the spirits o' generations.'

His father had smiled at him, placing the spectacles in their cracked leather case on the broken-down mantelshelf. They had remained there for almost half a century. But today the case had been flung into a corner where the wall had crumbled, and ferns intruded where once had sat a table or a cabinet. The glasses themselves lay in the middle of the floor beside the wood and wire of all that remained of an easy chair. They had been ground underfoot, the lenses, once almost intact bar a long crack from one end to another, were now smashed to smithereens, the thin metal frame bent and twisted.

This little act alone made his heart sore. Objectively, the spectacles meant nothing, but to him they conjured memories of his father, his mother, this place – *his* place.

Just as he stepped towards the bedroom where once a whole family had slept, a thrush flapped over his head from what was left of the old rafters and out through a hole in the roof. It made him start. He exhaled with relief when he realised what it was. He wasn't sure if it was the fact that he felt the cottage had been violated by unwelcome guests or simply the sight of the broken specs, but his heart was thudding in his chest, his face prickling in dread anticipation.

Then he stepped into the bedroom.

Alex Ronald stopped in his tracks. He'd played on that bed as a child. In those days it had been almost intact, the exposed springs of a mattress used as an improvised trampoline. A few years ago, a tramp had made the place his home. He'd laid a mattress the farmer had given him on the rusted springs, and spent a month of cold, uncomfortable nights in what bore only the slightest resemblance to shelter. The man had been old, and wandered at random around the area. Ronald had taken pity on him. He'd caused no harm, and he'd disappeared as suddenly as he'd arrived.

What faced him now was no wandering soul. He stood transfixed by the sight before him, surprised by his reaction. He'd been much more flustered by the fleeing thrush than he was by what he was looking at here. He realised that his response had been cushioned by sheer shock.

On what was left of the tramp's mattress lay a figure pinned to the bed like a butterfly in a display case. The face was white – pearlescent, almost. Unseeing eyes gazed at nothing, their spark long gone. The man's life had drained away, now gathered in a dark pool of blood and gore congealed on the floor beneath the bed.

For Alex Ronald, it was as though his other senses slowly

caught up with what he could clearly see. The smell of blood and faeces – the residue of violence and terror – permeated the little room.

Involuntarily, he doubled up and vomited over his favourite boots.

38

'You'll need to give me a hand pulling her in,' said Daley, as he grabbed a thick blue hawser tied to an iron stake that was thrust deeply into the rocky shore. It stretched out over a short expanse of water to where the RIB bobbed.

Brian Scott eyed the entire endeavour with great reluctance. Yes, the large cruiser was only a mile or so offshore, but for him it might as well have been halfway across the Atlantic.

'Come on, Bri! We haven't got all day.' Daley was impatient.

'I want it noted for the record that I'm utterly against this nonsense,' said Scott. 'You've as much idea o' sailing that thing as I have o' playing the harp.'

'I don't know. You spent plenty of time drinking Harp back in the day. You might surprise yourself.'

'I'm mair keen to see how much you're going to surprise me, big man. Aye, and hopefully in a good way.' Reluctantly – most reluctantly – Scott heaved on the rope.

The RIB glided towards the beach.

'There we are. No problem,' said Daley, as the craft bumped off the sandy bottom.

'We're no' in the bloody thing yet.'

'Correct, Brian. But no time like the present.' Daley strode across the sand, and with unaccustomed poise propelled himself into the RIB, by way of one hand on the gunwale. He turned to Scott, still rooted to the beach. 'See, easy-peasy.' He waved his colleague on.

Scott meandered to the water's edge, assessing the gap between the boat and the sand. 'You'll need to pull her in a bit, Jimmy. I've no' got great long arms and legs like yours.'

'Just jump. We can't pull her further inshore or we might damage something. It's just like vaulting a fence. I've seen you do that a hundred times.'

Scott decided to take a couple of steps back and take a run at the problem. However, as he jumped in the general direction of the RIB, a shallow wave chose that very moment to pass under the vessel. So instead of casually vaulting into it the way Daley had done he missed by a couple of inches and found himself slumped over the side, gripping on to a rope, while both feet remained dangling in the cold seawater. Daley grabbed him by both arms and pulled him properly aboard.

'Bastard! Look at this – I'm soaking. Look at my shoes!'

Daley looked about the floor of the RIB. 'There's a pair of wellies – you can wear those.'

Scott leaned across the crowded RIB's deck and dragged the boots towards him. He removed his sodden shoes, taking time to pour water out of each one, and pulled off his wet socks, doing his best to dry his feet with them. He dragged on the boots and got to his feet, already unsteady, despite there only being a foot of water between the RIB and the sandy bottom.

'See? No harm done.'

'What dae you mean? My feet are like two blocks o' ice. Aye, and these boots are three sizes too big. I feel like a clown – a cold yin!'

'Well, it has been said.'

'You can piss off, Jimmy. See when I think aboot it, the things you've put me through o'er the years wae your instincts and your plans. Och, too many to bring to mind.' Scott took a seat on the RIB, arms folded in disgust. 'So don't blame me when this ends up in a fiasco, and we both droon.'

Daley mumbled an acknowledgement. He was busy acquainting himself with the control panel at the helm of the vessel. There were some indicators he recognised, like speed and fuel level, of others he wasn't so sure. So he did what all sane adults of the twenty-first century did when they didn't understand something: got out his phone and Googled it.

Trim refers to the running angle of a boat as it makes its way through the water.

This little nugget of information was replete with notes on negative trim affecting fuel consumption and ease of passage. Daley identified the trim indicator and the lever used to adjust it on the console. Thinking about it, he was relatively confident that they could progress towards the cabin cruiser without mishap.

He inserted the key into the ignition then depressed the *Engine Start* button. The diesel roared into action, propelling the RIB forward.

Scott gripped the seat in front with growing terror. He trusted Daley in most things: driving a boat wasn't one of them. He mumbled an expletive that Daley recognised only by the movement of his lips over the growl of the engine.

The skipper took his bearings then turned the RIB in the general direction of the great yacht, further out in the bay. 'There, not so bad,' he shouted to Scott.

'Just keep at this speed and I'll no' be tempted to punch you right in the coupon!' shouted Scott in reply. They were meandering along at less than walking pace.

'I'll need to throttle her a bit or it'll take us hours to get out there.' Daley eyed the console again.

'No' before I throttle you,' muttered Scott under his breath.

Daley gripped the lever. It seemed reasonably straight-forward: push forward to increase speed, pull back to slow down. He pushed the lever.

The tone of the big engine changed in a split-second as, with a minimum of delay, the RIB shot forward. Scott's head tilted so far back he was looking at the sky as the boat bounced along, her speed increasing with every passing second.

Daley was holding on to the console with one hand, trying to engage the safety harness he should have secured before they set off with the other. With a great effort, he managed to click it into place. It pushed him into the contoured seat, from where he noticed that the horizon was fluctuating alarmingly because their passage through the water was creating huge bow waves. He was about to pull back on the throttle when a red light flashed before him, accompanied by an insistent bleep that modulated its tone like a car alarm.

'God help me,' said Scott as he tightened his grip on the seat in front until his knuckles shone white.

'Trim. It's the trim!' Daley shouted into thin air. Sure enough, when he pushed the lever above the alarm the bow rose in front of him, and though their view ahead was partially obscured, the RIB stopped banging off each wave, making its passage infinitely smoother. 'I told you, Brian. That's better, eh?'

'How can you see where we're going?' Scott's face was pale.

Daley didn't reply. He thought the RIB was still being tossed about too much by the choppy little waves in the bay, and decided that adjusting the trim had worked well the last time, so by force of reason should improve things further if he pushed the lever up some more. He did just that.

This time the effect on the vessel wasn't as he'd expected. The bow reared up like a bucking bronco. The wheel was wrenched from Daley's grasp as he was pushed back in the seat, clamped there by a combination of gravity and the tight safety harness. The vessel itself slewed dramatically, and Daley feared they were about to capsize. All along the console in front of him lights were flashing and alarms sounding. He realised that he'd adjusted the trim too far, and almost without thinking he reached out and pulled back on the throttle.

The motion of the RIB almost instantly slowed, the bow lowering now the force to push it up was absent. For a moment or two, Daley's view spun in front of him – first land, then sea. But as he pulled the throttle back as far as it would go, the craft settled completely and puttered towards shore no faster than as if it were propelled by oars.

Daley took a couple of deep breaths to settle his heart, which was thumping like a bass drum in his chest. Despite the chill of a December day at sea, sweat prickled his forehead, and he wiped it away with the sleeve of his jacket.

'Sorry about that, Brian. I got a bit carried away.' Daley blinked away some sweat and braced himself for some of Scott's particular brand of criticism. But no reply was forthcoming.

Daley turned to look at the seat where Scott had been sitting. It was empty. Quickly, he removed the safety harness that held him fast to the skipper's chair and shot to his feet, worried he'd see his friend lying in a pool of blood, having been tossed around the RIB when he lost control.

Not only was there no sign of blood, Brian Scott himself was nowhere to be seen. The only indication he'd ever been aboard was the pair of sodden shoes, one lying beside the console, the other wedged under a seat.

'Brian!' Daley shouted as he frantically scanned the bay. 'Brian!'

The only sounds were the gentle lap of water at the side of the boat, and the low hum of the engine.

ACC Cunningham had arrived at Semple's Hotel just as Daley and Scott were boarding the RIB. He was in full uniform, and the fairy lights placed round the bar danced in the silver braid of his hat and epaulettes as he and DC Morton stared out of the big picture window that looked over the bay from the rear of the hotel. 'What on earth are they up to?' he asked as the craft meandered from the shore.

'Not sure, to be honest, sir,' said Morton at his side. 'Though it might have something to do with the vessel further out in the bay, perhaps, sir?'

'That bloody pair! All this going on and they're messing about in boats. I didn't know Daley had any nautical experience. Aside from one encounter with a dentist, that is.'

The red-haired barman was busy laying tables. 'Aye, he says he knows his RIBs.'

Cunningham sneered, revealing his prominent teeth in a rather unpleasant fashion. 'He says lots of things, young man.'

They looked on as the boat's speed increased and the bow began to rise into the air.

'Is that normal?' asked Cunningham.

'Well, maybe a wee bit high under the circumstances,' said Angus, biting his lip.

But, in the next few moments, there was no mistaking that the RIB was behaving in a far from normal fashion. The prow rose further into the air, and instead of moving forward the vessel appeared to almost pirouette on its stern.

Angus's mouth gaped open. He flung down the cutlery he'd been holding and ran from the room.

'You know, this is the kind of thing I've come to expect from Daley and Scott.' Cunningham appeared irritated rather than concerned for his officers. 'I can't tell you how much I'd like to see the back of them both.'

'Sir?' Morton looked almost shocked.

'No, man! Not in a boating fiasco. Retired. Oh, don't worry, Morton. They'll emerge from this as they always do – smelling of roses.' He ambled off. 'Where does one find a decent coffee in this bloody place?'

Morton noted that Angus was now on the beach. He had his hands cupped to his mouth and was calling out to Daley on the RIB. The vessel itself had come to a halt. Morton – his loyalties divided between the Assistant Chief Constable and the wellbeing of his fellow officers – chose the latter, and hurried from the hotel to join Angus on the beach.

The RIB was now puttering slowly towards them, the single figure visible aboard turning frantically this way and that.

'What's up with DCI Daley?' asked Morton.

'There's a man overboard!' said Angus, hurrying to the water's edge.

Morton hadn't thought of that. He'd been so fascinated and horrified by the violent motion of the craft, he'd failed to spot that Scott was nowhere to be seen.

'Come into shore, Mr Daley!' shouted Angus. 'But don't . . .'

It was too late. Daley revved the engine in order to speed up the process.

'Why are you shaking your head?' Morton asked. 'The quicker he gets here, the quicker we can jump aboard and help find DS Scott.'

'Unless the missing man is lying just under the water and the propeller cuts him to wee bits.'

It took Morton a couple of seconds to process this. 'Sir! Slow down!' he shouted at the top of his voice.

Daley did slow, but only because he was nearing the beach.

'Quick, take your shoes off,' said Angus.

He and Morton removed their shoes and socks just as Daley bumped the RIB as close to the water's edge as he dared.

'Help!' he called, his face a mask of desperation.

Morton copied Angus by rolling up his trouser legs. Soon the pair were splashing through the surf towards the RIB.

'I don't know what's happened to Brian!' Daley's eyes were staring. 'What can we do?'

'Get back out there!' Angus shouted in reply. 'I'll take the helm, if you don't mind.'

Daley stepped away from the console. 'I don't understand where he could have gone.'

'Likely he was knocked unconscious when you reared up and she turned. What on earth were you thinking aboot?' Angus shook his head as he strapped himself into the skipper's chair.

'He's gone,' said Daley, his eyes brimming with tears.

'We'll find him, sir.' Though he heard himself say the words, DC Morton didn't believe them. He'd been looking from wave to wave and all he saw was grey sea.

He and Daley were pulled from their thoughts by a sound coming from the stern of the boat. It was a mix of coughing, sputtering and somewhat industrial language. Angus was already racing to the rear of the RIB. With one strong arm he helped what could only be described as a wet, miserable figure from the water.

'Brian! What a relief,' said Daley.

'It'll no' be a relief when I'm dooking your heid under the water and drowning you, Jimmy.' Scott coughed again, bringing up an unhealthy amount of seawater, but managed to glare at Daley nonetheless.

'I'm sorry, Brian. That thing is so sensitive. One touch and it was chaos.'

'It might have been chaos for you. For me, it was bloody terror. I got tipped oot o' my seat and the next thing I knew I was fighting for my life in the sea!' Scott spat out more seawater.

'Look on the bright side, Brian. You'll probably get the Police Medal for bravery.'

'Maybe not, sir.' Morton glanced back at the hotel.

Daley followed his line of sight. He could see a uniformed figure at the window. 'Tell me that's not who I think it is, son.'

'Yes, sir. ACC Cunningham.'

'Hope he didn't see any part o' this?'

'Just about all of it, sir. Until he went for coffee, that is.'

'Aye, good for the bastard,' said Scott. He was shivering with cold now, the adrenaline brought on by his near drowning having worn off. 'He'll need to move fast to beat me to resigning before he sacks me. Bugger you!' He raised two fingers towards the hotel.

'That's just what we needed,' said Daley, his feelings towards his DS veering from fear at the thought of losing him one minute to irritation at the sight of the gesture the next. 'Let's hope he didn't see that.'

'I've been shot – twice. Near drooned. I've taken who knows how many punches, kicks and put-downs; been blown up, blown doon, burned, spat at, kicked by a horse, bitten by a polis dug – aye, and the rest. I've had enough!' Scott began to plod up the beach in his bare feet.

'Hey! Where are my wellies?' shouted Angus, looking round the deck.

'They'll be halfway up your arse if you don't shut up,' said Scott. He turned to Daley. 'I don't care what's happening or who it's happening to, Jimmy. I'm never setting foot on another fucking boat again. Got it?'

'Got it, Brian.'

Daley was first in the lounge, where he found ACC Cunningham wearing a scornful expression.

'I went to Florida on holiday with Mrs Cunningham once. Most pleasant, it was. Warm, beautiful views out to sea, good nightlife et cetera. One day we visited an aquarium. They had two orcas that did tricks. Do you know, that's the funniest water-bound thing I thought I'd ever see – until now. What on earth did you think you were doing, Daley?'

'It's a long story, sir. Anyway, Brian could have been badly injured – or worse!'

'That was never going to happen. Brian Scott could walk

into a pyroclastic flow and come out with minor singeing. He'll carry on being an embarrassment to this force until he hands in his cards. And the sooner that happens the better.'

'I have a theory, sir. It's sound, I think.'

'Oh, I bet it is!' Cunningham snarled, revealing a row of teeth that looked like tombstones set in his wan, miserable face. 'I don't have time for your theories, Daley. You have a murder to solve.'

'They've found the missing lad dead?'

'Oh no. There's absolutely bugger all sign of him. This is another man. A farmer found him on his property just outside Kinloch when you were busy messing about in a boat.'

'Who is it?'

'How the bloody hell should I know? But I can tell you something, Daley. I have a bad feeling about all this.'

'I'll get on it straight away. Will you take the helm here, sir?'

'I'm bringing an MIT down to handle this. All you've done is have men meandering about the hillside in the middle of the night.'

'As per your orders, sir.'

Ignoring this, ACC Cunningham continued. 'Take that bloody drip Scott with you.'

'I was serious. We nearly lost him out there, sir.'

'Better luck next time!'

Taking this as a sign of dismissal, Daley left Cunningham to his coffee. Speaking to senior officers never changed. Always a mix of passing the buck and condescension. Cunningham was one of the worst, but Daley was used to it.

Scott was getting dried off in the toilet. He was – to say the least – unhappy. Daley found him some spare clothes and they left Semple's Hotel in silence.

39

She lay all alone now. The pain in her side was agonising. Outside, she could hear the trees whispering in the breeze, a seabird's cry, the waves crashing on the shore. Sounds that normally comforted her, but not today.

This was the end. She felt her life draining away. Its very last drops would be spilled on the floor of this old house by the sea: the place she'd always thought of as a sanctuary, her refuge from a world that could no longer understand her. That she'd been wrong was no real surprise. She'd made so many wrong decisions in her life; it was her default position.

In many ways, she'd died in the hot, grubby caravan all those years before. Her mind, almost no longer registering the pain, drifted back to that day. The hurry through the tourist-crowded streets. Checking her watch, conscious of the seriousness of the situation she faced.

In the distance, Kilvington thought she heard something. But her reality had already shifted. She was now far away from the here and now.

Kilvington could see the faces of her colleagues, feel the heat in the stuffy, enclosed space. She watched them leave, the last man shaking his head as he disappeared through the slit of light that was the open door into a bright summer day.

She should have listened to him.

Sometimes, being kind-hearted was a curse. She'd left herself vulnerable. A dead man on the floor and the children who killed him standing in front of her.

Until recently, she'd forgotten the face of the teenage boy who'd stood before her that day. Though she remembered that he had been tall for his age – a man, almost. In body, if not in mind.

But Emily Kilvington could never forget the face of the little girl, shrivelled and purposeful as she plunged the knife into her side, again and again. Her eyes spoke of pure hatred – an evil she could hardly possess at such a young age.

In that moment, Kilvington realised the mistake she'd made. It hit her as hard as the blade.

Too nice for your own good, my girl.

Her father's voice was still shrill in her mind. It was as though he was standing in the caravan, shaking his head as his daughter was being assaulted.

She closed her eyes at the shaft of light in the darkness that suddenly appeared in the periphery of her vision. The pain was almost gone now, as she slowly drifted away. The last thing she remembered was a voice she recognised, but it sounded different somehow.

Daley and Scott stood outside the little derelict cottage on the hill as the body was removed by mortuary attendants ready for a post mortem in Glasgow. SOCO men, ordered to the locus by ACC Cunningham, were already plodding about in their white suits, hoods and footwear covered by blue forensic bags.

Scott watched them leave as Daley spoke to the farmer who'd found the body, reassuring him there was nothing he could have done to save the victim.

'The beasts were unsettled that night,' said Ronald. 'I couldna understand why. Och, the thought such a thing could happen here makes me sick to my stomach, so it does.'

'If it's any consolation, this wasn't a theft gone wrong – nothing to do with the farm in fact. It just happened to be a handy place to kill,' said Daley.

'Puts a shiver right through me, all the same. Let me know when yous are ready and I'll take you back doon the hill in the Land Rover. I have a few fence posts to hammer back into the ground. They were near blown over in thon last storm we had. I'll just be over there.' Ronald stomped off through the muddy field in the general direction of a broken-down fence.

'He's lucky he never went to have a look to see what was happening, despite what he heard,' said Scott, sporting an anorak that was slightly too small for him over a jumper with Rudolph the red-nosed reindeer on the front.

'He was,' said Daley.

'Could you no' have found some decent clothes? I feel like a total arse standing here in this get-up.'

'You know what this means, don't you?'

'Aye. It's nearly Christmas.'

'I checked with the hospital. Alasdair Shaw has been discharged.'

'Aye, and?'

'Come on, Brian. That's the last remains of Andrew Mitchell they're taking away.'

Scott thought for a moment. 'Shit! No, Al could never do something like this, Jimmy.'

'You think? The man's threatened his family. Raped his wife. She only slept with him to keep her kids safe.'

'Nah, I'm no' having it. We should be glad this piece o' shit got what he deserved. It'll be some turf war. The whole west coast o' Scotland is going mad just now wae this fentanyl shit. You know that.'

'I know how I'd feel if it was my wife and kids.'

'We all know what you'd dae, too. Fae experience.'

Daley smiled mirthlessly. 'We'll have to speak to him, Brian. Better us than Cunningham's MIT mob, eh?'

'They're on the missing boy thing. They'll no' be interested in a murdered dealer, Jimmy.'

'Huh. I know Cunningham. He's a glory-hunter. Nothing would suit him better than to come down here and save the day. They reckon he's going to be the next Chief Constable. That, or head for the Met and get the top job there eventually. He'll be right into this the moment he gets a hint there's a cop involved.'

'Aye, same auld story. Nothing better than bringing doon one of your ain to get a boost up the ladder. And if the lad turns up dead, he'll blame us too.'

'Correct! At last you're getting it.'

'All this is getting me doon, Jimmy. Alasdair Shaw's a colleague, a mate. I don't want to collar him. This goes deeper, let me tell you.'

'It does go deeper, that's for sure. There's a feeling I just can't shake. I don't know what it is. I think we're missing a connection.'

'Eh? Posh kids getting kidnapped, deid scumbag drug dealers and some mental woman fae a big hoose? If you can join the dots wae all that, you'll be in for one o' they global peace prizes.'

'Nobel.'

'I like to think I have standards, aye.'

'No, the *Nobel* peace prize, Bri. Not *Global*.'

'Are you kidding? I've thought that for years.'

'Yeah, and I thought we were being sent to a dead-end job where nothing happened when we came down here.'

'And you were wrong. It's like the Bronx. I saw a TV show aboot this murder in a croft. Och, years ago, it was. I mind thinking, nah, that couldnae happen in such a wee place.'

'That was fiction, Brian. This is real life. C'mon, we'd better take a trip to see Shaw. But nothing goes on paper until we've spoken to him and made up our minds, right?'

'Here was me rushing to get some paperwork done. I don't know if I can stand being away fae the keyboard.'

'Touché.'

'You know, all these years, and I've never worked oot what that means.'

'I'll tell you one day.'

The pair hailed the farmer for a lift back down the hill to Daley's car.

40

Daley watched on a monitor in his office as Scott, with Potts alongside him, interviewed Sergeant Alasdair Shaw, a duty solicitor at his side. He knew his old friend would approach the interview as though he was talking to a mate – which he was. He'd been worried that Shaw would just clam up if he was present himself. It wasn't that they didn't get on, but the division of rank would always come between them. Strictly speaking, as Shaw's superior, Daley should have conducted the interview, but this was the way he wanted to proceed. If he was being honest with himself, he hated calling into question the integrity of a colleague, never mind a friend.

'You'll have heard aboot Andrew Mitchell?' said Scott.

Daley could view the questioning from three angles: looking at the interviewee, at Scott, or a raised overview above the table. He chose not to move from camera to camera, just watching Shaw's bruised, pale face.

'It was on the news. That was the first I heard of it, Brian.'

Daley was pleased that Scott didn't correct the informality and was keeping it friendly.

'You know what I'm going to ask, Alasdair.'

'Where I was yesterday evening?'

'Correct.'

'Either at the hospital or at home.'

'You weren't speaking to your wife – or the weans?'

Shaw hesitated. 'No, I didn't feel like it.'

'After being in the hospital . . . after what happened to you. Was that it?'

'Of course. What do you think, Brian?'

'I stopped thinking a while ago. You know that.'

They all laughed apart from Shaw's lawyer, a local man who sat taking notes, stern-faced.

'If you want me to say how sad I am that Mitchell is dead, that isn't going to happen.'

Scott smiled. 'I'm no' aboot to burst into tears myself. Professional curiosity, that was my only interest in him. Mind you, I didnae have an axe to grind wae him. Well, apart fae him being lowlife scum and that.'

'But I did.'

'You said it, Alasdair. The wife, the kids – the assault. Lots o' folk will have a grudge against Mr Mitchell. And you're definitely one o' them.'

'It wasn't me.' Shaw folded his arms and sat back in the chair.

'Okay, good to hear. But you know fine that's not enough, Alasdair.'

'Where are the boys from up the road – the MIT? You shouldn't really be interviewing me, Brian. I mean, I am the Federation rep. I know the rules, remember.'

'We're a bit pushed. You know how it goes.'

'Please shut up for your own good, Alasdair,' Daley whispered to himself while biting his nails. Shaw looked calm, which was good. But he was too calm, somehow. Like a man who had nothing to lose and was merely going through the motions.

'When I took my oath as a police officer, Brian, I meant it.'

'We all did,' said Scott.

Daley raised an eyebrow at this.

'He did tell me something, though.' Shaw looked Scott in the eye.

'Who?'

'Mitchell. You know, when he was busy turning me into a pin cushion.'

'What did he say?'

'That he wouldn't have to bother with the likes of me and my whore of a wife for much longer – he had *big plans*. I'm paraphrasing, Brian. I can't remember *exactly* what he said.'

'Aye, of course,' said Scott, with the conviction of a man who wasn't exactly sure what *paraphrasing* meant.

'They might be one of the reasons he finds himself dead – these big plans?'

'But he didn't say any more aboot them?'

'No. I was being beaten and drugged, Brian. Hence the paraphrasing.'

Daley watched Scott squirm in his seat and cough on his overhead view.

'Maybe one thing.' Shaw looked pleased with himself. His expression changed from beaten and downtrodden to conviction.

'What's that?'

'I'm pretty sure he mentioned money coming from an "unexpected source" – not the "shit dough that keeps your wife topped up".'

Daley's brain was already whirling. Across from his desk

was a whiteboard. Images of students Salazar and Nate were connected by a red felt-tip line. They hadn't had time to update the schematic with Mitchell's rough features. But mentally Daley pictured him as he stared at the students, pondering the last few days.

Scott was winding things up, too. 'Okay, so you suspect that our man Mitchell had some scheme on the go, but you have no idea what, eh?'

'No. I've told you all I know.' Shaw swallowed hard. 'I just want to restate for the tape that I have nothing to do with this. Absolutely *nothing*.'

Daley lost interest as Scott went through the closing formalities of the interview. He was about to re-read his notes on all that had happened prior to the discovery of Mitchell's body and their little escapade on the RIB that morning when the door to his glass box burst open. A rather harassed-looking detective stepped into his office. She gathered herself before speaking.

'Sir, Ms Kilvington – you know, the woman we had in custody?'

'I do,' said Daley, rather put off his stride by this sudden interruption.

'She's nearly dead, sir.'

'What?' It was all Daley could do to stop his jaw from dropping.

'When I say dead, I mean she could die, sir.'

'Wait, calm down, DC Carmichael. What has happened to Ms Kilvington, and where is she now?'

'Sorry, sir. I just had ACC Cunningham on the phone at the front desk. I said I'd put him through to you. But he said he didn't have the time.' She blew out her cheeks.

261

'Just tell me what he said.'

DC Carmichael paused for a moment, gathering her thoughts. 'Ms Kilvington was found in her home by the man from the Taindale shop. I think his name is Wanley, sir.'

'Yes, it is. Go on.'

'She'd been badly beaten. The helicopter – air ambulance, sir – took her to Glasgow right from the locus. But she's in a really bad way. Head injuries, lost a lot of blood – maybe internal injuries.'

'Okay. Find out as much as you can about this. Get hold of Wanley and get a proper statement.'

Carmichael looked suddenly uncertain.

'What is it?'

'I think the Major Investigation Team are handling it, sir.'

'I see.' Daley was deep in thought. Cunningham had given the order for Kilvington to be released. Of course, strictly speaking, he'd been correct. But Daley would never have sent her back to the big lonely house given her prevailing mental state. That Kilvington was fragile had been obvious for all to see. Apart from Cunningham, it appeared. No wonder he wanted his own men investigating. They would be sure to cover his backside while they were at it.

'Do you still want me to speak to Mr Wanley, sir?'

'Yes, I do, please. But keep it to yourself, okay?'

Carmichael smiled. 'I will do, sir' She was about to leave when something else crossed her mind. 'She kept saying something over and over again when she was found. *Tango Charlie*, sir. Traumatised, likely thinking about her time in the police. That's what the ACC thinks. But he told me to pass it on.'

'Good. Thank you, DC Carmichael.'

Scott bumped into the detective on his way into the glass box.

'What's her hurry, Jimmy?'

When Daley told Scott about Kilvington, the latter shook his head.

'Ever get the feeling we're spending too much time interviewing polis? Docsnae matter whether they're serving or not. You never leave this job, as far as I'm concerned.'

'You know who released her, Brian.' This was a condemnation rather than a question.

'Cunningham. To think that useless bastard could be the Chief Constable.'

'Why would she be saying *Tango Charlie*?'

'Beats me, Jimmy. Let's face it, the woman's as mad as a box of frogs. Anything could be going on in her heid – especially after what she's been through. Fuck, who's doing all this shit?'

'I don't know. What links her to Mitchell? Or are we to think these things are just happening in isolation?'

'Aye, and the missing lad and his pal wae nae fingers.'

'Mitchell is the key to it all. There has to be a connection.'

'He's deid, Jimmy.'

'I know.'

'Tell you what, though. Alasdair Shaw didnae touch him. I'd bet my pension on it.'

'So I saw. He's pretty composed for all he's been through.'

'He is, poor bastard. But he'll no' be famished like me. I'm starving, big man.' Scott's stomach rumbled in perfect time to match his complaint.

'Okay, quick bite at the County. Then I want to speak to Mitchell's wife.'

'It's the kids I feel sorry for. What chance have they got, eh?'

'Much better now their father is dead, I imagine.'

'You said it, big man.'

41

It was getting dark. Nathan Farringdon was tired, frightened and miserable. He'd been locked in a shed that appeared to be in the middle of nowhere, from what he'd glimpsed of it when they threw him inside. His captors had only spoken once. It was the biggest, roughest man.

'Stay in there – we're watching. Got it?'

Nate had mumbled his acquiescence, but that had been a long, cold time ago. He'd spent the night wrapped in stinking old hessian sacks on a beaten-earth floor. The only company he'd had was the scuttle of rats. Well, he supposed they were rats. What else would want to spend time in this shithole?

He'd had time to think. He wondered if Delph was okay. He was worried she'd been injured when he was kidnapped. He thought of his family – his brothers and sisters, his mother, even his father. He knew his mother would be distraught. She was a quiet, sensitive woman, so at odds with his father's bombast. He could see them sitting in the den back home, trying to keep each other's spirits up with lame jokes and pointless conversation.

But wasn't everything pointless?

His studies were supposed to lead to a career in politics. He'd begin his working life as a spad, slang for special adviser to a minister. From there, he'd eventually get a shot at a constituency, if they thought he was bright enough, that was. It would be somewhere the Conservatives stood no chance of winning, but he'd have to make every effort to run a promising campaign. He'd be watched, assessed, evaluated. The next time, if he was lucky, he might be given a shot at a more attainable seat.

Of course, his father's money would come in handy. He'd make the right donations to the party or to individuals, pull the many strings at his disposal, shake the right hands, buy the best of meals at the right clubs and restaurants, call in the appropriate favours. These things would be sufficient, Nate was sure.

Ultimately, he'd concluded, government was a veneer. A game for the well connected, rich and powerful. And though things might work slightly differently in the other political parties, it all amounted to the same thing: a political system populated by those who could scheme their way to get to the top rather than those who deserved to.

It kept him awake sometimes.

What did the future hold? A townhouse in Kensington for work, a decent estate in the home counties to which he could disappear when it was advisable to visit his wife and family. Of course, there'd be the obligatory mistress, the discreet consultancies, the same gladhanding bollocks at which his father was so proficient. All in preparation for the inevitable day his political career ended in retirement, a lost election or a scandal. Then he'd jump on the cab rank of cushy non-executive directorships, where he'd be tasked with lobbying old colleagues, friends and school chums, persuading them to hand government contracts to Shit Incorporated or whichever company of rogues he represented for doing as little as possible for the most lucrative reward attainable.

That's how Teddy had done it. His stay in parliament had been a short one, after he was caught in a compromising position with his secretary, but with his accustomed aplomb he had talked his way to a huge fortune due to his innate charm, his deviousness, an understanding wife, model children and access to his own father's influence.

That's what was in front of Nate. When he had become old enough to realise what had happened – in the whips' office, which made things all the worse – via a little pictorial piece put together by his friends at Eton, he despised his father for it.

The entire prospect seemed utterly worthless. Maybe he really did just want to be a Gary.

This made him think again about Delph – Delphine. He knew he liked her. She was pretty, quick-witted and had an edge most of the women he knew didn't possess. He wasn't sure that he loved her, though. Well, loved her *enough*. His father constantly complained that she didn't possess the right background to help him advance his career, his life.

'You might as well jump the brush with a common whore.' It was a saying of which Teddy was particularly fond.

But in this moment, Nate knew that he wanted her to hold him, wanted to feel the warmth of her body, the reassurance that someone cared – to know that she cared. Maybe it was love after all.

He'd been kidnapped for money – of that he was sure. He was equally sure his father would pay up. It was something they'd discussed as a family. They were a target, no question about it. Teddy's uncle had been kidnapped in the seventies from the family villa in Calabria, an incident which had definitely left a shadow over his father. For while being kidnapped in England was one thing, the Italian version had left Uncle Timmy with partial sight in one eye and a fear that never left him.

Still, though, Teddy was confident that anyone who wanted money in return for his children would be careful to bring them back intact or face the wrath of a man with wealth and influence. But that was England, and now Nate reflected that he found himself at the mercy of thugs in Scotland. He comforted himself with the thought that the man who'd told him not to move had definitely done so in a broad Estuary accent.

But where was the spirit of his forefathers? The men he could trace as far back as Agincourt? The ancestors who'd helped defeat Napoleon, Hitler – the Labour Party? As the light disappeared, and having heard nothing all day but the bleating of sheep, the distant lowing of cattle and the constant scratch-scratch-scratch of vermin, Nate decided it was time to do something positive. After all, Daddy was taking his own good time to liberate his son.

He approached the door. It looked anything but sturdy. He pushed at it and the whole thing moved. He was clearly imprisoned by a single padlock within a structure that a decent wind could blow over.

He remembered his rugby coaching. *Commit and execute*, that was the advice imparted to the Eton scrum. He took a deep breath, crouched, then leapt at the door, his right shoulder clattering against it with as much force as he could muster.

At first, falling through the air, he had the unsettling feeling of not knowing where it would take him. For all he knew, he might have been on the edge of a cliff, placed there for a laugh by his tormentors, who were happily watching him plunge to his death from a great height at this very moment. Hilarious!

The truth was rather more mundane.

The crash to the ground knocked the wind from his lungs. He gasped noisily for a second or two, propped up on one arm on what remained of the door that had imprisoned him.

But when he managed to gather himself, he was able to gaze out across a hillside, just as the gloaming began to settle across a small town far below in a little valley by the sea. Directly beneath sat the familiar lines of a council housing estate, rows and rows of tiny houses that all looked the same from this height. To his right, a flock of sheep gathered together, ready to face another cold December night. Lights flickered from windows; smoke drifted up from chimneys. Cars – like ants from this perspective – made their way along a labyrinthine pattern of roads beyond which sat a cluster of larger buildings. Churches, blocks of flats, industrial units, shops, all huddled around the shore of the loch.

He turned to look at his prison, which he now saw was little more than a shepherd's hut, or a feed store for the cattle and sheep that populated the hillside.

He was about to laugh when he remembered his circumstances. What if his captors were watching him, ready to pounce, set on removing his fingers, or throwing bleach in his eyes the way the Italians had done with Uncle Timmy. But as he edged his way round the side of the shed, there was nothing to be seen. No vehicles. No people. He had only a rough hillside and farm animals for company.

His relief was soon replaced by a feeling of shame. He'd spent a day and a night cooped up in a flimsy construction not robust enough to have contained a girl guide, within sight of a town full of people. Where was the spirit of Agincourt now?

A question nagged at him. Why was he here? Not the existential conundrum of a philosophy student, rather something more immediate. If this was a kidnapping, it was a half-arsed one. Sullenly, rather ashamed by what had happened, Nathan started to make his way down the hill while there was still light to see by.

In fifteen minutes, he was walking on a pavement past the rows of houses he'd spotted from above. The smell of burning logs on the cold air made him think of Oxford at Christmas. An old man was heading towards him, staggering slightly as he puffed on a cigarette.

'Excuse me,' said Nate. 'Could you tell me the way to the nearest police station, please?'

The old man squinted at him with distaste. 'That way.' He indicated over his shoulder with one stubby thumb. 'Just keep walking and you canna miss it.' He belched loudly. 'Sorry, son. I had one o' they mutton pies fae Michael Kerr's earlier. Coming right back on me, so it is. Likely filled wae a deid seagull.' With that, the man was off, only the lingering whiff of cigarette smoke left behind to indicate he'd ever been there at all.

42

The County Hotel was mercifully quiet. In fact, only Hamish and Ella were to be found inside. They were poring over a brochure at the bar, engrossed in it.

'Shop!' shouted Brian Scott.

'Well, hello, stranger,' his wife replied. 'Did you have a good night at the Semple Hotel?' She eyed him with well-practised suspicion. 'You didnae leave wae those clothes on.'

'It's a long story, Ella.'

'Summarise, dear.' She folded her arms.

'Okay. Jimmy near killed me.'

'What?'

'I was nearly drooned. My suit's ruined and I lost my shoes. It was yon Asda pair you bought me a while ago. Mind, they were always a wee bit tight roon the toe, to be honest.'

'Jimmy, what is he on aboot?' Ella turned to Brian's companion, deciding she was more likely to get sense out of him than from her spouse.

'He's right. I nearly drowned him.' Daley looked sheepish.

'On purpose?' said Hamish, sucking on his unlit pipe. 'Man, things are at a dreadful pass if that's the case. But you're still friends, I see.'

'No, not on purpose. We took an RIB out. It didn't go well.'

'Aye, you can say that again,' said Scott.

'What are you two so busy with?' asked Daley, hoping to change the subject.

'That's fine. Just tell me you near killed my husband as though it was nothing.' Ella folded her arms determinedly. 'Never mind what I'm at.'

'What happens at sea stays at sea,' observed Hamish. 'You should just be grateful he's back in one piece. I know plenty folk who'd gie the world to see their loved one walk through the door the way Brian just has.'

'Can we have something to eat, Ella? We're a bit pushed for time, to be honest,' said Daley.

'I'll get the truth oot o' you later, Brian.' Ella picked up a little writing pad. 'I'll no' bother wae the menu for yous know it inside oot. What dae you fancy?'

'It's like the Dorchester in here. Great service,' said Scott.

'I'm pleased you approve.'

'I meant the Dorchester Bar in Possil.'

Ella didn't think this merited a reply, considering a raised middle finger was an appropriate response. They both opted for the chicken curry, and she bustled off to place the order with the kitchen.

'So, what are you at, Hamish?' said Scott.

'If you must know, your wife and I are planning my going-away party. Man, I didna fancy such an event. But Ella persuaded me I canna just bugger off and no' say goodbye properly.'

'I don't think you should be going anywhere,' said Daley.

'Och, that's the problem in this toon. The folk here think it's the best place in the world, and the very idea of shipping out is akin to heresy. Well, there's mair places to sook a pipe than Kinloch. Minds need to be broadened, mine included.'

'You'd better be quick about it,' said Scott. 'There's no' much time for mind-broadening at your age.'

'Lessons in life carry on until the second it's o'er, Brian Scott. Why should a man like me no' sample a different culture before I pass on?'

'I thought you were going to Perthshire?'

'I am that.'

'It's hardly Uzbekistan, eh? I think you'll find that they do all the same shit in Perthshire they do here, Hamish.'

'That's no' true, Brian. For a start, you canna see or smell the sea. No matter how high the mountain is you stand on. Folk that don't live by the sea are different. I don't care whether it's Perthshire or Paraguay. For a start, the yarn will all be aboot coos and growing barley, I shouldna wonder.'

'Riveting,' said Daley.

'Don't scoff, Mr Daley. I've always felt I should know mair aboot the beasts o' the field. In these straitened times, a man never knows when he'll have to turn his hand to a different career. The pair o' you should take heed. Unless that was yous having a go at the fishing when you near drooned Brian.'

'If your mind's made up, it's made up,' said Scott.

'Aye, just as surely as I make up my mind to have a shave every morning.'

'But you don't shave every day,' said Daley.

'Well, that just proves what I've said. I would if I had a mind to.'

Ella returned. 'It'll be a few minutes, boys.'

'Good, I could eat for Scotland,' said Scott. 'Can we have a mug o' tea each, dear?'

273

'Dae you think this is a hotel?'

'Aye – occasionally, funnily enough.'

'It is for everyone but you.' Nonetheless Ella went about making tea for the harassed police officers.

'How's Delph getting on?' said Daley.

Ella looked confused. 'The girl from Oxford?'

'Yes.'

'Her room was empty this morning, according tae the lassie that cleans. Aye, and she hasnae come back, Jimmy. A bloke visited her in her room last night. She doesnae think I know. But I saw him sneaking up the stair then along the corridor to her room. She never checked oot or anything, just hasnae been aboot all day.'

'Typical, eyes everywhere. You're impotent, so you are,' said Scott.

'Omnipotent, dear,' said Ella. 'And no, I'm no'. But the CCTV in the office is. I was just tilling up in there when I spied him.'

Daley made a face. 'This man, what was he like?'

'Big, thrawn-looking. Kind o' a rough bugger, if you ask me.'

Daley was lost in his own thoughts for a while, until Hamish piped up.

'Nae sign o' her young lad then?'

'No, nothing,' he replied. 'The boy might be missing, but he's not on that hill.'

'You know, it's funny you say that, Mr Daley. I had a dream last night aboot ferrets.'

'Ferrets?' said Scott.

'Aye, just so.'

'So, you reckon he's turned into a ferret, Hamish? You've

been right aboot a lot o' things in your time. But you're off the mark wae this and no mistake.'

'Nah, not at all. You just don't understand the significance o' a ferret to me.'

'Which is?' said Daley.

'Those poor creatures spend too much time in bags and cages. Then, when they're let oot, it's doon some hole to flush oot a rabbit or suchlike. That's why I think this boy's like a ferret. He's being used.'

'I'm not going to dismiss what you say, Hamish. I've known you too long to do that. But as a fisherman, how much do you really know about ferrets?'

'Mair than you dae aboot the sea, and that's a fact. If you're in one o' they RIBS, you need to be strapped in. Aye, and, Mr Daley, trim is all very well, but it's a cruel master when things go wrong. Fae what I hear you could have flipped her o'er and both o' yous would have been killed. Horses for courses, for sure.'

'How do you know all this?' Daley looked bemused.

'Och, the whole place is on aboot it. I was telt that you were trying to impress a lassie on thon big cruiser wae fancy manocuvres. What nonsense, said I. These men are near auld enough to be grandfaithers. Their days o' trying to impress lassies are long gone.'

'No' so sure aboot that,' said Scott, casting the merest of glances at his boss.

'I'll never cease to be amazed by the way news travels in this town. I mean, how does it work?'

'It's an elemental thing, Mr Daley. We're like a collective. A hive mind. One soul in the toon senses something, and we all dae. It's quite a thing, so it is. You'll hear folk no' fae here say that it's a' nonsense. But you have to experience it to know.'

'Bollocks,' said Scott under his breath.

An urgent buzz ended the conversation. Both detectives automatically checked their phones, but neither had any kind of message. The buzzing continued.

'Here, that's coming from your direction, Hamish,' said Ella, as she placed two mugs of tea on the bar.

'Eh? What do you mean?' The old fisherman looked bewildered.

'From your pocket, man. It's coming fae the pocket in your dungarees,' said Scott.

'Oh, you're right enough. Man, there's nothing gets past you, Brian Scott.' Hamish continued sucking on his pipe as the buzzing continued.

'It might be important,' said Daley. 'Maybe your cousin from Perthshire about the move.'

The old man hesitated for a split second. 'Aye, you might be right, Mr Daley.' He plunged his hand into his pocket, produced a very old mobile phone and with some difficulty and much squinting answered the call. 'Ian, what can I do for you? I telt you, I'm in no position to take one o' your kittens. My Hamish would have it for breakfast. Aye, and maybe lunch, too.' He stopped, listening intently to his caller. 'Right. My goodness. That's odd, right enough. Fancy.' Hamish was nodding and shaking his head by turns. 'Aye, you never know the minute. Strange days, eh? Thanks for letting me know, Ian. Speak to you another time.' Hamish squinted again at the keypad, located the right button, pressed it and placed the phone back in the front pouch of his dungarees. He picked up his pipe from the table and carried on puffing at nothing.

'Was did Ian have to say?' said Scott.

'Ach, just gossip, that's all.'

'What gossip?' said Daley.

'You men must be well aware o' it already.'

'Try me.'

'Well, it sounds to me as though your man – boy, whatever it is you want to call him – has just walked off the hill. Ben Saarnie, as it happens.'

'What man-boy?' said Daley.

'The lad you've been looking for – the posh boy. Headed straight for the polis station, so I hear.'

'Cancel those meals, please, Ella.' Daley jumped out of his seat. 'Come on, Brian.'

'Hive mind, my arse,' said Scott, shrugging on his jacket. 'All thanks to Vodafone, eh?' He followed Daley out of the bar.

'I think your secret is oot,' said Ella.

'Am I the only man in the world no' entitled to a mobile phone? Another dram, if you please, Ella.' Hamish adopted what could be considered an angelic expression and drained his small glass.

'Entitled or no', Hamish, I hope you like curry,' she said.

43

The superyacht slipped through the dark sea. Above, the sky was a canopy of stars, the night clear and frosty. Pinpricks of light could be seen dotted up and down the peninsula beside which they sailed. These were cottages, farms, little communities huddled together against another winter on the edge of the great Atlantic.

On the vessel, though, all was warmth and light. Two men sat at either end of a long glass table, around which uniformed waiters and waitresses buzzed like flies, ensuring the diners had all they required. Bottles of wine sat amidst a veritable feast: dishes of fowl, beef and lamb, plates of sautéed vegetables, fruits, garnishes – even an ice sculpture.

Teddy Farringdon sipped his glass of red. 'That's a glorious drop, Werner. What the bloody hell is it?'

'It's a Montepulciano d'Abruzzo – Emidio Pepe. Too many people underestimate the Italians, don't you think?'

'I've been underestimating their wines, clearly. I suppose it comes with a traditional upbringing. My father wouldn't have anything in the house but the best French plonk. I suppose I followed in his footsteps.'

'You've always been more of a malt whisky man. I have something special for you on that front.'

'Steady on, old boy. I'll be pickled. Still not found that son of mine. I need to keep a clear head.'

'He won't come to any harm. Opportunists, local chancers trying to make a point. You know that. I'm sure we've addressed that little problem. This is what happens when the sons and daughters of privilege happen upon places like this. But leave it in my capable hands.'

'Very capable hands, too, I'm glad to say.'

'I like to think so.' Werner Brandt glanced at his hands as memories of plunging a knife through the chest of the man who had disfigured his son flashed across his mind. He smiled at the thought. He'd become soft. Being back at the rough end was good – invigorating. He snapped his fingers, and a white-jacketed waiter was at his side in a flash. He spoke quietly in the man's ear. The waiter rushed off.

'This business. Isn't it making you a bit jumpy, Werner?'

Brandt looked round the room. 'Leave us, please.'

One by one, the waiting staff filed out of the yacht's huge dining room.

'They are all hand-picked for their discretion. But we know all about the effects of temptation, yes?'

'Yes, I rather think we do.' Teddy took a sip of wine to banish memories he normally kept to the very back of his mind. Suddenly, he took the glass from his lips. 'You don't think this had anything to do with all that business, do you?'

'No, I don't. If it did, why here, why now? You're seeing things that aren't there, Teddy.'

The wine waiter arrived back in the room with a bottle wrapped in a snow-white cloth. He held it in front of Teddy, unwrapping it like a gift, slowly and deliberately.

'Nineteen nineteen Springbank? You must be kidding, Werner!'

'We are in the right part of the world – why not?'

'I wonder what it tastes like?'

'My dear man, we're not going to open it. It's a gift – for you. Add it to your collection.'

'I can't accept this. It's worth a bloody fortune.'

'Everyone raves about the nineteen twenty-six Macallan. One point five million US dollars for a single bottle. This will top that one day, trust me.'

Farringdon stared at the bottle for a few moments. 'It's a magnificent thing – absolutely. I don't know what to say.'

'Why say anything? We have been friends and business associates for many years. Can't I give you something?'

The waiter came back with another bottle and handed it to Brandt.

'We can have this for a digestif instead. It's the same whisky from fresh sherry butts – twenty-one years old. It probably tastes better than yours.' He smiled broadly. 'Let's take a wander on to the deck. They tell me the night sky is glorious in these parts. You'd better bring a jacket, though – it's cold. I'll have my man fetch one.'

Again, the waiter rushed off to do his master's bidding.

'This beast.' Teddy gestured round the large cabin. 'Where on earth did you get it?'

'Oh, it doesn't belong to me. But I have use of it whenever I want.'

'Unless whoever owns her needs a break on the briny, eh?'

'Then they give me another one. All it takes is twenty-four hours' notice.' Brandt clicked his fingers, something he clearly liked to do.

'I remember when we first met I was wealthier than you. I think our circumstances have changed.'

'Teddy, you know as well as I do that money is basically an illusion.'

'Only when you have enough of the bloody stuff.'

The waiter arrived back with a padded jacket bearing the crest of the yacht. In moments the pair were out on deck, leaning on the rail.

'It's like one enormous planetarium.'

'That's just what it is, my friend. The biggest there is – the real thing.'

'Is that Orion's belt?' Teddy pointed heavenward.

'Yes. They say it's where we came from and where we originated.'

'They do, Werner?'

Brandt nodded. 'But who really knows whence we come or when our end will be?' He placed a hand on Teddy's shoulder. Black water rushed beneath the keel of the boat, the moon and starlight reflected in the choppy sea like tiny diamonds on a black dress.

'Berkshire, in my case,' said Teddy.

Brandt stared at him for a moment then pushed him hard on the shoulder. Teddy staggered forward before being righted by his host's strong grip.

'You bastard! I thought you were going to push me in!'

Brandt was laughing heartily. 'I can't bear to part with my Springbank. But the look on your face was priceless. Worth every penny.'

Teddy shivered, despite the warm jacket. 'You've always been a cruel sort.'

The expression on Brandt's face turned as dark as the

night sky. 'You aren't a very gracious guest, Teddy. Has anyone ever told you that?'

'He's dead, you know. The boy.'

'He was no boy.' Brandt sipped on his whisky. 'I heard. Bloody shame for us. He had one job to do and failed.'

'Is this why our sons . . .' Teddy hesitated, 'is this why our sons are in danger?'

'We agreed, yes? You leave this to me, and everything will be fine.'

'But Nathan is still missing. And what about Salazar? Look what they did to him!'

Brandt stared across the sea at a flashing light. 'I told you, a local drug dealer, nothing more.'

'You don't expect me to believe that. This isn't the inner city. They've been targeted, and you know why. How is he – Salazar, I mean?'

'Weak and stupid. Perhaps this will make a man of him.'

'You really think being mutilated will turn him into a better person?'

'Why not?'

'You know that all cruelty creates are enemies, Werner.'

'I don't know. In my opinion a little cruelty serves as a good reminder. These days, everyone thinks they have the right to be safe and happy. Well, they don't. Everything has to be earned – everything.'

Teddy gazed at him as though seeing his host for the first time. 'Will I be the next one with my head in a box, Werner?'

'You really do say some stupid things.'

They both turned as a door swung open further down the deck. The head waiter hurried to Brandt's side.

'What is it?'

'A word, sir.'

Brandt leaned in to listen to the waiter's low tones. A smile spread across his face. 'Why on earth are you whispering? This is the best of news!'

'What is?' said Teddy.

'Your son is safe and well.'

'They found him!' Teddy Farringdon sighed deeply with relief, then took a great gulp of his whisky.

'No, they didn't find him. He escaped. Walked into the local police station, apparently.' He stared his guest in the eye. 'You see, all's well that ends well. We sail back to Kinloch, pick up Nathan, and things are back to normal. It's as if nothing happened. We can escape this – this place.'

'But something did happen, didn't it?'

'One last obstacle and it will be at an end.'

'We've said that before.'

Brandt stared back out to sea. 'We were too soft in the past. That was a mistake. No more.' He swilled whisky round the crystal glass.

'We don't even know where to look, Werner.'

'We don't?' Brandt's words slipped away on the wind, as evasive as their meaning.

44

Nathan Farringdon was remarkably calm as he sat in the family room at Kinloch police office. Given that he'd just escaped, this surprised Daley.

'You didn't get a look at the men?'

'No, not a glimpse. They were wearing ski masks – balaclavas or something. Just ask Delph, she'll tell you. They blindfolded me, threw me into the back of some stinking old van, and that was that.' He looked suddenly sheepish. 'I feel quite ashamed, actually.'

'Why so? It was a Land Rover, by the way – the van,' said Scott.

'Right. I should have known that by the bloody smell of diesel. Anyway, they pitched me into this place – little more than a shed. I can take you to it, if you'd like. When they left me there, they told me they would be watching – that I'd take a good beating if I tried to escape.'

'And that was a lot o' bollocks, eh?'

'Not the way I'd have put it. But yes. One decent shoulder charge and I was out of there in no time at all.'

'The capture aside, you weren't harmed, threatened in any way?'

'No. They pulled me out of the tent, shoved me in the Land Rover and that was it. I just sat there freezing, hungry and fretting until I summoned up enough courage to do something about it. I feel like a bit of an arse, truth be told.'

'So, no clues, no ideas as to why they snatched you or what they wanted?' said Daley.

'Honestly, none. I thought they'd be squeezing Teddy – my father – for money. My great-uncle was kidnapped, you know.'

'Nah, we didn't know,' said Scott.

'Back in the seventies, in Italy. It was all the rage in those days. Grab a rich person and make as much dosh as you can.'

'And you think that may have been the motive here?' Daley gazed at the young man.

'How should I know? Did anyone try to extort money from my father? If so, the miserable bastard can't have paid up. I had to escape.'

'No, we don't think anyone did ask him. If he was telling us the truth, that is,' said Daley.

'Listen, can I ask how Delph is? I asked one of your other officers, but they said you'd tell me. I was worried she got hurt – you know, when they took me.'

'She's fine, as far as we know,' said Scott.

'As far as you know?'

Scott cast Daley a glance.

'What aren't you telling me?' Nathan sat forward in his seat.

'Calm doon, son,' said Scott. 'She's fine, we're quite sure.'

'Can I see her?'

'Yes, as soon as we can arrange it,' said Daley. 'We think she's spent most of the day out looking for you. I've left a message at the hotel. I'm sure she'll be up here the moment she gets it.'

Nathan nodded his head. 'Okay, that sounds fine. As long as she's well, I don't mind. What about my father?'

'We've been in contact with him. He's on a yacht belonging to Werner Brandt, Salazar Brandt's father.'

'Really?'

'You look surprised, son,' said Scott.

'Yeah, I suppose I am a bit. I'd no idea they knew each other, to be honest.'

'Well, friends in adversity, that kind of thing,' said Daley. 'It looks like all's well that ends well. For you, at least.'

'One mair thing,' said Scott. 'See the drug dealer that cut your mate's fingers off?'

'Not this again.'

'He's deid.'

'He's what?'

'He was found murdered in a derelict cottage in the hills,' said Daley.

Nathan swallowed hard. 'Shit. I mean, I have no time for people like that. But murdered.' He swallowed hard. 'Makes me wonder what could have happened to me. You know what I mean?'

'Yes, I do.' Daley stood up, signalling the end of their interview. 'As I say, your father's on the way, and we've left a message for your girlfriend. So, if you hang tight here until they arrive, we'll do our best to make you comfortable. If you want a bite to eat, just ask the duty officer and something can be sent up from the hotel. If you fancy a lie down, just use the couch here. The tea and coffee's over there – help yourself. There's a TV in the corner here. Okay?'

'Yes, thank you. Please, the minute Delph turns up, I'm really anxious to see her.'

The police officers left Nathan Farringdon alone in the family room.

The young man picked up the remote control from the table at his side and flicked through what was on offer. Not much, by the look of things, he thought. In any case, he knew he wouldn't be able to concentrate. He turned the television off.

Nate had been ravenous when he was making his way down the hill to the police station, but for some reason the interview with Scott and Daley had rather soured his appetite.

Why was his father on a boat with Salz's dad? They knew of each other, yes. But though they'd been in the same room at various times, he'd never seen them exchange as much as a glance. In fact, he remembered his father being quite dismissive of Salz and his family, calling them *the gutter made good*. He supposed that adversity had indeed brought them together, and they'd pooled their resources.

If he was honest with himself, he was more worried about Delph. He'd envisaged her rushing into his arms. He remembered how she'd fought to stop him being taken out of the tent – the ferocious look on her face. Until now, love had been an emotion foreign to him. But now he only wanted to see his girlfriend.

He laid his head back in the chair. The room was warm, and he was soon asleep.

Daley and Scott were back in the former's glass box. Daley looked troubled, while Brian Scott was busy blowing on a cup of coffee to cool it down.

'If you ask me, we've won a watch here, big man,' said Scott, taking a tentative sip at the beverage.

'You think?'

'Aye, the boy's been found, Cunningham's MIT will take care o' the heid in the box, and we've got rid o' one nasty bastard.'

'Mitchell?'

'Aye, of course. Who did you think I meant?'

'Once you've finished your coffee, I'd like you and Potts to take a trip down to see his partner, wife, whatever.'

'Aye, nae bother. How's Alasdair?'

'At home, on police bail, with a cop outside the house.'

'Good move, Jimmy. We don't want any o' these bastards getting to him again, eh?'

'Not for that reason, Brian.'

'You're no' telling me you're keeping tabs on the bloke? Mind, he's one o' oor ain, Jimmy!'

'Then tell me, who else killed Andy Mitchell?'

'The man was a drug dealer. Any number o' bastards could have had it in for him. Good for them, that's what I say.'

'You know we can't leave it at that, Brian. I want to get into this. Now Nathan's back safe and well, it's only a matter of time until Cunningham's all over us. And you know what that means.'

'Aye, less work for us. His Major Investigation Team will be on the case. Job done.'

'You know this is a man who would happily see me put in charge of car parks or office furniture, don't you?'

'I knew the bloke wisnae very fond of you, right enough.'

'That's an understatement.'

'I'll miss you, big man.' Scott laughed.

'If he dislikes me, he absolutely hates you.'

'Steady on, Jimmy. Anyway, what can the bastard dae?'

'Guys like Cunningham can do anything, and you know it. You'll be on the beat in Drumchapel before you know it.'

'Ach, you think too much, big man. You know these drug gangs. Can't wait to spread the word they've topped this one or that one.'

'He'll try and pin it on Shaw just for a result and to get back at me. No, we need to get on this now.'

Scott drained his coffee mug. 'Aye, I'm on it, Jimmy. But once I've seen this Mitchell lassie I need some kip, big man. I'm fair knackered.'

'Yeah, yeah – of course. We've been up for two days, basically. Take a statement from her, check out the lie of the land, then get some shut-eye. I'll do the same.'

Scott left the glass box to find DC Potts, and Daley was left to his own thoughts. He flipped open his laptop. In a few moments he was staring at the faces he'd placed in this case file. Emily Kilvington, Salazar Brandt and his father, Delph, Nate and Teddy Farringdon all stared back at him.

He searched and added an image of Andrew Mitchell to the collection. Last of all, he took the photo from Alasdair Shaw's warrant card and set it with the rest.

There they were, a collection of people from very different backgrounds. The students and their rich parents; a deceased criminal; his detective sergeant, and the unfortunate Kilvington, now languishing in a Glasgow hospital.

He pondered on the well-to-do portion of those before him. All were connected by Oxford University. But he'd noted the surprise on young Nathan's face when he heard his father was spending time with Brandt senior. From what he'd managed to discover, these were two very different men, one old money, the other a shady businessman with connections within the UK government and security services, not to mention some very powerful friends abroad. They made for odd bedfellows. He resolved to look further into both of them.

Mitchell was a lowlife, whose end – violent as it was – would come as no surprise to those from the criminal fraternity. Live by the sword, die by the sword. It was clichéd, but true nonetheless.

He stared at Alasdair Shaw's even, dependable features. Daley was angry with himself for not noticing the man was under severe pressure. It was his job as senior officer in the sub-division, and after all his kingdom wasn't so large that he didn't know every police officer under his command. Was this man capable of revenge?

His mind flashed back to scenes from a moored yacht, when he'd half killed the man who'd raped Liz. It was strange. He could recall almost nothing of what he'd done, apart from the Journey track that had played away in the background, and the moment his world went black as his heart condition had rendered him insensible.

Don't stop believing.

Then there was Kilvington. A police officer attacked and nearly killed by two children, a trauma so great it ended her career – had turned her mind, quite clearly.

The more he stared at the faces on the screen, the more they seemed to dance before his eyes. There was something, something he couldn't quite fathom, nagging away at the edge of his consciousness. He just couldn't grasp it. Instead, he held his head in his hands and yawned deeply.

Then it came to him.

Quickly, he wrote an email to the forensic unit responsible for the post mortem on the severed head. The next part of his thought process would have to be completed in the morning. It was too late now to contact anyone outside his own force.

Wearily, Jim Daley left his office and made for his SUV. It wasn't only Brian Scott who needed his beauty sleep. His back was aching – again. And he was more than aware that he needed another prescription for the painkillers upon which he was now so reliant.

It was another problem. But problems were something to which he was more than accustomed.

45

Andrew Mitchell had lived in a renovated cottage just outside Kinloch. As soon as Scott turned his car on to the narrow driveway, security lights burst into life round the building, about fifty metres away down a narrow drive.

Scott parked the car as near to the front door as he could. This patch of gravel clearly served as car park and front garden in one, as it was littered with children's bikes, toys, shoes and a large doll's house, big enough to have children as residents, a rusty metal table and some similarly distressed chairs. Rather incongruously, an expensive BMW SUV was parked in the midst of this tumble of detritus. Scott shaded his eyes against the security lights, his face close up to the front passenger window of the vehicle as he looked inside. The interior of the car was as chaotic as the front of the house. Old cigarette packets jostled for position with empty crisp packets and cola cans. A half-eaten pie discarded on the passenger seat had taken on a rather unhealthy-looking green tinge, and a pale stain adorned the black leather dashboard.

'See shite like this, they don't deserve anything decent,' Scott remarked absently as DC Potts approached the front door. The house was in darkness. Blinds were pulled down on every window at the front, and not even a chink of light escaped the dwelling.

'Looks as though they've done one, sergeant,' said Potts, opening the letterbox to try and see inside.

'We'll check roon the back. Hey, it suits me if they've buggered off. It means I can get to my bed,' said Scott.

Potts pulled a small torch from his pocket and flicked it on. Tiny though it was, the beam of light illuminated the side passage leading to the rear of the property. Strangely, this area seemed to be utterly devoid of the bright security lights that lit the front of the house up like a birthday cake.

Potts passed the beam of light across an ill-kempt back garden. Basically, a large washing green.

'Fuck, I didnae think grass could grow that high,' said Scott as the beam from Potts's torch flicked around. 'There's likely soldiers in there still fighting the last war. Why light the front o' the place up and no' the back, eh?'

'I think this is your answer.' Potts pointed the torch at what remained of the housing of a security light, hanging just under the guttering. It was mangled beyond use. He ran the beam along the length of the roofline. Sure enough, there was another broken light, rendered just as useless.

Scott examined them both. 'They've been shot oot. See, there's a bullet hole in the rendering just behind this one. We need to get inside.' The look he gave Potts said more than enough.

'The file said he lived here with his wife and three kids. All young, too.'

Scott shook his head. 'Sometimes I really hate this job, do you know that?'

Scott and Potts made their way up the steps leading to the back door of the property, where Scott tried the handle.

Stout as it was, it had been given three hard bashes by something heavy enough to mark the wood, break the lock and splinter the jamb.

'That's a sledgehammer job,' said Scott, as he pushed. Though the door moved slightly, it was clear that something behind was preventing it from opening fully.

'You don't think . . . ?' Potts gulped, his meaning clear.

'If there's someone lying deid behind it, we still have to get the thing open, son.' Scott put his shoulder to the door, and slowly – almost agonisingly so, for the onlooking Potts – managed to push it open far enough for them to enter.

The detectives stepped into a large kitchen. Scott felt for a light switch, found one and flicked it on. The room was in turmoil. A big kitchen table was turned over, as well as some chairs and cooking appliances. The pair crunched their way over broken glass and crockery until they reached the door leading out of the room.

'Take a look, gaffer,' said Potts.

Near the door the wall was splattered with blood. A large bloody footprint – a heavy boot, by the look of things – was plain against the light wood of the floor.

'Better get the cavalry here, son,' said Scott. He began to move deeper into the house.

'Shouldn't we wait? I mean, this will need to be examined by forensics, won't it?'

'Aye, it will. But what if there's some poor wean dying in there desperate for help? Rules are all very well, but sometimes you've got to use your heid. We can tippy-toe, if you're that worried. Don't touch anything. Be useful and get on the blower and get bodies oot here. Aye, an' gie me that torch. Did you buy it yourself, aye?'

'No, it was issued. Didn't you get one?'

'Naw. I never get bugger all, by the looks o' it. Jimmy's got one o' these too.' Scott made a face, grabbed Potts's torch and stepped over the threshold into the hall. He reached out again, and sure enough the hall was soon illuminated by bright light from pin-spots in the ceiling.

The carpet here was light beige. There were more gory footprints, and a streak of blood slathered across one of the white walls. It was as though someone had been dragged along the hall, clearly injured. The unfortunate Mitchell, Scott supposed, though he couldn't be sure. Whatever had happened in this house had been swift and violent, of that he was certain. He could hear Potts in the kitchen on the phone to the office. But there was something else, like a low whisper, the swish of a door being opened.

'Don't move or I'll shoot you, ya bastard.' The voice was high-pitched, almost juvenile.

Scott spun round in the direction of the voice. Before him stood a tiny boy, dressed in red Wellington boots, blue pyjamas and a white cowboy hat. He was standing in the doorway of a darkened bedroom, pointing a toy gun at the detective, his face set in a determined frown.

Scott knelt before the child, his heart still pounding at the surprise. 'Hey, are you the sheriff, eh?'

The boy cocked his head to one side and looked bewildered. 'What?' he said, rubbing snot from the end of his nose.

'You know, the man who catches the bad guys. Like the polis, you know.'

The boy screwed up his face. 'Fuck off. I'm no' a polis!'

Scott heard Potts hurrying to his side and waved him to stop. 'Here, that's no' a nice thing for a wee boy to say. I'm a polis.'

Unexpectedly, the child sniffed loudly, turned on his heel and disappeared into the darkened bedroom. 'Mammy, it's the fucking polis!'

'Are you in there, Mrs Mitchell? I'm DS Scott from Kinloch Police. I need to come in.' In the distance he could hear sirens, no doubt answering Potts's call.

There was movement from within, a scraping noise then a click. Scott stopped in his tracks. He waved Potts back with one hand, his finger to his lips in a hushing motion.

'I've got a gun. And it's no' a toy yin neither. If you're the polis, you'll need to prove it or I swear I'll blow your fucking heid off.'

'Listen, Mrs Mitchell. You'll need to turn on a light. Then you can see my warrant card. Anyway, I've met you before. Mind, when your auld faither was doon on holiday fae Glasgow and stole they sausages fae the Co-op?'

'You!' The bedroom was suddenly bathed in light. 'How many times? He didnae steal them – he's just got dementia and forgot.' She stared at him from a huge bed. Two small heads peeked from under the duvet, both with masses of blonde curls. The oldest child – the one with the cowboy hat – was standing by a wardrobe picking his nose.

'Can I come in?' said Scott.

'Aye, you can come in.' The bold look on her face changed to one of frightened vulnerability. 'I don't suppose you're here wae good news?' Her eyes filled with tears, the role she'd played to try and protect her children at an end, the performance over.

Scott shook his head.

Mrs Mitchell gathered herself and addressed her offspring. 'Yous go into the living room and watch some cartoons.

Joshua, you know how to work the thing. Take your wee sisters, come on.'

Two little girls appeared from under the quilt in matching dressing gowns. They looked up at Scott with wide blue eyes as they followed their brother out of the room.

'I telt him – I always warned him. Don't bring it hame here. I don't want the weans to see what it is you dae. Honestly, I'm no' lying to you.' She burst into tears. 'He's gone, aye?'

'Aye, he's gone. I'm sorry.' Scott heard the sound of engines to the front of the property; the help Potts had summoned.

'Who's that?' Mrs Mitchell produced the pistol from under the duvet.

'It's mair polis. Hey, dae yourself a favour. Wipe that bloody thing clean o' your prints and put it in that drawer on the other side o' the bed. You don't want a firearms charge on top o' everything else.'

Meekly, she did as she was told, wiping the gun clean of her fingerprints with a hankie then placing it in the drawer. 'He changed. Really changed in the last few months.'

'How so?' said Scott.

'I dunno. Got in tow wae new people – worse folk than he was already in wae. It was shite, but the bastard wouldnae let it go. He was never here, and when he was, he just acted like an arsehole.'

'I can believe that,' said Scott. 'But who were these new folk, eh?'

She shrugged. 'How should I know? I had nothing to dae with it. All I know is, I had to leave all my family and friends and shift doon here. I hate this place. I don't know why we couldna have just stayed where we were. I was happy back in Easterhouse.'

'Aye, I know – in Glesga, but no'.'

'That's where I'm fae. You cannae beat the countryside. Well, you know what I mean.' She wiped away a tear. 'And the bastard was having an affair.'

'How do you know?'

'I caught the end o' a conversation he was having wae her. Bold as brass, too. Had his phone on loudspeaker. He didnae hear us coming in. They were fighting like fuck anyway. But I caught him.'

'What did she sound like?'

'I wisnae bothered what she sounded like. I just knew he shouldnae have been talking to other women behind my back! You don't have an argument like that wae some lassie unless you're shagging her.' Mitchell calmed herself down again. 'But now you ask, she sounded posh, like.'

Scott found it hard to not to wince at this information. Alasdair Shaw's wife was from a comfortable background and was well spoken into the bargain. The call could have been from her. He didn't enlighten the newly widowed Mrs Mitchell.

'These poor weans. No kid should see their father being dragged oot the hoose and battered. Oh, I'd to pretend it was all a game – he was just playing wae his big mates. But kids are no' stupid, especially Joshua. Shandy and Melody, aye, they maybe believed me. But they were still scared shitless.'

'You've been in here since it happened?'

'Aye, what would you dae?'

'Call the polis, no?'

'Come on, gie me a break.' She started to sob again. 'I hoped he'd come home. Despite everything, I still loved him. I've been stuck in here heating tins o' spaghetti and shit in that microwave. I didnae want the weans to see the kitchen. But Josh had to go in. Too much o' his faither in him.'

Scott had a mixture of emotions. How could this woman live with a man she knew to be rotten to the core? Worse still, how could she subject her children to what was happening? He remembered Jim Daley's warnings about trying to see life through the eyes of others – putting yourself in their place. He settled on that.

'Right, get yourself dressed. You'll need to come doon the station and give a statement. Don't worry about the weans, we'll bring them too. They'll be looked after.'

'Thanks. You're one o' the decent ones – polis, I mean.' She wiped the tears from her face.

Brian Scott left her to get changed and walked back into the hall. Two officers wearing forensic suits had already laid a little plastic walkway down on which those not properly dressed could walk without destroying crime scene evidence. Things moved quickly these days, he thought.

'You didn't leave her in there with the gun, did you?' Potts looked alarmed as he stared between Scott and the bedroom door.

'Nah, she was only bluffing. I didnae see a gun.'

The detective sergeant made his way along the plastic walkway and out into the cold night air. He pictured the wee boy with the cowboy hat and the cap gun and remembered his own son at that age.

'What a world.' Scott shook his head and made for his car.

46

Under a full moon the superyacht's sleek lines looked out of place against the old hills and the big stone houses scattered on the north shore of the loch. A cold wind was gaining strength from the east. It hadn't whipped the waves into white horses yet, but it soon would.

As most of Kinloch lay soundly asleep, very few noticed this new chill from the east. But from the big picture window of his house high on the hill, Jim Daley watched the vessel's progress into the harbour. Despite his thick dressing gown, he shivered. He took another sip at the mug of hot milk in his hand and tried to calm his restless mind.

He knew who was aboard, knew them from the endless files and reports he'd read as he tried desperately to make sense of what was happening. People missing then not missing, his desk sergeant blackmailed by a drug dealer slain while his young family hid in the bedroom of his home. Scott had called to report that he'd found Mrs Mitchell and her children safe and well, if somewhat traumatised. He could be thankful for that, at least.

The yacht was nearing the harbour now. It looked like an object from another world, and in many ways it was. The people who occupied it lived lives of extreme privilege, their wealth cushioning them against life's buffeting. No worries about paying the bills, about keeping a roof over their heads or food in their bellies for them. But, he supposed, they probably had a whole set of cares of which he had no knowledge.

He'd managed two or three hours of sleep due to sheer exhaustion, but the pain in his back wakened him. Try as he might, Dalcy hadn't been able to get back over. He hoped the hot milk would work. He searched in the pocket of his dressing gown and found the little leaf of opiates that were the only thing making his life bearable now. There were only four left. He'd tried to eke them out, but he'd have to take two now and leave what remained for the morning. The doctor had warned him about addiction. He reckoned he might have a problem getting a prescription for more. But how could he function without them? Anti-inflammatory medicine had already been ruled out because of his heart condition. Nobody seemed able to offer a solution apart from swimming and stretching. He resolved to make an appointment to see a specialist, but how long would that take? The whole thing was dragging him down.

He popped the pills out and swallowed them with a gulp of warm milk. He'd give them twenty minutes or so to start working before he tried for more sleep – sleep he desperately needed.

Liz had been acting strangely. She was unhappy about his approach to Alasdair Shaw, who'd confided in her. He was angry with Shaw for involving his wife in this way. But he realised the man was desperate.

This thought brought him back to the 'posh woman' on the phone to Andrew Mitchell that Scott had talked about.

Yes, Shaw's wife was well spoken, and would definitely be considered *posh* by the likes of Nadine Mitchell. He pictured her and her children holed up in a bedroom, not knowing if their husband and father was alive or dead. The trauma of seeing him being dragged from the house by brutal men, the fear they would return.

He felt guilty for having thought that Shaw could have been behind the dealer's murder. There was no way he could have been responsible, of that he was certain now. Though he was still to read Mrs Mitchell's official statement on the matter, the conclusion that this was professionally done, a visceral message sent, was obvious.

He heard James junior cry out in his sleep, and padded out of the lounge into the hall. His son's door was ajar, as always. A dim blue night-light sat on the table by the little boy's bed. James was mumbling to himself in his dreams. His round cheeks were flushed red, his dark hair flopped over his forehead. But though he had his father's hair, he was the image of his mother.

Daley sighed at the thought of his own flesh and blood facing the harsh reality of the world. Things were bad enough now. What on earth did the future hold for the little boy?

He kissed James on the cheek, rinsed the empty mug in the kitchen and returned to his bed in the hope he'd manage another few hours' rest before morning.

Now moored at the New Quay, the cruiser sat alone there apart from the orange and blue lifeboat, which it dwarfed. Crewmen spilled over the side and secured the vessel, while silhouetted figures were busy on the bridge. On the quayside, a large Range Rover had drawn up alongside the yacht. People dashed here and there on deck as the gangway was slowly lowered on to the pier.

In a few minutes, two men, wrapped up against the cold Kinloch night, made their way down the gangway and into the vehicle, which reversed at speed up the quay and took off along the little dual carriageway leading into the town centre.

Nathan Farringdon was worried. He'd dozed for a few hours but was now wide awake. He had asked the police officer at the desk five times in the last couple of hours if there was any news from Delph. Each time, the man had shaken his head. Now he stood in the front office and demanded that the hotel be called, or he would go there himself.

'I'm not sure I can let you do that,' said the harassed duty constable.

'So I'm under arrest. Is that it?'

'No, sir. But you're helping us with our inquiries. And your father still isn't here.'

Nate was exasperated. 'How old are you, constable?'

'Twenty-two. Why do you ask?' The constable looked confused.

'Tell me, do you still do what your father tells you – wait for his permission, I mean?'

'Ha! No, not at all. Me and the auld man don't rub along too well, as it goes. Anyway, I live with my fiancée. We're getting married in the spring.'

'Well, congratulations to you both.' Though Nate sounded sincere, he wasn't. 'I'm twenty-three. Did you know?'

The constable shook his head. 'No, not really. I could have looked it up, I suppose.'

'Now, why would I – at twenty-three years old – have to wait for my father to help me out of here?'

'Right, I see.' The penny had dropped.

'I'll say it again. If you don't phone the hotel, I'll go there myself. Do you understand?'

The constable busied himself with a list of numbers, while Nate drummed his fingers impatiently on the counter.

A buzzer rang behind the desk. The constable stared at a bank of cameras. 'Is this your father, by any chance?' He pointed to one of the screens.

Nate leaned over. Indeed, there was Teddy, wrapped up in a thick scarf and long overcoat. 'Yes, that's him.'

'Good.' The desk officer clicked open the door, and two men walked into Kinloch police office.

47

Though Jim Daley had managed to get back to sleep, it hadn't lasted long. He was rudely awoken by a very harassed constable, who didn't have a clue whether Nathan Farringdon should be permitted to leave Kinloch police office or not.

In the end, Daley decreed that whether the young man removed himself from the office to Brandt's superyacht was his decision, as long as he made himself available for further interview. After all, he was still involved in investigations, and the police needed their witnesses to be within reach.

Fortunately, young Nate was in no hurry to leave the area before his girlfriend was found. She, it was revealed, had failed to return to the County Hotel. As it was now the middle of the night, Nate was understandably worried about her. He wasn't moving an inch until she returned.

Daley resolved the situation by informing the young man he would visit him on the yacht later that morning, and assuring him that every effort would be made to find Delph and ensure her safety.

The detective was reflecting on all of this as he sat amongst a cluster of locals in Kinloch surgery, waiting his turn to see the doctor. Scott was looking into the whereabouts of Delph, as well as keeping an eye on the forensic search at Mitchell's cottage and taking the relevant statements. To make matters infinitely worse, ACC Cunningham was at the office, and he wanted to speak to Daley as soon as he'd seen the doctor.

All in all, it was going to be another hard day. He'd run countless investigations, but this one was so fragmented – unfathomable, almost.

The faces of the main protagonists flashed through his mind again. The Oxford set, Kilvington, Shaw, Mitchell, the head in the box. He shook his head and sighed at the complexity of it all.

'Aye, you've nae troubles to seek, eh?' said the man in the boiler suit sitting next to him.

Daley smiled. 'Part of my job, I'm afraid.'

'It canna be easy. I'm glad I'm a plumber. It's true to say that I find some o' the mair dirty jobs no' quite to my taste. But when you've got your arm doon a U-bend, at least you know fine what you're after.'

'Shite,' said an older woman sitting opposite.

'Nae need to be so coarse, Jackie. I think Mr Daley knows fine what I was meaning.'

'No, I'm saying you're talking shite. I remember you had your arm, not to mention all manner o' rods an' other contraptions, doon oor toilet and you didna find bugger all. Me and Bobby had to go next door to use Mr Paterson's. Aye, and he soon got fed up wae that. We ended up on one o' they camping lavvies.' She addressed Daley. 'You know the ones wae the bit you pull oot to get cleaned?'

'Yes,' said Daley, desperate to be spared the toilet debate but in it nonetheless.

'It did for a wee while. Mind you, there's nothing mair

off-putting than trying to get a handle on *Line of Duty* while your man's busy dropping his load in the chemical toilet in the corner. And all because this one here took two weeks to fix the proper one.'

'Surely you'd just put the chemical toilet in the bathroom,' said the plumber, an expression of deep distaste across his broad face.

Jackie pursed her lips, adopting what could only be described as a superior look. 'It's a bit like having your dinner on your lap when you're watching something good on the telly. Bobby was into the programme, and he didna want to miss any o' it away in the bathroom.'

Even Daley raised a brow at this exceptional televisual solution.

'Was the room no' stinking, Jackie?' said the plumber.

'I opened a window! He didna dae his business on the carpet. He was on the chemical toilet. And in any case, don't blame oor Bobby. If you weren't the worst plumber in the world, he widna have needed to go in his ain living room. Don't gie Mr Daley the idea you've never been flummoxed by your work, because you have.' She crossed her arms purposefully. 'And that's all I have to say on the matter.'

The plumber turned to Daley. 'A convenient convenience, eh?' He laughed at his own joke. 'And there was bugger all I could dae aboot their toilet. The problem was under the street. And that's the council's affair.'

'James Daley, you're next,' called the receptionist.

In the time it took the policeman to leave his chair and head for the doctor's consulting room he heard the argument continue.

'Have yous no' heard of watch-on-demand?'

Daley was grateful he had to play no further part in the discourse.

He was pleased to be seeing Dr Wilson, an older practitioner he felt might be more sympathetic to his plight than some of the younger clinicians. He'd worked with him, most local physicians doubling as duty doctors for the Kinloch police at one time or another.

'Mr Daley – Jim – do take a seat.' The man was in his early sixties, balding, and peering through his half-moon glasses at Daley's records on a computer screen. 'Feeling no better, I take it?'

'No, unfortunately not, doctor,' said Daley.

'Yes, backs can be difficult beasts. Especially at your height – and weight, if you don't mind me saying. My first advice would be to lose a stone. For the sake of your back and your heart.' He stared at Daley over his glasses. 'I think it seems clear that this problem isn't simply going to go away. Let me examine you, please.'

Daley removed his shirt and stood with his back to the doctor, who poked and prodded up and down his spine.

'Nothing to be found here. But you'll need a scan and a proper consultation with a specialist.'

'How soon?'

The doctor was back on his chair typing on his keyboard. 'Now, we don't have anyone down here until April, so it'll have to be a trip up to Glasgow. How does the sixteenth of March sound?'

'What?'

'The earliest appointment there is. I'll put you down for a consultation, but no guarantees, I'm sad to say.'

'It's very painful, doctor. As you know, I can't take anti-inflammatories, so all I have are painkillers.'

'Yes, we must have a little chat about that. I see you were prescribed with twenty of the strong opioids recently. How many do you have left?'

Daley was relieved. At least it looked as though Dr Wilson was willing to write a prescription for some more.

'I can let you have another ten. But after that we must taper them off, you know. We'll have to think of something else.'

'Ten?' Daley felt his heart sink, which surprised him.

'I know a bad back isn't pleasant. But it's nothing like as unpleasant as these things once you begin to depend on them. How many have you been taking a day up until now?'

Daley considered lying, but what was the point? 'Six – eight some days when I can't get to sleep. Because of the pain,' he added hurriedly. But even as he said the words he knew this wasn't the complete truth. Yes, they made his back condition – whatever it was – bearable. But he enjoyed the calming feeling of wellbeing they imparted. It seemed to Daley that he'd been able to relax for the first time in years while taking the medication. It was a feeling he didn't want to lose.

'You should have another appointment to see our physio and the pain management nurse. They'll be able to put together a regime of stretches and exercises – perhaps a TENS machine. I wonder, have you ever tried yoga?'

'No,' said Daley emphatically.

'Worthwhile for anyone with problems like yours. Strengthens the muscles, adds suppleness. You should think about it. In the meantime, only take the pills if you simply can't bear the pain any longer.'

'Can't you give me more of them? Just to see me through until I see a specialist? You know what my job's like, doctor.

I need to be on the ball, fit for the day-to-day stresses and strains. That kind of thing.'

'Ten is all I can do. I'm unwilling to see any more patients going down the road of addiction. Everything has its place, Jim, but we've been over-prescribing this type of medication for far too long.'

Daley stood. 'Great. So why was I given them in the first place?'

'You'll thank me in the long run. Just stop at reception and they'll arrange for you to see the physio and our pain people. Hope things improve, Jim.'

Daley left the doctor's office with his prescription. He couldn't help but feel let down. There was no doubt he had a very real problem with his back. He'd never given waiting lists on the NHS much thought. But now it seemed that anyone unfortunate enough to fall ill would be condemned to months of agony before they would even get to see a consultant.

Nagging at the back of his mind, though, was the thought of trying to make it through the day without his pills.

'No, go if you want, please. But I'm staying here until she turns up.' Nate faced his father in one of the private cabins of the yacht.

'I swear, I don't know what you see in that girl. How do you know she's not buggered off with some other chap? Trust me, it happens all the time. I know you think you have everything going for you – money, good looks, a decent education – but there's no fathoming the female mind. I can tell you that from experience.'

'Oh, yes. Your wide experience of treating Mum like shit. Good one, Teddy.' Nate's face was red with anger.

'Listen, we can be back home by this afternoon. You spend a couple of days getting over this trauma, then we'll go somewhere hot. You'll like that. I could do with a break, that's for sure.'

'Wait, I want to understand you. You're suggesting that I pack my bags and take off on holiday, not just without Delph, but also not even knowing where she is or what's happened to her?'

'Yes, that's the kind of thing, Nathan. It's time to stop mooning about like a lovesick teenager.'

'Well, you can bugger off! In fact, I'm not spending another minute on this ridiculous pleasure palace. I've had it with you – and with Brandt. Did you know I saw Salz earlier? He looks like shit. But he's still frightened to say anything against his father. How on earth did you get involved with this man?'

'Lower your voice.' Teddy spoke quietly, slowly, for emphasis. 'Werner has been very generous with his time and the resources at his disposal.'

'This big fucking yacht, you mean?'

Teddy was standing by the large window that looked out over the harbour. He was trying to keep his patience, but his son was pushing him to the limit. 'Tell me, Nathan. How do you judge yourself? I mean, your prospects, your talents – your place in the world. How do you think that's all going?'

'What are you talking about?'

'You depend on me for everything. Do you really think you'd have made it to Oxford if I hadn't crossed some – too many – palms with silver? Do you really think you're clever enough?'

'I passed the interview. Grades aren't everything when it comes to Oxbridge. They talent-spot. Everyone knows that.'

Suddenly, Nate felt unsure of himself. Coming from the school he'd attended, getting into Oxford or Cambridge was expected, like night following day. Yes, there were some dropouts, idiots who wanted to travel the world on a mountain bike or do good works in the middle of war zones. But they were the exceptions.

Teddy smiled at him, but there was no warmth in it. 'You have no idea the money I spent to get you into that bloody college. You were so far behind in the admissions process that you might not have ended up at any university at all. Solid Cs aren't the making of a great mind. And, yes, you will graduate with a mediocre degree, and my influence will help you into a job as one of these pathetic political advisers or suchlike. Snotty-nosed little rich kids who don't know their collective arses from their elbows. Or maybe a newspaper or the broadcast media? How does that sound?' He swung round, and in a flash gripped the collar of Nate's shirt. 'None of it happens without me. You'll be a nothing. A little prick with no wit or purpose. So get this fucking girl off your mind and try to live up to the large pile of cash I've spent on you while you still have the chance!'

Nate pushed his father away. Without a word, he turned on his heel and left the cabin.

48

Mr and Mrs Hunter were walking their two terriers by the loch. Though it had been a relatively dry night, a cold east wind enveloped Kinloch in an icy embrace. Indeed, there were flurries of snow in the air, fluttering down from the ominous sky.

The couple shivered as they made their way down the little path that led from the road to the foreshore. Mr Hunter let the little dogs off their leads, and they snuffled and pawed at the stony shore, well used to their surroundings.

Across the choppy waters sat the local graveyard, a great monument to Kinloch's dead. Being a certain age, Tommy Hunter stared at it, wondering when it would become his new home. As was his almost daily habit, he wiped away a tear at the thought of those he'd known so well who now lay there at rest. He pictured his parents, sitting happily at a Christmas dinner when he was a boy. His elder brother, who lost his life on a capsized fishing boat, was as plain in his mind's eye as though he stood before him that very moment, with his thick shock of red hair and his big smile. But his parents had been gone for almost fifty years, his brother more than thirty.

'Are you getting maudlin again, Tommy?' said Betty. 'We're going to have to take oor afternoon walk elsewhere if this is going to be your caper from now on.'

'I don't know how you keep so detached fae it all, Betty. I've been in the glums since I turned fifty. Aye, and it gets worse every year.'

'I prefer to enjoy life while I've got it, no' worry aboot when it's going.' She loosened a pebble with the toe of her boot and sent it trundling into the loch.

'You're right, I know that.' But despite his words, Tommy Hunter saw old age as one endless passage to eternity. His life these days seemed all about sad nostalgia for the past, or fear of an unknown future. He found it hard to experience joy in the present. What was joy, anyway? He wasn't sure he'd ever known. Yes, he'd had happy times – lots of them. But joy should surely be a less ephemeral affair than a passing state of mind. He knew people who exuded joy, who found something new and magical in every day. He'd always wanted to be like that but knew it just wasn't the way he was – the way reality was.

'It's your mother's fault, all this misery. She was forever lamenting the past and a' the folk she outlived. Miserable old soul, so she was.'

'She was no such thing. You've never had a good word for my poor auld mother. Man, she was an improvement on that battle-axe o' yours, and that's a fact.'

Betty Hunter had known that a mere mention of her husband's late mother and her well-known melancholy would be enough to rouse Tommy from his torpor. And so it proved.

'She'd a lot to put up wae, let me tell you. I loved my faither dearly, but he could be a right thrawn bugger. Tight wae money, too . . .' But before Tommy could launch into his father's merits and demerits, one of the terriers started to bark, followed immediately by the other. 'Sheena, Kyle, that's enough! Come here this minute!' But the little dogs, normally obedient to a point, refused to stop.

'I think they're barking at something in the water, Tommy.' Betty walked towards the loch and narrowed her eyes. 'Aye, look, there's something yellow oot there.'

About six metres off the shore, something bright, an almost luminous yellow, was floating. And though Tommy put the leads back on both dogs, they were reluctant to be pulled away from the sight and smell of it.

'I hope it's no' a body,' wailed Betty.

'Nah, there's nae body there. It looks like a jacket, likely fell off a boat or something. The tide's pushing it to shore. Here, gie me o'er your stick and I'll pull the thing in once it gets close enough.' Tommy turned to his dogs. 'At least it'll show you two there's nothing to be barking at. I know what you're like, you'll be whining all night if yous canna work it oot.'

In a few moments, the yellow object was close enough to the shore for Tommy to stand on the pebbles near the water's edge, lean over and hook it with the handle of the walking stick. With the dogs reaching a veritable frenzy, he pulled it towards him. A sharp tug, and the garment was out, dripping from its soaking in the loch.

'See, there you are. Just an old jacket, nothing to be feart of.' He brandished the sodden garment before the terriers.

Betty screamed.

'Don't you start. What's the matter?'

'Look!' She pointed to the jacket. 'Turn it round and you'll see.' She sounded distressed.

Tommy did as he was told, swinging the front of the object towards him on the walking stick. The little dogs backed away, Kyle whining, his ears flat against his head. The front of the yellow coat, despite its dousing in the waters of the loch, was slathered in crimson blood. Tommy could see slits in the fabric. It took him a few seconds to realise that they had most likely been left behind by thrusts of a knife, repetitive thrusts, leaving the garment almost in tatters.

'Betty, get that mobile o' yours oot and phone the polis. Quickly!'

Daley arrived in the office in less than good humour. On his way from the surgery, he'd been trying to work out for how long he'd manage to eke out ten tablets to stave off the pain he was already feeling in his back, only a couple of hours since he'd taken the last dose.

'Sir,' said Constable Cummins at the front desk. 'The ACC is here. He's in the boss's office, sir.'

Ever since Daley arrived at Kinloch he'd eschewed the sub-divisional commander's office, once occupied by his wretched predecessor Inspector MacLeod. He preferred the familiarity of the CID suite and his glass box. Inevitably, any visiting officer of rank gravitated towards the other.

'What's he doing?' said Daley.

'He was on the phone the last time I looked.' Cummins checked the internal switchboard. 'He's still on the line, sir.'

'Good,' said Daley, ready to make for his own office and delay his meeting with the ACC until after he'd consumed at least one strong cup of coffee.

'Another couple of things, sir. DS Scott says he'll be back soon from the Mitchell residence, and an inspector from

Suffolk Constabulary left a message for you to call him back.' Cummins passed Daley an official memo sheet with the caller's name and number written in clear, bold letters.

'Thank you, constable. Keep this up and there might a full-time job for you.' He made his way quickly through the corridors of the police office in case ACC Cunningham finished his call and cut him off before he could reach his own domain.

To his relief, he made it to the CID suite without any unfortunate encounter. He grabbed a coffee from the machine, kicked open the door to his glass box, dumped his briefcase, placed the paper cup on his desk and prepared to face yet another difficult day. Sitting in his big swivel chair, he took a sip of coffee, grimaced at the bitter taste, then picked up the memo sheet.

Call Inspector Uxley, Suffolk Constabulary. Daley did just that and waited as the dialling tone sounded in his ear.

'Uxley.' The call was answered sharply and efficiently.

'DCI Daley – Jim – from Kinloch police. Thanks for contacting me, DI Uxley.'

'Ah, good man. Give me a couple of seconds, please.'

Daley heard the call muffle. True to his word, the inspector was soon back on the call.

'Sorry, DCI Daley. We're breaking in a new cleaning contractor. It's been absolute chaos here.'

'Nobody knows the perils we face every day.'

Uxley chuckled. 'Now, you wanted to speak about the caravan case – Emily Kilvington.'

'Yes, please. It would be very helpful with something I'm currently up to my neck in.'

'I don't envy you. I remember Emily – when she was herself,' he added, a note of sadness in his voice.

'Yes, she's been through the mill by the look of things.'

'Of that there's no doubt, Jim. I'm Ron, by the way. I remember that day as though it was yesterday. Bloody hot it was. I was in the control room in Skeggy – Skegness – when the call came in. At first, we thought it was a joke – you know, little girl calling to say she and her brother had killed their father. But it was no bloody joke, as you know.'

'I don't quite understand why Kilvington managed to get attacked herself. Surely she wasn't alone with them?'

'Ah, now that's where things get tricky. One of our senior cops was first on the scene with his partner, Terry Dalton. He's retired now – you know the type, old-school, called a spade a spade, wasn't averse to breaking the odd rule here and there. But a sound copper, if you know what I mean.'

'Oh yes,' said Daley emphatically. 'I know the type very well.'

'Anyhow, when Emily arrived, she dismissed them – wanted to speak to the kids on her own. You know, to try and gain their trust.'

'It came back to bite her, clearly.'

'It did that. She lost a lot of sympathy because of it, too. You know what this job can be like, Jim.'

'Definitely.' He paused. 'The kids, what were they like?'

'I think they'd had a hard time right enough when their mother died. By all accounts, their father – George Broughton – was a real bastard. He was a cop in Manchester. We put together some background reports on him. Not a nice man, by all accounts.'

'Not Happy Families.'

'Most certainly not. The whole thing was a tragedy. As for the kids – well, they were odd. In my opinion, of course.'

'I suppose stabbing your father to death indicates you might be a bit unstable.'

'You said it. When I heard your message, I looked out the psychologist's report on both of them.' Daley heard a knocking noise and rustling pages. 'Here it is. The boy, Samuel – Sam – he wasn't very bright. In fact, they reckoned he was educationally sub-normal. Their words, not mine. He was a big lad – strong, you know? But he didn't have much about him. I remember seeing him when they brought them in.'

'And the girl?'

'Charlotte, though she preferred to be called Charlie, now I think about it. Her report was very different. It says here: *Bright, and well above average intelligence for her age.* She had a personality disorder – they don't come to a definitive conclusion in this report, but it was likely sociopathy, narcissism, that kind of thing. You'll probably need to go into later evaluations to find out. But she was the one who stabbed Emily – made a right job of it too.'

'Did you come into contact with her?'

'Saw her in passing in the office. I was just a constable then. Just passed my promotion exams. But something did strike me about them both.'

'What?'

'The boy looked scared. I suppose that's natural, given what had just happened.'

'But?'

'But she was bold, unrepentant. I was standing on the door when she was being interviewed. When they told her Emily was fighting for her life she laughed. Not just normal laughter – manic. You know what I mean?'

'What happened next?'

'Both children were placed in secure care. It took time for them to organise a hearing, because of their age. By the time it happened, Emily was fit enough to give evidence. Charlotte just stared at her, never said a word the whole way through, just stared. It shook me up a bit, to be honest. No remorse, no tears, no sense of guilt, nothing. For someone so young it was scary.'

'What was the result?'

'Sam was sent to a juvenile offenders' unit. Charlotte was put in a secure home – because of her age and the state of her mental health. I never heard what happened after that. Just watched my colleague try to come back to work, fail . . . well, you know how it ends up, Jim.'

'It's really sad – tragic, as you say.'

'Yeah. I hear Emily is in a bad way. What happened?'

'Attacked in her own home – stabbed.'

'I see. I know you'll be thinking what I'm thinking, then?'

'Yes. What happened to Charlotte Broughton?'

'I can tell you a bit, but not much. The home she was sent to was somewhere in Cheshire, I think. I can find more details for you. Separated from the brother, I know that. They'd had a big fall-out for some reason. Give me a few hours. I'll make some calls.'

'Very kind of you, Ron. I appreciate it, really I do.'

'We've got to stick together in this job. Especially these days. Don't know what it's like with you, but more brass than coppers down here.'

At that very moment, the stern figure of ACC Cunningham appeared at the glass door. Daley signalled for him to come in and take a seat.

'Do me a favour, if you will, Jim.'

'Yeah, surely. What can I do?'

'If Emily pulls through, please tell her I was asking for her. I liked the woman. Something like that could happen to any one of us, eh?'

'Very true,' said Daley. It was a sobering thought. He ended the call and made his apologies to Cunningham.

'Who was that?' snapped the ACC.

'A DI from Skegness. I'm looking into what happened to Emily Kilvington when she was a police officer, sir. In the light of recent events, of course.'

'I see. Well, you needn't worry about any of that. I'm taking charge of the whole case.'

'By whole case, what do you mean, sir?'

'I know you can't sail a boat, Daley. But I thought you at least had a minimal grasp of the English language. By whole case, I mean just that. The kidnapping, the Brandt boy, the decapitated head, Mitchell your drug dealer – everything. I want you to get everything you have together and hand it to DCI Birkenshaw. He's heading up my Major Investigation Team – do you know him?'

'No. Should I?'

'Bright young man, straight out of the Met. Thirty-five. Headed for big things, let me tell you. I might even have to look to my own laurels.' Cunningham's face was transformed by a sickly, insincere smile.

'Good luck to him. So, what do you want me to do?'

'Whatever you and Brian Scott do down here every day.' Cunningham was about to say more when the door swung open, revealing DC Potts.

'Apologies, sir – sirs.' He nodded to Cunningham shyly. 'Something you should be aware of, chief inspector.'

Cunningham raised his brows. 'Well, I'll let you get on with it, Daley. Birkenshaw will want everything you've managed to piece together by close of play.' He stood, and unceremoniously ignored Potts as he swept out of Daley's glass box.

'Come in, DC Potts. What is it?'

Potts explained the circumstances behind the Hunters' discovery of the bloodied jacket.

'Where is it now?' Daley asked.

'Sir, DS Scott is looking at it at the locus. I redirected him when you were busy with the ACC.'

'What size is it? I mean, is it designed for a man or a woman?'

Potts consulted his notes. 'Small size, I think, sir.'

Daley dismissed him and called Scott on his mobile.

'Aye, Jimmy. You know aboot this jacket, aye?'

'I do. What are your impressions?'

'I dae a no' bad Jimmy Cagney, but otherwise I'd say if this isn't blood, I'm a fish. But I've just got here.'

'And it's punctured, Potts says.'

'Aye, good an' proper, too.'

'What's it like? I mean, a zip-up, a fleece, a rain jacket?'

'One o' they posh jobs, Jimmy, no' a Primark special. The ones that cost about four hundred quid.'

'Send me a pic of it, will you, please? Oh, and keep this to yourself, Brian. Especially if you come across a DCI Birkenshaw.'

'Been there, done that.'

'Eh?'

'He was at the Mitchell hoose. In charge o' Cunningham's MIT.'

'What's he like?'

322

'He's a prick. Will that do?'

Daley asked Scott to meet him at the quay in half an hour. He still needed to speak to Nate Farringdon. But he wanted to stop at the County first, though he hoped his first instincts were entirely wrong.

49

Daley shivered as he paced down Main Street. With every jarring step, his back throbbed with pain. But what could he do?

Tiny flakes of snow showed bright white against the red sandstone building as he turned into the familiar doorway of the County Hotel. As he made his way through the lobby, the enticing waft of bacon, eggs and coffee made him salivate. Maybe later, he thought.

Though he didn't have much time to chat, he was pleased to see Hamish at the bar. It was too early for alcohol, so he was nursing a large mug of tea, sitting at his usual table.

'You're up and about early, Hamish.'

'I'll have you know that despite retirement I'm still up wae the lark every morning – while most folk are still abed, you included, I'll wager. I just find myself in the toon a wee bit earlier than normal today. A business matter.'

'Right, I see.' Daley looked round the bar. 'Is Ella about?'

'The last time I saw her she was making heavy weather o' it wae four plates o' bacon and eggs. She's at the waitressing when she comes in every morning. Man, I remember this place when it employed half the toon.' Hamish took a contemplative slurp of tea. 'A lot o' them didna dae much, mind you. But it was considered a duty to the community, keeping folk in work. Aye, and folk were grateful, so made sure they made use o' the place in return.'

'Changed days, Hamish. It's the same everywhere.'

'I daresay you're right. But the passing o' decency and doing the right thing is much lamented. At least in my book it is.'

The door behind the bar swung open, revealing a tired and careworn Ella.

'Jimmy, how are you today? I swear, if I lay eyes on another full Scottish breakfast I'll scream.'

'Like that, eh?'

'Aye, just like that. Where's Tweedledummer?'

'I'm just going to meet him. I popped in to see if you could help me, actually. It'll only take a second.'

At the table, Hamish raised his brow in suspicion, and cocked his ear in the direction of the conversation.

'I need a smoke. Whatever it is, can we do it oot the back?'

'No problem, Ella.'

She ducked under the hatch, and the big detective followed her out of the bar and along the corridor, through a door, down some stone steps and out into the car park at the rear of the hotel. She fished a packet of cigarettes from her pocket, lit one, and drew on it with evident pleasure. 'Now, how can I help you? Mind, if you're here to drag me away fae all this and set up on oor ain wee island, I'll go get my bag packed.'

'Island? I just want to go back to bed.'

'Now you're talking, Jimmy. I knew you were a man o' action rather than words.' Ella winked at him.

'I need you to look at this for me, if you don't mind.'

'What?'

Daley took his phone from a pocket and pulled up an image. He held the phone out in front of Ella. 'Did you notice if Delph the student was wearing something like this?'

Ella stared at the image. 'Aye, I did. And I can tell you where she bought it, too.'

'You can?'

'Hall's at the bottom o' the street. She arrived with it in a bag when she checked in. You know this place, nosy as they come. The receptionist asked her what it was. She telt her that her last jacket got ruined, so she just went an' bought a new one. The receptionist was telling me when I came in. Here, you know she didnae come back last night, don't you?'

'Yes, I do.' Daley put the phone back in his pocket.

'Are you saying that's the same jacket? It's in some state in that photo, Jimmy.'

'It is. Keep this to yourself, Ella – you know.'

Ella put one hand over her mouth. 'You know, sometimes I don't wonder that my Brian drank like a parched camel. The things yous have to cope with. It's enough to drive anyone to the booze. I hope she's okay, Jimmy.'

'Me too.' Daley checked his watch. 'I'd better be off, or I'll be late meeting your nearest and dearest, and that would never do.'

'Tell him it's sausages and mash for his tea. If he doesnae like it, tough.' She finished her cigarette, wished Daley good luck, and returned to her bacon and eggs.

Daley hurried off, appreciating the fresh air. He spent too much time in stuffy offices. It was good to be out and about, though at the same time his heart was heavy. He'd only shown Ella the back of the jacket, not the bloodied, ruined front. He pictured the bright young woman as he turned back into Main Street, heading towards the harbour.

'Find one, lose another,' he muttered to himself as his back twinged yet again.

From across the street Amy McKay and Flo MacMurchy followed his progress.

'Do you know, that man's aged since he came here. Walking like an old man, so he is,' said Flo.

'Aye, and she looks younger every day – the wife, I mean,' replied Amy.

'No' a happy marriage. It just shows you, beauty's no' everything.'

Amy nodded, observing a hair growing from a mole on her friend's face. 'Mind you, you widna mind a shot at it, eh?'

A flurry of snowflakes spattered against the young woman's face as she sat on the bench cooing into a small pram. So swaddled was the child, any passer-by would only have seen a huddle of blankets.

She stared into the oily grey waters of the loch. Two swans floated past gracefully, seemingly untroubled by the snow. She watched them as they headed to the lee of the New Quay where sat the sleek superyacht. Passing her hand over her ample belly, she wondered what was happening inside: what fine food was on offer, what wine, beer – luxury. Two crewmen passed her on the promenade, chatting excitedly in foreign accents. They were tanned and well dressed. She pondered on the inequity of the world.

She heard footsteps, and to her right saw an older woman marching towards her along the path.

'It's a cold one,' the newcomer said, her hands thrust deep into the pockets of a thick sheepskin jacket. 'I hope the wee one's wrapped up well.' She smiled.

'Of course she is! What kind of mother do you think I am?' The young woman made no attempt to hide her irritation at the remark.

'Very sorry, I'm sure.' The passer-by hurried on.

The young woman pushed the pram back and forth, apparently soothing the infant following the impertinence of a complete stranger. Why people could never see fit to mind their own business she didn't know, but that was the way it was.

Looking back towards the town, she noticed a large man with dark hair hurrying along the promenade. Every now and again, he grimaced as though in pain. A car door opened, and another man got out. They exchanged a few words, then made their way to the head of the quay, disappearing behind some buildings, then re-emerging at the bottom of the gangway which led up to the yacht.

She got to her feet, wiped some loose crips she'd enjoyed from her old pink anorak, leaned into the pram and cooed again at the huddle inside. Unable to take her eyes from the superyacht, she continued her walk back into Kinloch, head nestled in her deep hood against the snow and wind.

Daley and Scott took in the yacht from the quayside.

'Bigger than the *Waverley*, I'd say, Jimmy,' said Scott as he ran his gaze along the length of the vessel.

'Are you kidding?'

'No, why would I be kidding?'

'It's much bigger than the *Waverley*. Anyway, it's like comparing an old Rolls-Royce to a supercar. The *Waverley* is for a leisurely sail down the Clyde. This thing – well, it feels as though you could take off in it.'

'That doesnae sum up the *Waverley* to me. I've only ever got pished on it.'

Daley looked to the heavens as they approached the gangway.

Before they could make the climb, however, three figures appeared above, clearly intent on heading down to the pier. This they did, two burly men in dark suits fore and aft of Werner Brandt, who was wearing a long dark overcoat.

'The local constabulary. Well, better late than never, I suppose. But sadly too late for my son, who will be disfigured for the rest of his life.' Brandt was on the quayside now, beside Daley and Scott, his bodyguards stepping back from the conversation.

'Mr Brandt, we have reason to believe that the man who attacked your son was murdered. I hoped we could speak to you about it – when it's convenient, of course.'

Brandt put one forefinger to his lips in mock puzzlement. 'Why on earth would you want to talk to me about the murder of scum like that? I just wish someone had had the good sense to kill him earlier. Maybe then Salazar wouldn't have to spend the rest of his life minus fingers. I find it quite incredible that men like that can flourish in a community like this. I shall have words with the Chief Constable.'

Undaunted, Daley continued. 'Do you have time to talk about this now?'

Brandt smiled mirthlessly. 'Does it look as though I do? And as I said, I cannot see any reason why you'd wish to speak to me about the death of a local criminal you singularly failed to bring to justice.' He clicked his fingers. 'Card, please.' One of his assistants stepped forward brandishing a business card. He passed it to Brandt, who in turn gave it to Daley. 'My lawyer. If you have further questions for myself or my son,

I suggest you call him first. Now, does that conclude your business at my vessel?'

Daley took the card and read it: by the looks of things an exclusive, expensive lawyer based in London of whom he hadn't heard. 'Thank you, Mr Brandt. Please tell him to expect a call soon.'

Brandt nodded, but before he could walk off Daley went on, 'I need to speak to Nathan and Teddy Farringdon. I believe they've been staying with you onboard?'

'They have indeed.' He looked at the loch, then back at the detectives. 'Is this absolutely necessary? I mean, both father and son have been through so much – we all have. It feels, DCI Daley, as though you are spending more time harassing victims than catching criminals. But if you must.' He held his hand out towards the gangway. 'Ask any member of my crew and they'll take you to them. Now I must be about my business, if you'll excuse me.'

Daley watched him step into a black Range Rover. The exchange had been polite enough, however critical of the way he did his job. But the detective had sensed unadulterated malice in the man. It was easy to believe that this stemmed from what had happened to his son. But Daley felt there was something else at play. That the late dealer was responsible for the mutilation of Salazar Brandt was mere conjecture. He was the prime suspect, but they'd had no time to establish the identity of the true perpetrator.

'Are we going up here or no'?' said Scott. 'I'm freezing, and I'll bet my last shilling they've got a cracking cup o' coffee on this thing.'

Daley and Scott made their way up the gangway.

50

DC Potts was typing up a report when a tall man in an expensive suit appeared at his side in the CID suite. He was in his late thirties, as straight and smart as a guardsman.

'Potter, isn't it?' he said in a cut-glass accent.

'Potts, sir.'

DCI Birkenshaw inclined his head in acknowledgement of his mistake. 'Well, Potts, I had hoped to speak to your DCI Daley, but I was told at the front desk he's not in the office and I should speak to you. Tell me, is that whatshis-name about?'

'Sir?'

'The one who sounds as though he's speaking a foreign language.'

'That'll be DS Scott, sir.'

'Yes, that's the man. Met him at the Mitchell residence. Anyhow, where is he?'

'With DCI Daley, sir.'

'They can't be far away. What are they up to?'

'I have no idea, sir,' said Potts, lying his head off. He was well aware that Daley and Scott were interviewing Nate Farringdon on the yacht.

'I see. Well, I'd like to wait for them.' Birkenshaw looked round the CID suite. 'Not in here, though.'

'The family room is quite comfortable, sir. There's a telly in it.'

'The family room? Who do you think I am, the father of some errant teenager? Don't be ridiculous. What about there? Looks like the boss's office.' He pointed to Daley's glass box.

'I'm not sure DCI Daley would be happy about that, sir. I mean, it is his office.'

Birkenshaw fixed Potts with a glare. 'I'll be talking to ACC Cunningham shortly. I'm sure he'll think it absolutely fine that I'm where I should be. After all, I'm taking charge of these investigations. Need somewhere to bloody well sit.'

He strode across to Daley's office, tried the door, which was unlocked, and disappeared inside.

Potts bit his lip, not really knowing what to do. His sense of unease increased when, one by one, the blinds inside the glass box were closed, and he decided his best course of action would be to call the sub-divisional commander and alert him to this incursion. But just as he picked up the phone Birkenshaw's head appeared round the glass door.

'Be a good chap and grab me a cup of coffee, would you? Black, no sugar.' He noticed Potts, frozen like a statue, with the phone in one hand. 'And please, if you're about to call DCI Daley to tell him I'm here, don't. I'm sure he's very busy. That's an order,' he added absently.

Beaten, all Potts could do was get on with his work and hope he wouldn't be hauled over the coals for allowing such a breach of his boss's privacy.

Now inside, and with no prying eyes, Birkenshaw did

exactly what ACC Cunningham had ordered him to. One by one, he pulled open each drawer in Daley's desk. He flicked through the papers he found in the first but found them to have no relevance to recent events. They were mainly in reference to a past case involving the late police officer DS Dhar. Though he'd heard about this, and had a passing interest in it, it wasn't why he was here.

In the drawer below he found the transcripts of an interview with Emily Kilvington. He had begun to read them with great interest when a knock sounded on the glass door. 'Come!' he shouted.

Potts appeared with a mug of black coffee and placed it on a coaster beside him.

'Found something to read?' he asked rather timidly.

Birkenshaw looked him up and down. 'You seem inordinately interested in finding out what I'm doing, Potter. Thanks for the coffee. Now bugger off, there's a good chap.' He waited until the door had closed behind the DC, then turned back to the transcript. He had to admit the questioning was thorough enough, if somewhat stilted at times – especially where the baleful Scott was concerned.

Meaning to carry on his search of Daley's desk, he turned the transcript over, ready to place it face down in the drawer as he'd found it. He wasn't sure how he'd missed it when he'd first picked up the document – probably too keen to read its contents – but scribbled on the back in pencil he noticed a mobile number, beside a short note that read *Lincolnshire Constabulary – Kilvington*.

Though he was relatively new to the case, Birkenshaw had absorbed enough to know that the unfortunate Kilvington had been injured while working as a police officer in Skegness.

He found his mobile phone in his pocket and dialled the number.

Brian Scott was sitting on an extremely comfortable couch examining a spherical ornament he'd found amongst others on the table beside him. He held it up to the light, turning it around in his hand, seemingly captivated by the piece. The stern cabin of the superyacht was magnificent. Huge windows from floor to ceiling looked out across Kinloch. The experience was rather like looking at the place on a large cinema screen, but the scene was most definitely real.

'What would you say that's made o', Jimmy?' said Scott, still intrigued by the little sphere.

Daley, who had been stretching his back beside one of the full-length windows, went to investigate. Scott threw it to him. After a fumble his boss caught it.

'Cold to the touch, light green. I'd say it's jade, Brian.'

'Right. I might have known you'd have a handle on it.'

Daley returned the ornament, and Scott continued his perusal of it. 'You seem impressed. I'd never have had you down as an admirer of this kind of stuff, Bri.'

'See, you don't know everything. It reminds me o' this marble ashtray my cousin Billy half-inched fae Gleneagles. Fabulous thing. Massive – I don't know how the fuck he managed to steal it. Man, I wanted that ashtray.'

'You have a big marble ashtray on that coffee table in your lounge,' said Daley. 'Couldn't resist buying one for yourself, eh?'

'No. That's the one I'm talking aboot.'

'Did he just give it to you?'

'Billy, are you kidding? He wouldnae gie you a cold if he

could help it. He's a miserable bastard. Dae you know, he goes roon all his friends and gets they wee bits o' soap that are left o'er? Melts them together and uses them in his ain hoose. Hey, doesnae sound hygienic to me. When we go roon there, I always tell Ella to bring some of oor ain soap.' Scott nodded grimly in order to underline just how seriously he took the matter.

'Wait. So, this Billy wouldn't piss on you if you were on fire, yet hands over this big marble ashtray. An ashtray, I may add, that he *stole* from a hotel.'

'That's just it, big man. He was showing it off like the cock o' the north, you know. I just telt him I was going to arrest him for stealing it, but if he gave me the thing, I'd make sure it got back to the hotel, no questions asked.' Scott smiled, still pleased with himself.

For a moment or two, Daley tried to calculate the number of offences that were involved in Brian Scott's possession of the marble ashtray from Gleneagles, but gave up at theft, reset and any number of internal disciplinary breaches. In any case, Teddy Farringdon and his son Nate appeared in the cabin just then, the latter looking utterly miserable, and the subject was dropped.

Scott eyed them both with a critical eye. 'Better digs than Semple's Hotel, eh?'

'Just a bit,' said Teddy. 'Trust Werner to have access to this bloody thing. Fabulous, isn't she?'

'She is that,' said Scott.

Daley knew his old colleague so well, he realised he was poised to ask another question. Something forensic, likely to get to the nub of what was going on. Scott was a master at putting people at their ease before moving in for the coup de grâce, so he was happy to let him continue.

Scott nodded, his expression grave. 'See this.' He held up the little ball of jade. 'What dae you think it's worth, eh?'

Daley sighed, while Teddy looked rather nonplussed. Nate, on the other hand, had a very different reaction.

'Oh, for fuck's sake! Delph is missing and all you want to know is the price of some ridiculous bauble from this floating expression of bad taste. Come on!'

'We have people looking for her now, sir,' said Daley. 'I can assure you of that.'

'Maybe tell your sergeant, then.' The young man's face was a mix of righteous indignation and trepidation. Clearly, Delph's whereabouts were of great concern. Daley's opinion of him changed. He'd initially considered him a rather arrogant, vacuous young man; yet again, it showed just how wrong first impressions could be. Though by the look on Farringdon senior's face, he didn't have the same concern for the missing student.

'Steady on, Nathan. I'm sure the officers are doing all they can. You're back safe and well, aren't you?'

'I rescued myself, Teddy. It had nothing to do with them.'

Teddy turned to Daley. 'I'm sorry about this, chief inspector. He's been under a lot of strain, as you know. It's not been an easy time – I'm sure you appreciate that.'

'I do. Please sit down. I'd like to speak to you, Nate.'

While Teddy sat lounging on one of the long leather sofas, his son positioned himself at the edge, working away with his hands as he stared between the two police officers. 'I need to know where she is. Please, I'm beside myself.'

'Did you know she had a male caller to her room?' Scott had divested himself of the ornament and decided to take part in the conversation proper. He was – as ever – the battering ram.

'Who was it?' said Nate.

'We were hoping you'd know, son. Big guy, thickset. Went to her room at the County Hotel – was there for quite a while, according to our witnesses.'

'Not somebody from the university party?'

'No, we don't think so,' said Scott. 'This guy had a friend. If we're right, the pair o' them had drinks in the bar when your lassie was in there. Rough-looking guys. You know, no' the kind that would be at Oxford.'

'And there we have it. Just as I predicted, Nathan. Nothing but trash. First sign of another man and she's in bed with him. I told you, you're wasting your time with this girl. Just forget all about her and let's go home.'

Nate ignored his father. 'Do you think this guy had something to do with her disappearance, DCI Daley?'

'That's the six-million-dollar question. We hoped you might have some idea. We're looking for these men, obviously. We have some images screen-grabbed from the hotel's CCTV.' Daley, with no little difficulty, got to his feet, pulling his phone from his pocket. 'Take a look. We think the man on the right of this picture was the one who visited Delph in her room.'

Nate took the phone and stared at the images. 'I have absolutely no idea who these people are. None whatsoever.' He handed the phone back to Daley with a bewildered look.

'If we don't find her soon, we'll have to contact her family. We could explain away her absence overnight by way of her search for you. But now she hasn't returned we are becoming concerned, I must be honest. Do you have their contact details?' Daley refrained from mentioning the bloody jacket that had been found in the loch. It was being tested for DNA, samples of which had been taken from Delph's hotel room. As it stood, though he suspected that the jacket did belong to her, he didn't want to tell anyone – not until he was certain.

'You'll think this a bit strange, but I've never met Delph's family.' Nate blushed. 'They're a bit staid – you know, old-fashioned. I don't think they'd have approved of our relationship. Delph's had quite a sheltered upbringing.'

'You don't even have an address?'

'Oh . . . I do, as it happens.' He thumbed down the screen of his phone. 'I was going to surprise her during the last holidays. This is her address in Wiltshire. I'm ashamed to say I took it from her phone when she wasn't looking. I'm not sure she wanted me to have it.'

'But you didn't visit?'

'No, as it turned out. She arrived at our house instead.'

'Yes, delightful,' said Teddy sarcastically.

'Give it a break, Teddy. I'm getting sick of your little digs.'

Daley handed Nate's phone to Scott, who noted down the address and passed it back to the student.

'But you're going to hang around until we find her?' As Daley said the words, he felt rather ashamed. After all, he had reason to believe that Delph could well be in serious trouble.

'Yes, absolutely. I'm not going anywhere until she's back safe. In fact, I'd like to help with the search if that's okay?'

Scott shot Daley a cautionary look that only the other detective would have noticed. Having known each other for so long, theirs was an uncanny relationship, both men likely to think roughly along the same lines at the same time – on most things, that was.

'I appreciate that, Nathan, I really do. But we like to keep these things in-house as long as we can. I'm sure there's nothing to worry about.' Daley felt bad about the deceit. But if something had happened to the girl, he had to rule out both father and son as her possible attackers. He turned to Teddy. 'It seems fair to say you don't have much time for the young lady, sir.'

'Listen, I don't wish her any harm – quite the opposite. But I don't really want my son being involved with a family like that. I've always thought they sounded quite odd.' He turned to Nate. 'I'm sorry, but it's true.' Nathan said nothing, so he turned back to Daley. 'However, as Nathan wishes to stay here in Kinloch until she's found, then I must support him.'

'Please! I'm old enough to look after myself.'

'Really? Were you telling yourself that when you were locked in the sheep shed?'

Noting the less than cordial atmosphere between father and son, Daley decided they'd got as much from the Farringdons as they were likely to. He stood, ready to bring their brief encounter to an end. He was dreading the time he'd have to come back and tell Nate what he feared, but now his duty lay with Delph's parents. Since the MIT had taken charge of just about everything else he should have had little enough to do, but ACC Cunningham hadn't reckoned with DCI Jim Daley.

Just as the detectives were about to take their leave, the door opened and Salazar Brandt appeared, his hand still heavily bandaged.

'I beg your pardon. I'll leave you to it.'

He started to close the door again, but Nathan stopped him. 'It's okay, Salz, the officers are just going.'

Salazar Brandt took a seat near his friend and looked around the room. 'Any news on Delph?'

'A search is in progress, Mr Brandt,' said Daley. 'While you're here, I don't suppose you've remembered anything about your attack?'

'No, not a thing.' He lowered his head, as though the very mention of what had happened to him was too much to bear.

'You know where I am if you do.' Daley zipped up his thick winter jacket. 'Now, gentlemen, if you'll excuse us.'

Instead of following his lead, Scott addressed Salazar. 'Here, this is your faither's boat, aye?'

'Well, he has the use of it when he wants.'

'See this, how much do you think it's worth, eh?' Scott held up the jade sphere again.

'Oh, yes, those are beautiful. My father bought them from the Lizzardo collection. So tactile – as you've found out. I think this set cost over two million.' Salazar smiled.

'Right. Aye, very good.' Carefully – very carefully indeed – Brian Scott placed the little sphere on top of the other four where he'd found it. He patted the table in front of the objects ever so gently and quickly followed Daley out of the room.

51

The pristine light sand of the long beach contrasted with the gunmetal-grey sea. Here the sky was a great dome, seabirds hovering almost motionless on the breeze. In the distance, a huge cargo vessel looked like a toy on the horizon. Clouds scudded hither and thither, while in the east a huge bank of pearlescent grey indicated that more and heavier snow was probably on its way.

ACC Cunningham huddled into his thick overcoat against the cold wind. After years in the CID, he'd become accustomed to wearing a uniform again, and when – as now – he found himself in civvies, he felt almost naked.

Far along the other end of the beach he could see a dark figure walking in his direction. He set off across the sand, cursing his decision to wear his good John Lobb Oxford shoes. He looked down at their high blood-red polish and desperately hoped the sand wouldn't ruin the most expensive pair of shoes he'd ever owned.

As grandiose as he was, he couldn't bear such unnecessary clandestine behaviour. They could just as easily have met in a warm car in some discreet location, rather than on this desolate stretch of beach. The rugged, beautiful charm of his surroundings was lost on a man whose only goal in life was to advance his career and get to the top. He knew the man he was meeting was well connected. So well connected, in fact, that he could easily advance Cunningham's aim of becoming Commissioner of the Metropolitan Police. The very thought of this lofty eminence was enough to make him salivate.

Cunningham stomped on through the sand, the wind making his eyes water.

'ACC Cunningham!' said Werner Brandt. 'I'm sorry to drag you here. I like to keep my business private.'

Cunningham studied Brandt with a practised eye, pleased to note that he too was wearing an equally expensive-looking pair of shoes. Though, he reflected, a man who'd sailed into Kinloch's harbour in a superyacht could purchase such shoes without a thought.

'It's my pleasure, Mr Brandt. When I had the call from Whitehall to say you wanted to meet me, I must confess to being rather intrigued.'

'I find that face to face is still the best way to do business, yes?'

'Absolutely. Nothing like getting up at close quarters to make sure you can trust a man.' As soon as he'd said this, Cunningham realised that the remark could easily be taken the wrong way. It was also hypocritical, as he enjoyed nothing more than sitting in the comfort of his office doing business over Zoom rather than having to share a space with someone he inevitably wouldn't like. Then there was travel, nothing more than an irritation – unless the meeting were to be held in an exotic location, that was.

'So beautiful, don't you think?' Brandt was gazing out to sea.

'Stunning, absolutely stunning.' For effect, Cunningham took in his surroundings with a noble smile on his face. 'You can travel far and wide and never come across anything as majestic as Scotland's scenery.' He hoped he'd carried the lie off, as he'd much rather have been in the Adriatic or better still the Caribbean.

'I want to talk to you about a couple of issues.' Brandt removed a cigar from his pocket and determinedly puffed it into life with a powerful lighter, sheltering the gasping blue flame from the wind with the collar of his jacket.

'I'm at your service, sir. Please don't hesitate to ask anything.'

'I'd be happy if you could persuade Nathan Farringdon that there's nothing to be gained by his hanging about waiting for the girl. I have many things to do, and I can't stay here as a glorified nursemaid. I dearly wish I hadn't invited them aboard.'

Cunningham thought for a moment. 'That won't be a problem. I'll give them some spiel. I'm sure we'll find her soon, anyway. I must say, these students have proved to be a bloody nuisance – with the greatest respect, of course.'

Brandt took a long draw on his cigar, then let the smoke drift from between his lips to eddy on the wind. 'Of course, Mr Cunningham. From what I hear, she may have wanted out – you know, away from the boy.'

'That puts an entirely different slant on things. I'll have a word with him and his father as soon as we're finished here.'

'Your DCI Daley has already spoken to them this morning. I thought he was off the case?'

Despite the cool of the day, Cunningham felt his face redden with rage. 'What?' He realised that sounded rude. Also, as though he didn't have control of his officers. He pretended to remember something. 'Ah, of course. Daley just has to pick up a few details, addresses and so forth. That's why he'd have been at your yacht.'

'It takes a detective chief inspector to pick up an address and a phone number in person? I'm not sure that's an efficient use of manpower, Mr Cunningham.'

'You know what it's like in these rural areas. Nothing to do, so they make work to justify their existence.' This was the first excuse that came to Cunningham's mind. It was reasonably good, he thought.

'I hear DCI Daley is a top detective. He's been at the centre of some major cases over the last few years. He has to justify his existence? I doubt that.'

'He's been there or thereabouts. But I think you'll find that the significant work in those cases has been done at a rather more senior level.' Brandt's withering look made Cunningham realise that he didn't believe the statement. He felt he must embellish. 'Daley has had a few problems – health, discipline. And while I hate to criticise any of my colleagues, I think his race is just about run, to be honest.'

'I don't really care what his career path is to be. He's been asking questions about me I don't like. I'm sure my friends in Whitehall wouldn't be too pleased either. If he's off the case, he's off the case, no?'

'Most certainly he is. I'll see to it right away.'

'That is good. It's been pleasant to meet you, assistant chief constable. I'm sure I shall do so again.' In a flurry of cigar smoke he turned on his heel and made off from where he'd come.

Cunningham stared after him for a few moments, until he realised he was still holding his hand out for the handshake that had not been forthcoming.

As he stumbled through the sand on the way back to his own car, he cursed Daley out loud. 'And you'll pay for these bloody shoes if they're ruined,' he muttered, planning the detective's demise with each step.

52

As soon as Daley arrived back at Kinloch police office, he knew something was wrong. He was met with furtive glances, lowered heads, worried faces. He and Scott had used the back entrance via the car park, so hadn't been briefed at the front desk.

But when they arrived at the glass box, Daley immediately saw that the blinds were closed – something he rarely did.

'Sir,' said Potts, looking whey-faced. 'DCI Birkenshaw let himself into your office. I did try to stop him.'

For Daley, decorum was in order. 'That's fine. Nothing to worry about, Potts.'

'He's one cheeky bastard,' declared Scott, rather spoiling the calm sense of order Daley had been hoping for.

When he opened the door, Birkenshaw – a long, tall man – was leaning back in Daley's chair with his feet on the desk. His attention was apparently fully taken up with a phone call.

'And there we have it, sir. I made the call, and we know where we are,' he said into his mobile. As he swung round, he noticed that Daley and Scott were standing in the doorway. Rather than removing his feet from the desk or looking

346

remotely embarrassed at his unauthorised presence in Daley's office, he smiled broadly and pointed to the phone at his ear. 'Yes, sir. In fact, DCI Daley has just arrived. Do you have any message you'd like me to pass on?'

'Just let me knock this fucker oot, Jimmy. It'll be my ticket oot o' the job. You know it makes sense,' whispered Scott.

'Yes, sir, absolutely. I'll make sure that DCI Daley is aware of that. Thank you.' Birkenshaw ended the call, sliding the mobile into the inside pocket of his jacket. 'Hello, people. How did you get on down at the *Queen Mary*?'

'The boat's no' called that, is she?' said Scott.

'Just my little joke, sergeant. But all is well, I take it?'

Daley nodded. 'I'd like to sit down, if you don't mind – at my desk.'

For a split second, Birkenshaw glanced over at the guest's chair, as though he expected Daley to sit there. But once more he smiled, and with the lithe energy of his relative youth bounced up without the support of his hands.

'Thank you,' said Daley.

'No problem. Oh, by the way, that was ACC Cunningham. He wants to meet you here at five, if that's okay. Sounds a bit put out.' Birkenshaw rolled his eyes. 'I've to *remind* you that your official involvement in the Brandt case is over. Also, anything involving Emily Kilvington, the Mitchell murder or Nathan Farringdon. Though he recommends you find that girl – whatever her name is. Clear?'

'You're getting good money for being a message boy, eh?' said Scott.

'And – in my opinion – you're in a job for which you are utterly unsuited, DS Scott. But you know what opinions are like: everyone has one.'

Daley sat down in his office chair, feeling the unpleasant warmth left behind by someone else's backside. 'Is that you done, Birkenshaw?'

'Yes, quite done, thanks. I'll leave you and your colleague here to – well, whatever it is you get up to in such a place. Oh, and by the way, I spoke to your friend Uxley in Skegness. He'll be dealing with me from now on. All the best to you.' With that, he was gone.

'Aye, fuck off,' said Scott when the door closed, loud enough for Birkenshaw to hear him.

'No point, Brian. It's birds of a feather flocking together. Him and Cunningham, I mean. Just unfettered ambition. They don't care who they stand on to get where they want.'

'We've got nothing left to be at, anyway.'

'We still have a young woman to find. But you know what I think about that.'

There was a quick knock at the door and Potts appeared. 'Sir, thought you should know, we've had a DNA match in for the head in the box.'

'You'd better tell his lordship there,' said Scott.

'Not before you tell me,' said Daley. 'Who is it?'

'It's a bit of a shocker, sir. Samuel Broughton. If I'm right, he was one of the children who stabbed Miss Kilvington, wasn't he?'

Daley's eyes were wide. 'Yes, he was. Thanks, Potts.' He looked at his watch. 'Give it half an hour before you let our friend know – you know who I mean. Good work.'

Potts left them to it. Brian Scott was deep in thought. 'So, someone sends that Kilvington lassie the heid o' the lad that assaulted her. Don't get it, Jimmy.'

Daley was up at the whiteboard. 'We have Kilvington

348

and Broughton – there's the link.' He drew a line between their names.

'How come she didnae recognise the boy?'

'Severed head in a box. Remember, he was only a kid when he and his sister killed her. Plus, look at the state she's in.' Daley bit his lip. 'I want to find out more about what happened to them both after the Kilvington incident – the Broughton kids, I mean.'

'We're off the case, Jimmy. We have men oot looking for the Delph lassie.'

'Just what you'll be doing. I'll get on with this – out of curiosity, you understand.'

'Whatever you say, big man. I'll go and see how things are going – chase up the DNA on the jacket, see what's happening with the search.'

Daley was left to his thoughts. He returned to the whiteboard, adding the names of Nate Farringdon, Salazar Brandt, their respective fathers, and Delph Harker. He remembered the name Beovan, the company who owned the secure children's home to which Charlotte Broughton had been sent. The financial squad back at Gartcosh were looking at the company in detail for him. He wanted to know more about the homes they ran. Initially, this had only been of passing interest. But now – he wasn't sure why – something about it was calling to him.

He searched for Beovan on his computer. The company, it seemed, had been wound up after a major public inquiry. But the results of the search didn't only produce financial results. Entry after entry, many from newspaper and other media headlines, filled his screen: *Horror at Children's Homes; Abuse Widespread at Child Hostel Group; Beovan Limited:*

Directors Culpable. The list went on and on. The last article he read was simply entitled, *Shame!*

Daley read through it all, the bile rising in his throat. Accusations of the physical, mental and sexual abuse of children on page after page. He placed the articles in a file on the laptop, sent a copy to Scott, and searched for the results of the inquiry and resultant court case that must have surely followed this catalogue of horror. But try as hard as he might, he found nothing. There was no sign of any criminal investigation, never mind a court case. It appeared that the directors of Beovan had been left to quietly walk away from it all, free from any taint of wrongdoing.

Daley sat back in his chair, feeling nauseous. He thought of his own son; pictured him alone in an institution where he faced abuse of the most abhorrent kind. The thought of it all became too much, and he had to focus on something else to banish the revulsion he felt.

He rechecked a couple of articles. They were from almost eight years before. But one name jumped out at him: Brandon Kemp, a fearless campaigning freelance journalist he'd met during protests outside an oil company based in Glasgow more than ten years before.

Daley was an old-fashioned cop. He still had a little black book, one that had been replaced again and again and had grown exponentially over the course of his career. He kept it locked in a drawer in his desk. Suddenly, he was glad to have taken this precaution. He had no doubt that Birkenshaw had rifled through his desk. How else would he have managed to find Uxley's contact number?

He thumbed through the pages of the 'little' black book that was now a hardback desk diary, painstakingly copied out from iteration to iteration. Not for the first time, he was grateful for his neat handwriting, and he soon found the name Brandon Kemp. The number was a landline, reflecting the changing times between then and now, when any contact would be an email address or mobile phone number. He picked up his phone and dialled.

'Hello?' The voice on the other end of the phone belonged to a woman. She sounded rather frail and tentative. Daley introduced himself and outlined why he'd called.

'I see, chief inspector. I'm Mrs Kemp, Brandon's widow.'

This revelation made his heart sink slightly. He hadn't known the journalist well, but here he was trying to commune with another dead man. That, and the missed opportunity to find out something more out about Beovan.

'It's funny to hear his name after so long. People called for a while after he died. You know the life of a freelance journalist. But that stopped. It's interesting to hear you mention Beovan. It was a passion of his.'

'I'm not surprised. From what I've read, it's a national disgrace.'

'Yes, very much so.' The frailty in Mrs Kemp's voice had almost disappeared. It was as though her late husband's fervour for the subject had also galvanised her. 'Of all the dreadful injustices he wrote about, this upset him most.'

'I'm sure,' said Daley. 'He was very passionate about his work, I remember that.'

'Ah, yes. He became consumed by everything he worked on. I miss him so much.'

Daley, being a typical west of Scotland male of a certain generation, felt her pain, but had little idea how to express this empathy. He mumbled something again about being so sorry and other expressions of regret.

'He wrote a book about it, you know. Didn't earn him very much, but he did all he could to expose what he'd found.' Mrs Kemp sounded proud.

'He did? Is it still in print, do you know?'

'Yes, yes, it is. I get a tiny royalty every year. It always makes me smile. But then a feeling of great sadness washes over me. I can send you a copy, if you'd like?'

Daley was thinking. His source was dead, but he had written a book, and if Daley could get his hands on it quickly . . .

'It's available electronically, too,' Mrs Kemp went on. 'What do you call these fancy modern things?'

'Ebooks?'

'Yes, that's it. The book is called *Horror with a Smile on Its Face*. He wrote it under his own name. And though he was always rather proud of it, he carried the disappointment that it failed to achieve what he'd hoped to his deathbed.'

'If you don't mind me asking, how did Brandon die?'

'A car accident. They never found who'd hit him. Only just in his sixties. The local police tried their best but got nowhere. A truly dreadful time.'

Daley expressed more regret at what had happened, thanked Mrs Kemp for her help and ended the call.

The residual sadness of it all haunted him. First what he'd read about Beovan Homes, then the discovery that Kemp had died. It was odd, he thought, how the death of a stranger he barely knew could be so affecting. He realised quickly that it was an expression of his fear of his own mortality. Selfish, in a way, but there was nothing he could do to stop the feeling.

But his work never ended. And soon DCI Jim Daley was searching online for an eBook he knew he'd find very difficult to read.

53

Though it was only just after four thirty, the sky was dark and the lights of Kinloch held sway, illuminating the town and making the loch shimmer with the ghosts of their reflections.

The woman had no pram now, though she was still huddled into her pink padded anorak, zipped up over her belly. She stood by the railings that guarded the promenade, gazing across the loch to the lights on the other side, the town's north end. The air was fresh and cold, with a hint of burning coal. For many, this would have been nostalgic, but for her it conjured up nothing but misery, sadness and regret. A regret so deep that it gnawed at her every day like a cancer. She spat into the dark oily water to banish the memory.

Her arm was itching again. She pulled up the sleeve of her jacket and the jumper underneath, revealing a dirty bandage wrapped round her right forearm. The dressing needed to be changed, but she didn't have time for that.

She removed her phone, checked the time and searched her contacts. She sent one simple message: *be ready*.

The phone made a swooshing noise as the message was sent. She waited for a reply. The single letter *K* was enough for her to know that what she'd sent had been received, and, more important, understood. She pushed herself off the railings and carried on to the quay where the great yacht was still moored. Somehow, it looked even grander at night, all lit up by spotlights on the superstructure and a warmer glow coming from the cabins dotted around below. She could see people moving in the stern cabin, behind the big picture window. They seemed ephemeral, seen as they were through a shade, as though they weren't real, disguised by smoked glass. The passengers on this ship were like spectres, she decided.

She paced to and fro along the promenade, never straying too far from the vessel. Now and again, a figure would appear on the gangway. She'd identified most of the crew, recognising even individual gaits. The cold was chilling her to the bone now. Surely it would happen soon.

It had been interesting at first, studying the movement of the passengers. One man never left the vessel alone, but was always accompanied by at least two large men. Bodyguards, she reasoned. Why not? If she ever owned a superyacht, she'd have bodyguards too.

She hadn't counted how many times she'd focused on the gangway. It must have been hundreds. Only twice had she seen what she wanted. But now, in a split second, it all seemed worth it.

A tall figure stepped jauntily on to the quay.

She was off the promenade in a breath. Making sure not to appear hurried, stopping for a moment to type something into her phone, the screen momentarily illuminating her face in a pale blue light.

The man walked away from the yacht. He stopped and sniffed the air, drawing it deep into his lungs. She could see he was of middle age, good-looking, tanned, his grey wavy hair streaked blond and neatly cut. She stepped towards him.

'Excuse me, do you have a light?' she said, looking at him from under the rim of her hood.

'Yeah, sure,' he replied, delving into his pocket for his lighter. 'Us smokers, we have to stick together . . .'

The last sentence Teddy Farringdon would ever say was left unfinished. The knife flashed in the lights of the pier as she stabbed him twice in the throat. As he gurgled his final breath, she pulled him to her like a lover, plunging the vicious blade under his ribs. She twisted the knife once and let him go.

In desperation Teddy reached out and managed to grab her, his hand pushing back the sleeve of her pink anorak, his nails running down her forearm, making her yelp in pain. But his strength was gone. He fell to his knees, wide-eyed, dying.

She was off, running to the road just as a car screeched to a halt in front of her. Smoke and the smell of burning rubber soured the evening air as the car took off again, heading for the darkness at the edge of the town.

On the quayside, the victim fell forward, twitched for the last time and was still.

Jim Daley should have gone home, but his sense of duty wouldn't allow it. He had a missing girl, and as he read Brandon Kemp's book about the Beovan Homes scandal he grew more and more depressed.

Daley remembered Kemp as an honourable, intelligent man with a hatred of injustice. These qualities shone out from the electronic pages he was reading on his tablet. The homes were wicked bastions of neglect and abuse. Routinely, children and young people were physically, mentally and sexually abused within their walls. The big detective's heart sank as he read about case after case: traumatised kids, ruined families. *Case X*, as it was called, was particularly harrowing: a young person sexually abused and beaten. Kemp returned to it again and again. Though the gender of the victim was never revealed, it appeared that their refusal to back down had made it the worst example of so much widespread abuse.

Eventually, it all became too much. Daley knew everything he needed to. It was gut-wrenching. He sat back in his chair, thinking about what he'd just read, trying to be objective and not allow the contents of Kemp's investigation to cloud his judgement. But though he could be accused of many things, Jim Daley's sense of right and wrong was as strong as his desire to see good triumph over evil.

He decided to skip to the end of the book to take in Kemp's conclusions. If anything – and he'd thought this impossible – they disgusted him even more. Despite the evidence given by residents, blameless members of staff and those charged with the regulation of such establishments, nothing happened.

Kemp's investigation had come up against a brick wall of silence. A silence so stark and desolate that even his powers of persuasion and gift for uncovering the truth were rendered useless.

And here we reach the end. Despite hundreds of hours of testimony from children, as well as the testimonies of those employed by Beovan, police officers, doctors and social workers, nothing has come – will ever come – of this investigation. There will be no day in court, no inquiry allowing those so, so wronged to look into the eyes of the people ultimately responsible for these disturbing, unacceptable and disgusting events.

You may ask why. I've asked it myself, often. The truth is, we don't and will never know who they are.

Throughout the writing of this book, I've tried to make sure that every accusation I make, every revelation I've made, is backed up by hard evidence from not one, but multiple sources.

Now, however, I enter the realm of conjecture. But not that of speculation or wishful thinking. What I say to you now is based on thorough research, and evidence passed on to me from people unwilling to verify what they were saying. Facts that hang in the air like wraiths, their ultimate truth destined almost certainly to be obfuscated for eternity.

I shall summarise in as unsensational a manner as I can. I'll do it by asking this question.

Who or what is powerful enough to subvert the true course of justice to such an extent that its pursuit becomes futile?

As I write, I have been threatened with all manner of consequences for having had the gall to champion those desperately unlucky enough to find themselves within the Beovan system. This has occurred throughout my research for this book, and for the many articles I've written for newspapers and magazines on the subject.

Will I complain, yet again, to the police?

No, I won't. Because it has been made clear to me that

should I continue to do so, I myself will end up on the wrong side of a set of bars – or worse.

To seek out evil, one must follow not money, but the reason. The reason why such things happen at secure homes run by Beovan have happened and will happen again. The thought is abhorrent. But the will to cover this up, to obscure it, must go straight to the top.

Beovan as a company is a chamber of secrets, some of the most wicked of their kind. But whoever is responsible must be so precious to those who control our nation that they can never be exposed.

This is the most chilling thought of all.

Daley had read enough. He slapped the tablet down on the table, his face white with the detail of it all. Whoever had chosen to hide the secrets of the Beovan homes had done a good job. He'd never even heard of them, despite two of their establishments being located in Scotland.

Quickly, he wrote an email to the Economic Crime Unit. If there was anything to add to Kemp's findings, he wanted – needed – to know. And, notwithstanding the author's advice, if he wished to expose who had benefited from years of abuse of the most vulnerable, money was the conduit. It would never be enough to convict. But someone, somewhere, knew.

The door to his glass box was flung open with such force it was almost removed from its hinges.

'Brian, what the—'

'It's your man – Teddy whatever – he's been murdered, Jimmy.' But even as Scott brought Daley up to speed with the details, the latter couldn't take his eyes from the tablet and the distressing things he'd read. As his old mentor Ian Burns always said: everything happens for a reason, whether apparent or not in the first instance.

The pair left the warmth of the glass box for the cold, murderous quay.

54

By the time Daley and Scott reached the pier the place was illuminated by the blue flashing lights of police vehicles and ambulances, their crews busy about their business in the flickering shadows. An attempt to save Teddy Farringdon's life had been made by members of the superyacht's staff, but to no avail.

Daley – with no little difficulty – ducked under the yellow police tape cordoning off the pier and stared at the mound of a body under green medical blankets.

'Just shows you,' said Scott. 'It doesnae matter how much cash you have, you're just a piece o' meat at the end o' the day.'

Before Daley could reply, a paramedic was at his side. A man he didn't recognise.

'He was dead when we arrived. Simply bled out.'

'Mr MacDonald,' said Daley, reading the name tag on his green uniform. 'Thank you. I'm sure you did your best.'

'It's my first week on the job here. Didn't expect this, I must admit.'

'You'd better curdle your loins, in that case,' said Scott. He was rather surprised when both Daley and the paramedic looked puzzled.

'*Gird* your loins, Brian,' said Daley after a moment.

'Aye, well, yous know what I meant.'

Sergeant Carney from two shift appeared before Daley. 'Just waiting for the force doctor, sir. We need SOCO, obviously. From what I'm told, the victim was approached by someone on the quayside. I've got a member of the crew – a Mr Marquez – who saw it unfold from the bridge. Said it all happened in a flash, before anyone aboard could do anything.'

'Thanks, sergeant. Everything secure?'

'Yes, sir. We were just coming down Main Street when the call came out. We were here in a couple of minutes.'

'Anything on the perpetrator?'

'Sir, just a rough description.' Carney produced his notebook. 'It's a woman, stout, around five feet four or five, wearing a pink anorak with the hood up, dark leggings and trainers.' He shrugged. 'Apparently, once the job was done, she made off to the road. Picked up by an SUV that came round the corner just at the right time. I've got the rest of the shift scouting about. I hope we'll get something about the vehicle from CCTV.'

'Team effort. She had help,' said Scott.

'Thanks, Carney. Carry on.'

'Yes, sir.' The sergeant hurried off back down the pier.

'Okay, Brian. We'll get Potts down. Ask him to source any CCTV available from the pier. We can see what we've got from the town's system as far as the escape vehicle is concerned. You speak to this Marquez guy, see if we can't rouse some more witnesses. I'll go and speak to the son.'

'The boy will be devastated, big man. Girlfriend missing, now his faither's copped it. Tough holiday, eh?'

'Daley!' The call came from behind. Both detectives

turned round. ACC Cunningham was making his way on to the pier in full uniform, his braid and shiny buttons flashing in the light of the blue emergency lights. The tall figure of DCI Birkenshaw was at his side.

'Sir, Mr Farringdon has been stabbed. He hasn't made it, I'm afraid.'

'Thank you. But from now on it's none of your concern. DCI Birkenshaw will be SIO on this, starting now. I'll need your men until I get more bodies down here. Please make sure he is given any assistance required. And you'll do as you are asked by Birkenshaw, got it?'

'Isn't he SIO on the Mitchell case?'

'Yes. Your point being?' Cunningham glared at Daley. 'I want to see you back at the office.' His tone was low, threatening. Seeing Daley about to speak, he snapped, 'Not here, the office! You and your sidekick get back there now.' Cunningham stomped off.

'Keep that seat warm,' said Birkenshaw with a grin. He followed Cunningham towards the yacht.

'There we are,' said Scott. 'Early louse for us, Jimmy.'

'You, maybe. I'll have to wait for Cunningham.'

'Fuck that pompous arsehole, Jimmy. We're only here to investigate this. He and his big dog are doing it now. Come on.'

Walking away from a murder scene was alien to Daley. But he'd been replaced; his orders couldn't have been more pointed. 'Yeah, home, I suppose, Brian. Fuck him.'

Daley looked back at the scene as they walked back to their car. Cunningham was deep in conversation with Werner Brandt, newly appeared on the quayside. The ACC gazed at them for a moment.

'What's up, Jimmy?' said Scott.

'Nothing, Brian. Just a wee notion of mine.'

'Right, well, you can have it about something else. We're toast as far as this case is concerned.'

'When we get back to the station, I want to give you something for your bedtime reading.'

'Cannae wait,' said Scott. 'If it's anything like the usual stuff you read, I'll be out like a light.'

Martin Cook had just finished mending his tractor. He was in a shed a hundred metres from the farmhouse, on a hill a mile or so out of Kinloch. He'd heard the wail of sirens carrying on the air about an hour before. The place was trouble; there always seemed to be something going on. He spent as little time there as he could, despite its proximity.

He closed up the tractor and blew on his hands. Even with his fingerless gloves on, they were almost frozen stiff with the cold.

One of his sheepdogs went scurrying off into the darkness. The bitch, one of his most intelligent workers, began barking with sufficient urgency to persuade Cook to follow rather than call her back. He pulled a torch from his pocket, flashing the beam round the fields in front of him. He picked the dog out in the beam of light, and she ran a few metres towards him then back again, indicating she wanted him to follow.

'Aye, right, Jess. I'm coming.' Cook hoped that he hadn't lost another sheep on the single-track road that twisted up from the town. The SUV brigade had been out and about and they didn't give a toss about his livestock, just looking for the thrill of driving fast in his muddy fields. Having spent a lifetime on these same fields, he found the whole thing bewildering. And though he'd reported the latest offence to the local police, he was sure they'd be too busy with what they saw as real crime to do anything about it. It irritated him.

Puffing as he took the rise, Cook was soon upsides with his dog. 'Now, what's all this, girl?' he said, directing the beam of the torch down to where she was still barking. At first, he thought it was nothing more than a huddle of discarded clothes. But in the torchlight he saw the glimpse of a face.

'Help me, please.' The words were weak, a woman's voice.

'Come here, lassie.' Cook bent down and helped her to her feet. 'What's your name – and mair important, what on earth are you doing out here?'

'My name's Delph, Delphine Harker. I'm so cold.'

Cook held on as the young woman fainted away in his arms.

55

Hamish was sitting in the light of the blazing fire, the cat – his namesake – curled up on his knee.

The old fisherman felt strange – disoriented, almost. Though he'd reasoned with himself at length, he felt as though he was slowly fading away. Not in the physical sense, but spiritually; his purpose in life now over, he was merely meandering to the end. This feeling had begun when Annie died. He thought it part of the grieving process he kept hearing about, and imagined the whole thing would eventually stop. But he'd been wrong. If anything, the sensation was growing.

'Aye, Hamish. What's to become o' us, son?'

As though it understood, the cat looked at him through narrow, yellow eyes and hissed.

'Here, there's nae need to be like that. Never bite the hand that feeds you.' But, he reflected, Hamish the cat fed himself. He habitually dined out on rabbits, birds, rats and other small mammals, his wildcat instincts never sated. 'You'll miss a' that fish I get from the pier. Aye, you're no' so good at catching the fish.' In all truth, Hamish wasn't really sure if his pet could catch fish or not. But the cat regularly brought home the odd rabbit's leg or half-eaten rodent to prove he wasn't slacking.

The animal settled back down, his head on his master's right hand.

Hamish thought back on his life – on Kinloch. It was the only place he'd ever lived. Yes, he'd visited here and there: Glasgow, Edinburgh, County Antrim, and the many ports up and down the west coast he'd put in to as a fisherman. But he couldn't say he'd really taken to any of them. So the question remained: how would he take to upping sticks and moving to Perthshire?

'I'll need to ask for a sign, Hamish,' he said to the cat. He laid his head against the antimacassar on the back of his chair and closed his eyes. Soon, in front of the roaring fire, with the warm bundle on his lap, he was fast asleep.

Hamish woke cold and alone, just as dawn was breaking in a thin line above the hills across the loch from his cottage. Hamish the cat would be out on the prowl. His owner had cut him an improvised cat flap simply by upending the back door and cutting a sufficiently cat-sized gap at the bottom of it. Now the animal came and went as he pleased, but his owner had regretted the deed. The wind, he was dismayed to discover, blew through the hole with alacrity. That was, until Hamish rethought and nailed on the bottom of a soft-haired brush to act as a baffle. Though it hadn't pleased his cat, he was proud of this elegant solution. And, eventually, his feline companion had become accustomed to the inconvenience.

He thought back on the vivid dream he'd experienced in the hours he'd spent asleep before the fire, now little more than a few glowing embers. It was as though he was flying over mile after mile of rolling fields, with cattle, sheep – even horses – grazing far below. But it had been one of those dreams that left a residue in the soul. And though he recalled those somnolent meanderings in great detail, something nagged at him. It was as though he'd been searching for something he couldn't find.

Hamish creaked his old bones from the even more venerable armchair. He was stiff from sitting all night in the one place. The room was cold, so he got up to put some more coals on the fire. As he stepped past the window, he stared out at the loch. The water was an odd bright green colour under the pale light from the east. He watched a large gull circle from the heavens and land. It fussed at its plumage for a moment, then fixed its gaze firmly upon him. Man and bird engaged briefly in a silent communion, until – having made its point – the gull flapped its great wings and flew high into the sheltering sky, to disappear over the emerging horizon.

Hamish shuffled to the coal scuttle. He mended the fire, rousing the dying embers into a flash of bright red with the poker, then carefully placed the coals atop. Rather a master of the task, he made sure to leave sufficient room for the fire to breathe, prosper and grow.

He straightened up with what could have been either a hefty sigh or a weak groan, depending on the point of view of the listener.

'There you are then,' he said to nobody in particular.

It wasn't that Daley had slept badly; he hadn't slept at all. Thoughts of the man lying dead on the pier, Cunningham, Birkenshaw, the long sleek yacht, his pills, the pain in his back, all combined to form an unbreakable barrier between him and repose.

It was a few minutes after six, just as his eyelids were

beginning to feel heavy, when his mobile began buzzing on the bedside table. He reached out for it quickly, not wanting to wake Liz who was sleeping soundly beside him.

'Sir, sorry to waken you so early.'

'Don't worry, Cummins, I'm awake. What can I do for you?'

There was hesitation, as though the man on the other end of the phone was unsure of himself. 'ACC Cunningham said you had no need to know. But I thought I should tell you that Delph Harker turned up last night. She was found near Breachan farm. I'm sending you the details by email. If you could keep them to yourself, I'd be much obliged, sir. Well . . . you know . . . not tell the ACC it came from me, please.'

'No need to worry, Cummins. Thank you,' said Daley. He ended the call, then checked his inbox. Sure enough, there was the farmer's statement and details of the young woman's condition.

He lay back and thought it all through again, adding this new information to his considerations. The report stated that Delph was cut and bruised. That would certainly account for the bloodied jacket, though some of the slashes in the garment would have to be compared to her injuries.

Quietly, he slid off the bed and tiptoed from the bedroom. To his relief, Liz was still fast asleep.

After putting the kettle on to boil, Daley stretched to try to rid himself of the pain in his back. He knew he'd soon be forced to take a painkiller from the small supply he'd been prescribed. For some reason, the thought made him feel anxious – hopeless, almost.

'My precious things,' he mumbled to himself wistfully.

Despite telling himself not to be angry at being sidelined

by Cunningham, now he was up and about Daley felt it niggling away at the back of his mind. He tried to reason that things were different now. Major Investigation Teams were the norm, arriving at almost every significant crime scene. But in his experience to date, the man on the ground had always been trusted to head such a team, local knowledge being to the fore in remote areas like the one he policed. Though his career had been tarnished by a tendency to push back against his superiors, as well as the odd misdemeanour, he knew that his skills as a detective were highly regarded. So why was he being replaced by Birkenshaw?

The image of ACC Cunningham and Werner Brandt, cheek by jowl in the flashing light of the pier the previous evening, told him all he needed to know. He had gleaned enough information about the latter to know he was a player on the international stage – and that meant power and influence. If Daley's theories were correct, Brandt was a man of less than few scruples. What he'd read about Beovan played out in his mind again. Who had the power to keep such an awful secret quiet, to hush things up? Whoever it was would had to have help at the highest level; from governments, no less.

Daley wasn't naïve. He knew all kinds of misdeeds escaped the public gaze as the result of cover-ups. He thought of both Brandt and the late Teddy Farringdon.

It could only be revenge. The same revenge that had been meted out to the unfortunate Emily Kilvington.

But what could he do? He was off the case – out of the picture.

As he stirred a teaspoon of sugar into his black coffee, he reasoned that while he was persona non grata in the major investigations, as head of the local CID, as well as remaining sub-divisional commander, he had every right to investigate Delph Harker's reappearance. It had happened on his patch, the place for which he was responsible.

Daley decided this would be his best course of action. And if any of his forays into the other bones of this case came to fruition, well, so be it. Ultimately, two men lay dead. He wasn't prepared to have it swept under the carpet – regardless of Cunningham's intentions.

Just as he drained the last of his coffee to wash down the dry muesli bar that was his breakfast, something clicked in his mind. It was inspiration, but from where, he didn't know.

DCI Jim Daley's heart was beating rapidly as he stepped into the shower. If he was right, he'd have to be both creative and quick. *If he was right*, everything took on a new, deadly perspective.

56

As Daley drove through the very early Kinloch morning, he noticed all the things he'd become accustomed to in his time in the town. Fresh morning rolls were being delivered from the van outside Michael Kerr's bakery. Across the road, the elderly newsagent was supervising unloading of the morning papers, all in bundles held together with blue parcel tape. He waved to the detective as he drove past. One of the town's less sober figures was propped up by a lamppost, pawing at the pavement with one worn boot. He was holding a can of super lager, his face gaunt with a complexion known as a drinker's tan.

Though drinking alcohol from an open vessel was an offence, such matters had never concerned Daley. This man had chosen his passage through life. Who knew what tragedy and pain he'd had to endure? As long as he was causing no disturbance – and he wasn't – the officer in charge of policing Kinloch's streets let him be. The whole thing was regrettable, but then, he reasoned, did anyone really know when they'd find themselves propped up by a lamppost? Life could change in an instant – he'd seen it happen. In Daley's experience, nobody had the right to expect their life to be a bed of roses. Even the loftiest individual could find him or herself coming a cropper. Nobody should look down on others because they thought themselves superior.

As he headed up the brae to Kinloch police office, he saw a large black SUV parked outside the local court building. Two men were sitting in the passenger seat behind the tinted windows. Daley noticed that they observed him closely.

He was surprised by a few things when he arrived in the office. The place was a hive of activity. This was reasonable, given the simultaneous murder investigations now being conducted, without his participation. The whole idea was still an alien one.

Daley was relieved to note that his glass box was unoccupied. He'd fully expected to find Birkenshaw in situ, but there was no sign of Cunningham's arrogant puppet. As he sat down behind his desk, the exhausted figure of DC Potts appeared at the door, opening it with a knock. The detective was pale, with great bags under his eyes.

'You look bloody awful,' said Daley.

'Up all night, sir. His master's voice, if you know what I mean?'

Daley did, and nodded his understanding.

'Sir, I'm under strict instructions to tell you nothing about the case. But just let me know what you want to know and I'll be happy to oblige.'

'Good man. First off, where is Delph Harker?'

'Last I heard, she was in the hospital getting the once over. She's lost blood and is dehydrated, apparently. Some minor injuries. DCI Birkenshaw took her statement, sir.'

'Okay, good. Any progress on the killer?'

Potts shrugged. 'If there is, they're not telling any of the local officers. They've set up an incident room in the canteen. Their team are in there. Can't even get a bacon roll. Birkenshaw and ACC Cunningham are working from the boss's office.'

'That makes sense,' said Daley with a sigh.

'And there's somebody to see you, sir.'

Daley furrowed his brow, puzzled as to who would want to see him so early – especially as he'd been marginalised from all that was going on. 'Who is it?'

'Mr Werner Brandt, sir. He's in the canteen. Should I go and fetch him?'

'Yes, please do.' DC Potts turned to leave. 'And listen, son,' said Daley.

'Sir?'

'Go home and get some sleep. You're out on your feet.'

'What about the ACC, sir?'

'Last I looked, you were one of my officers. The ACC can drive his own team to distraction if he wants. He won't do it to my people.'

Potts smiled. 'Thank you, sir.'

Daley thought about the man who was about to step into his office. While the DCI was sure he'd used his influence to put Cunningham and Birkenshaw in place, he must keep an open mind.

When Potts showed Brandt into the glass box, Daley noticed a stillness about the man. It was something almost intangible, but it afforded him an almost sinister air. He took a seat opposite Daley.

'Good morning, Mr Brandt. I'm not sure what I can do for you. You'll be aware that ACC Cunningham and DCI Birkenshaw are in charge of this case.'

'Oh, yes, I am indeed aware of that. I put them there.'
Brandt's face was blank.

'I thought as much. Though I'm not sure how pleased the
ACC would be by your broadcasting the fact.'

Brandt took a deep breath. 'I don't care whether he's
pleased or not. In any case, he's an ambitious man, and
ambitious men are like paper in the wind. They blow in the
necessary direction without too much fuss.'

As a man in the habit of observing details, Daley noted
that Brandt's knuckles were scarred. Old wounds: the sure
sign of a past that did not match his present, the DCI
considered. 'I see. Well, that's a matter between you and
Cunningham, sir. None of my business.'

'You're an interesting man, Daley. Wasted on a life in the
police. I've been reading up on you and your exploits. Most
entertaining and informative.'

'Funny, I've been doing much the same on you.'

'Beovan. Oh yes, I heard. Poor Mrs Kemp has had such a
struggle to survive since her husband died. So unfortunate.
It's the least I can do to help out here and there. I enjoy being
charitable.'

Daley's blood ran cold. The implications of Brandt's
statement were obvious. Kemp had strayed too close to the
truth – a truth Daley was certain he knew. He'd become an
inconvenience; that inconvenience had been eradicated.

'I wonder what you are thinking, DCI Daley? I can't
possibly imagine.'

'I'm thinking what a prick you are, if I'm honest.'

'Now, come on. If it wasn't for my son, you'd still be
plagued by that dealer – what was his name? Mitchell, yes,
that's right. Dreadful creature.'

Daley cursed himself for not seeing it earlier. Mitchell wasn't the victim of a turf war. His vicious murder had been a case of violent revenge. He took in the man before him, his impassive face, expensive suit and scarred knuckles, as he pictured the dealer skewered to the rusty bed. But he knew he'd never be able to prove it. He wasn't even on the case.

'You see, life is all a matter of power, both soft and hard. I've learned this over the years. Some things, well, you need to take a sledgehammer to them, while with others a little persuasion is more than enough.'

'Really?'

'Absolutely.'

'You'll forgive me, Mr Brandt, but I'm not sure why you're here. This isn't a confessional.'

'I'm sure I don't know what you mean. There is a purpose to my visit.'

'I'm all ears.'

'To begin, you needn't worry about Miss Harker. She was examined in your local hospital. In my opinion, the place isn't fit for purpose. She is now in the care of the doctor and nursing staff I was forced to bring in to look after my own son following the vicious attack on his person. The streets here – so unruly. I blame the local police. Looking after Miss Harker is the least I can do for poor Teddy's grieving son.'

'I see. Good for you.'

'I'm glad you understand. I am doing so with the full agreement of your ACC Cunningham: a fine police officer. Going places, too. I shouldn't be surprised if he becomes Commissioner of the Metropolitan Police one day.'

There was the pay-off, Daley thought. 'I'm sure he will. After all, it helps to have friends in high places.'

'It does indeed.' Brandt slapped his hands on his knees. 'So, our little exchange is at an end.' He stood, holding out his hand to shake Daley's.

The big man stared at it for a moment, then gripped it firmly in his and jerked his visitor towards him, almost toppling him over. 'Remember, Mr Brandt, complacency and hubris have always been the enemy of great men.' He let go Brandt's hand.

'Something you too should remember, DCI Daley.' Though his manner was as smooth as when he'd first arrived in the glass box, Brandt's green eyes blazed. 'I bid you farewell. We sail shortly. Take care, Mr Daley. You and your lovely family.'

57

Brian Scott was not a happy man. Though he was up early, he arrived in the kitchen to find that the bread was stale. Leaving the house without his customary toast and Marmite was an alien prospect. He resolved to find some sustenance in the canteen when he arrived at work, but when he got there he was faced by a roomful of people he didn't know and absolutely no movement behind the counter.

'Can I help you?' said a detective, a stranger to Scott.

'Only if you can rustle up a bacon roll in the next ten minutes.' Scott left the room, not waiting for his unknown colleague's reply.

When he appeared in the CID suite, things were no better. The place was deserted, save for Daley, brooding in his glass box. Scott was well used to his old friend's moods, but it didn't make them any easier to endure. He could tell he faced a day of heavy silence, punctuated by unpredictable, often petulant displays of irritation or anger.

'I don't suppose you fancy a roll, big man?' he said, hoping the prospect of breakfast might be enough to shift Daley's mood.

'No, thanks, Brian. I don't have any appetite right now.'

'Okay.' Scott thought for a moment. 'I read bits o' that book last night – the one Kemp wrote. Horrific. To think that some bastard profited fae all that cruelty and pain. Makes you wonder who the real gangsters are, eh?'

'We all know what a soft spot you have for certain members of the criminal fraternity, Brian.'

'I see. Like that, is it?'

'Like what?' Daley was more than sullen; he was confrontational. Scott had seen this before too, but not often. Not directed towards him. Something was preying on his mind, something big. 'I know what this is aboot, Jimmy. You don't think I'm stupid, dae you? Surely no' after all these years.'

Daley's head shot up. 'What is it you know?'

Scott detected something behind the big man's eyes. If he hadn't known better, he'd have thought the emotion was fear. 'This Beovan company. You think that Brandt and Farringdon were behind it, don't you?'

Daley's shoulders lowered; the tension left his face. 'I should have known you'd get it, Brian. You're right: I do think it was them. But proving it – well, that's another matter.'

'It'll no' matter to Brandt. His guts are spread all o'er the pier.'

'No, I daresay.'

'Still no' justice, Jimmy.' He hesitated. 'You think it was the Broughton lassie, don't you? The girl fae the caravan that stabbed Emily Kilvington all those years ago.'

Daley stared Scott in the eye. 'Why, don't you?'

'I do. I cannae work oot why her brother ended up wae his heid in a box, but you're right, I'm sure o' it.'

'They fell out for some reason. Who knows? Any other theories?'

'Maybe he was dangerous – frightened her. I don't know.'

'Maybe he was getting in the way of her plans, Brian. In my experience, blood isn't always thicker than water.'

'You can say that again. My brother sold me that heap o' shite motor. Remember the Sierra? That burgundy thing?'

'You paid him well for it too, if I remember.'

'Aye, well o'er the odds. He stuck a Cosworth badge on the back. I found oot it was just a sixteen hundred. Bastard's no' to be trusted – never has been. Me and him didnae speak for years after that.'

'I remember that too.' Daley drummed his fingers on his desk restlessly. 'Come on, we're no use here. We'll go down and get bacon rolls from Michael Kerr's. How about it? Your hungry look has melted my heart.'

'Now you're talking. I could eat an auld shoe.'

The pair left the police office, passing ACC Cunningham's car as they headed down Main Street. At the wheel, Daley looked straight ahead, ignoring his senior officer.

'That's right, big man. Sling the bastard a deefie,' said Scott.

'I'm going to do more than that.'

'What are you on aboot, Jimmy? I know there's something.'

It was clear that Daley was going to say nothing further on the matter. He pulled into a parking space near the bakery.

'My treat,' said Scott, unclipping his seatbelt.

'It's okay, Bri. I need the fresh air. Bacon roll and coffee, right?'

'Don't forget the broon sauce, Jimmy. None o' that salad nonsense.'

Daley nodded and left the car.

In his absence, Scott took the opportunity to call Ella, no doubt getting ready for her work at the County Hotel. 'How you doing, darling?' he said as the call clicked on.

There was silence on the other end of the line.

'Hey, what's up? You there?'

'What's this, Brian? You only left the house a while ago. If you must know, I'm shaving my legs.' Ella, as was often the case with her errant husband, sounded most put out.

'I'm very sorry. I just had a few minutes spare and thought I'd gie my wife a wee bell. Seems as though I've done the wrong thing.'

'Aw, poor Brian. You never get a break, dae you? Oh, now look!' Ella cried out, forcing her husband to remove the phone from his ear.

'What's happening, doll? You near blew my heid off there.'

'I nicked myself with the razor, if you must know.'

'Come on, honey. I'm just aboot to have a bacon roll. I don't want to picture you wae blood running doon your pins while I'm eating it.'

'Have you ever heard o' unreconstructed males, Brian?'

'No.' He paused. 'It sounds painful. You've had your heid in they magazines again. I've telt you for years they do you no good. Bonce filled wae nonsense.'

'Right, what's really up? You never phone me just for a chat – even when I'd like you to.'

'Don't be like that. I pride myself on being quite an attentive husband.'

'In the same way a tiger's attentive to a goat, dae you mean?'

'Eh?'

'Never mind. Just tell me what you're after. And don't say a Chinese and an early night. You know fine how knackered I am after a full shift behind that bar. It's eleven to eleven tonight.'

'Aye, they shifts must be terrible. What are they really like?'

'Don't be sarcastic, you're no' clever enough.'

'I'm worried aboot Jimmy.'

'Has there ever been the time you've no' been worried aboot him?'

'Aye, sometimes.' This answer didn't sound too convincing. 'He's no' himself. It's as though his mind is elsewhere. I know we've had a tough time wae that arsehole Cunningham, but if Jimmy isnae used to the odd scrap wae oor senior officers, I don't know who is.'

'You are, Brian.'

'Aye, well, apart fae me.'

'I had her on the phone yesterday. He's mooning aboot after mair o' those painkillers. The doctor telt him he could only have a wee drop o' them.'

'I knew it! I warned him aboot they things. How many o' my family are addicted to painkillers?'

'Brian, half your family try to sniff toothpaste. Near every one o' them is addicted to something. Look at you, for a kick-off!'

'Och, this is just turning into a slagging match. I should have kept my powder dry and no' phoned at all.'

'Good. So, can you go, and let me finish my legs?'

'Nae bother. Mind and no' cut yourself.' Scott ended the call as quickly as he could to avoid the barrage he knew was to come from his wife. He laughed as he pictured her shouting down the phone at nobody. 'It's the little things that matter,' he muttered to himself with a smile. Still, his worry about Daley's withdrawn state persisted.

He checked his messages and emails and was pleased when he saw Daley making his way back across the road with their breakfast. 'Great, Jimmy,' he said as the big man passed the bag to him and got back into the car. 'Only one roll and two coffees. Have you eaten yours already?'

'Didn't fancy it, Brian. Just having a coffee.'

Scott looked at his old friend doubtfully. 'What's up wae you?'

'Cunningham, all that's gone on – you know. It preys on my mind. But they're his problems now.' Daley started the car. 'Let's go down the front and have our breakfast, eh?'

'I'll have mine, you mean,' said Scott.

They drove the short distance to the promenade. Daley parked the car and stared out at the superyacht. Members of the crew were busy with ropes and bollards, water churning at her stern as they readied to leave Kinloch.

'Life's no' fair, is it, big man?'

'It certainly isn't, Brian. And sometimes it has a habit of biting you in the arse,' said Daley, still staring at the yacht.

'I'm here to testify to that.' Scott set about his bacon roll with gusto. 'Here, sure you don't want a bite?' He held the roll out in front of Daley's face.

'No, thanks.'

'It's no' like you to be off your food.'

They both looked on as, very slowly, the superyacht pulled away from the quay, and sailed out into the loch.

'Good riddance!' said Scott, taking a slurp of coffee.

'For once, I agree.'

From the corner of his eye, Scott took in his colleague once more, still puzzling over the distant look on his face.

58

Werner Brandt was in the big forward cabin – the superyacht's main lounge, as he preferred to think of it. Only in the roughest seas did he ever think of this vessel as anything other than a floating hotel.

Soon, Kinloch slipped away, and they entered the sound. He had business in Dublin: political business. He'd offered to fly Nathan Farringdon and his newly rediscovered girlfriend back to London from the city, and they'd agreed.

Though he'd expressed his shock and sympathy at the murder of Nathan's father, it was all for show. He'd known the man for over thirty years during their long business relationship, but in all honesty he felt not the least twinge of sorrow. It was his default position when it came to death. The person was gone. What was the point of wasting one's own life in grief?

The whole episode was an embarrassment. He'd ensured that the repellent Cunningham let them leave as soon as they could. The police had their statements: what else did they need?

Brandt was thinking about his reason for having been in Kinloch in the first place. He blamed his son for everything, and cursed the moment the boy had set foot in the town.

'What a bloody awful place,' he mumbled to himself. He knew Cunningham would wrap things up satisfactorily. An anonymous gangster would be blamed for Mitchell's death and never brought to justice. As for the girl who'd stabbed Teddy, he couldn't imagine there would be any difficulty in finding the perpetrator in such a small place. If he thought about it at all, he reckoned the incident had been motivated by jealousy or greed, though in reality he gave it very little headspace. After all, death was his business, and business was good. Brandt was more interested in making sure that the incident was given as little publicity as possible, or rather that his name was removed from any it did receive.

'John,' he said to the hefty man sitting near the door, 'we're out of port. Go and have some breakfast.'

The man thanked him and left.

Being in this lounge was rather akin to standing on the bridge of a great ocean liner, he always thought, with its picture window, and the fact that it was indeed located directly under the bridge. It was as though he was captain of all he surveyed, sailing the vessel by his will alone.

He watched the Isle of Arran pass by as they made their way out into the Irish sea, thinking he'd soon be rid of snivelling Nathan Farringdon and his unprepossessing other half. He spent a few more minutes letting his mind drift along with the motion of the ship. It was like meditation, after which he regularly had his best ideas. But memories of his younger years in Austria often crowded in. The pains from sheer hunger; being knocked onto the cobbles by an older child when he was little more than a toddler; his mother's gaunt, grey features as she lay dead in the casket, and he not yet ten years old.

She was the last person he'd ever grieved for. The only person he'd ever truly loved. His wife, his son – they were mere encumbrances, necessary accessories. His big regrets, as he liked to think of them. But the world was the world. It spun on. And as always in his life, he just had to make the best of it.

He was still in this meditative state when he was aware of the door opening behind him.

'Good morning, Mr Brandt.'

The voice belonged to a female. He turned to face her.

'Miss Harker, how are you? I hope that you managed to get some sleep. I know what a difficult time it's been.' He gazed at the young woman, thin, pale, wearing a long cardigan, wet hair straggling down her back. 'At least you managed to have a warm shower. That always makes me feel better about the world.'

'Yes, very comforting. I remember always wanting to have a shower when I was young. We didn't have one when I was a child.'

Brandt thought of the cold latrine on the Vienna apartment's main stairs, a facility they shared with seven other families. It was all he could do to prevent himself from shuddering at the passing memory. 'And how is poor Nathan? I've been awake half the night, just wondering if I could have done anything to stop what happened to his father.'

'He's bearing up. He couldn't get to sleep.' She sighed. 'Understandable, I suppose.'

'Yes. And what about you? I still don't know the details of what you went through. It must have been terrifying.'

'It was awful. More awful than you can imagine. Nobody should have to live like that.'

'I'm sorry?' Brandt looked puzzled.

'Sorry, just ignore me. I think I'm still coming to terms with it all.'

Brandt smiled benevolently and turned back to face the window. 'Take this all in, my dear. I find there's nothing more relaxing than watching the world go by from the sea. It takes your mind off things. Lets it drift.'

'I intend to. Drift, that is.'

Brandt opened his mouth to speak, but no words came. His mouth gaped, his eyes widening, desperately. With one hand, he reached round to his back, as though trying to scratch some unseen itch. But before his fingers flicked against the handle of the long blade now embedded deep in his back, it was too late.

Werner Brandt fell forward, right through a glass table. He lay motionless, his eyes still staring, his mouth wide open. Death had been his business, and that business now consumed him.

Delph Harker stood above Brandt's body and spat.

Quietly, she turned on her heel, left the cabin and made her way out on to the cold deck. There, as a fleck of sea-spray brushed her face, she took a moment to smile. This was not the wan smile she'd worn for so long, but a smile of triumph and sated revenge. It was Charlotte Broughton's last smile.

As someone screamed within the yacht, she levered herself up on the guardrail, jumped, and disappeared under the cold grey waves.

59

It took three hours for ACC Cunningham to burst into Daley's office without bothering to knock, imparting the news that Brandt had been stabbed to death on the superyacht. He then launched into a barrage of abuse and accusations. Daley sat passively as his superior ranted and raved.

'You'll pay for this, Daley. Your actions, or lack thereof, have left a very important man dead. Not to mention the other consequences. This will end your career. I'll make certain of it.' Cunningham spat the words, his features red and twisted.

'Have you finished, sir?'

'No, not by a long chalk!'

'If I could interrupt for a moment, then?' Over Cunningham's protestations, Daley spoke: 'I had nothing to do with this case. You removed me from it and all of the related inquiries, remember? And I don't know what you expected me to do to prevent the death of a man in the middle of the Irish Sea.' Daley stood to his full height and looked down on Cunningham. 'If all you want to do is berate me, I don't feel much like hearing it right now. In any case, I think you'll have some questions to answer yourself.' He stepped out from behind the desk, sending Cunningham back a couple of paces. 'I don't particularly care for my career, sir, but I know very well how much you value yours. Go and save it, if you can. Before I pick you up and throw you out of my office!' The DCI yelled these final words with such force and conviction they appeared to blow Cunningham from the glass box. Daley slammed the door in his wake, and sat back down, breathing deeply. For the first time in days, he felt no pain in his back. It was as though a magic potion had been applied to his spine.

Scott poked his head round the door.

'Is it safe to come in?'

'Be my guest, Brian.'

Scott walked into the glass box and closed the door behind him. 'You telt him, anyway. Must have been quite satisfying, even though you might just have signed your ain resignation, Jimmy.'

'I don't really care, to be honest. But think about it, Brian. He came and took charge. Maybe if I'd known more – continued our investigations – maybe I'd have worked it out. But as it was, he and Birkenshaw were in charge. You know we gave them all we could.'

'Aye, we did that.' Scott leaned forward in his chair. 'Jimmy, even I'd worked out that Brandt and Farringdon owned Beovan. You knew it too.'

'Suspected – I didn't know. I doubt anyone will ever find that out for certain.'

'I worked it out aboot the lassie, too.'

'You did?'

'No' until this morning, right enough. I knew there was something up wae you. It clicked just as I'd finished my roll.'

'You should have told Cunningham.'

389

'Only a suspicion, Jimmy. I didn't *know*.'

'Touché, Brian.'

'And the brother – the heid in the box. Why did she kill him?'

'Who knows about families? My guess is he was keeping tabs on her. Waiting for his own chance. These were profoundly disturbed kids, remember.'

'She was smarter, mind.'

'She sure was. Ended it all in the sea. Used her university mates as lures. It worked well, too. You read Kemp's book. Those children were put through hell. Who could survive that intact? It's a tragedy, but not for those who caused it. They deserved to die.'

'Naebody gets oot o' something like that without scars, Jimmy. Had us fooled, though, eh?' He stared at his old friend. 'I know what this will take oot o' you, big man. If I'd been smart enough to work it oot when you did, I'd likely have done the same thing.'

'I suppose you would.'

'Those pricks profited fae the misery o' kids. Millions and millions made off ruined lives. They're not alone, though. There're bastards like Brandt all o'er the world.'

'Can't win them all, Brian.'

'True. There was nothing to win really, when you think aboot it.'

'No, losers at every turn.'

Scott rubbed his chin, deep in thought. 'Tell me something – as an old pal.'

'Surely.'

'If that prick had left you on the case, what would you have done?'

Daley smiled. 'Luckily, I'll never have to find out.'

'Hard days ahead, big man. Cunningham won't lie doon. He's no fool, neither. He'd have seen this if he'd no' been so busy trying to climb the greasy pole. He'll realise you knew.'

'He might suspect that, Brian. He doesn't know.' They both smiled, and Daley stood. 'One thing, it's as if I've been given a new back. Not a twinge, Brian.'

'Don't worry, that won't last. You just gave yourself a shot of adrenaline, so you did, when you threatened to fling Cunningham oot the office. It'll be even mair painful when that wears off, trust me. I've been shot – twice.'

'Thanks, Brian. You're a real rock.'

'Don't mention it, DCI Daley.' He winked.

Epilogue

Scott was right. The days that followed were amongst the worst in Daley's career. Cunningham fought, made accusations, inserted himself between Daley and the PIRC team. He threatened and cajoled, using all the dark arts at his disposal. But ultimately there was nothing he could do. He'd taken Daley off the case – off *all* the cases. As the officer in charge, he alone took the blame. In the corridors of Kinloch and Gartcosh, the general consensus was that Cunningham was bound to take the hit. What promised to be a stellar career looked like ending in shame and ignominy.

As the only man who knew his secret and his motivation, Brian Scott was as solid as a rock. Daley had expected nothing else. Though he found himself, at times, exasperated by his friend's antics, there was no doubt that a better, stauncher friend could not be found. As they both knew, there was no way those investigating the incident could ever police their heads, their thoughts. Cunningham had made it easy.

As the days rolled on to Christmas, more and more was revealed about Werner Brandt. It was the inevitable process of organisations big and small – even whole countries – divesting themselves of responsibility, making sure that any wrongdoing in their name was firmly placed upon the shoulders of the man who had merely acted as a conduit for all that was bad about world politics.

As Daley relaxed in the County Hotel at Hamish's going-away party, he reasoned that Brandt himself would have understood it all. It took more than a modicum of pragmatism to live in the shady world in which the Austrian had spent most of his life.

In fact, Daley was feeling quite mellow. He'd been exercising with Liz, spending time with his wife on a yoga mat. And though he had absolutely no aptitude, Daley felt that the stretching had strengthened his back.

He looked across the bar as Brian, Ella and Liz nattered away to Alasdair Shaw and his wife. Shaw himself was still pale and gaunt, but though Cunningham had virtually applied thumbscrews to him in an attempt to connect him with various offences Shaw had batted it away. He was just glad that Mitchell was dead and his family was safe.

Mrs Shaw glanced over at Daley and smiled weakly. He raised his glass to her. He supposed that many years before he'd have judged her addiction to drugs a sad indictment of her character. But he'd known the pull of opioids, the sense of wellbeing and euphoria. *His precious things.*

Hamish was sitting amongst a bastion of his own friends and a wall of cards and gifts. He had a massive rubber fish hanging from his neck on a chain, a gift from a well-wisher. But Daley still fretted about the old man's removing himself from all he knew – especially at his time of life.

He also spared a thought for Emily Kilvington. It had pleased him when he heard that she was no longer in danger after the beating administered by Charlotte Broughton.

But her scars ran deep, and for now she was being kept in a secure facility in the hope that her demons could be banished. And though he hoped she could be helped, he wasn't confident.

He looked on as Hamish made his excuses by holding his pipe in the air and making for the front door. Then he settled back in the arms of a good single malt and bathed in the warmth of his wife's warm lips on his cheek as she gave him a kiss on her arrival back at the table. Despite Hamish's sad farewell, there was still love in the world, despite all the horror.

Hamish stood at the door of the County Hotel. He puffed his pipe into life, wreathed in billows of blue smoke.

The snow, which had been little more than a flurry when he'd arrived at the party, was now falling in great, fat flakes. He stepped from the doorway and took in the view down Main Street to the water of the harbour. All was a white blanket: cars, roofs and the steeple of the town hall. The snow ringed shop windows, making them look even more festive than the flashing displays within. It hung from lamp-posts, it hugged road signs, and clung to the festive lights strung across the street. They still shone, but the snow diffused it all, turning the wee toon into a Christmas-card-perfect scene. With everything soft, all hard edges blurred by the white stuff, it could have been a moment from any part of his life, the passing of years swept away.

The old man gulped back a tear at the beauty of it all.

There was his mother with her shopping basket. Across the street, Sandy Hoynes, a half-bottle of whisky poking out of one of the pockets of his oilskins. There were huddles of his friends, the lassies he'd taken out – all with little success.

There was his family, appearing before his mind's eye as though they were there in front of him. His father – gone for so many years – winked at him from a doorway, his image dissolved by the tears that welled up in Hamish's eyes. This was his home – his town – a place where folk still smiled and said hello, where community meant something, and to be a member of it held you fast, sheltering you from life's squalls.

It was Kinloch.

He turned away, his attention caught by the scent of perfume on the air. She was standing across the street, her face wearing the same smile he'd known for so long, snow gathering on the furry hood of her jacket.

'Annie, it's you.' A smile spread across his face.

'Aye, me, Hamish, you daft auld bugger.' She shook her head. 'You'll never leave this place. I needn't tell you, for fine you know it.'

'Ach, you're right enough. But there are so many ghosts, lassie.'

'Not ghosts, Hamish. Just the ones you love, that's all. We live in your heart – we always will.'

'But what aboot all they presents, eh? Some fine whisky, into the bargain. I'll have to gie it all back when I tell every bugger I'm staying put. There's going to be a riot.'

Her laugh tinkled across the street and echoed off the walls of the hotel that had been her home. 'You'll think o' something. You always do. And anyway, it doesn't really matter.'

Then she was gone.

Hamish pondered on the long road home. There would be no taxis tonight.

The sky was dark, and the snow was deep. In this white deserted place, the old fisherman thought only of sleep.

Acknowledgements

This, the eleventh Daley novel, marks something of an end, and a new beginning. It will be the last in the series to be published by Polygon in Edinburgh. To Hugh, Jan, Neville, Alison et al I owe you a great deal. Without you, Daley would still be a far-flung dream languishing on a slushpile. We've done great things, and I thank you all from the bottom of my heart.

Thanks also, to my dear wife Fiona, who lives with a man whose head is firmly in the clouds. To my effervescent agent Jo Bell, for whom failure is not an option – *fabby*! To my friends far and wide, God bless you all. Even Douglas Skelton and his daily mantra, 'I have a bad feeling about this.' And to David Monteath, who has brought the books alive through his matchless vocal talents.

To editors Alison Rae and Nancy Webber for trying to keep me on track. No, we can't have Daley in space!

For the good folk of Kintyre, who continue to inspire, thank you. And lastly, for you, dear reader. Fear not, Jim and Brian will return.

Denzil Meyrick
London
2023

The DCI Daley thriller series

Book 1: *Whisky from Small Glasses*
DCI Jim Daley is sent from the city to investigate a murder after
the body of a woman is washed up on an idyllic beach on the west
coast of Scotland. Far away from urban resources, he finds himself
a stranger in a close-knit community.

Book 2: *The Last Witness*
James Machie was a man with a genius for violence, his criminal
empire spreading beyond Glasgow into the UK and mainland
Europe. Fortunately, Machie is dead, assassinated in the back of a
prison ambulance following his trial and conviction. But now, five
years later, he is apparently back from the grave, set on avenging
himself on those who brought him down.

Book 3: *Dark Suits and Sad Songs*
When a senior Edinburgh civil servant spectacularly takes his own
life in Kinloch harbour, DCI Jim Daley comes face to face with the
murky world of politics. To add to his woes, two local drug dealers
lie dead, ritually assassinated. It's clear that dark forces are at work
in the town.

Book 4: *The Rat Stone Serenade*
It's December, and the Shannon family are heading to their clifftop
mansion near Kinloch for their AGM. Shannon International, one

of the world's biggest private companies, has brought untold wealth and privilege to the family. However, a century ago, Archibald Shannon stole the land upon which he built their home – and his descendants have been cursed ever since.

Book 5: *The Well of the Winds*
As World War Two nears its end, a man is stabbed to death on the Kinloch shoreline, in the shadow of the great warships in the harbour. When DCI Daley comes into possession of a journal written by his wartime predecessor in Kinloch, he soon realises that he must solve a murder from the past to uncover the shocking events of the present.

Book 6: *The Relentless Tide*
When Professor Francombe and her team of archaeologists find the remains of three women on a remote Kintyre hillside – a site rumoured to have been the base of Viking warlord Somerled – their delight soon turns to horror when they realise the women tragically met their end only two decades ago.

It soon becomes clear that these are the three missing victims of the 'Midweek Murderer', a serial killer who was at work in Glasgow in the early 1990s. DCI Jim Daley now has the chance to put things right – to confront a nightmare from his past and solve a crime he failed to as a young detective.

Book 7: *A Breath on Dying Embers*
When the luxury cruiser *Great Britain* berths in Kinloch harbour, the pressure mounts on DCI Jim Daley. The high-powered international delegates on board are touring the country, golfing and sightseeing, as part of a UK government trade mission. But within hours, one of the crew members vanishes and a local birdwatcher has disappeared.

Book 8: *Jeremiah's Bell*
Teenager Alison Doig disappeared from Kinloch over thirty years ago under mysterious circumstances. Her reclusive family still live in a remote part of the Kintyre peninsula, amidst rumours of wrecking, smuggling and barbaric cruelty.

Now rich American hotelier Alice Wenger has arrived in town, determined to punish those who made her suffer in the past. But someone has vowed to keep hidden sins concealed for ever.

Book 9: *For Any Other Truth*
When a light aircraft crash-lands at Machrie airport, DCI Jim Daley and his colleague Brian Scott rush to the scene. But it soon becomes clear that both occupants of the plane were dead before take-off.

Meanwhile in Kinloch, local fisherman Hamish is unwittingly dragged into danger when he witnesses something he shouldn't have, and hotel manager Annie is beginning to suspect her new boss may not be as he first appeared. And just as Chief Superintendent Carrie Symington thinks she has finally escaped the sins of her past, she finds herself caught in an even deadlier trap.

As the action spills across the sea to County Antrim – all under the scrutiny of the Security Service – the search is on for any other truth.

Book 10: *The Death of Remembrance*
Glasgow, 1983, and a beat constable walks away from a bar where he knows a crime is about to be committed. It is a decision that will haunt him for the rest of his life.

In the present, a fisherman is found dead by Kinloch's shoreline and a stranger with a deadly mission moves into town.

Meanwhile, DCI Jim Daley must confront old friends, new foes and ghosts who will not be silenced.

Short Stories and Tales from Kinloch

One Last Dram Before Midnight: The Complete Collected DCI Daley Short Stories

Published together for the first time in one not-to-be-missed volume are all Denzil Meyrick's short stories. Discover how DCI Daley and DS Scott first met on the mean streets of Glasgow in two prequels that shed light on their earlier lives. Join Hamish and his old mentor, skipper Sandy Hoynes, as they become embroiled with some Russian fishermen and an illicit whisky plot. And in present-day Kinloch Daley and Scott investigate ghosts from the past, search for a silent missing man, and follow the trail of an elusive historical necklace.

Dalintober Moon: A DCI Daley Story

When a body is found in a whisky barrel buried on Dalintober beach, it appears that a notorious local crime, committed over a century ago, has finally been solved. However, the legacy of murder still resonates within the community, and the tortured screams of a man who died long ago still echo across Kinloch.

Two One Three: A Constable Jim Daley Short Story

Glasgow, 1986. Only a few months into his new job, Constable Jim Daley is pounding the beat. When he is seconded to the CID to help catch a possible serial killer, he makes a new friend, DC Brian Scott. Jim Daley tackles his first serious crime in an investigation that will change his life for ever.

Empty Nets and Promises

It's July 1968, and fishing-boat skipper Sandy Hoynes has his daughter's wedding to pay for – but where are all the fish? He and the crew of the *Girl Maggie* come to the conclusion that a new-fangled supersonic jet which is being tested in the skies over Kinloch is scaring off the herring.

First mate Hamish comes up with a cunning plan. But they will have to face down a vindictive fishery officer, a suspicious exciseman and the local police sergeant – not to mention a ghostly piper and some Russians.

Single End: A DC Daley Short Story
It's 1989, and Jim Daley is now a fully fledged detective constable. When ruthless gangster James Machie's accountant is found stabbed to death in a multi-storey car park, it's clear all is not well within Machie's organisation. Meanwhile DC Brian Scott must revisit his past in an attempt to uncover the identity of a corrupt police officer.

A Large Measure of Snow: A Tale from Kinloch
It's December 1967, and the town of Kinloch is cut off by heavy snow. The only way to feed and water the townsfolk is for the fishing fleet to sail to Girvan for much-needed supplies. But the skipper of the *Girl Maggie*, Sandy Hoynes, has a problem. First mate Hamish has, to everyone's astonishment, been chosen as Young Fisherman of the Year by a Glasgow newspaper. Marooned in the town and with one eye on a scoop, their reporter decides to join the fishing crew on their mercy mission.

As the blizzards worsen, the crew of the *Girl Maggie* embarks upon a trip like no other, encountering ghostly Vikings, gigantic crustaceans and a helpful seagull.

A Toast to the Old Stones: A Tale from Kinloch
It's 1968, and the fishermen of Kinloch are preparing to celebrate the old New Year on the twelfth of January. The annual pilgrimage to the Auld Stones is a tradition that goes back beyond memory, and young Hamish, first mate on the *Girl Maggie*, is chuffed that he's been invited to this exclusive gathering.

Meanwhile, it appears that the new owners of the Firdale Hotel are intent upon turning their customers teetotal, such is the exorbitant price they are charging for whisky. Wily skipper Sandy Hoynes comes up with a plan to deliver the spirit to the thirsty villagers at a price they can afford through his connections with a local still-man.

But when the Revenue are tipped off, it looks as though Hoynes and Hamish's mercy mission might run aground. Can the power of the Auld Stones come to their rescue, and is the reappearance of a face from Hoynes' past a sign for good or ill?

Ghosts in the Gloaming: A Tale from Kinloch
Having cheated Sandy Hoynes out of a rowing race and navigation certificate when they were young, Dreich MacCallum makes an unexpected return to Kinloch. With the *Girl Maggie* up on the slip awaiting urgent repairs, Hoynes takes to his bed, the memory of it all too much. When first mate Hamish persuades his skipper to get up and put the fishing boat back into the water, there are unexpected consequences that put Hoynes' liberty and reputation at risk. Has Dreich won the day again?

Denzil's three Tales from Kinloch will be published in one volume, *On Yuletides: The Collected Tales from Kinloch*, in October 2023.

For up-to-the-minute news
and information about
Denzil Meyrick's books
and projects find him here

f DenzilMeyrickAuthor

y LochLomonden